As Marilyn Lay Dying

Stories of the Primal Scene

As Marilyn Lay Dying

Stories of the Primal Scene

Richard Geha

Library of Congress Number: 2005907755
ISBN :   Hardcover   1-59926-241-X
                Softcover   1-59926-240-1

This book was printed in the United States of America.

To order additional copies of this book, contact:
Xlibris Corporation
1-888-795-4274
www.Xlibris.com
Orders@Xlibris.com
27432

CONTENTS

For Danielle Geha
To whom this book owes its life

Acknowledgments

For assisting with this project, I wish to thank *Danielle Geha* whose loving devotion and intelligence helped steer me through those emotional twists and turns which otherwise would have misled me in the course of writing these stories. She is a superb editor and one of Rilke's Angels. *Walt Stepp* expended many hours both editing these stories and discussing their ideas. Before such generous assistance as his, Hamlet speaks for me: "Beggar that I am, I am even poor in thanks." My gratitude to *Lynn Park* for her warm support, sense of humor, and excellent work in carefully reviewing and critiquing my work. Thanks also to *Roberta Kramer Luttrell* for reading several of these stories and offering such cogent commentary.

"The Appearance of the Father" was first published in *Pangolin Papers* (1997). The version that appears here is slightly modified.

The Rilke quotes are from *Ahead of All Parting: the Selected Poetry and Prose of Rainer Maria Rilke,* edited and translated by Stephen Mitchell (New York: Random House, 1995), pages 371 and 373.

Temples are no longer known. It is we who secretly save up these extravagances of the heart. Where one of them still survives, a Thing that was formerly prayed to, worshiped, knelt before— just as it is, it passes into the invisible world.

—Rainer Maria Rilke, *Duino Elegies*

Mr. President, the Late Marilyn Monroe

"Mr. President, the late Marilyn Monroe." And Gladys Pearl once again resigned herself to watching it on television. It was the star-studded celebration of President Kennedy's birthday, but since only this one segment was being repeated, it seemed more a commemoration of this Marilyn Monroe than the president. Yes, and didn't they do it last year too? Yes, it was early August, hot like today . . . and yes, the August of the year before, and . . . oh maybe not. Why remember?

Gladys tipped back and forth in the uncomfortable iron chair as she and several other patients looked at the TV in the Community Room. Again they were watching that movie star, Marilyn Monroe, hurry on to the stage, take the ermine jacket off, and pose before the crowd at Madison Square Garden. She was radiant as a bolt of lightning, with gleaming platinum hair and a skintight silver-sequined gown. Gasps of astonishment and sighs of unease rippled through the Community Room. The room was airless and the heat nearly insufferable. Gladys grunted and rolled her thumbs over and over the tips of her index and middle fingers, calloused now where blood circles used to form. (Mr. Graves called it *pilling*. Drugs did that to her. "Hey," Mr. Graves sometimes said, "look at all that pilling you're doing today, honey. Busy, busy lady.")

This Marilyn Monroe was really quite dazzling, and perhaps Gladys had noted that before, but she couldn't quite recall. Things slipped out of her memory so quickly. Gladys figured that was why they doped her up—to erase memory. But she remembered she had been seeing this scene all week. And for some reason, everybody just kept watching it, including Gladys. But why? She had asked this question and been given some answer—but what was it? Gladys Pearl couldn't remember the reasons for things very well. Yet here everyone was, glued to the TV set. Why? After all, this spectacle had happened . . . well, Gladys guessed, at least a few years ago, hadn't it? She couldn't remember. Hadn't President Kennedy been shot? Yes, it was a pretty old movie by now. Oh well, there was nothing else to do except watch movies. For Gladys, everything was a movie, and she wondered who was playing President Kennedy, that handsome dog!

Gladys rolled her thumbs rapidly over her fingertips as she watched this Marilyn Monroe begin again to sing "Happy Birthday" to President Kennedy. Oh yes, how handsome the president was, with that mischievous smile—the cat that snatched the canary—seeming so enticed by this woman flaunting her glittering figure in front of him, in front of millions, in front of everybody in America, in fact. A thought flashed through Gladys's mind, "The children—they shouldn't be watching this." Oh well, how do you hide the world from children? Certainly, no one had hidden the world from Gladys.

Gladys found the Happy Birthday song eerie. Such a familiar little song, but this Marilyn Monroe was singing it with such a breathy voice, oozing nothing but sex, that the song was scarcely recognizable. It was meant to be funny, yet it wasn't funny at all—not to Gladys anyway. No, she supposed that when you got older, this sort of nonsense wasn't amusing anymore. She knew what this Marilyn Monroe and this king of America were doing, and doing right under everybody's nose. Gladys could see right through the makeup.

"Oh, Gladys Pearl—who's that, honey? Know who that is?" someone behind Gladys remarked with teasing affection, as someone always did when this program played. As always there was snickering. Of course she knew who this Marilyn Monroe was, didn't everybody? She was Marilyn Monroe, that's who. And so? Why are we watching this over and over years later? The king is dead, isn't he? Or was it merely the actor who played the part that died?

And where, pray tell, was the queen of the land? What was her name? Gladys grimaced. She couldn't even remember the first lady's name! Oh yes—*Jackie*, sweet Jackie, as flat chested and brittle as a peppermint stick, Gladys recollected, nothing the king would want to munch on—oh no, not while the birthday boy was feasting on this, the world's most scrumptious cake. Gladys felt sorry for Jackie, probably off someplace in her own private nuthouse, watching this Marilyn Monroe on the TV, tilting back and forth like Gladys, keeping time to the beat of a runaway heart.

A young woman named Phyllis Albright rushed over and stood too close to Gladys. "Look who that is! See her? My god, Gladys!"

See her? How could you not see her? And damn, did this Marilyn Monroe want to be seen. Gladys scowled, irritated, and someone barked at Phyllis, "Shut up, bitch!" Who said that? Ruthie Sloan? Probably. She was ninety years old and thought she was immortal. She also thought she was a witch who could fly anywhere she chose because when she was ten, the devil had shoved a magical broomstick up between her legs. Ruthie thought Gladys also had one of these broomsticks tucked away. Oh how wonderful, if it were only true. She'd be up and away and flying forever, never landing. Gladys realized that Ruthie was down the rabbit hole, mad as a hatter. She heard it again—"Shut up, you bitch!" Yes, it was Ruthie.

Gladys's body leaned forward and backward in one of the hard metal chairs built to withstand any abuse. God, it was hot. Hard to breathe. There flickered across Gladys's vision the image of a flaxen-haired little girl—maybe the child was five years old—screaming in the middle of the night for her mother. "Mommy, stop, stop crying. Stop hurting Mommy." The child had golden hair; Gladys knew that, even though it was pitch-dark. She could see the screaming child perfectly because she glowed in the dark.

"Shut up and go back to sleep."

"I can't sleep."

"Too bad. Then don't sleep. But get the hell outta here. Can't you see a guy's in bed with Mommy right now? Can't Mommy have a drop of fun? Dear lord, ain't there no privacy anywhere? Get out of my hair. Go on, go back where you came from."

That wasn't a memory, couldn't have been. The drugs washed away memory. So was that a movie Gladys had seen? Sure—wasn't everything a movie?

Gladys rolled her fingers, making thousands and thousands of little pills.

"She's so beautiful," Phyllis whispered right in her ear. Gladys continued to frown and say nothing. Gladys didn't talk much anymore. The Thorazine dried out her mouth and made her bite her tongue. She didn't like Phyllis because she was so nosy. Gladys didn't much like anybody; they were all nosy, especially nosy about this Marilyn Monroe, who would now and then visit. And all the screwballs would swarm like flies, pestering her for an autograph, and getting a scribbled—"Love, MM." It annoyed the daylights out of Gladys. Sometimes the looneys even begged Gladys for her autograph, to which she'd just flip up a middle finger in front of their busybody noses. For god's sake, couldn't they see Gladys was a nobody? Evidently, this Marilyn Monroe couldn't see that either. For some reason, she paid special attention to Gladys, pretending that they knew each other. Gladys would look at the photographs she showed her. Yes, they were pictures of a movie star, spilling out of her clothes. No matter what this Marilyn Monroe did, sex spilled out of her. But so?

"Don't you recognize me?"

"They're you. You said you're Marilyn Monroe. These are pictures of Marilyn Monroe."

So? It was like a joke that Gladys just didn't get. And a very cruel joke too because this Marilyn Monroe at times appeared—in the oddest manner—to be impersonating Gladys's lost daughter, Norma Jeane, her daughter who got tired of life and went back where she came from. And this Marilyn Monroe kept asking where her father was. Well, how would Gladys know where this movie star's father was? Somewhere along the way Gladys's daughter had also disappeared without knowing who her father was either. Ruthie Sloan claimed that Norma Jeane had a broomstick up there she got off on. Sometimes Gladys would feel her daughter kicking inside her belly, alive, dying to be born. But that lasted about a second.

"Oh my god—look at that! Our president, he's looking up her dress. Nasty, nasty! Shoot him! *Bang, bang!*" someone exclaimed.

"Shut up, bitch!"

A rustling permeated the heat of the room. Everyone seemed uneasy about something. These women all wanted to jump right out of their skin, Gladys believed. They all had brooms between their legs, brooms that didn't fly.

Gladys rocked like someone riding a horse, although she never for a moment believed she was going anyplace. It gave her something to do with her body.

Of course Gladys caught on damn quick that it was around the name Monroe that this movie star sought to forge a connection between them. How utterly ridiculous! Monroe—a name as common as table salt. True, Gladys Pearl's last name had once been Monroe. But then it changed to Baker, then to Mortenson, and most recently to Eley. Names—slippery and as changeable as shoes. Sometimes the things names were attached to were even more slippery. Things altered or ceased to be or never even existed in the first place. Having sashayed around the block a time or two, Gladys was thoroughly schooled in the mercurial nature of reality. No, things and names often failed to link up. Why, this institution alone housed half a dozen nymphos calling themselves the Virgin Mary. And the name Marilyn Monroe—well, it labeled nothing related to Gladys Pearl. Sometimes nothing seemed related to her.

Gladys could tell that this Marilyn Monroe was so deeply into fabricating that only what was fabricated was real. Not that Gladys didn't believe that herself, but endeavoring to cast Gladys in a part that Gladys wasn't auditioning for—well, that made her want to vomit. Let's pretend. You play Mommy, please, please, please. No, no, no. That role poor Gladys had already played and relinquished years ago, having gotten damn sick and tired of it.

Gladys studied this woman, gleaming like a light bulb on the TV screen, singing to the king, making obscene love to him. Oh yes, she saw what these two were doing, as did everyone in the Community Room. And there were children all over the country getting an eyeful. Where were their parents? But it was all a bit dreamy to Gladys because she felt sleepy. The Thorazine that the nice attendant, Mr. Graves, insisted she take often made her sleepy. Not that it mattered; sometimes it seemed to her that she was sleeping all the time, that everything was just a big old dream. Sometimes in the dream you believed you were awake, but of course you weren't at all; dreams could make you believe anything.

But this Marilyn Monroe—just look at her! Gladys was certain that she was a fake of some kind, presuming to be someone or something she wasn't. Who made this Marilyn Monroe? Whose idea was this Marilyn Monroe? So made up. This woman wasn't anything real. Well, of course, this Marilyn Monroe was a *real* fake. Anyone could poke a hole in her. That's what Gladys had told Mr. Graves after one of this woman's visits. Mr. Graves merely replied, "Oh I don't think so. Here, try some candy, dear." Thorazine pills resembled pale brown M&Ms. The patients called them M&Ms—yummies. Jesus, in this place even the candy was unreal. For the longest while, all Mr. Graves would say to her whenever the topic of this Marilyn Monroe arose was, "I'm so sorry for you, love. Here's some candy."

But why? Gladys Pearl wasn't a fool easily taken in. Everybody thought old people were so gullible and dumb, but they weren't. No, and yet this Marilyn Monroe, with her cruel joke, did confuse Gladys whenever Gladys happened to let anything count enough to confuse her, whenever her meds wore off enough. Why didn't this Marilyn Monroe leave her the hell alone, stop haunting her, stop claiming to love her, stop bringing her stupid presents? Stop visiting, stop appearing on television, stop appearing in her dreams. In and out—talk about a witch on a broom. Get out of the inside of Gladys's life.

Actually, Marilyn Monroe had stopped visiting some time ago. But that hadn't registered with Gladys. Occasionally, events of her past got mislocated into the present. Things that had passed away had an uncanny way of rising from the dead. No, the visitations of Marilyn Monroe hadn't ended; unbidden, she was always reappearing.

The other night Gladys dreamed that this Marilyn Monroe was sucking milk and blood out of her breasts, draining the sweet life right out of her like a dead person would want to do; a vampire, sucking away every last drop of her beauty, stealing Gladys's looks away and transforming her into this monstrous creature—this Marilyn Monroe. It was a terrifying dream, too much to bear. No one on earth could have nursed this Marilyn Monroe—even though the night of the dream Gladys had been lactating, her nipples dripping with milk. (Mr. Graves had explained that the M&Ms caused that too.) Oh, why couldn't she shake this woman out of her head?

Gladys was startled, as though awakened, by Phyllis's voice. "She's so naked," Phyllis sighed. "If I had her bod, I'd be too. She looks like a mermaid. God, *you* made her! Gladys—you did! Aren't you proud?"

"Quiet, bitch, or we'll rip out yer tongue," someone shouted.

"She's a slut!" someone else shouted. Gladys was unsure whether they meant that Phyllis was a slut or that this Marilyn Monroe was or that someone else was, or maybe they meant that Gladys was a slut. Not a new idea. Years ago, back in the Roaring Twenties, hadn't Gladys, more than once, been accused of being one? Back then, herself all awash with sex and booze—well, hadn't she been? Who remembers?

But yes, this Marilyn Monroe was definitely a slut. How could she not be? No doubt the king had had her often. He was having her now. Oh yes, look at that shit-eating grin on his pretty face, his eyes ogling this naked woman, ogling this blinding body of light, drinking down this heat into his loins. The radiance of this woman—made only of see-through gossamer, with no core at all, no navel.

Naturally, the king was also a fake; Gladys saw that too. Actors, all of them. He had used this Marilyn Monroe, and this Marilyn Monroe had used this king. Climbing around on each other like monkeys. Very amusing really; Gladys had to smile. Who did they imagine they were mounting anyway? What were they getting? There was no meat on these bones; there were no bones. Makeup, thin as shadows, transparent as light—splicings. All film. Gladys knew this game. She had once been employed at Consolidated Film Industries, cutting up millions of miles of the film negatives movie directors used to compose worlds as thin as paper. Not that she ever bothered to recall any of that mind-numbing work, but looking now at the king and his glistening paramour, she knew, as any wise old soul would, that they really were nothing real—only "the chimera of desires, overwrought," as Gladys had once heard Jean Harlow described.

Gladys rolled the invisible pills—thousands of them.

And yes, of course this Marilyn Monroe was naked—crazy Phyllis was right. Every woman in this asylum understood this; Gladys knew no one here was fooled. Everyone in America was pretending that this silver woman was dressed so that she could go about as naked as a jaybird, as naked as a mermaid swimming about in the black, dirty waters of everyone's mind. Gladys Pearl understood. She wondered if this dirty little mermaid was swimming around somewhere inside Mr. Graves. She would ask him when he came round with her meds tonight. But when Marilyn Monroe would visit, Gladys could see by the bulge in Mr. Graves's pants exactly where it was this mermaid was swimming. Damn right. Gladys had always had a keen eye.

The birthday song concluded. Someone turned off the TV. Gladys heard two or three women sobbing. They always did after this program played. How strange. Why? Gladys always inquired, and each time, she vaguely remembered, she had been told why. But she forgot immediately what the reason was, probably because it didn't make any difference. Usually nothing mattered if the meds worked.

All this weeping. Gladys suddenly became aware of the dank, fetid stench of urine that had, over the years, permeated the walls and floors of the hospital. She hardly ever noticed it because, she supposed, she had herself become a part of these very walls and floors, become what life had pissed away. She had once overheard Mr. Graves comment to another attendant, "My god, this place, it smells like what life's pissed away."

After the program, several of these weeping women came pressing up to Gladys, milled around her, stroked her with their filthy hands, and kissed her lovingly, and said how awfully sorry they were. Most assuredly they meant to be consoling, but Gladys found them revolting. As always, Gladys glared at them, bewildered. And as always, she asked, peevish and perplexed, "For what? Sorry for what? Get away from me. What's happened?" Each time she almost knew what they would say before they said it. Of course, they again told her the reason for their sorrows.

"Marilyn Monroe—she died, honey."

"The *late* Marilyn Monroe—don't you get it?"

"She killed herself. Drugs. Too many pills—thousands. Killed her, killed us."

"Couldn't stand life. Like you, like us."

"She was murdered, honey. Like us."

"Your daughter—Marilyn Monroe. Dead."

Oh no, not my daughter! Gladys screamed deep within herself. How disgusting—these crazy bitches, acting so loving, flinging these vicious lies at her like rocks that cracked open her poor skull. She must remember (she had resolved this many times before) to kill all these filthy wenches so that she would never have to suffer this caterwauling again. *Never! No, no, no!* She closed her eyes tightly, but with all these crazy bitches knocking at her head, she couldn't prevent the appearance of Marilyn Monroe—white, burning light, naked as the day she was born, singing "Happy Birthday"—fatherless, motherless, her own creation, her own creation: *hers*. Gladys surrendered to what she knew. Her pale brown nipples were lactating hard, beaded pills—yummy M&Ms. Her leaking nipples—what were they doing? Stop! Stop! But they wouldn't. They had a mind of their own. Gladys couldn't help herself: Gladys took the enormous sight into her arms and pressed the hungry lips of it against her bare bosom and flowed into it like a river into the sea. She was filled. For as long as an instant, she was filled.

Then Gladys again felt the violent thud within her chest, and she knew, remembered but for an instant only, that this was what occurred when your heart broke and your blood gushed forth like a fountain, or when you gave birth to a child. Marilyn? Norma Jeane—is that you? Oh yes, Gladys knew (old people weren't stupid). Yes, and either her water had broken or she had again wet herself, pissed herself away. It didn't matter. She couldn't remember how to cry like a mother. The mother within her had been too long ago buried alive; a mother now good for nothing, now not even worth a nod of recognition to a daughter too fabulous to own. Dead. Her baby. Gladys knew she couldn't give birth to a dead child. My god— how horrifying! Don't cry, don't cry—just fly away, get that broomstick humping. And in an instant, she forgot what had just happened.

Gladys Pearl rocked back and forth, rubbing the numb tips of her fingers. She stared at the blank, gray TV screen. Nothing was on. Her head ached because some bitch had hit her with a rock. In the sultry August heat, she waited, without knowing for what—not for visitors. No one came to visit anymore. Waiting had become a habit divorced from anticipation. A thought crept like a ghost into her mind: *That woman will never die.* Inexplicably, it soothed her. She resisted focusing on who that woman was. Of course Gladys knew that woman was Marilyn Monroe, but the full grasp of that awareness lay beyond her reach. The M&Ms squelched so much, she felt nearly as empty and gray as the television screen, just so shut off, so little of her left. But somewhere buried deeper within, who else this actress was besides being Marilyn Monroe wavered like a ghostly image in a mirror, smoky and mottled with age. Wherever that woman was . . . no, she would never die. Strangely soothing. Never, never. Back and forth, back and forth, unending . . . nowhere, nowhere.

Dear god, it was hot enough to fry an egg on the floor. And at some point—

"Mr. President, the late Marilyn Monroe."

The Appearance of the Father

A warm late afternoon in June:
The little girl watches him sitting hunched over on the stone steps of the abandoned chapel, stealing swigs from a whiskey bottle sheathed in a brown paper bag. He's a pathetic sight, but he doesn't stand out in this part of town. She thinks he sometimes acts guilty, gulping that stuff (her mother calls it *poison*) and then glancing from side to side. But nobody really pays attention to what he does. The other derelicts rarely concern themselves with him, unless to mooch a nip of poison; otherwise, they idle about, exchanging a few perfunctory words.

Tracy wonders how many even know his name. The girl guesses that he needs to believe that somebody still cares enough to regard the bad thing he's doing, squatting alone in this dissolute neighborhood on the steps of a forsaken church, poisoning his life. Yes, because he needs such regard, he behaves as though he's under solicitous surveillance. Is that why he's on the lookout? Or is he anticipating an arrival, perhaps the tall, attractive woman who visits occasionally? Hopefully, she is not the one for whom he waits; hopefully, he awaits his daughter.

The girl has stared at him, hour after hour, as she would a captivating image in a dream. She can't get enough of him. To observe this man as often as possible, she has had to dash here after school. But now that it's summer, she comes almost daily, sometimes lingering even into the evening, until he dissolves into the night. She's been spying on him for two years.

She usually finds him alone, sitting on the chapel stairs. Rolled up neatly beside him is a black trench coat, frayed and torn in places, that he wears if it rains or the temperature drops, as frequently it does in the late afternoon. He carries the coat wherever he goes; on these streets, coats are precious commodities, second only to alcohol. He always looks tired and old—lifeless. But he isn't old, not to her anyway. No, he's the age she recalls her father being before he left them—left because, her mother has explained, "He drank too much and was a no-good rotten bum, darling, who never worked a day in his life. Neglected us, treated us like we hardly existed. He was cruel, Trace."

"Not to me."

"No, to *me*."

Occasionally, the child overheard her mother tell her aunt that he slept with other women. Therefore, she hated him. Hence, he had to go. And he did.

"What's *betray* mean?" the child asked.

"Nothing. Never mind about that now, Trace, my love," her mother said. "Someday you'll understand all too well."

Thus far, however, it is all beyond the child's comprehension, except that she knows what it means that her missing father slept with other women because he often appears in her dreams. Sometimes he nestles in close and sleeps with her. With her secret inner eye, like a pussycat that could see perfectly in the dark, she will gaze at him snuggled against her.

"Where is he?" she asked her mother.

"Oh, he's nowhere, Trace," Mother replied. "Forget about him. Stop dreaming your heart out over him."

Tracy found a newspaper clipping in her mother's chest of drawers. The headline read *Death by Defenestration*. The article mentioned her father's name several times and seemed to address whether he had committed suicide by leaping from a window or had been pushed— murdered, it said. She pointed to "defenestration" and asked what that meant. Her mother said she didn't really know, "But it doesn't matter anyway 'cause the person in the paper's not your daddy, but just some guy with his name. That's all. Stop nosing around, Trace. It's making you sick. Don't you understand me?"

She is eight years old and has a boyfriend. When she tells him that she intends to hunt for her father against her mother's wishes, he grins and says that if she is cautious enough, only the pussycat's eye will see her. She giggles, knowing that he hints, as he so often does, at their intimate secret. He is two years older than she and so smart he has already been skipped ahead in school a year beyond his grade level.

Recently, he showed her a small, beautiful marble he called a *pee-wee*. Embedded in the marble was a delicately configured circle of fluorescent green.

"It looks like a pussycat's eye," she exclaimed. "Can I have it? Please, please." Excited by something, he unzipped his pants and a pale pink worm thing wiggled out, rose up, and its one tiny eye leered at her. She was amazed, aghast.

He said, "Why, sure, Trace, you can have this pussycat eye if you let me tuck it away in the very safest place of all."

"Where?"

"*There.*"

"*What?*"

"Is it a deal?"

"*No.*"

"Please."

"Okay, okay, you can," she screeched. So with some awkward posturing of her quickly stripped body, and a little worldly-wise patience on his part, and a little virgin pain on hers, the eye got deposited.

"Now you're cockeyed, Trace," he said.

"I'm what?"

"It'll guide you, bring you luck."

"Honest?"

"Honest." He added, "It's also a seed."

"A seed?"

"Yeah, that'll duplicate you—an eye for an I. Someday it'll grow into a baby. When that happens, I'll be the father. Get it?" No, she didn't.

He is *sooo* smart she often can't understand a word he says, but she has his eye in her, all to herself. And if it remains *there*, at the center of her, she believes, because her companion has promised her, it will see her through the search for her father. She doesn't understand but she believes him. Her mother has said that her boyfriend is crazy, that she should stay away from him.

Tracy's father left when she was five. Afterward, a thick fog settled over most of her recollections of him. But of the few memories she has preserved of him there was this. When she was a toddler peering through the bars of her crib, in a rage, he had hoisted her mother above his head and thrown her, kicking and screaming, through the large living-room window. The crash of the shattering glass mingled with her screams.

Quickly, even while her mother plummeted down ten stories from their apartment, her father snatched her up out of the crib, but instead of also tossing her through the window, he hugged her tight and kissed her. She forgot her mother's plight and, wrapped in her father's embrace, drifted asleep. Later, after he had left them, she asked her mother if she had been hurt when she hit against the ground. Her mother seemed taken aback, but she smiled, stroked her daughter's long golden hair as she always did when the child was obviously perplexed, and answered that she couldn't honestly recollect that particular fall, but she felt just fine now.

"Oh my precious Trace, you shouldn't worry about stuff you aren't old enough to understand," her mother told her for the hundredth time. "It's making you sick, darling." The child declared that she would find her father, and her mother said, "You can't find him. Quit!"

To avoid being discovered, or rather, as a pretense at concealment, the girl sometimes sits on a bench down the block from the dismal shape slumped on the chapel stairs—not so far that she can't observe him, or that he, if he chooses, can't observe her as well. She wants very much for her father to recognize and come to her, as he almost nightly does in her dreams. Night after night, he finds where she lies waiting for him to ambush her with hugs and kisses.

Occasionally, she hides across the street from him in a narrow passageway, called *Blind Alley*, squeezed behind two big trash barrels that no one ever moves. This section of town is always quiet—no traffic, no crowds, no stores open for business, no noise, although at times she does hear voices or distant laughter or someone will shriek as though assaulted or a window will break. But mostly, a hollow silence prevails. Her mother has explicitly forbidden her to hang around this part of town because awful people lurk here and bad things can happen.

That description and that warning, perhaps, served as the initial signposts directing the quest for her father. Moreover, it was here—from the window of that high building only a block from the chapel—that he had fallen. The very window through which he plunged to his death was, in fact, still broken. She often stared, disbelieving, at a discolored gray stain at the spot on the sidewalk. Once, she had dreamed she was gaping up at that window when her father lunged forward from it, falling and crushing her. She woke paralyzed, panicked by sensations of suffocation. Crying and frightened, she told her mother how she'd been killed. Her mother stroked her yellow hair and whispered in her ear that she must stop fretting about all this because, "Your dream's right. It's crushing the life out of you. Wake up. And stay away from that creepy little friend of yours. He's nuts."

When the girl related the dream to her friend, he just smirked and said that the eye of the pussy never closes, and that when she sleeps, what it sees, she dreams. She giggled as usual because of the juicy secret they shared, the one that she had sworn she'd never reveal until the eye blossomed into a version of herself, and he, because of the seed he'd sowed, became the father. She giggled too because she knew her mother would say, "That's crazy. He's crazy. Keep away from him, hear me?"

At times, she yearns so for the man whom she takes for her father to notice her that she will sit herself on the curb directly in front of him.

When he walks or staggers down the street, she tags after him. Whenever he has collapsed unconscious on the pavement or out in the road, she has ventured up to him, inspecting him before bending to stroke her hands over his unshaven face that is always scratched or scabbed, and now and then, bleeding in spots. She has even kissed and cuddled him, as she still does her worn-out black-and-white stuffed panda bear.

She knows that he is very ill; frequently he spits up blood or passes out. Sometimes his eyes are flat and lusterless, unclosed but unseeing. At such times, she wonders if he's just dazed by the proximity of his faithful daughter. She's afraid that he might die before he truly sees her, truly acknowledges and reclaims her. Once, she dreamed of herself wandering naked and lost over a parched sandscape so vast that she could never hope to reach its end before her blistered body expired from thirst or exhaustion. The barren land was called the *Father Desert;* no one was ever found in time out there. She was fairly sure such a region existed because they had said something about it in Sunday school, hadn't they?

The man evidently likes this abandoned church because she almost always finds him here. Often he will enter it, as the doors are never locked. A few times she has even followed him. The musty interior, cool and dark, is vacant except for the pews and the framework of the altar. The walls are bare; all the icons and paintings have been removed. Miraculously, none of the stained-glass windows are broken. He sits there, in the muted church light, hardly more than a shadow, drinking, and now and then peering around, as though to check if anyone has caught him.

Sometimes he will talk to himself, gesturing, mumbling words she never quite grasps; it's like eavesdropping on someone talking in his sleep. She makes sounds herself, usually accidentally, but sometimes quite intentionally too. She has even spoken to him—"Here I am, Daddy." But mostly, she speaks to herself because he has never once seemed affected by noises she makes. She watches him, follows him, tries to speak to him, none of which he appears to notice.

The pussy's green eye rotates deep inside the dark chamber of her confusion, and it comforts her somewhat to remember that cats can see in the night.

Outside the church, he drinks continually, either sitting curled into a ball on the hard steps or pacing about, zigzagging, sometimes tripping or falling. Sometimes he will read a paperback. Or occasionally, with his eyes closed, he'll hold a book in front of his face upside down, as a blind man might. She wants him to read to her as her mother regularly does at bedtime.

He doesn't do much of anything, and mostly he's alone, although not always. Sometimes he chats with a bedraggled woman who will drop by and sit next to him, either partaking of his bottle or sharing hers. Slovenly dressed, she is tall and curvy, her face pallid but attractive. She scoots close to him, rests her head on his shoulder and talks to him. Or she laughs or cries, and he will also laugh or cry. Sometimes they nestle so close, the child can scarcely tell one from the other.

The woman's presence makes her jealous. And yet, these two figures fascinate her. They always act as though they are doing something wrong. When they kiss or joke or bawl like babies or dance on the sidewalk to songs they sing to each other, they sneak glances up and down the street. They cause the girl to feel she's peeking through a pinhole in a wall at things she's both forbidden and unprepared to view. At times, guilt and excitement mingle with such intensity the child drops her head in her hands and stares into a darkness out of which the two lovers quickly rematerialize, not unlike the way they occasionally do in her dreams.

She cannot take her eyes off them. They, however, seem never to perceive her, even when she stations herself a few feet from them, and they stare directly at her. One day the woman walked past her—indeed, would probably have stepped on her had the girl not darted aside. She wondered briefly if the woman was blind because evidently she had failed to see the child blocking her path. Either that or the child could not make her presence real enough, a possibility that compelled her to distrust her own tangibility. To reaffirm it, she raced home and inspected herself in the full-length mirror of Mother's bedroom.

Her mother once declared that, "You can't see yourself in the mirror, Trace. The appearance in the mirror's not you, sweetheart. It's an appearance. You never see yourself; in fact, the self's never beheld 'cause it's inside, clear outta sight. I don't expect you to understand this, my darling."

And she didn't understand, although she now suspects that what's been happening to her in this dilapidated part of town relates to whatever Mother meant. But the luminous eye within her that rolls around surely sees her, along with so very much else. It must, because night after night, do her dreams not show her all the mysterious things the eye has seen— just as her boyfriend told her would happen?

In any case, she has been concealing and revealing herself, or believing that she often reveals herself, for two years. It is the most important thing in her life because she is convinced that this man is her absent father. She believes, even though she remains unsure why she's so convinced. Not that she has *no* reasons; weak and ambiguous though they may be, they have nonetheless persuaded her.

Her mother described her father as a drunkard. But down here, near where she and Mother lived, many of those roved around. Her mother cautioned her to stay away from this area. Why did she do that, if not for the fact that he was here, that he had fallen from that window to his death? Moreover, the child deciphered in this man a resemblance, probably undetectable to any scrutiny except her own, to photographs of her father that her mother had shown her. One of these pictures was of her mother and father on their wedding day, smiling and happy in front of that very church which he had, according to his daughter, continued "attending." She could see through the man's mask, through the tangled overgrowth of beard, the dirt, and the dried blood splotches. She could detect in this vagrant her father on his wedding day.

But all of this merely suggests to her that this man *could* be her father. Mainly her conviction rests on this: About a year after her father departed, she had been passing along this very street and noticed a man sitting on the church steps. She doesn't know why, but for some reason she ducked down Blind Alley and concealed herself behind the two trash cans. From there she spied on him. Soon a woman in an elegant black dress came strolling down the street. As the woman neared, the girl thought she recognized her mother, although she had never seen her mother in a dress like this. The woman also appeared much younger than her mother and more attractive or—she didn't have the word for it, but—sensual. The child was sure she knew her. It was odd—baffling to her, really. How could she be *almost* certain of her own mother's identity?

The woman, or her mother, halted in front of the man and looked down at him. He lifted his head and squinted. Neither spoke. Minutes passed. He then smiled and offered his bottle to her. She shook her head no. And then she slowly gathered her dress up over her hips and stepped as close as she could to the man's face. He stared at her nudity briefly and then lowered his head as though ashamed. Motionless, she sustained her pose a long while. Neither spoke.

The woman shifted herself even closer and touched the middle of her exposed body to the top of the man's bowed head. Then, spreading her legs wide apart, she stretched her skirt over the man's head and let it drape over him. Then she pressed him to her and stood perfectly still.

He stirred slightly. Her mother (or whoever this was) tilted her face upward and fixed her sight on the glistening globe of the church's golden bell tower. The girl looked up too. The spire was blinding in the sunlight. Quickly, she returned her stricken sight to the woman's bloated belly. Heat waves from the pavement circulated around the couple; the outline of that distended body shimmered. Throughout this scene, the girl had become dizzy and begun to sweat with fever. She felt trapped by the large trash cans that flanked her. Soon her mother undraped the man, or no, didn't undrape him, because he was not there to be undraped. He had disappeared. The woman flung up her hands like a triumphant circus magician and strode away in the direction of the girl. The child gaped and began laughing, frightened and enfevered, perhaps delirious.

(The woman's trick completely mystified her until she recalled her boyfriend inserting into her that marble. Yes, the woman probably carried a concealed pocket up between her legs, not unlike the one that she herself possessed, into which articles such as glass marbles could be implanted. Marbles . . . or an entire person. Well, the woman undoubtedly possessed a pocket larger than hers.)

After this episode the woman now passed within inches of her. The child tried to muffle her nervous laughter. She lost her balance and shoved one of the trash cans, sliding it across the asphalt a short ways. The woman turned slowly and seemed to glance expressly at her. The girl thought she had surely been discovered, but she hoped that her mother would discern how ill she was and forgive her. Trembling and giggling, then sobbing, wasn't her distress obvious? Anyone, certainly her own mother, would reach down and pick up such a child and dispel the mysteries of the world. Then she'd understand and not be afraid anymore. But the woman never responded and simply kept walking. When she was far away and no bigger than a wavering black dot, the child fainted. And out of the gray mist she had sunk into, she beheld her mother emerging, bewitchingly beautiful in a new black dress, approaching the slumped figure of her father who appeared as little more than an empty silhouette before a church. He had all but disappeared. From that moment on, Tracy determined this man to be her father. She intended to never let him escape from her sight for long, to never lose him again, and ultimately, to bring him back home to live.

He habitually crouches here by the church, his old coat bundled beside him. He is usually alone. And she much prefers him that way— alone—to those times when the tall, slovenly woman comes to call. Sometimes, when the child sits surveying him there drinking, the woman will appear. The girl then becomes agitated and often stomps right out in plain sight, as though this will scare off the intruder, or at least inhibit the drunken pair's displays of affection.

Everything about their conduct has by now become, for the girl, objectionable—not just the kissing and hugging and stroking, but also the talking and weeping and laughing, also the strolling along or the standing together or even the mere passings by exchanging a nod or a smile. Everything manifests affection of the worst kind—love displaced from its rightful recipient. Even more tormenting than any of these exchanges, however, is that neither of them has ever betrayed the slightest awareness of her presence. She might as well have been a ghost.

A warm, late afternoon, now in June.

She follows the man and the woman into the chapel. Several yards behind, but openly in view, she trails them as they sway up the aisle, arm in arm, humming "Here Comes the Bride." At the altar, vandalized of all its sacred details, they enact their mock ceremony, uttering vows and saying "I do's," and sniggering like blasphemous children. The girl finds none of this amusing; she doesn't want this woman even pretending to wed her father. She stares at them as they kiss and entwine. She sees their hands fondling, sees their squirming bodies, sees their obvious hunger for *something*.

The girl's blood races, her skin burns, as she watches the man spread his coat on the site of the altar. He and the woman swiftly undress. The girl sees a balloon enlarging from between the man's legs that points at the dark triangle of hair between the woman's legs. (The girl has seen that strange feature jutting from her boyfriend the day he poked oh so painfully the pee-wee into that hidden pocket of hers.) Lying down on the coat covering the hard floor, the woman stretches her thighs apart. The man lowers himself between them and begins bouncing on her body while she pushes back against his brutal thrusts. She writhes, wrapping her long legs around his midsection and raking her fingernails across the glistening skin of his back. They gasp and cry out as their tangled limbs rock violently.

The girl sees the bright red lines the woman has clawed across the man's back. She fears they are hurting each other, but she enjoys thinking of the man inflicting pain on the woman. In fact, she wants him to kill her, send her away forever.

She realizes that the middle of their bodies is the spot generating all the couple's fierce motility. For some reason she so identifies with this screaming woman that she feels as though it is against her own heated body that the man exerts his pounding weight. The girl lowers her cupped hand between her legs and rubs her damp flesh gently up and down, up and down. She edges her panties to the side and eases her middle finger up inside herself and works it around, the way she does when seeking to touch that green, elusive eye that her clever lover embedded in her.

She sucks in and exhales air in rhythmic pants, as though she's been running a long distance. A warmth floods through her and a trembling vibrates through her body. She shuts her eyes and thinks she's dreaming. It's like the warm chill of a fever sweetened by delirious visions. She gulps in the air of the dark church, as sounds of heavy breathing and sighing and crying out encircle her. The man's jabbing strokes penetrate the fragile body of her comprehension, violating its narrow boundaries and cramming more into her than she's able to receive. More than a marble is going in. Overwhelmed, she nonetheless craves to hold forever this fantastic place she's now uncovered, to be pumped and filled everlastingly with desires that must exceed all understanding if they are to remain desires of this nature. These desires *must* remain. How she knows this—just knows it with all her heart—she can't say. To her it seems that hours are passing and that maybe this ecstasy will indeed never, never terminate. Blinded by too much sight, no, no, she can't see an end to this; she doesn't want to. The eye within sees for her.

Still naked, the man and the woman stand and embrace. Their eyes are shut, as though they're sleeping. Is her father sleeping with this woman too? The girl watches, still breathless, still dazed like one awakened from an entranced state of ravishment—her soul permanently unsettled. Soon, the woman reluctantly unclasps her arms from the man's neck and steps back; each stares at the other's face. The girl suspects that this will be her last encounter with the woman. Of course she wishes this, but she has also inferred it from how the two sob, cling to one another, then release, and then cling again.

This desperation the child's never before noticed. But then, neither has she ever before seen them perform as they have in the church. It's difficult to comprehend what anything foretells. Yet the girl senses that this event is too special not to signal a conclusion. She discerns it in the way they're acting. They grip each other as though each is about to perish. For these two, the girl can imagine nothing that can follow.

So saddened by what she sees, the girl bursts into tears. She cries now so loudly she's positive the lovers hear her, but no, they don't, or they act as though they don't since they continue to caress in front of her despite her grief. Heartbroken, she wants her father to fling this naked woman out the red-yellow-blue stained-glass windows. But curiously, an opposite wish arises as well. She also envisions the three of them living happily together right here in this shell of a sacred house. A family—as it once was before he went away.

Eventually, the woman and the man dress. Afterward, he picks up a whiskey bottle from a pew and guzzles. He offers the woman the bottle, indicating she should keep it. He folds up his coat, and they walk outside. The child follows, weeping. The sun shines so brightly, it seems she has crossed into another world. The woman begins stepping hesitantly away from the man, swaying from side to side—after all this, still inebriated.

The girl races down the street ahead of her and stops and waits in open view. The woman carries in her right hand the green bottle of whiskey that the late afternoon sun strikes with a bead of emerald light. To the girl, the tall woman is now very pretty despite her crumpled clothes, tattered and ill fitting. A little too large, the clothes sag the way the girl's mother's do when, imitating her mother, she models before a mirror articles of mother's clothing.

In fact, as she studies this poor woman, the girl begins to detect a likeness in her features—her long, begrimed blonde hair; her soft, uncertain smile; the quick, uneasy movements of her watery-green eyes; her overall despair. She embodies an eerie reflection of the child herself, disguised, bedraggled, older certainly, but not unlike an aged image of herself that a dream of hers once projected years into her future. The dream revealed that she would one day look like her mother. She wonders if *this* woman is her mother. Has she gone in search of her father and along the way chanced upon her true mother?

No—no, because that is impossible. Nonetheless, the child's hardened heart has softened toward this woman who is now approaching closer and closer, her stride always a bit unsteady, as though reluctant to trust the stability of the earth itself.

Finally, a couple of paces from the girl, she halts and turns back, to again view the man seated on the church steps. He raises his hand slowly and waves. In response, she lifts the bottle, tilts it, and lets a few drops spill on the ground. He cups his hands as though to catch the spillage and smiles. She returns the smile. He reaches behind his back, and magically, another bottle appears. The woman shakes her head and turns away. As she does, her gaze lands exactly on the spot where the girl stands staring, her confusion showing in rapidly shifting facial expressions. Although their eyes seem to meet, the woman appears not to observe her.

Peering into the woman's green eyes is for the girl like staring into a mirror seeking to recapture a reflection that has escaped all recollection, just as she herself has stood—searching over the figures of mirrors for something she can't recall. The woman's unseeing gaze seems to pierce through the child and yet to focus on nothing, as though staring absently backward at a memory, the girl guesses; or perhaps at a dream that foresaw this sad place of departure. Young though she is, the girl understands that you must always keep a sharp eye peeled for the aftermath of dreams.

The woman extends the green whiskey bottle toward her so deliberately the girl assumes that she's supposed to take it. So persuaded is she of this that she reaches to grasp it, but the bottle shifts, or she misjudges its location, because somehow nothing touches her outreaching fingertips. It would have seemed very peculiar, except by now the child expects everything to elude her grasp. She looks again at the woman's face and finds that her vacant eyes still point at her and that the woman is now smiling toward her, yes, but not really at her. The woman then proceeds on, eventually disappearing around the corner.

The child feels that everything disappears. She believes that the woman has gone forever; that is what her mother said "passed away" meant—gone forever. Everything is passed away; nothing stays put. Does it? *Does it?* She wants to yell out her question. But to whom?

She is sorrowful because what she's just witnessed is, after all, another divorce. Someone else has lost this man. Is he only there to be lost? The woman has departed from him but (so the child wishes to understand) passed him on to his daughter.

She looks up the street at the man sitting there. The eye of the pussy strains to make him out. His head hangs down touching his knees, his hands clasp as if in prayer, no doubt beseeching God to return his daughter to him. The weather has become cool. His old trench coat drapes over his back like a shroud, the way the child recalls her mother's (or someone else's) skirt once did when she tucked him into her pocket as easily as you could a marble. The girl imagines that he must need love desperately because the woman has just abandoned him. The sun has sunk enough to once more leave the man's body only a shadow. The street, except for the two of them, stands deserted.

The girl decides that the time has come for him to reclaimed her and for her to resume her rightful role. The events of this day—the spectacle in the chapel, the woman's sightless vision and final departure, her own thrills and fears, sorrows, self-caresses, her own memories—the compounding of all these has vanquished any lingering indecision. Oblique realizations that have stirred within her impel her toward him, and the space vacated by the woman has, as well, made an immediate confrontation with this man imperative. The time is now. She is ready; so must he be.

Without hesitation, she strides toward the shadow. Through all the days she's been attending to him, whether she hid or revealed herself, she's believed that he not only knew of her presence, but that he also instantly recognized her, yes, even from the moment she ducked behind the trash containers in Blind Alley.

It's like a game of hide and seek you play with your father who at once unerringly apprehends where you're hiding but pretends you've duped him until you've had all the time you require to either allow him to uncover you, or all on your own, disclose yourself to him. Yes, she imagines, it's something like that. How precious this long-anticipated recognition is to her. She's nearly made it. All the obstacles she's endured—the dreams, the frightening spectacles all bravely entered, the unending maze of confusions survived—yes, and perhaps with the help of her internal eye she's managed to even glimpse her own transparency, her own invisibility. Oh, if only the little that remains to make it all worthwhile is not impossible to attain. The hour of revelation lies at hand.

As she approaches, her eyes rivet on him, as they would an object in a dream, an object which belongs so absolutely to you or you to it that you're incapable of looking elsewhere. Her heart pounds. He will tell her (of course he will, she reassures herself) why they who had lost each other have had to wind through this labyrinth of seeking and refinding; or at least, why *she* has had to. He will explain simply so that she will at last comprehend. He will explain why he left, why he jumped or was thrown out of a window, why the newspapers claimed he had died, why he did that animal thing with the woman on the chapel floor, why he's played this pitiless game with his very own daughter, even why the world's the way it is. He will address these strange desires that have been circulating inside her, circulating with unintelligible fears. If, as her father, he looks but fleetingly upon her beseeching face, she's convinced he will dispel all the world's dreadful perplexities. In that interval of absolute rest, they can fold into a perfect sleep together; they can dream on and on together.

She does *mostly* believe this, and yet, as she nears the culmination she has sought, a cloud of doubt darkens her hopes. What if her wishes and all her dreams have misled her? What if this man is *not* her . . . No, that possibility is too painful to entertain an instant longer. It's far too late for *any* second thoughts.

Trembling, she now stands before him, this shadow of her father, perhaps, by now, hardly more than a wraith herself. She waits, apprehensive, waits for him to lift his head. She is so very tired now. The uncertainty she vanquished only a short while ago surges up anew. But it is too late for any gloomy misgivings. And yet, what if he fails to acknowledge her, to joyfully greet her? What if he embarrasses her or is embarrassed himself? Perhaps they do not share a secret as she presumes. Embarrassment or shame could also surface from something other than a blood affinity that never existed. It could issue from an emptiness, the sort of emptiness that fills this hollow church that entombs only ghosts, the sort of emptiness that engulfs this neighborhood where people vanish or decompose, where only shadows or recollections linger throughout the space that he and she occupy.

She waits, shivering, as one condemned to death for crimes too complicated to fathom. But she's convinced that this too—the anxious, interminable waiting—constitutes part of the rediscovery, the recognition of the lost father, recognition she must earn, must earn by painfully expending herself to the very brink of extinction. Only then will he truly believe that he is all her life. Persuaded by this perilous conviction, she waits, as she has for so awfully long. She waits, exhausted, for him to see her, waits for a bright light to radiate her existence. A bright light from one shadow to another. But he fails to budge, locked as he surely is in agonized prayers for his daughter.

She waits. The night seems to darken. That's all that's happening: the dark getting darker. She wonders why he acts as though he doesn't even know of her presense, right now, here, before him, his very own loving daughter; even acting as though no one is standing here. She waits. The dark thickens. Even as a shadow he is fading out. She waits, suspended between this longing for her father and a hopelessness nearly too profound to tolerate.

What else can she do? The game's finished. What can she do? Nothing she knows of. She can hardly even see now the shadow of all her yearning. A photograph of her father once effaced itself in a dream, blurring into nothing. And here before her again, he resembles an amorphous ball, the mouth of a cave that she could enter and walk through straight to the heart of the earth, where all dreams either conclude or start over. Her heart's about to break.

She hears the words before she realizes she intended to say them. "Daddy . . . please." The shadow fails to move. She waits. She hears her own breathing. His shadow seems to enlarge, as it spreads and thins out, becoming evermore one with the engulfing night. She hears something—paper, glass rolling—that bottle must be rolling down the steps. She hears it break like the pane of a window. The sound is too familiar to startle her; it makes her sleepy. She extends her trembling hands into this expiring shape.

"Daddy . . . please," she repeats herself. Or maybe she doesn't. She doesn't know whether she's awake or not. But at last she feels the dark surrounding figure of her dream embrace her with a suddenly suffocating presence. Breathless beneath the weight of so much fulfillment, her heart bursts. And the eye within gazes blindly at itself.

The Trancing of the Toad Prince

A deep hypnotic trance, wherein I regressed beyond my birth to a former life, unearthed the most startling revelations about my prior existence during the Middle Ages. This knowledge revises the famed but false narrative of me that has been so long preserved. I divulge this now, not because the truer version unveils a finer, nobler picture (it doesn't), nor because of any altruistic devotion to historical facts, nor to deprive children of lies—no, but because *she* deserves a more revealing account. After all she did to me, I owe her this.

I became a fairy tale—the Frog Prince. Of the many extant chronicles of my life, only the great adventure has proven notable: the encounter with the princess. I am a tragic figure—misunderstood, abused, made over, calumniated—but to deceive children, anything's condonable. For one thing, I wasn't a frog, not one of those smooth-skinned fops whose succulent legs everyone chops off, cooks, and gobbles like candy. No, I was rough and bubbled, a manly toad; so manly my hide could exude a potent poison when I felt endangered. An animal who gulped a toad got a dose of death. (No human had ever wolfed down a living toad, so the septic effects of such excretion were, in those benighted days, entirely unknown. Humans had, of course, touched toads and developed warts after being peed upon.) Such details matter. Why, even the Grimms misreported me. (*The Grimms*—a life recounted by the Grimms!) And the day of the great adventure, I lay ruminating inside an old hollow log, reconsidering, as oft I would, the trauma of my early life, the circumstance that cast me into this earthly perdition. First, a word about that.

Before being metamorphosed, I was a prince. When I was twelve, my saintly mother died, presumably of a broken heart, after discovering for the umpteenth time Father fructifying the castle maidens. Following Mother's death, my father, king of Bumley, hastily remarried a woman ravishingly beautiful. This stepmother, apparently to "befriend" me, encouraged me to sleep in her bed. There, she would tease me or bestroke my brow whilst reciting poems of love. I was *sleeping* with her (how inexact language can be). Actually, she seemed to prefer me to Father. Very strange.

To decipher her intentions, I needed other categories of understanding, let's say. Not everything about the world any longer fit beneath a blanket of innocence. I was clumsy, but as you know, at that callow age, the sex drive spouts forth like a reckless weed. So, with such inner impetus, I let her go ahead and bediddle me; all of which, I shamefully own, quickly dissipated any melancholy surrounding the loss of Mother.

How swiftly I fell in love with her replacement. I changed overnight, and almost immediately I couldn't stand my new mother near Father, especially in bed with him, laughing and panting away at things that I fancied she indulged in only with me. More and more she excited me, explored me, and journeyed me over all the undulating terrain of her body; with mature guidance, escorted me around all her crevices and fissures. I discovered the wonderments of my penis, learning all the thrilling adventures rendered by its tumescence.

She also taught me the words: this was a *prick;* that, a *cunt,* a *tit,* an *asshole*—terms that never lose their wallop. "What's 'fuck' mean?" I inquired, guileless as a child (which I was). "Let me show thee, my son." Laid in the lap of an immense intelligence, I learned. Yes, inevitably, one evening she extended her thighs and drew me into her burning cavern. (Alas, at such a time, who can distinguish the gates of hell from those of heaven?) Yes, I did question whether I should be doing *that.* But Mother, perceiving the perfunctory nature of these doubts, reassured me, "Yes, yes, thou mayest, my child. 'Tis okay to fuck thy mum, so long as thou tell'st no one." Yes, yes. And *poof!*—all doubt flew off like a bird that never was. The sex was fantastic; the pleasure huge as the vaulting sky, magnificent as a shooting star. Indeed, for a child, too fantastic, because afterward, exhilarated beyond all constraint, I foolishly shouted that I must proclaim to the whole world what had befallen me, what I had become—a man—as my mother had made me.

Unfortunately, at that consummate height, matters took a decidedly downward dip. Grinding her teeth, Mother informed me that never— *never,* did I comprehend?—would she permit that. No! And moreover, neither could she even chance its possibility, especially now, after she'd heard my declared intention. "But, Mom, why?" I whined, perplexed and pitifully deflated.

"Because Mother's an evil witch who poisoned thy own mom, and who's also gonna kill thy own dad and usurp his kingdom. Time for Mom to snatch the reins."

Without a second thought, I said, "Fine!" (Nothing could be done about my deceased mother, and ruining Dad was, lately, a really superb proposal.) "We'll rule his kingdom together?" "No way, babe. You might squeal on Mummy and blemish her image." Wow! Imagine that—blemish the image of a witch! I saw her scowling, her now surprisingly ugly face twisted by a stern verdict against me. I was in over my head, flabbergasted. Quickly, she seized my balls and cracked them like acorns. I screamed. I vomited. I might have fainted. I felt myself changing, being rapidly transformed . . . somehow. Jesus, god—shrinking, imploding! And then I was catapulted through the air. Somehow she had pitched me out of bed like a piece of junk. She was either superstrong or I'd gone light as a feather. Dizzy, wobbly, I looked in the mirror and beheld what I had become: *a toad!*—squalid, ignoble, shit-green.

I stared long and disbelievingly at this grotesque rendition of me. Shocked, seeking consolation, I kept repeating, "'Tis but a dream. 'Tis but a dream." Yet there I was, as clear and distinct as I'd ever been, so the hideous "I" in the mirror appeared as real as anything ever is. After a frozen moment of speechless dismay, I finally spoke. (Thank the lord, my voice remained.) "What dost this mean, Mother?"

"It means thou art a toad, stupid." She—the first object of my love and lust—two-faced as Janus!

"What must I do," I tearfully beseeched, "to eradicate this heinous curse?" Ah yes, fully I grasped that this was an old-fashioned curse, and worse, maybe one thoroughly deserved. Maybe I was corrupt to begin with, a bad seed. Had I not only fucked my father's wife but also wished him dead into the bargain? Incest, patricide, regicide—what a malevolent day! Woe unto me. Then, however, was hardly the time to equivocate about my guilt. No, I desperately needed to know how to retrieve that comely prince of a lad I was.

Laughing maliciously, she replied, "When you come again as a man."

"But how canst a toad do that?"

"As a toad may go a progress through the guts of a princess." Huh?

So much for my origins, whether dreamed or not, for years (centuries, maybe) I pondered the conundrum: *When you come again as a man and go a progress through the guts of a princess.* Alas.

There I was the day of the great adventure, abiding peacefully by the well at the end of the world, minding my own business, hopping about, snagging dragonflies, swimming, lounging atop a moss-covered rock, croaking seductively to females, or hunched inside a rotted-out log, meditating philosophically—loafing, basically. Was I awaiting some momentous, transformative event? Who isn't? But perhaps I wasn't, because mine wasn't what you'd call a grievous life. Of course things could always be better; even in Eden we thought so. Yet as the representation of a prince too disguised for anyone ever to recognize . . . well, frankly, it was a curse I could live with if I had to. I did ponder the riddle of the curse, but the relentless pursuit of my restoration had long ago lost much of its urgency. Besides, eventually we make the most of our damned state—*if* temptation leaves us undisturbed.

But that fateful day: summer it was, noontime, when she came skipping merrily along, the happy, happy princess with her golden, golden ball. Right off, I suspected that this ball was a symbol. And she—too beautiful, too happy, too sparkling with innocence and fun—had to be a symbol too. Christ, I had to read, to translate! Things were not what they seemed. No, quick as a gnat in your eye, the situation imposed demands. Not an auspicious beginning.

Many a day I'd watched her from my grassy lairs, riding her white stallion, her long golden hair aflow in the breeze. Oh how oft I envied that lucky horse. And now here she was before me, sitting herself down on the green grass (damn, and near enough to jump!). Then, all asmile, she spread her white-as-snow virgin legs—shapely limbs that instantly caught a bulging eye. Naturally, I gave a goggle befitting any earthly male. As yet unnoticed, I avidly watched her playing with the gleaming golden ball 'twixt her thighs, dribbling it gleefully up/down, up/down. Cute as fuzz on a bug. Ah, the beguiling sweetness of little girls. I admit, toad that I was, eye-bopping with that golden ball did rouse me. But I knew my place. Boundaries prevailed here, socioeconomic, species, etc., that forbade trespassing. Yes, I was bedeviled with normal masculine thoughts, but a good citizen of the kingdom I was—insectivorous, yes, yet evil I was not.

Now, *there* would have been an end to the matter had she not lost control of her dribble and bounced the golden ball squarely into the well at the end of the world. I ducked adroitly as the shining orb sailed over my head to splash and then sink in the black well like a brick or a ball made of gold. Right off we're into depth, I thought. (I was like that—a thinker, an interpreter, a fool in many ways.) But she apparently wasn't. She wept for the loss of her precious jewel, her plaything, her bauble, that was all. How sad, as always, to see a princess cry. No, a princess weeps and you, *tout de suite*, leap like a knight to her rescue.

So forward I sprang, and at her feet inquired, "What ails thee, mistress? May I assist?" Startled, she gasped and gawked at me. You would have thought me some kind of inscrutable text or a gob of spit. One of her tears actually splashed on my forehead. For a moment I expected it to somehow transfigure me, but no, it didn't. (Naturally, women, to me, possessed awesome mutative powers. They make us, and twice they had made me. The tear that hit me, however, left me unfazed.) At once I discerned that my appearance shocked her. But around here, all toads spoke, so it wasn't just that.

"What? What—*you* assist *me?*" Ah yes, not a humble princess; but how few ever are (as I recalled from my former life)?

"I didn't mean to intrude. I live in the well. I merely wished to offer my services. That's all." Believe me, at this stage, I meant well.

"Ooh I see—your services." Suddenly, she seemed . . . eh, a bit flirtatious, I must say. "Whilst playing with my golden ball it bounced from me and disappeared in thy inky well, Monsieur Toad. I do bemoan its loss. Help me, please help. 'Tis my birthday."

"Your birthday? How wonderful. How old?"

"Twelve. A woman."

"Yes . . . a woman, indeed." I think my prick came *then* into play. I can't say for sure, but something beneath was astir that remained just a squint out of sight.

"Please, please help me. I'm distressed."

"Of course . . ."

"I'm destitute." (*Destitute?* Do twelve-year-olds use such language? Well, this one did.) "I'll reward thee handsomely, I swear."

"Handsomely?" Mind you, I would have done the boon for free, but when a princess proffers herself—though as obliquely as the instigation of a dream—well, you snap the bait and risk the hook. How often does this happen? Mostly never.

"Yes, yes, whatever," she replied impatiently.

"Whatever?"

"What*ever*. Please hurry, before it sinks too deep for even thee, great swimmer, to retrieve. Go and return to findest whatso'er thou dost desire." What phrasing! A savory sweetness oozed from her words like honey. But still too unschooled in these manipulative arts, she failed to entirely suppress her annoyance. Vaguely, I sensed myself getting carried away, things taking an ominous, mysterious direction. Something, I sensed, floated above my comprehension. But heedless I was as an ocean swimmer, paddling away, reckless as a fool with nothing to accomplish beyond drowning himself. Hm . . . that golden ball . . . for a second I considered the dense symbolism. Of course some things that are lost can't exactly be redeemed, and yes, I did suspect that this was possibly the situation here. Had I promised more than I could deliver?

"Not too deep for me, Princess. But you said *whatever I desire?* How 'bout dinner?" A spasm of revulsion contorted her throat, as though she were about to gag.

"Dinner? You mean you want to eat me?" *Eat her!* Where, oh where, was I being led? Before I could clarify myself, she said, "Sure. Dinner's fine. Drop by anytime." Real jocular—eat her anytime.

So I took the plunge. What had I to lose? "And . . ." I paused, enjoying, I confess, the power—or at least the illusion of it—I exercised over her.

"And? And *what?* Anything, I said!" Pissed as a spoiled brat she was. You daren't keep such a damsel hanging while you measure your courage.

"Let me sleep with thee."

"Sleep with me?" Now did she seem truly perplexed. "*Sleep* with me?" Words were a problem here, but the proposition in fact sounded so gross, that exactly what I meant befuddled even me. Sometimes words exceed us. "Sleep with me? Oh . . . yes, yes. But please hurry now. Yes, sleep with me, thou mayest. Please!" I felt like someone in a drama he hadn't rehearsed. This wasn't me. Fleetingly, I wondered if my extending prick now showed beneath my belly.

"Don't cry, Princess. I'll fetch that ball back. I can manage it. Trust me." She clutched her hands to her breast, and looking upon me with pure blue, imploring eyes, sealed the deal. I trusted her. I was her knight. So into the well's underworld I dove. Down, down I swam, with great strength and fortitude. Down, down into depths that seemed interminable—miles it was. Hours, months it took, perhaps years. (Remember, in Magical Land, Time was warped; it played with itself.) Indefatigably I plumbed those airless confines. Finally, I stopped the errant ball's descent. Handling it as carefully as you would an egg, breathless, practically suffocated, I resurfaced. Having all but drowned myself, I surged skyward—water gushing high as a geyser and brilliantly into the summer light, as though a miracle had been performed. Triumphantly I placed the precious golden toy in her eager, outreaching hands.

Then, weary as the nearly dead and trembling at her feet, I closed my eyes, puckered my broad yellow-green lips, and waited to be swept aloft and hailed with grateful kisses. I waited and waited. Nothing. Years could have elapsed. I opened my eyes. *Nothing.* She had vanished. It was as though I'd been dreaming. I admit it: I started to bawl like a baby, heart broken, betrayed. Not even a "Thanks. Now go fuck thyself." Oh, the hurt! Yes, even a tough, bubbly-skinned toad hath feelings. I reconsidered the episode. Maybe I *had* dreamed it. No . . . yes/no—it didn't matter.

I rallied, pulled myself together like a man. Hey, I was a contender, by god, I had a shot. I cast off self-pity, cleaned and spiffed myself up, and journeyed forth to claim my precious rewards. Oh, how little did I dream what would befall me. Perhaps, "Fool" *was* my nature. But upon how many toads had fate bestowed such opportunity as now was mine? So onward I sallied—small, but like a prince made for love.

The castle, a mile away, I reached by evening. Tired—but so what, with such glittering prizes beckoning? I thumped the castle door. Merriment issued loudly from within. Yes, the princess's birthday party. How uncanny that on this very day I had come to receive my gift. Waiting for admittance, I pondered this curious detail, scouring for undercurrents of elusive meaning. Things felt a little off, a little too coincidental; I searched for the plot. Birthday . . . expecting gifts on the day of someone else's birth . . . losing and retrieving the golden orb . . . water . . . awaiting entrance. Hm, yes, something worth reflection suggested itself, but—. The door opened.

"The princess expects me," I declared, feigning more confidence than I possessed.

"The princess? Expects *you?*" Such disdain. This very servant had flung a mallet at me in the palace garden a couple of days ago. Nothing personal, just ridding the environs of vermin. "I'll inform her. Wait right here." His tone, a bulldog growl, insinuated he might return with a club to bash out my brains. Don't ask why it never dawned on me that I might receive less than a joyful welcome here, but now I did begin to doubt the wisdom of my undertaking. (Was I a fool? Admittedly, that would explain a lot. Well, I was what I was, so a fool eats his folly. Pity me, if nothing else.)

So there I stood, poised at the threshold, already having come face to face with a would-be assassin. Was this woman really worth such endangerment to life and limb? But would any other than a true fool forego such alluring connubial bliss? In any event, I elected not to linger, exposed at the threshold. *Tout de suite,* I ventured inside; and like a dormouse, hid. Sure enough, the guardian of the threshold returned, concealing an ax behind his back. An ax! Funny, isn't it, how you just know these things? At his heels strode a sassy white cat with black hind legs, named Puss 'n Boots. A very perilous situation, indeed. Of course if Puss 'n caught and killed me, that would be the death of Puss 'n too. But not a trade-off that held any appeal for me.

They stepped outside to track me down, and mightily pissed was the guardian of the threshold. Incredible, the offence you can evoke with no malice aforethought. And he didn't even know me.

Anyway, off I sped to find Her Highness. What a sumptuous banquet, everyone eating lavishly, guzzling ale, and laughing boisterously. Hundreds had assembled to honor her birth. Tapers burned everywhere. All these people overjoyed she'd come into the world. What splendorous revelry. Awed, I nonetheless wondered: does anyone need this much celebration?

Damn, and there I stood, as good as nothing; a miserable outcast, despised; down on all fours, as intimidated as a rat; less than human. What, oh what, did all this superfluous grandeur mean, and me next to nothing, a zero? Prick me, don't I bleed?

I spotted her at once, as you would a fire in the dark. Hurriedly, I hopped right over to where she sat and jumped up beside her. She didn't notice me, but others around her, startled and taken aback, assuredly did. The maidens gasped as though they had espied a slithering snake, and the boys grabbed their dagger hilts and poised themselves for war. Quickly, the princess glanced down, her mouth contorted in revulsion, and she gagged. Not at all glad to see me. How awfully awkward and embarrassing.

"I have come to share this meal with thee, Princess, as thou didst promise." She leaned down; her flowing golden locks curtained around me, not to warm and comfort my shivering body, but to conceal me—an object of disgust.

With teeth clinched, she whispered, "Get away, thou vile, *vile* creature, or I'll have thee beaten and thy legs hacked and fried." This was very hurtful, even though through my toad life I had grown rather callous to such unkindness. But I had certainly noticed on the banquet tables mounds of fried frog legs (my poor, poor brethren!).

Swiftly I licked her earlobe, my long, sticky tongue flicking out as it would for a buzzing mosquito. Don't ask why. Call me "Fool." Maybe I felt I'd never get another chance to kiss a princess, that the ear of a princess passes within reach once in a lifetime, if ever. Aghast, she darted back, emitting a shriek, as though bitten by a venomous viper. Silence fell throughout the grand hall. Everyone gawked wide-eyed at us. You would have thought bloody murder had been committed. Terrified, but confused, I leaped to the table, anxious to flee if I could. Dear god, how easy to slip into scraps you can't escape! But the princess plainly intended to extricate herself from what she evidently regarded as a very nasty mess—the deal she'd cut with me.

Here the king bolted up like an unsheathed sword.

"*Silence!*" he shouted, although never have I experienced a silence as profound as the one that already prevailed in that immense room. The queen also flew up, scowling, ready to sentence whoever needed it to death. There I sat—a pinpoint beneath the angry, glowering eyes of all this royalty. Not a situation devoutly to be wished, believe me. "What is it, my beauteous child? Who troubles thee? Speak," intoned the mighty king.

"This toad's out to eat me, Father," she announced, pointing at me, as though I were not visible enough. Actually, she sounded fairly cool for one about to be eaten.

"Off with his head!" the queen shouted. Jesus, god . . . I confess I wet myself. A growling outrage rumbled around the regal multitude. The king, however, amidst this adversity, remained admirably composed, clearly a leader conversant with perverse negotiations.

"Be this so, Toad?"

"Your High . . . Highness," I stammered, "she . . . she invited . . . me to eat w . . . w . . . with her."

"Invited? What's this, beauteous one? Didst thou promise a toad thou wouldst dine with it?"

"No."

"No?"

"_____ _____ ean it. So that meant I needn't."

_____ en screechingly iterated.

_____ as her ass." What? What? *What* did he

_____

_____ th the toad."

_____ by her. We have decreed. Be it so!"

_____ ughtlessly blurted out, "King, my father, Your _____ ere's more." Undeterred by prudence, a fool plays _____ ghout.

_____ flash, the princess cupped a hand and swept me up to her _____ cious, luscious lips and again whispered in my ear, "Utter another word and I shall geld thee myself!" I was transfixed, more by the prospect of the princess fingering my toadly prick than the terrible threat of losing it. (Fool, granted—but was I also demented?)

"King, King, heareth me!" I bellowed, going for broke. She squeezed me. My aching balls lay on the chopping block. "Please heareth me, Lord."

"Let the toad talk."

"She promised to admit me into her bed as well." Another silence, this one as soundless as a bottomless sea. A benumbed incomprehension reigned. And then—

"*Off* with *her* head!" the queen, beside herself and totally distraught, screamed at the top of her lungs, flailing her arms like a mad woman flinging a hatchet. (It was the only handle she had on life.)

The king, although himself momentarily speechless, was ultimately unswayed by these menacing hysterics. "Speak, daughter. Didst thou vow to bed a toad?"

"Yes, Father, but I meant the opposite of what I spake; I spake the language of dreams, as We are ofttimes wont to do when such suits Our royal inclination." Such a mouth on her!

Richard E. Geha, Ph.D.
PSYCHOLOGIST/PSYCHOANALYST
1224 HOW LANE
NORTH BRUNSWICK, N.J. 08902
BY APPOINTMENT
(732) 249-2386
(609) 397-1368

The king grimaced, as though he had bitten into a pill of extreme bitterness. "No, that gibberish is unsuitable for lowlifes, of whom the toad beest one. Thou hast determined thine own ordeal. Live through it."

"Huh? What canst thou mean, Father—speaketh plain."

"Bed the toad."

The queen, as bleached as a turnip, fainted; the princess turned livid. But everyone else, after a brief interlude of disbelief, actually appeared to accept the princess's fate fairly well, even (dare I say?) with some bemusement. And down we sat to our repast. Shorter than others, I brazenly plopped atop the table (had I not the king's permission?) and fed from the princess's very own dish (mine the only amphibious limbs unsevered!). She glared with blue-blooded revulsion. Her face drenched with disdain, adamantly she refrained from barfing. I grinned foolishly from ear to ear, a Cheshire cat as scared as a yellow-bellied sapsucker. Scared and exhilarated, in the plate of the princess, with legs alive! *This* my fifteen minutes of fame.

"Everything about thee sickens me!" Her darting words stung like poison-tipped arrows.

"Such as?" I barely managed to respond.

"That bumpy vomit-green skin, thy size, and stupid shape! Thou squattest, always relieving thyself. Yuck! Pip-squeak! Defecating dwarf! That asinine grin, thy gait—canst thou not even walk right? That moldy smell— yuck!—and penniless as a louse, as groveling as a worm . . . dung-eating riffraff pretentiously mimicking thy betters. Selfish, selfish, selfish, trying to bully and . . . and *mount me!*—*bully* and mount *me* as would a studly knight. Thou art abnormal, mad as a hatter . . . a creep. Thou art—"

"Please, enough. I get the picture." Then, most philosophically, I added, "To thou, I beest what thou dost thinkest me."

"Yes, a slime bucket."

"A slime bucket?"

"Thou art," she sighed, "he whom I must survive." He whom she must survive. If ever a twelve-year-old spoke like an old soul . . . At least she recognized me as a thing worthy of regard, like horse shit in her path.

"Dost thou hate me so because I'm *other?*"

"Other? Thou dost speak like a creep, too. I'll kill thee when I can, hack thy balls off and throw them like pig nuts"—*pig nuts!*—"in the well at the end of the world. I'll—"

"Please, my lady, spare me . . . thou dost rend mine heart in twain."

"Haw! A reptile's heart? Don't make me laugh." Daintily she picked up two succulent, fried frog legs from her platter, and dangling them before me, remarked with sinister glee, "Here's thee."

"But I love thee," I said, quivering, but whether with love, lust, or fear, or just a bloody brew of all these, 'twas impossible to determine.

"What! Don't make me laugh. The lowly can't love. You little bunghole!" But she did laugh, and then hesitated before asking, "What dost thou love?" Oops, I felt I'd accidentally struck a very, very sensitive chord. She gazed into my enormous toad eyes as into a looking glass. I'd seen that searching expression in my own eyes when I peered into ponds at my own indelible ugliness.

For this princess, there existed only one reply: "I love thy beauty."

"But you barely know me."

"But I've watched thee every day from many a grassy hideout 'round the castle. I'm enthralled."

"Enthralled?" she repeated. I could detect the viscous substance of the word spilling and seeping into her vanity. She actually smiled and seemed at last about to utter . . . well, something kind.

Unfortunately, at this delicate juncture the king rose. He glanced at the queen, who now rocked woozily, pitifully unable to sober up. He nodded to four servants, who carried the poor, sagging mother from the room. "Thou hast supped enough," the king then declared to the guests. "Go now to thy next carousals. Remember, *when We pledge Our Word, to princes and toads alike, We honor it,* if necessary with Our blood, virgin or no. We have spoken. Go—be ye merry."

Since I didn't wish to frolic further with this bunch, exposing myself beyond the king's wise and just purview to additional insult and possible mishandling, I said to the princess, "I must depart. Later, to thy bed shall I come."

"Do, and dead meat thou art," she hissed. As I glimpsed her hand sneaking toward a knife that lay near, I leaped speedily away, deciding that for now I'd really enjoyed enough. With great vigilance I maneuvered through a throng of scurrying feet that seemed not disinclined to stomp out my existence.

Once out of the castle, I hightailed it like a toad on the lam. I managed eventually to make my way back to my mossy rock near the pond—home! Exhausted, and still achurn with that odd compound of exhilaration and trepidation, I collapsed, totally bewildered by my adventure. What did it all mean? To cool my fevered brain and soothe my fatigued body, I dove into the well's dark but familiar waters, trying to rejuvenate myself for the amorous eve that I prayed awaited me. Surely the princess would not defy Father, and cheat me of my just desserts. Surely not, not if filial piety yet retained a shred of worth!

For an hour I floated meditatively, feeling more than usual the blood of the curse coursing palpably through my misshapen body. To woo this princess, oh what a difference a princely appearance would make, to flaunt all the trappings of royalty. The form mattered to her, not the substance. After an hour, I drifted into sleep and seemed to sink into the well's murky depths. I dreamed: *When thou dost come may go a progress again as a man through the princess's guts through the guts come as a man through a princess when . . .*

Eventually, I awoke, surfaced, and with haste lit out for my rendezvous, as though moving from a dream full of babel into waking necessitated no adjustment at all. Indeed, the realm of waking, whatever else it might be, is simply less real, that's all.

As usual, guards encircled the castle, standing watch for greater dangers than I—a toad in lust. Yes, *lust*—surely that best described that inner drive directing me, a propulsion old as life itself, older than love.

I slipped quietly past Puss 'n Boots, asleep inside fur-coated dreams. How fortunate for both of us this pussy hadn't swallowed me. Then easily, as though escorted by an invisible hand, I found my way into the princess's lavish bedroom. Nothing stops a fool's folly. Everything seemed to unfold outside my awareness, as though I were playing in a plot not my own.

It was a little past midnight, August, very hot. A full moon hung shining all too brightly through the window like a demon's lantern. She lay naked, *more* than naked, as only a princess in a myth or in a dream could possibly be. I perched upon the bed railing, entranced at her glowing moon-white skin, a nimbus of beauty, still as death. My throbbing heart hammered warnings too overbearing for reason to heed. To and fro my eyes roved over the curves of her young body, only twelve and as perfect as any body could be.

Whether God or devil sent, her beauty glowed in heavenly light. I rocked back and forth, shamelessly pumping my ding-a-ling like a loon. Odd, but while satisfying myself, I decided that with that I'd put an end to this bizarre liaison—yes, jack myself off and leave princess dreaming of her fair prince. Naturally, I felt sorry for myself, but after all, who was I to disturb the slumber of a princess? I, a nobody, just as she had asserted. She was right after all. So in secret I'd merely indulge this harmless self-pleasuring and then scram.

But no, fate had decreed otherwise. She woke! Why? She heard the bed creaking? Heard me panting? Heard my regret groaning like a dying dragon? Felt a moon shadow slip weightlessly over her too-delicate complexion? Felt my thoughts tickling her privates? Or in a dream, stroked by her lover, wakened with hopes of his incarnation? However it occurred, she woke, moon glazed and dreamy eyed, stretching her radiant limbs. Oh yes, surely expecting some lover (other than a toad). Abruptly, she spotted me; stunned, her mouth dropped open with a gasp. Naked as she was, she could not, did not, move a muscle. What an effect—I must confess—

Beauty paralyzed by moi. *Me!*—as good as a gorgon's head. The choice?
Clear as day: pounce now or forever pound your pud! But no . . .

"Good evening, Princess. 'Tis I," my deep baritone as courteous as
one can be while pounding one's dick, skipping scarcely a beat.

"Fiend! What art thou doing here?"

"Here to enjoy the rest of my reward. But—" Bone hard and cranking
like a backward lunatic, I was about to explain my intentions to take my
leave (oxymoronic as that may have appeared while pecker pounding).

"Not on thy life. Not a drop of this virgin's blood for thee, Buster."
(*Buster!* So ahead of her time. A woman not easily bested, no sir.) She
actually bared her teeth at me. My god, she hates me, really hates me, I
thought. For a thinker, I was slow, but her hatred . . . that much was evident
enough. Could ever I have doubted it? Hated me, yes, wanted me
annihilated. I could tell, just tell. She elevated herself on her elbows, and
now she herself became aware of her bedazzling nakedness. She looked
down at her outstretched body, seemed to appraise it, and a strange calm
settled over her moon-pale complexion. A weird moment, indeed. What
was going on as we both gazed at her loveliness—both, I think, equally
impressed with the spectacle? (And I had not stopped wanking. Paying so
much attention to *her*, I guess desisting never seriously occurred to me.)

She glanced up at me and at what I was doing, then back at her own
luminous body, then back up at my busy activity, and then she smiled.
Smiled! I don't know what came next. I think I wanted out of there. Then
why did I say, "Thy father bade thee comply, to keepeth thy promise"?

"Oh yes . . . yes, my father did. I remember that now." She raised her
head and . . . and kept smiling at me. What, oh what, did that smile
mean? Derision merely, or welcome? I detected in her expression
something dangerous; inviting, yes, but with malevolence. However, there
wasn't time to study this fully. For a toad, meat's a flicker; snag the bee
on the fly or it's lost.

"Art thou sure this be thy wish?" she inquired, in tones melodious
with lust. Twelve years old! My god, had my ever-acute hearing betrayed
me? She glanced down again at her lunar-clad body and slowly spread
her legs wide. What? Did I dream? Spooky. Here again unfolded one of
those scenes that spelled doom because I had unthinkingly consented
to pay any price. Art thou sure this cunt be what thou desirest most?

I blurted, "Yes." *Brilliant!* Said *yes!* There it was—the toad-
transcendent moment of my life. "Yes" was the only possible response.
Incapable now of distinguishing my pecker from the rest of me, my soul
in my hand, I yanked away shamelessly. "Yes, yes," the pecker roared.

"Yes?" she echoed, with a gleaming moon-smile as hard as silver.

"Yes, yes, yes, mine own dear love. I say *yes*."

"Thy own dear love? Thou sayest yes. Then cometh unto me. I keepeth my troth." She arched her hips (my god!) and extended her arms toward me, me—frozen as the bone I had sculpted into polished stone. But, I'm ashamed to admit, I now didn't know exactly what to do. Yes, what to do and how to do it? It dawned to me—as though for the first time!—that I was a toad, not precisely configured for this invitation from a goddess as she was humanly embodied before me. But I took the great leap and landed betwixt her thighs. And there, there in the vale of milk and honey, I froze again. I waited! For what? Instructions? Divine intervention? And what occurred? The lips of her vagina opened! Imagine—the gates of paradise! For a moment, because I was too dumb or terrified, I seemed not to comprehend. No—I didn't get it.

But she kept simplifying *le texte*, until even a half-wit could decode the message. Okay, but how was I to handle this? Her opening had enlarged gigantically, comparatively speaking. Horrifying temptation accosted me. My toadhood scarcely measured up to such daunting insertion. This was not a female toad before me, whose butt I'd bound in two shakes of a toad's tail. No. I heard her snickering pitilessly.

"Well, what's holding thee up, lover?" she taunted. Speechless, I longed to scat back to the pond, and beg one of my own kind to nurse my wounded pride. The princess was right, I could now acknowledge: I did fare from the wrong side of the pond. Yes, therein lay the *whole problem*. Very well, but right now another *hole problem* confronted me. A *void* to avoid. Yes, ready I was to turn tail and end my little fiasco, with nothing gained certainly, but other than a little face, nothing lost. That was still possible. Don't monkey with Pandora's Box. But no, it was not to be. She continued to present the orifice of lust, the wet bloodred lips breathing heavily, gasping like a fish on dry land. Riveted, I just hunkered there, too stupid and ill equipped to perpetrate the deed. Sweating it out, frantically rubbing my magic wand, I awaited a miracle.

Well, what do you think happened? I squinted, as one would at the most impenetrable and feared of all texts: *the void*. But there's nothing there, I thought . . . except (I was confused) . . . . the *absent*. What is that? Nearly everything. Stunning! She, doubtless perceiving that at this decrepit pace a hundred years could lapse before I budged, reached down and cupped me solidly by the butt. Thinking my life kaput, fear paralyzed me. She giggled, giggled like a fucking twelve-year-old at my humiliation, amused by my impending extermination. What, oh what, had she in mind? Gradually, she goosed my inert body, inching it forward, nothing but dead weight. One inch, two inches, three . . . then I got it. I got it! And like a crocodile, at the vestal casement, I crashed. *Arrivé!* With legs and arms bent and tensed (the swimmer), I plunged with all my worth—a veritable battering ram. First, in-barging my head, then, with maximum force, the body—foot-long in length and diameter—big as an infant. By god, and I was in! *Was in! In!* Surprisingly, it was totally dark. Hmm . . . The womb is not, as you've imagined, well lit.

Submerged, I felt the vibrations of her groans and cries, like echoes in a cavern, or screams reverberating through a deep ocean. I felt the rippling walls of her diaphragm, her pelvic muscles release and contract, the up-and-down bounce of her abdomen, the swing of her hips tossing me like a tongue in a bell. *Bong. Bongbong. Bong.* What a wild, bucking ride. Ecstasy—mine, hers, nothing but breathless sensation. The blood of her hymen tasted like cherry wine. My penis bulged hugely with a tumescence that assumed the entirety of me. Every few seconds I blew my wad. (I know, I know, I couldn't believe it either.) But, my god, I'd come again as a man! As a total prick, even a toad can do that. The curse was not so crazy after all. Configured by desire, my prick was I, as hermetically sealed by the powerful walls of her stomach as an entombed mummy. Jarred and galloped, the rider or the ridden—from ecstasy to ecstasy I was cast. *Bongbongboing.*

Presently, however, a mild apprehension emerged, which then began rapidly to increase. Like hurling yourself from the parapets of a castle, exhilaration quickly turned to dread. What was she doing? Vertigo engulfed me, as I spent the juices of my body in quick, continual spasms. My depleted lungs were starved for oxygen. How long could I endure this breathless rapture? Toad though I was, and renownedly adept at aquatics, after a while, some air I had to have. Then the horrible truth hit: My god, she wasn't going to let me out. She had taken my cock at its word. She would drown me in my own cum. Suckered again—framed by the view of a woman. *Déjà vu*—into another grave plot of my undoing. She had squeezed her thighs together to impound me—a fly corked in a bottle, bandied and shaken, practically beyond endurance. Had she misunderstood my desire? Had I? There I was, seemingly given what I had craved, and now in possession of it, totally possessed *by* it! Fucked to death! I had gotten what I asked for. Had she? It was astounding. Pained as she undoubtedly was, she used me for a fabulous screwing; she got off on me. Dildoed I was by her sweet revenge. Buried alive, I swung like a pendulum in the pit of my own lust. Rocked and locked in place. For her, it must have furnished the perfect delight. Bound and disciplined . . . but not your usual B & D by any means. What, oh what, was I thinking when I barged into this, the mouth of all life? My very own cunt-coffin!

Sex had ruined me once before and now again it paved my downfall. I became frantic, twisting and turning with all my might in this death-hole. I blew myself up, straining to burst the seams of this womb-tomb. I licked her savagely until she bled, tongued the tip of her heart. All, unfortunately, only further enhanced the little princess's insatiable appetite. *Bang. Bang.* Everything I did accelerated her excitement; the totality of me excited her, my every movement—if only I had been having a less harrowing time of it. So *in uteroed,* I lost all sense of time. I may have passed out.

Strange, but even amidst my terror it all felt stupendous. I must have shot off a hundred times, one explosion igniting another. If, indeed, ecstatic deaths occur, surely a dozen were mine. Or was I being blasted unto death by the rapid fire of her countless orgasms? Who could explain this? I had lost my mind. Perhaps terror circulates through all our joys, sometimes as silently as the blood streaming through our veins. When Death embraces, maybe a benevolent masochism o'erfloods us—the psyche's last loving deed.

Inner-coursing with the princess, these contradictions commingled—the bliss of terror, the terror of bliss. Meteorites burst in my addled brain. But other than those stellar lights, I saw nothing. What was *she* going through? I couldn't see inside the woman I was in. The longer I resided in her—the way I was in her—the less I seemed to conceive her. Perhaps I was blindly immersed in her for months. Time was a thing of the past. Awash amid the beatitudes of an eternal sea, ecstasy interfused with terror. Static as a turd I flew. I smelled and tasted blood, piss, sweat—both hers and mine. My burning skin bubbled with greasy exudation. Ecstatic death! Ruptured, imploded with a myriad little deaths, I shit myself too. Well and good, but how much of this could *you* take? Who is made for this much pleasure, for the actuality of dreams? The gods? Maybe so. But for us sublunar lovers, such ultimate rapture annihilates, crushes the fuck out of us like a suffocating nightmare.

All I wanted now was out, out into that life beyond these unrelenting walls of flesh. She groaned, as her embrace steadily squashed my guts and broke my bones. Like Jonah, bellied in that gigantic fish, afloat in the midst of his nether world, my soul fainted within me. Apparently, I'd committed some egregious act and this fucking-unto-death was the punishment imposed. Yes, that's always the way to make sense of the inexplicable: blame yourself (and of course, you're rarely wrong). So, I was sorry for whatever I'd done. *Whatever.*

This was no time to split hairs. "Dear Lord," fervently I prayed, "release me from this jam and I'll never do again another wrongful thing. Never will I tolerate—if this be my crime—myself being goosed into the princess cunt." Desperate as a cat some sadist had tied in a gunnysack and chucked into the river, I meant what I said.

Forlorn and god-forsaken, only a drop of life remained, a moment more and I would have been snuffed. And then—

The vigor of her paroxysms slightly abated. She began to simply tremble, as though a diminished electrical current sang through her nerves. And that went on and on, for who knows how long . . . years, perhaps. But done so nearly to death, was I hallucinating, or was she indeed relinquishing . . . weakening? Was I, finally, too much for her maidenhood to master in one grueling life-death bout? Was I more than she, so young and untested, had bargained for—my size, my power, my own tenacious determination? After all, I was fighting for my life.

But who could tell about Her Highness? Through all this she'd been pretty speechless. Immured in the middle of her as a total prick, sightless, I saw nothing of her. What a prick I'd turned into—everything about me. I was her prick—her very own. How complete she must have felt . . . to herself or to me? Or was she a whole without me? Is it for me to speak for her? Did I know what she felt while fucking herself with me; fucking herself, and who knows what else—digesting me, perhaps? She was an extraordinary woman, I must say. Who but she could have schemed this: kept her word to her father, enjoyed the screwing, and killed the jerk who raped her? Twelve years old!

Still, for whatever reasons, she was letting up. Then, suddenly, her contractions reintensified. Yes, but oh with a vehemence quite oppositely directed. Now she writhed more as a snake struggling to disgorge a toxic clot that its gluttonous hunger had disastrously ingested. Had her own abysmal urges proved too ferocious? She'd nearly eaten me to death, and yet, she shrieked and moaned as though she (!) were about to perish. Maybe she was.

Terror permeated my jumbled thoughts. Twisted about, having been unable to tell up from down, pressed and wrung out, tangled as a Gordian knot, flooded and choked by virgin blood . . . nothing made sense. But, oh, I *was* re-forming. My alteration here was spiritual; certainly it was, but somehow physical too. Not just reformed of soul and character, I was also turning around in her belly. Topsy-turvy. And not just rotating like a wheel, either, but re-forming—physically, I mean, my very substance, cell by cell. (You do know this when it's occurring, believe me.)

Jesus, jesus, joy springeth eternal. Her crack was cracking, slightly, ever so slowly, but cracking. I glimpsed a gleaming sliver of light of—yes, the lovely world I'd always known. I pushed; she pushed. God's hands served as the forceps here. I pushed with all my living might. Yes, and now reversed, head down, I was definitely heading out; every fiber of my being revivified, my energy redoubled. Still, you don't consummate this task alone. She was, thank god, laboring mightily to deliver me. I could sense her great pain, her own fear and ecstasy, but did these feelings have the same meaning for her as they did for me? Bonded now in this together, it seemed we wrestled toward a common end.

Then, both of us in rhythmic accord—*boom!* I flushed free! Bursting forth, gasping, oxygen-starved, my lungs were infused with new air, and I wailed with boundless gratitude.

She was panting, as though she had climaxed not only me back to life, but herself to freedom. Exhausted she lay, her legs asprawl, with me a bloody ball betwixt, pulsating and bawling. I was so happy. We had made each other. *How a toad may go a progress through the guts of a princess.* Did it all at last make sense? Not then; I was not all there. *What had happened?* My god, surely a miraculous birth if ever there was one. Oh this holy virgin. She couldn't help herself; she had been, unwittingly, the fated instrument of my deliverance. Yes, she had been, against all her premeditated intent, not the death of me, but the salvation. Although probably as confounded as I by this grotesque affair, she may not have viewed it this way. (I hated to believe that I, whom she had so voraciously incorporated into her very being, had simply become too revolting to contain, and ultimately, too hard to even kill. I hated to believe that aborting me brought happiness to anyone.) Still, I was glad to be alive.

Yet something was wrong with me. I was different; I felt it. Felt what? Peculiar . . . somehow newly made. I'd gone in, survived the ordeal, been birthed, and redeemed. But of my former self, I could detect no recognizable trace.

I couldn't think. While I was struggling to recall who *I* was, she unexpectedly lurched forward, groped urgently between her thighs, and quickly finding me, squeezed firmly, harshly.

Oh no, not again! What . . .

Exerting her last ounce of strength, she flung me against a wall of stone. In her mind, I'm sure, she was trashing the filthy toad for good. What unwavering determination my mistress displayed! She had done all she could, by god, to rid herself of me. I crashed. In blinding pain I plummeted over the edge of consciousness again into utter darkness. I remember thinking, "Mother of mercy, she's killed me."

How long my unconsciousness lasted, I can't say—a minute, a day, a century . . . Maybe I'm still sleeping. I dreamed of snakes shedding their skins, caterpillars unwrinkling into moths, tadpoles squiggling into frogs, sinners ascending as saints, vaginas losing their teeth and softening into the crimson lips of loving mouths. I dreamed of myself changing in front of a mirror, and what I saw reflected was amazing beyond belief. *Déjà vu*—dear god . . . . I woke, so stunned by the image I had faced, an instant amnesia veiled the dream.

More of the incredible ensued. The princess was clasping me warmly in her arms, caressing me, stroking my fevered brow, kissing me tenderly, and murmuring into my ear. "I love thee, love thee with all mine heart, now and forever. Unto thee I do render my body and soul, do betroth mineself. Thou hast made me thine. Thou art my dream, mine own dream that I hath made come true." I understood the words, of course, I just couldn't decipher their meaning. What was she saying? Who was this to whom she spoke thus? And . . . and . . . and who was this whom she embraced as her lover?

"Princess, please, I don't understand. How canst thou love me? Thou hast murdered me."

"Oh, my darling—yea and nay, I did and I didn't, thou art who thou art and not whom thou wert. 'Tis all so clear now. Forgive me for not recognizing thee. After splattering thee against stone—oh, my poor, poor darling—I rose to scrape thee up and dump thee down the hundred-foot-deep commode of my bedchamber. It was then I beheld thee, my brave, my handsome prince. But hadst I immediately discerned the truth of thee, wouldst thou be here as thou now art, released from what I know was the curse of some wicked bitch? I thinkest not. Through travails thou hast been returned to thine own self. Both aborted and resurrected thou hast been. Sometimes, sweet love, we just gotta go through hell to enter heaven. Sorry, but it wasn't easy for me either. Killing thee proved more burdensome than I'd conceived."

"Please, of what art thou speaking?" She stood up, as nude and bewitching as when last I beheld her; through everything her incomparable beauty had prevailed undiminished. Moonlight still glowed hauntingly throughout the room, though whether it was the same moonlight, the same night or year, I knew not.

"Come, my love. Let me show thee thine own true self." Taking my hand, she led me to the mirror. How uncanny . . . yes, it was the same mirror that had appeared in my dream. And the second before I looked into it, I knew precisely what I'd see: my lost-and-found self. And sure enough, there . . . the prince. Tall, handsome, twelve years old (recommencing at the age of my first termination). I was dumbfounded. She had vanquished the animal aspect of me and annulled the curse inflicted by the evil mother. The pale smiling face of my princess, dyed with moon-white luminance, stared at me in the glass; all the happiness in the world spread o'er her features. My god, she had delivered me!

She reached down—I cannot say I didn't flinch—and lightly grabbed my golden balls. My prick at once erected and I reentered her. (Wouldn't you think I would have given a moment's pause? No—you know me well.)

The embrace was divine. Two twelve-year-olds. In the mirror I witnessed our wedding as in the reflection of a dream.

But sadly, ours was not the joyful ending you've told to children. Our divine coupling lasted perhaps a minute before she convulsed violently, quivering as though struck by a streak of lightning. Stark panic seized us both. She then froze and stared at me; her shocked blue eyes, suddenly moon-gray, glassed over with bleak consternation. Within moments, she sagged, and I eased her dead weight to the floor. Heart-stricken, I instantly realized what had occurred. How oft had I witnessed in the predators of toads this excruciating attack of septicemia. By accident she had committed suicide. By inserting me into her vagina and then nearly strangling me to death, she had compelled me—in an instinctive response—to exude through the ducts of my skin that protective toxin. Dear god, I did not mean to poison her (or maybe I did). So profoundly interred within her flesh, I had been beside myself, struggling desperately for life, for a gulp of air. She was surely the first human being to die thus, and surely the last to have so totally engorged a living toad. She could not have known the risk she ran. And how could I ever have foreseen these tragic consequences?

Lovingly, I hugged lifeless beauty, magnificent even in death. I wept until it was nearly dawn. Then, I left her there, and like a murderer, slipped from the castle, passed Puss 'n Boots, still asleep, hunting through dreams for a toad to devour. When the sun rose, the weight of its light was almost unbearable. I saw too much of the world illuminated, too much of myself.

I decided against returning to Bumley where Mother undoubtedly now reigned. The pleasure of being roughhoused again by almighty woman, I could actually now decline. Self-exiled, I wandered from town to town, continent to continent, century to century, from one lifetime to another, grief-sickened, sorrowing for her and for myself, for what we had both lost—her life.

No one ever discovered what had happened; no one ever knew the price or the means of my ghastly redemption. The events of that day have been enough to permeate the timelessness of history. Through all the years that have followed the day of the toad and the princess, the story (expurgated beyond recognition) has been told and retold to children. Mythic, timeless, she and I have thereby remained narrated, kept alive, even though merely as distorted, bowdlerized remnants. This new edition of ourselves I dedicate to the princess. And now *you* know the whole story imparted in a trance wherein I was reengendered. Tell your children, if you dare, but a curse upon whoever tries to alter or rebury me.

Amid Loss and Disorder

Do forgive me. I must say, I'm *so* disoriented. Awakened by two such handsome gentlemen, unfortunately for such dreadful purpose. I *do* hope this nightgown's not too see-through in this light. I can't tell, myself. But if I can be of use . . . I'll try to be coherent for this.

Oh my lord, the poor, dear, darling child! How dreadful to imagine. Well, yes, but even so, even given what you gentlemen already have implied—oh yes, we think you *have* implied and very explicitly too. But then, an old woman finds distress everywhere. We've sobbed our eyes out.

Anyway, where did we last see Lea? Through this pane—oh, how neglectful! I do forget myself. May we serve you a cup of hot tea? Coffee— no, I'm sorry. We don't drink coffee here. It abnormally arouses the mind, and here that's quite unnecessary. Besides, we sleep most of the time. You know; you found me. My hair . . . oh, I'm such a muss. But tea . . . perhaps a biscuit? No? As you prefer.

Yes, that's right. Looking out our living-room window. *That* window, directly facing No-Place Lane. It *is* funny, isn't it? Called *No-Place*, I've always assumed, because it's the shortest street in our little nowhere town, and after three quick blocks, it simply dead-ends at the bus depot. Odd, isn't it? From there you could, I guess, travel anyplace. Busses go everywhere. But where's there worth going? What? Hm . . . Oh we're sorry. My mind wanders. We're old, you see. But pretty well preserved, as you can tell. Oh, thank you for your kindness.

But yes, *that* window. Gazing out I was, as you two are doing now, at precisely 6:30 AM, Saturday last . . . Oh! Well—when was it, then? Just continue? Say what I have to say? Very well. Sometimes it seems I can't tell yesterday from today. You know how that is, of course. After a while, it's all one. I hope you gentlemen can write your notes all right. A little overcast today, I'm afraid. Nothing's clear. Like last Saturday. Remember? Hard to see in here. If there's a drop of natural light, we never switch on our lights.

But why take notes? A strange question? Really? Do you think so? What's actually occurring here you're not jotting down anyway, are you? Besides, if you want, we'll retell it all to you. What have we better to do than recount events that maybe happened to me? Stay awhile . . . please. I'll recall everything . . . just for you. You two . . . you're too busy to properly remember, though, aren't you? Too young, too wickedly handsome. I know your sort. Hunters. What do I mean? Why, nothing, my dears . . .

Too factual, too. Facts have nothing to do with remembrance, I always remind myself. What? I mean nothing. Forgive me. I'm so distractible . . . was, even as a child . . . Lea—the centerpiece—yes, that poor forsaken life. That's right. I saw her from there, as we said. I recall the exact hour, you must like that, "the *exact* hour," because my husband, Frank, had departed only minutes before, rushing off to work as usual, catching the early-bird bus. I had been watching him walk away from me toward the station, walking slowly, poor man, because he was tired and unwell and also unhappy—unhappy with me. Yes, I can say he was; *he* said he was, if that matters.

It was snowing fairly heavily, as you boys probably recall. Well, I *certainly* recall, because he disappeared after a single block, vanished as into a soft white blanket, like a phantom into nowhere. A small red feather was tucked in the band of his hat. Funny, the trivia that sticks for years in memory. He considered that feather very attractive, thought that it attracted women. Lea loved to stroke her fingers along it. You could easily detect the effects of her allurements upon him. I think he even wet himself once. Pardon me for being so crude, but do men think we're blind? He remarked, he'd like to eat her up. I laughed, naturally. I was always afraid he'd leave.

When I was fifteen, my father ran off with a girl (a *trollop*, my mother called her) three times younger than himself. Her name was Lea too. Mother claimed it was because she too often caught him "peeking on" me, as she phrased it, or "eating out your private parts," she said. What did she mean by that? I'm not sure. When your mother was as crazy as mine, you're never entirely assured of what she meant. But he left. A terrible loss.

So he looked at me. So? Look your fill. I used to charge the boys in the neighborhood a buck a shot.

But she—the Lea *you're* after—was indeed lovely. No, I haven't seen him since, if that matters. That morning I really missed seeing him off . . . I mean because usually I can, if I choose, and I often do, follow him with my keen eyes every step of the three blocks down No-Place. At the end, he always turns and waves goodbye to me. Sometimes I wave back, although we realize that the reflections of the pane probably make it impossible for him to ever see me, or for us to definitely know if he ever does. Seems like yesterday. So he can't be sure, can he, whether or not I'm here watching him leaving me? Go ahead, walk to the other side and try peering in, if you'd like. You'll see how differently things appear. I'll wave to you. It's like a shadow behind a mirror, a mirror with depth. Yes? No? All right. Yet, I'm convinced that my beloved, Frank, wherever he is, maintains an abiding faith, and I'm glad to believe he does, that we shall always be there, here, watching and waiting. And mostly he's been right. We've stood there, stood here, faithfully, watchfully waiting fifty years, not going anyplace. Waiting, fifty years—can you imagine? Why? You ask, *why?* Oh, my poor darlings. You're too young to understand what loss, a particular sort of loss, can do. Waiting forever's really not at all too long! Eventually, you become afraid of never again . . .

Oh yes, *again*, we beg your pardon. At that moment, the moment he faded from me, Lea and I stood there staring into the blinding snow— yes, now and then refocusing on big flakes that would strike the window and cut jaggedly down the pane melting—yes, leaving me again staring back at that benumbed whiteness—yes, it was then, precisely *then*, she appeared, materialized, as though from nowhere. Posed, she was, at first, a wraith, within the window's frosted frame, streaked with lines of melted snow drops, for several moments absolutely still, slightly obscure, like a faded photograph of someone remotely familiar. When I recognized her, it seemed she had occupied my presence for a long time and that I had been, as one entranced, mindlessly gazing at her, rather the way you relentless hunters are presently staring at me. We can't detect what you now think you perceive, can I?

I was a homecoming queen once. Yes, I was a sight to see, then. The night before they crowned me their queen, I strutted like a peacock, waltzed, struck dozens of poses, nude before my bedroom mirror, practicing for that great day. I knew that everyone would peer through my exquisite white gown . . . strip me bare. And they did! What's a queen for if not to disrobe? Everyone wanted a piece of me. You can imagine; I can tell by your searching eyes. Besides . . . you're neglecting to scribble your notes. Isn't this noteworthy?

Later, Mother informed me that she caught Father peeking at me through a crack in the door—"misusing himself," she alleged. Back to *her?* Lea . . . of course. A lovely golden-haired girl out of a fairy tale . . . oh yes, lovely, and I'm afraid, seductive too. And now—my god, you can't allow it!—all that loveliness, youth, seeming innocence, lost, defiled. It makes you want to cry, doesn't it? Cry till nothing remains of you. No, no, it's lost. The same as dead. I heard *you:* "We can't be sure, ma'am." But can you hear *me?* Dead. I just know, that's all. I feel it tingling in my bones, an aching apprehension.

Stop writing! Listen. Please. Thank you. She wore a heavy red coat, like Little Red Riding Hood. About thirteen years old—yes, I remember, thirteen—ah yes. Thirteen, approximately, although already curving womanly . . . *very.* When she stood near my dear Frank, you could detect—should we say?—the outlines of arousal in him. Shame's so passé these days. She was young, but not *that* young. She knew how to pet the feather, if you take my meaning. Not what you'd call a virgin. I myself matured early, as well; I know the awkwardness, the embarrassment, the hunger, the danger. Once, I was she.

I'm positive you gentlemen comprehend me quite correctly, now don't you? Yes, too fast . . . too inciting, boys already circling like mongrels sniffing the damp heat. Hunting you down, like a bleeding injured animal, betrayed by your own blood-tracks. Does a young girl fight to escape or does she merely surrender to the threat and excitement washing through her veins?

Oh . . . look! Do we discern a thin, mischievous smile creasing your charming lips? No? Of course not. What am *I* suggesting, you ask? *I* have no suggestions. What? Do *I* think sex is everything? My, my, I was right about you boys, wasn't I? But then I can't be too wrong; the risk wasn't that great. You're men after all. But is sex everything? No, not always, but when it's not everything, it's never totally absent now, is it? It's in everything, more or less.

Look. So *there!* Anyway, if I could only have been more certain, perhaps we would have known what to do. Is that a motive? What? All right, I think I see what you mean. It's not the victim who has the motive. Hm . . . well, all right, not usually, I'll own.

Anyway, there she stood, that gray December morning, paused in front of the window, all bundled up in red like a Christmas package ready for somebody to cut open, waving warmly, friendly as she always was. Silent, pretty, covered up. But I could read her hungry heart. I scrutinized her, wondering: Does she realize what she's doing? I believe we read in her moving, silent lips, "Good Morning." A little disingenuous, I might say. Like this: Good Morn . . . ing. I don't know, how can we say for certain? It was snowing. Who could be sure of anything? But I see her clearly now. Strangely dislocated now, torn . . . so bleeding, so out of context.

There—two hours, at least, too early for school she was; and besides this is not the direction to school. There she was. Just there. Misplaced.

A piece. She offered herself, a missing part to a puzzle. If you possessed a sharp mind you could put two and two together, of course. Afterward, anyway. Life makes so little sense without hindsight. This street goes only to the bus terminal, as I've mentioned, so plainly that's where she was headed—besides, she carried a small suitcase. Obviously, the one in which you found some portions of her. My god—like carrying your own coffin.

I see her, right on the heels of my Frank. It's amazing! Stopping and waving at me, as she would to her mother, no doubt. Amazing though! Really amazing! Of her loveliness and sweet innocence, my Frank used to remark, "Here today, gone tomorrow." And of her sweet life—well, you two know, that's the size of it. Yes, heartbreaking. Who knew we'd never again lay eyes on her? Yes, we remember exactly what you said and what you also didn't exactly say. Still, I feel she's ruined, beyond all remedy. If she's not yet dead, she certainly soon will be, except as she's sustained in me. How long can you go without your—*oh how horrible!* I see her still.

Here she was, barely more than a child, toting that suitcase, walking too early in the wrong direction, too cold, too silent. Waving at me. I returned her greeting, vaguely, imitatively, like a reflection in a mirror. We even motioned for her to come forth, come inside. Frank would have beckoned her in from the cold for warmth. He could be so generous that way. Somehow, so out of context she appeared; she seemed not really there at all, like my own lost girlhood, displaced—yes, so coldly alone, forlorn and confused, amid my own restless desires, going nowhere I should have gone, but going where I *had* to, because I could not stay— wherever . . . well, wherever I imagined I was.

She was I. What was mine was hers. Do you inquisitive gentlemen follow the wanderings of an old woman's mind? I'm all over the place. Oh thank you. How kind, for saying that. You warm a cold heart. I talk to myself so much when I'm awake I occasionally forget I'm not always alone. I'm old but—look!—pretty well preserved. If you could see your gleaming eyes rolling over me.

Oh, don't be so nervous. It's in everything. You haven't done anything you shouldn't have. I'm only teasing you. It's in everything. But you do see, don't you? In a way, I was also discovered after I had been cruelly murdered. Found too late. I shouldn't have passed away when I did. No one deserves to die so young. And yet, we all do.

I know, I know, she hasn't been discovered yet, ma'am. No, not totally. Where was I? Yes, I said I motioned to her. Maybe she didn't see my invitation. I can't tell. Or maybe she did, and that's perhaps what turned her decidedly away; maybe that gesture to come forth set more decisively

in motion her ill-fated direction, which was simply away, you understand—
in the direction of Frank.

What? No, it's not ambiguous, if you can read. The street only has
one destination. You'd have to be an imbecile to conclude otherwise.
Are we talking too fast, my dears? I'm doing the best I can. I'll repeat all
this if you wish. Just don't go. All we do is go over it anyway, endlessly. We
either sleep or piece the world together.

Stay with me awhile, will you? Ooh, before your piercing eyes I feel
so exposed. I know whose hands I'm in. There was a time you would
have loved me in this state. Oh, there it is again, the glint in your eyes.
Wolves. My god, do these savage hungers ever leave us? Lea . . . Where is
she? I told you I did observe how resolutely she turned from me. I mean—
she must have. However, I don't actually know that, I confess, because
apparently at that very instant, the instant of the invitation—it's blurry
here—I turned away from the pane and started groping my way back
through the house, moving almost blindly because the white snow had
so bedimmed my sight. There's a blank in here, a hole.

Oh look at you! Your ears all cocked. I suspected that part would
interest you boys most. The hole in the woman. That's what all you
inspectors are into, isn't it? Oh nothing. I mean nothing. I'm teasing—
sort of. It's everywhere. I'm sorry. Old . . . I've gone all agray. Winter
time. Ripped off. Fill me in with your green imaginations. I need a favor.
I'm sorry. I do prefer to be of use. But what good am I? Unused. Not
beautiful anymore. Oh thank you. You touch me so. That makes me
want to kiss you right on the mouth. Thank you, sweetheart. But since
the day he abandoned me, I've been more or less blind, split, robbed,
less by half. So I'm used to this, the hole in me. Empty—but everything's
in there.

Look. After enough's been lost, I suppose you mostly make up the
world, don't you? Still, the blank is here. I can't fill everything completely
by myself. I'm not a whole; I'm one side. But that's the side you've come
to inspect, isn't it, the side you woke? Hey, was that wink for me? I was a
beauty once. Remember that. You would have chased me down, a mere
sixty years ago.

Men—devils all! You know. Ooh, I love your smiles. Did you lick your
lips just then? Oh, I'm imagining, am I? It doesn't matter; I've sold myself
for less. Where am I? I said, we turned from the pane, groping along,
blinded by having witnessed too much. I was too weak to protect her
from the tragic fate that befell her, befell us all. I feel for her. But I
needed help myself. Look at me! I feel for her in me. So I turned away
from her sight and headed into my own dark hallways.

Did she foolishly follow? Isn't that question awfully peculiar,
gentlemen? I moved slowly. Did she follow us? Slowly . . . every object of
furniture, every doorway confronted us as a heavy shadow obscuring our
progress, our understanding, our intentions. In fact, we seemed lost within
my own house, groping along among suddenly unfamiliar shapes, down
a dark passageway that I could only trust led to my empty bedroom,
slowly, like a sleepwalker, back toward our bed, where you, patient
hunters of a wounded maiden, found me sound asleep on the other
side of the pane, dead to the world.

You kissed my parched lips, and they dampened and filled and
opened. Red. Oozing. Wet. And then you two . . . . What? No? *No!* Oh .
. . how embarrassing! All this while, I thought you had . . . Dear me! How
humiliating! What have we been imagining? I must have been dreaming—
yes, that's it!—that I was a princess, bewitched in a snow-covered castle,
asleep for a hundred years, awaiting the embrace of a prince, who today,
I mistakenly imagined, turned out to be the two of you. Well . . . there. If
I ever need an alibi, that's it. We've been asleep a hundred years! At
least you found me, the part that's left. Oh well.

You're quite welcome—certainly. But . . . ah . . . please—don't go.
Will you not? Time never passes; we do. I mean it. Please—could I be of
further use? We've watched you seeing through these sheer coverings.
I'm well preserved. Parts have broken away, but it's all here, as far as I'm
concerned. I'm whole in part. Have you uncovered all you're looking
for? The body you're hunting lies hidden beneath this hazy undergarment.
Look in. Is anything remaining? I can't tell.

Santa Teresa's Angel

It was October 1614. In Ávila, the birthplace and the site of most of Teresa de Jesús's religious activity, the lengthy celebrations of her beatification had been both solemn and jubilant. It had all fairly exhausted Padre Juan Pérez. Having known and loved Teresa, he had participated actively in the ceremonies, but now he looked forward to some relaxation. So the letter from Angela Lomas stating that her brother, Enrique, was gravely ill and begging him to come at once to hear the ailing man's confession did not gladden him. She added that should he consent, he must please avail himself of her coach. The coachman (who had delivered the letter) would await his decision.

Padre Pérez was very fond of Señora Lomas, a beautiful woman who, because of her admiration of Teresa, contributed generously to his parish. The Lomases, an aristocratic family, lived in Madrid, but sometime ago they had resided in Ávila. Occasionally, Angela would visit the town lately made famous by the sanctity of the Carmelite nun, Teresa de Jesús. Madrid abounded with priests, so it greatly puzzled the padre why they should insist on him as the confessor. But how could he refuse her?

The next morning after celebrating early-morning Mass, he boarded the coach and embarked for Madrid. The journey would occupy most of the day. It was warm, but thank the Lord, not as terribly hot as it had been. Rolling along, beneath a glorious blue sky, Padre Pérez relaxed into a reverie. He did not know Enrique Lomas, although he had certainly heard of him. He was a man of considerable learning, but a philanderer, gambler, drinker, seducer of women, who squandered most of his time in France and Italy. He was also an accomplished swordsman, rumored to have dueled with and slain several men. Evidently, all that was concluded now, and the adventurer, grown old and infirm, had returned home to die.

Considering this gossip, Padre Pérez groaned because to him it seemed such a dissolute life. But of course, who was he to judge? The Lord could forgive anyone for anything at any time. He wondered what this decadent rogue would confess, and whatever it was, why it had to be confessed to *him*. After a while, he fell asleep.

He arrived late in the afternoon, stiff from sitting so long, but fairly rested from all the napping he had done. The house was huge, more like a small castle than the residence of a single family. As soon as he stepped from the coach, he noticed Angela Lomas standing on the veranda smiling at him, her large black eyes gleaming.

"How prompt! Thank you, Padre, for coming. I did not doubt you would. It's been too long since last we met."

"It has indeed. I had hoped the commemoration of Teresa would attract you to Ávila."

"No. On that day Enrique's health swiftly declined. I did attend some of the festivities here in Madrid. Come, Padre, let me show you to your room so you can freshen up. Afterward, we will dine and then you'll meet my dear brother."

"Bless me, Padre, for I have sinned . . . sinned much."

"Why must you confess to me in particular, Señor Lomas?"

"Because my sister speaks highly of your sympathy and kindness, and because you are from Ávila . . . and because you knew Teresa de Jesús. Perhaps as well because you are a Jesuit."

"Because I am from Ávila and I knew Teresa? Because I am a Jesuit . . ."

"It will become clear."

"What do you wish to confess?"

"All, I cannot say—time prevents—and besides, I can't even recall all my sins. My memory's unreliable. But sins . . . well, they've constituted my life. God has noted down everything. Held in a certain light, Padre, perhaps everything's a sin . . . or not a sin. How a jewel strikes the eye depends on how you turn and hold it to the light."

"Sins are not jewels, señor."

"For me, some have been. For most of my carrying on, I cannot honestly say that I am sorry. In my heart I am not a religious man, although at this late date, when I can no longer deny the nearness of death, I fear damnation. I dedicated my life to the pleasures of the flesh. I'd be a hypocrite to denounce all that. I'd live it over again if granted the opportunity. That I was a fool, that I still am, I admit. The devil won me early."

"God will forgive you if you wish for him to."

"Why must we struggle against desires, Padre?"

"Forbidden desires? So that our resistance may attest to our glorification of the All Mighty."

"Does he need such glorification? Ah well, however that may be . . . So—when was the seed of my wayward life implanted, Padre? Was it during the incident that I am now compelled to divulge, the memory of which haunts me with a deranged joy and a dread that my memory is nothing but a record of distortions? I am not even positive that what I am about to reveal counts as something for which I should entreat God's forgiveness. Confusion, you will see, permeates this story I have to tell. Braggart that I have been, it is my only exploit that I have wished no one to discover. And no one has learned of it from me. But the other with whom I shared it . . . well, in her fashion, she told everyone—even you, Padre. I see you are perplexed."

"Of course. You are about to relate something, señor, which I already know?"

"To *reveal* something more nakedly than you know it. Yes. It is, in any case, something that I must now disburden my soul of, disclose what occurred as I saw it. Strip the covers off the bed. Why I must do this will perhaps become evident in the telling. Perhaps it is a love story. Can an old reprobate such as I have known love?"

At this point, he began coughing violently. He reached quickly and drew a white handkerchief from a pile stacked near the bed. He covered his mouth with it, spit up a thick wad of blood, and released it to the floor. "Excuse me, Padre. This has been going on for days." He chuckled. "If it continues, I'll perish of blood loss."

"Your heart is troubled, señor. Tell me what happened."

"I was eighteen, a university student here in Madrid. Sometimes I would visit my family in Ávila. Late one afternoon, while strolling through the forest that borders the Carmelite nunnery of the Incarnation, I saw a nun standing in a glade, motionless as a statue, staring seemingly at nothing. An aura of luminous silence encircled her. She was stunningly beautiful . . . as you know. I was young, Padre, and innocent—not, I am sure, of unclean thoughts, but certainly of deeds. That moment doomed me to the influences of alluring women.

"Evidently, my approach had gone unheard, so I continued to spy on her. How can I explain? I felt bewitched. My heart beat as though I had stumbled into the presence of something prohibited, possibly dangerous . . . exciting. The spell lasted several minutes, until her body abruptly started to vibrate; her limbs jerked and flailed about. It was a dance of weird distortions, a *danse macabre*. Shocked, I had been yanked from an enticing dream and dropped into a nightmare. She needed some kind of help, but I feared she was possessed, and that the demon who inhabited her might decide to spring into my own body, as I knew

demons did if you associated too intimately with those they infest. She
stumbled to the ground. Agog, I watched her groan and writhe about as
though wrestling to untangle herself from the coils of a serpent.

"Finally, my paralysis broke and I flew to assist her. Not knowing what
to do, I clasped hold of her. She gripped me with the desperate strength
of a drowning swimmer. She gasped and gagged, but her eyes rolled
back white in her head and she appeared unconscious. Her nose bled.
Confused and aroused, I rocked her back and forth—the only thing I
could think of to soothe her. She trembled in my arms until she eventually
calmed down. She then lay so still I thought she was dead, but in a few
minutes she revived.

"Still clinging firmly to her, I described what had happened. With
my handkerchief, I wiped the blood drops from beneath her nose. She
listened rather absently, seemed not at all dismayed, and said, 'Thank
you for watching over me, señor. God will bless you.' Only that, and then
she cupped her hands around my face and leaned forward. I shut my
eyes, Padre, and tenderly she kissed my eyelids. She got up then and
walked toward the nunnery. I watched her. The black habit swayed
gracefully, and soon her figure melted into the dusk like an apparition.
Stunned, I could scarcely believe what had occurred. Had I, in fact, been
dreaming? Strange . . . she never asked my name. The memory of those
soft kisses even now brings tears to my eyes."

"It is very moving, señor, but nothing that warrants confessing, does it?"

"Please bear with me, Padre. This is merely the prelude to the most
remarkable and perhaps most—you must decide—unforgivable episode
of my life."

"Pardon my interruption. Present your story as you choose."

"Thank you, Padre, for your patience. It is important that I relate all
of this to you and to myself . . . to myself in the company of you, God's
representative. Only then can it be fully realized."

"Fully realized?"

"Unless someone hears of it, serves as witness, it has not been fully
realized. I've always needed witnesses. But what I mean will perhaps
later become clearer to you and to me as well. I shall continue.

"Afterward, I now and then met her in the forest, at first making it
seem accidental. She always seemed pleased to encounter me. She jokingly
called me her 'guardian angel.' Eventually, we arranged rendezvous, in
the evening when possible. Very surreptitious. Both of us knowing—without
open acknowledgment—that we should not be doing this. Although for a
while what *this* was lurked as a shadow in the background. She would talk
at length only of religious matters, about her yearning to embrace her

Savior, about the salvation of the soul. No doubt, Padre, foreseeing that mine would soon sorely require tending to.

"Often, as though enthralled, she would stare at me, I think not perceiving me at all, but staring through me into the immensity of eternity. Her eloquent speech intimidated me. A boy—what did I know? Awed by her, I hardly uttered a word. I listened enraptured to her passionate adoration of Christ. I had never heard such affirmations of love. I'm ashamed, Padre, to say so, but a jealousy of Christ soon besieged me. Oh, a demon had indeed invaded me. I was obviously captivated.

"Her gaze, Padre . . . gleaming black eyes burned into me. Often too much to endure, they forced me to avert my eyes. She stared intently at me, yes, but absently, as though all of that intensity focused on something or someone other than myself, something more worthy—I presume, more compelling. But at the time, I didn't quite comprehend matters that way. I was too flattered by what I simply perceived, or misperceived, as her adoring attention. How very peculiar that attention actually failed to register. No, I felt only the ardent effects of her words, her eyes. Padre, hers was a starving gaze, a ravenous hunger, a hunger that greatly bewildered and excited me."

"Yes, but all this expressed a hunger for our Savior, did it not?"

"Yes, she spoke endlessly of her fervent attachment to Christ. Yet, to me, it seemed rather—but what did my callow heart know?—more of a lust for him, something that one could, in a secular context, easily construe as indecent. How can you discriminate, Padre, whether the fire of passion issues from Christ or the devil? It occurred to me, even then, that if an inquisitor had been privy to these torrid outpourings she would have been condemned to the stake. But I needn't worry that any of my revelations will accuse her. The disclosures of confession are sacrosanct, are they not, Padre?"

"Yes, they are."

"Even the tortures of the inquisition could not coerce such secrets from you. No, but you can see how I felt she was imparting a fatal secret, even that she had implemented me—and oh, made such a willing accomplice by my own desire—in a conspiracy of unholy passion. I realize now much that I didn't then. She extolled Christ, but sitting near and staring so directly at my face, I believed then that she was addressing me, no matter how imperfectly concentrated upon me and wavering her regard actually was. Sometimes she stroked my cheek, seemed to fawn over me as a mother or a lover would. I am not sure I clearly distinguished the two. Did I misunderstand everything? How did God intend for me to be used by her? Is the way we are used ever any other than the way he

intends? Do you know whom I am speaking of, Padre? Must I speak her
name?"

"I know her name. Continue."

"At some point, Padre, she began describing her visions. How
profoundly that affected me. I was in the presence of someone touched
by the finger of God. She claimed that God had shown her his hands . . .
then his face! And more! She beheld what no one else could—the
invisible immanence of all existence. Can you look upon God's face,
Padre, and escape annihilation?"

"No, ordinarily not, but some have—Hagar, Jacob, a few others."

"She—among those few, no doubt. Well, it was the recounting of
these visions that set the stage, because through them, Padre, she
informed me of how things were to befall her. So I was fairly specifically
instructed as to what she expected. You understand me, Padre? No? Let
me explain.

"They were radiant visions bestowed by God, not fabrications of
imagination. No, she insisted, not in a million years could anyone dream
up such fantastic sights. She exercised absolutely no control over them.
This she vehemently defended, as though interrogated by Thomas de
Torquemada himself—buried so near where we rendezvoused, he must
have defecated in his grave. But such distinctions meant nothing to me
then. Now I appreciate how much hinged on that point. Was all this the
eruptions of an insane mind—devil work? Not a question I asked at the
time. I drank her words in like honey.

"She avowed that her visions transported her beyond the temporal
order. Yes, but *only*, only by God's grace did she witness Christ crucified,
witness his wounds as priceless stones, more priceless than any earthly
gems, witness the dazzling brilliance of his resurrected body. Oh, how
she longed to view again, to view forever, Christ resplendent . . . an ecstasy
plunging like a lightning bolt into her bowels. With my imagination—
human and young, and I'm afraid, infected with lust, I tried to envision
all this magnificence. Of these sights, she sighed in remembrance of the
delicious pain that had surged through her, a pain too . . . I don't know,
Padre—too enigmatic for mere words to convey. A pain sublime—again,
beyond all imagining. She told me this . . . but was she speaking to me?
No, never entirely, this I now know.

"She said that sometimes amid these raptures her body contracted.
Smothered, unable to breathe, she could only moan, begging to be
ravaged by love unto death. She felt stabbed to death by love. She said
she was not herself, or too much herself to recognize the person whom
she had always known, whom the world had always known. Filled with

joyful suffering, she pleaded that the sacred flames would culminate and reduce her flesh to ashes. Her overflowing passion bewildered me. What was she talking about? I listened, beside myself with wonderment . . . and yes, Padre, with profane desire. I gazed upon her beauty, enslaved, at the beauty of her transfixion, gazed as though captivated myself by a divine vision. Padre, you know the beauty that I speak of, do you not?"

"*Her* beauty, you mean? Yes. However the beauty that she beheld was not of this world."

"Yes, *that* she often stressed. Then one day, Padre, she told me of God's lustrous angel who would soon descend upon her and drive into her heart a flaming spear that would sear the vile sin within her and liberate her imprisoned soul. The consummate miracle. Like all celestial beings, angels are incorporeal. For such visitations, they disguise themselves because no one could withstand the luster of their unrestrained splendor. Upon this she enlightened me, as a mother would a child. Seraphim could assume any incarnation they chose, but the one who would visit her—whom she seemed to have glimpsed the distant approach of in a dream—would don the guise of a young man bursting with energy—not come as a shower of gold or a swan to a Greek maiden. No, nothing so alien.

"Then she added: 'Yes, my dashing young savior—a man, perhaps a humble student, such as yourself.' Me, Padre—an angel, an avatar of God! The angel's arrival was imminent. She emphasized this with breathless anticipation. In that moment I froze. In that moment I apprehended what all this had been leading to, or at least as all that my own appetites had construed it. Padre, have you ever known such a situation yourself?"

"Señor Lomas, please, it is not for me to confess to you."

"No, of course not. Forgive my impertinence. Like all reprobates, I long for understanding . . . as well as limitless indulgence. Where was I? Yes . . . She smiled at me—or rather at something over my shoulder, perhaps far off in the heavens—and repeated that she had been forewarned to ready herself for such a visitation that very night. My heart raced and leapt, as it is doing now—a wild stallion vaulting over a chasm. All this revives itself so vividly inside me, Padre, as though I am dreaming while awake. I have spent much of my life recalling and trying to preserve the memory of it. Memory—how like an unfaithful mistress: the tighter you try to clasp her, the more she betrays you. Maybe I'm telling you this story so that it will remain on the earth when I'm beneath it. Perhaps, but I also relate all of this, Padre, because I am uncertain what it is exactly that I am confessing. Even as I speak, I seem afflicted with some kind of pride . . . that I was chosen. A pride suspiciously akin to some demented sense of power . . . that upon this tale of mine rests the very foundation of her sainthood or her damnation."

"What do you mean, señor?"

"Never mind, Padre. Excuse the digressions of a muddled old man." Again he coughed, and a burst of crimson stained another handkerchief, and again it was dropped to the floor, atop refuse that resembled a bouquet of red-white flowers.

"I am sorry you suffer so."

"I do not feel as bad as it sounds and appears, but I suspect it is that bad. Appearances, Padre—what to make of them, Plato's shadows on the cave wall? Ah well, I must finish my story."

"Yes, I am following everything you say, señor. Please resume."

"I've asked myself, could it be that she flattered me into the role I enacted? *I* had been chosen. But I was only eighteen, a student absorbed in the unrealities of books and daydreams. The only woman whom I had ever known intimately was Angela."

"Angela?"

"Yes. Of certain childhood indiscretions with my sister, I am heartily sorry—sorry, that is, only if I caused her any harm."

"So you were not quite as innocent as you professed a moment ago?"

"No—I discount such childhood iniquities . . . shouldn't I? If not, that's another story, Padre. Time is brief. I cannot relate all in a single breath, and hardly more than a breath remains. In any case, of such follies with her, I long ago confessed and was absolved. But again I stray. My mind, how desultory . . . my life, nothing but wanderings.

"I was saying? Yes—she was convinced that the angel would materialize that night. She had explained that all was to be accomplished with a fiery spear. Well, you can easily guess, Padre, how a boy's overheated brain transcribed all this. For the grandeur of such an undertaking, I possessed meager means. I would utilize the only staff I owned. What can I say, Padre? I intend no disrespect. I desired her: her extravagant view of herself, her communions with God, her forbidden beauty, her envelopment of me, the rapacity of her own desire, and—what else?—those early intimations of her transformation of me."

"Transformation?"

"One that I never entirely measured up to. You've seen her, Padre. You must understand. Brimming with desire she was. I know now that hers was a desire beyond anything I could comprehend—not then, not now. I translated it into a language which, doubtless, perverted the quintessence of everything about her. She and I, we each seemed molded by the hands of some other: she by God's hands, I by hers or the devil's. Everything eluded my control. She seduced me. I do not blame her. What boy does not crave to be so used by such a holy mother as she? I was used by her to receive God; I lay like a bridge between them. Through me the Father came." Again he coughed, and again a rose of blood fell to the floor.

"Pardon these vile interruptions, Padre. Did you know her well?"

"Only briefly and not well, no. Does that matter?"

"Perhaps not. I wondered how she affected you, that's all. You saw her enormous eyes—not unlike Angela's, wouldn't you agree? Try to refuse anything they ask! But no matter. So, Padre, that night I did what I believed she anticipated, what my desires fancied she wished. I watched her enter the clearing in the woods. It was midnight. A bright moon silvered the stage. A ghostly white silence engulfed her. She swayed from side to side as though dancing to music which she alone heard, a spirit attuned to some ethereal sphere.

"And I, rooted in the soil of my physical being, felt enlarged by a blood-rush of excitement. I wanted to pounce upon her like some frenzied satyr . . . or a werewolf, but held spellbound by her, I couldn't budge. Perhaps I would have stayed in that state indefinitely had she not begun to stagger. As though struck in the back of the head, she reeled, lost her balance, and collapsed. Frightened, I expected her body to again contort in paroxysms. But that didn't occur. Although nervous, I hurried to her. She moaned, half conscious, like one intoxicated . . . and oh yes, so intoxicating.

"She looked directly at me, those black eyes agleam with moonbeams, unmoving eyes scarcely aware or entirely unaware of my presence. In recollection, her gaze was curiously blank. Eerie. No, she was not really observing me. I wonder now, Padre, was she ever fully aware of me? Would she even have recognized me outside the theater of her vision? Through the years this question has grown increasingly troubling. How do you love someone who looks at you *as* someone else?

"Anyway, she had obviously fallen into a swoon. She writhed a bit, sighed, whimpered like a wounded animal. Oh yes, how very lovely in her abandonment, more lovely then than ever. She appeared, in fact— I have to say it—luscious. You know what I'm talking about. I feasted on her helpless beauty, on her hunger, a hunger that animated her body. I devoured the undulating curves of her desires. Oh, the way her desires shaped her! Do you see her, Padre?"

"Señor, I . . ."

"Yes, of course, you do. You have seen the deadly snake, have you not, Padre, that twists inside the sinuous body of a woman? But too young and eager at the time, I failed to decently savor anything. However, over the years I have savored every morsel of her, dining on those succulent memories. Do you follow me, Padre? The wolf wanted to leap upon her, but too overwhelmed, I just watched, dumbfounded by the delicious feast that fate, with inscrutable intentions, laid before me. Did I believe that she would actually do this? Probably not. Perhaps until that instant I considered it all merely a game, a bit of harmless teasing on her part, as a mother does with a child. Nonetheless, I did show up, didn't I? Yes, on the remote chance that . . . well, maybe, just maybe, this—"

A harsh cough broke his sentence. Blood discolored another handkerchief. "Forgive this mess, Padre. You see the blood this tale costs me."

"Yes, I do. You need not recount all these details if it too distresses you."

"No, the details matter. This is a journey, Padre. Accompany me. I passed through it alone as a boy, and also as a man alone, through a landscape of refracting memories, and with age, untrustworthy understanding. How altered things become when what we did becomes what we remember. Do not abandon me."

"I am here as you wish me to be. Continue."

"You must see what I saw. Tolerate me. So . . . I stared at her; she stared at me, or at something that occupied the same body as mine. She began removing her habit, staring up from the ground into my bulging eyes, into my eyes or the eyes of one whom she conceived me to be. Into the eyes of an angel—her heavenly lover. That was whom she fixed upon, Padre. This she had already disclosed. I do not doubt the reality of the vision she lived, a reality compounded of nothing I could fathom then . . . then or now. She, a Carmelite nun, a bride of Christ! I, a sinner, heedless that he was perhaps about to consign his soul to perdition. Oh, did I do that, Padre? You will decide.

"As still as a stone, I watched her undress. Once unwrapped from the encasement of all that black cloth, the whitest skin I've ever beheld appeared. Oh, her long hair cascading like a waterfall, glossy black in the moonlight. Look, Padre! Do I see your eyes widen? No . . . Perhaps not. The gray moonlight surely intensified the haunting effect. My agitated nerves responded to the seductive surfaces of everything. Padre, you could have resisted this; I could not. Yet, I discern—is it merely the reflection of candlelight here in your eyes?—that you are not unaffected. All the lust of youth sped through my veins. Who choreographed that magical setting, Padre—God or Satan? To her, it was God. If the evil one can so deceive a saint, then surely the rest of us grope in utter darkness. We can use only the poor tools God provided."

"Those tools, yes, plus faith and the guidance of Holy Mother Church are all we require."

"Of course. I meant not to blaspheme. You are listening to an ignorant old man, still wishing—no matter what he otherwise claims—to justify his misdeeds."

"God knows all we've done."

"Yes, God knows . . . better than we do ourselves. Finally, my paralysis abated and I commenced with what I believed she yearned for. I too undressed and then I knelt over her. I touched the long, hard spear's hot tip to her swollen breasts. It pierced her flesh. *Pierced her!* This was the way she had depicted it would happen to her. Yes, I pierced her . . . at first a mere pinprick. A tease to warm her up. I laugh at such a notion now. *Warm her up!* She, the molten furnace of the Lord. Pathetic boy! Perspiration oozed from her. She perceived it as scarlet droplets of blood. Blood. This was how she had foretold it, Padre. Everything for her unfolded within the terms of her vision. And of the essence of that, what can I tell you? Nothing. An experience composed by God for his chosen ones, who among the rest of us can apprehend it? Color to the color-blind. I translate her—my gibberish, a fool's translation of poetry. Do you understand me, Padre?"

"It seems to me a story of translations."

"Yes . . . how do you mean?"

"She translates God; you translate her translation. And then, señor, you retranslate everything, don't you, into the language of the body, the ordinary language of lust."

"Do I detect the metaphysical bent of the Jesuit mind here? Oh, the way she so willingly opened her body . . . yes, Padre—ordinary language. Indeed, back to that! We know a naked maiden when we spot one, don't we? Unless she's a saint in disguise . . .

"Enough! Where is she? Ah, *there!* How long had she yearned for this moment? Surely, all her life, wouldn't you say? Was I the first? Ah well, be at ease, my jealous heart. She knew what she was doing. I can't pretend I did. I proceeded as a man reading instructions. She raised herself up on her elbows, grunted, and arched backward, as flexible as warm wax, uplifting her ripe breasts to receive the . . . the pain. Because for her it all amounted to some kind of exquisite *pain.* Oh, she had practiced as best she could for this blessed agony. In hindsight I know, Padre, that she had. But she had always realized that no amount of preparation would ready her for this. I think she told me that. Some things you can't rehearse. No, for this she could never have adequately readied herself, not for the ineffable: God injecting his love like acid into the wounds that he had cut in her flesh. Unwittingly, I simply served as host to an angel, either sent by God or cast by him down to earth."

"You struggle to unravel mysteries beyond human capability. She said that God bestowed understanding upon her. She wrote of these matters in her books. We cannot tear answers from his hands."

"No. But I ask nonetheless. Who was I? What was done to me? Did I impersonate an angel, or did an angel impersonate me? In her eyes, I *was* made over. To her, *I* was not in disguise, an angel was. *I was* what I mistakenly believed I only feigned, someone other than whom I thought myself, something more—an angel of God! God's love by indirection. It has to be that way. Who can withstand such an undiluted infusion of sacred love, the naked spectacle of a god? What maiden, seduced by Zeus masquerading as a man, was then burned to death by the sight of him candidly disclosed?"

"Semele."

"My memory . . . unreliable as the length of life! Yes, poor Semele. More than she could handle. A tricky business being exposed to what exceeds comprehension. As in a nightmare, appetites are aroused too fantastic to endure. And yet, this Carmelite nun asserted that God had revealed himself to her; first his hands, then his face, she had beheld God and lived to tell of it. Nonetheless, God's love means to destroy however it arrives, does it not, Padre? Destroy the beast . . . disembrace the soul from the beast within. Yes, she told me his love meant to demolish her, his vassal. She got that right, didn't she, Padre? And to that fate she stood as resigned as a martyr. Only sacrifice gave worth to anything. That obsession of hers over discalced nuns . . . the pain of going barefoot everywhere . . . the distraction of the earth that must be overcome . . . ever-present sacrifice. She lived within the visions she proclaimed, fully embracing the consequences. Yes, she knew that she needed to be destroyed, or rather consumed, burned down to cinders, cleansed by God's purifying love. Is this terrible purification the only means of escaping hell, Padre?"

"God determines what we require and he provides. Trust him."

"Provides, yes, but often in ways too obscure to recognize. She told me of the sin within her—within her, within the body of a saint!—sin that only God's merciful fire could purge. She prayed fervently for God to inflict upon her this divine violation. I was merely the instrument of its enactment. She believed in extremes. All saints do."

"The Church has yet to confirm her as a saint, señor. You know this."

"Yes, but it nearly has and soon will. At least during her lifetime she avoided the torments of the inquisitors, didn't she?"

"Not all of them, but some—the worst."

"Yes, hard to manage once the curiosity of those rabid hounds begins to sniff you out. How I despise those Dominican witch hunters. As a Jesuit, do you despise them as well?"

"As a Jesuit, I despise none of them; as a man who hates cruelty—some of them."

"The Jesuits defended her. Who was that young, learned Jesuit who—"

"Baltasar Alvarez."

"Yes, he defended her. I trust the compassion of the Jesuits for her, a compassion I hope will here extend to me."

"You may take that for granted, señor."

"Thank you, Padre. My sister spoke truly of you. Dominicans or no, our saint held staunchly to her convictions. She dwelled as in a dream amid Christ's amorous flames, the fumes of which smelled to high heaven of sex. The inquisitors knew this. Sex and heavenly ecstasy were as synonymous for them as they were for me that night. And yet they never condemned her to the stake, neither as witch nor heretic. She outsmarted her persecutors, escaped by a hair. Not an easy job for a suspected woman, even when sex is not so flagrantly at issue. In France and Germany they burn more witches than we in Spain. Think of that pitiful wench . . . what was her name?—my memory . . . so unreliable—Jean d'Arc. She, too, professed that she did only what her voices dictated. Voices! Women—they're too much for us . . . attuned to another world."

"Have they been too much for you, señor?"

"Some. She was. Oh, if the inquisitors knew what I'm telling you—

"Where was I? Yes, Padre, in the woods that night I witnessed her consumption, a little of it, as much as my human eyes could. Her life had been an act of being burned alive, stabbed to death—a spear, as in the side of Christ, a spear as the nails of the cross. Sacrifice. Sacrifice . . . only through pain could she give herself away. Pain made the consumption of herself real; no reality existed outside it, no sacrifice held value without it. This she proclaimed repeatedly; this she demonstrated. But, Padre, these meanderings of an old man . . . Where was I?"

"Kneeling over her body."

"Ah yes—you recall . . . yes, indeed. Her breasts—do you also recall those?—ignited by my spear rose as two torches lighting up the night. You see her, Padre? All these years later, I can picture everything. She spread her legs, just in case—I sometimes must guess her thoughts—oh yes, just in case God wished to enter her *there*, at the virgin's door.

"But for a moment longer I continued to pound my godly shaft into her throbbing bosom, glistening with blood-sweat . . . her bosom, my spear, the implement of her sweet torture. Stabbing her like a man deranged by another's vision. A bloody death, a death that revivifies—ecstasy. She and I differently lost in our own transformation . . . my imagination unable to expand into the enormous image that she had fabricated for me. Who comprehends these impenetrable mysteries, Padre? The doctors of the Church? Perhaps you do. I understood nothing of the part I played. I did as directed in the drama of another. A slave, used by her divine comprehension. Have you ever played a role written for you by another, Padre?"

"I strive to fill the role God has assigned me."

"So did she. She saw herself aflame with blood, with pain sublime. She gasped, barely able to breathe, suffocated by herself, by her god, by her angel. She made me what I was. You see this, don't you, Padre? She twisted about, incapable of ingesting everything at once. Overpowered, breathless, her lungs unable to keep pace with the intensity of her expectation . . . She created more than she could cope with. Part of her resisted—who does not?—what she begged for. We are never at one with our prayers.

"She was too full of her god; she had overeaten. God was everywhere, in every ounce of air, in every fiber of her being. 'Oh yes, oh yes,' she moaned. 'Take my breath, take my soul!' You can see her, can you not, Padre? Look—there! Sprawled, impaled. Forgive me, Padre . . . forgive me if I was not the Lord's emissary but the devil's. I took her word. I did not see what she saw but I believed blindly in her vision, the truth of it for her. Was I beguiled—by her, by myself? Everything an illusion? Can we ever know how thoroughly we hoodwink ourselves? I believed in what she believed in. No—I believed in her. Did she hoodwink herself?"

"The inquisition exonerated her of all suspicions."

"I know, but did she fool the grand inquisitor himself? Magdalena de la Cruz duped him, at least for a time, until finally she stood humiliated before her judges with a rope around her neck and a candle in her hand. My addled brain. Who am I to pose such questions? Look at her, Padre. The firebrand further penetrated the pallid skin of her firm, voluptuous breasts, and deep, deep into her heart I dove. *Trasverberation*, you call it, do you not, Padre? Strange, vibrating word—heartless. She saw her nipples leak fire-red blood. Ecstatic, she lunged forward to assist her own sublime wounding. 'Please, please, please, oh sweet Jesus,' she prayed, begged. With thighs widely parted, she planted her heels and uplifted her abdomen." Again he coughed and another blossom fell. "Something within aims to kill me, Padre. Is it her spirit? I pray not."

"Do you wish to discontinue, señor?"

"*Discontinue? Here?* No, unless, if I must, I'd choose this as a place to die. But no. I was saying—yes . . . the spear sliced down her belly, eviscerating her. Her words, not mine—her own depiction, Padre. Believe me. Sliced down to the open lips of her vagina. Look, Padre! Glistening red lips . . . I remember as though it were but an hour ago. Insufferable pain gushed through her as I gouged the path of God's entrance. Pain, pain, because God was knifing though every strand of resistance to him. I know now what was happening to her. She had foretold it all—told me . . . told someone—and I overheard every word. At the time, I was only half there, an actor playing the part scripted for him by another, a part ill understood. Over the years I've pieced it all together. I was exploited by a plot too outlandish for a boy's mind to encompass. Still, I admit, even now the performance amazes me."

"Is this a performance I'm attending right now?"

"Why, which performance do you mean, Padre? Are we not all actors in somebody's play? God's play, the devil's . . . you in mine, I in yours? I took my cues; I listened with a lover's ear. I played the angel, to the hilt, you might say. She felt set ablaze—she said so—set burning inside with God's immaculate fire, she a boiling pot. Look at her, Padre."

"Señor, I'm afraid I must—"

"Burned alive, after all—cremated. A saint on fire. What a sight! Look at me, Padre—the bridge from God to her. The bridge! I too felt set ablaze. Not like her, of course. I was merely a man, like you, Padre . . . weaker, much weaker, but like you otherwise. Not like her. She inhabited another world, as in touch with God as flesh could ever be, suffused with him. Look closely. Your eyes widen, Padre, your jaw drops. We are brothers. See—"

"Señor, this is not—"

"She—*there* . . . aburst with gratitude; with spread thighs upraised as high as possible, she tried with those once-virgin lips, the lips of her loins, to kiss the very face of heaven. Once-virgin lips . . . oh, was I the first? Had God or Christ or other angels before me entered her, perhaps many times? Who am I to ask? Oh, she lunged upward again and again. Padre, she desired to return something to Christ, give back all of herself, ashamed, knowing all of her amounted to less than a trifle. All of her was nothing—she often bemoaned that. God was branding her, branding what he knew he already owned so she would know as well.

"I slid the spear in slowly, ever deeper, the sacred knife slicing its route to the core, liberating the caged soul. Her breasts . . . burning torches—you see them, Padre?—fueled with her blood, her womb a fiery oven. Her eyes blazed with the sight of herself. She saw herself in her vision, as in a mirror or a dream we watch ourselves. She was overcome with the spectacle, the drama of herself that she had created . . . that God had created of her, of her infused with him. She was so totally affected, so totally on fire. Until the end—more alive the more she was consumed, consummated.

"She ate fire and was by fire eaten. God was in her; everything going on was in her. I jabbed the spear into her, once slowly, then twice, then fiercely, again and again. I repeat; she groaned like someone being murdered. I think that even at the time, I sensed that all of this had something to do with death—*dulce Cristo*, something else beyond my grasp! You knew of her 'little deaths,' didn't you, Padre—when she lay for long periods, sometimes days, in a coma, everyone believing she was dead?"

"Yes, I knew of those."

"I heard that once they nearly buried her. Is that true?"

"Yes, it is true."

"Her physical illnesses were very strange, were they not?"

"Yes. She was often unwell. She suffered greatly."

"Yes, she was unwell . . . she suffered greatly . . . burned alive, her own *auto-da-fé*. She could not locate the exact site of the searing spear's point of insertion. I knew little then, but that much I sensed. Or do I sense it only now? The jabbing must have seemed to occur at a hundred different sites. She felt entered everywhere, every pore of her skin. She was only made of holes—open, empty until now. Without God within, nothing is whole.

"She said that everything that occurred within her trances was invisible to the world, that the things of the spirit resided invisibly, that only the eyes of the soul could apprehend them—when God allows. Mystics, I suppose, have always asserted this. But transported as she was, she saw nothing of me. I amounted to nothing 'midst the burning of her being. She felt that burning throughout. She forced her thighs ever farther apart . . . nothing but access for him, for the angel of him. Gored, stabbed with flaming pain . . . she suffered greatly. Have you ever witnessed someone burned at the stake, Padre?"

"No, I never have. How horrible!"

"I have. How horrible, indeed. Anyway, in her eyes—eyes that had envisioned the living God, the Lord crucified—she bled profusely. She ran her hands over her bleeding chest and moaned; her hands burned with a holy fire. No doubt. She believed that she was going to die. All those little deaths—how many deaths had she endured? Oh, she suffered, all right. I saw the ecstasy in her moonlit face. Through all of this, I was myself as one possessed, possessed by the sight of her rapturous desire. All my life she has possessed a part of me. I've stared at her all my life. Some things you can't stop seeing, like those I saw burned alive, like the moonlit body of her inflamed passion. Do you see her, Padre?"

"How do you mean? I remember her sometimes—yes."

"Of course you do. Who cannot who opens his eyes? She meant herself to be seen purely exposed—naked. She stroked my face, the angel's face. Saw that her angel saw every bit of her. She set my bedazed countenance afire. Fire inflamed whatever lay near her. Yes, I shared a little in the conflagration. I believe I still do. You too are now near her, Padre; you too partake of her."

"No, señor, not I. Not that way."

"She knew that God was answering her prayers through me, her savior . . . no, not *I*, I was nothing in myself . . . through some kind of intercession, a bridge that she had conceived—no, that God had conceived; she had conceived nothing, nothing had come from her doing. She even convinced the inquisitors of that. Remember, all this, to her, extended beyond the reach of any human imagination. Yes, even as she felt the blood fountain gush from between her thighs. Her guts spilled forth, exactly as she had foretold. Even then I too may have pictured it. I certainly do now. As you do, Padre. We are brothers . . . *in flagrante delicto*."

"We are brothers, yes, but not in this, not in the way you mean."

"Yes. What gratitude she showed, to someone if not to me. How grateful she was that I consented to be so used. No, no, she knew nothing of me. I was a mere reed, a spear, a lightning bolt in the white palms of God. I, a passageway. A bridge. It was so strange. What can I liken myself to that I know? Impaled on God's shaft from womb to heart, disemboweled, she exploded with gratitude time and again, gratitude to God, to Christ, for taking her, possessing her. I was merely a body immersed in a huge expanse of gratitude. That is the most divine answer to any prayer, is it not, Padre—to be possessed, taken over? She was beside herself. Burned alive, she wailed into the moon-silver night like an animal.

"Long into the night we fornicated, Padre. That's what I did, anyway. She screamed; she dug her nails into my back. Her strength at times was greater than my own. I could not have disengaged from her even had I wanted to. I erupted with my own gratitude, a few driblets, nothing compared to the immense effusions of her passion. I was a stick consumed in the conflagration of the forest.

"Selfish in all my bones, nonetheless I sought to please her. I got what I got out of it . . . more, oh so much more than I realized at the time. I, a mere mortal. Within such mundane boundaries, how much can we ever attain, Padre? I couldn't keep pace with her. She had bounded over the edge of the world. She loved in a realm beyond, eternal, outside our time and our space. She wore me out, melted my spear down to nearly nothing. Deflated, empty, yet joyful, I withdrew from her scalding body.

"Infused with everything of me, everything that God had passed through me to her, she fainted. She threw me away when she had finished. Outside her vision, I counted for nothing, nothing, if not God's angel, discharging his will. I think I understood that much even then. Strange, in some ways it's harder to recapture now what I experienced than to imagine what it was like for her, because she told me what it was like for her before it had all even occurred. The story was made up before it happened. We lived the story she had composed. It's still being written. You are now in there, too, Padre."

"*You* are telling this story, señor. I have no part in it."

"How can you listen the way you are listening and have no part? Yes, I am telling her story, but stories are elaborated by everyone who hears them, don't you think? No? Well, she neglected to inform me what the angel experienced. Perhaps that didn't matter. She was totally centered on God, on Christ, on an angel . . . from my vantage point, totally centered upon herself—pleasured though I was in the process. Everything circled around her, as those lunatics Copernicus and Galileo have alleged the earth does the sun—do you know of any nonsense too incredible to believe? These times—a paradise for charlatans!

"But yes, she, the visionary, was the mirror of it all. When I looked in the mirror, I saw, if only imperfectly, what she saw. She was both the mirror and its image. Do you see what I'm saying, Padre? Afterward, I disappeared from her vision, like a moonbeam off the body of a lake. Perhaps I just flew off. Did she see me with wings, Padre, fanned out and beating powerfully around her, sweeping us up and lowering us down in a flight of divine copulation? Did she? She didn't say. Emblazon me with them if you wish, Padre . . . an artist would. But weak as I am, scarcely able to raise hand to mouth to wipe away this blood . . . it must be hard to picture me thus. Wings—incidentals she never specified. In any case, it was done. I was left with the years to grow into the enormity of it." Again he coughed and the refuse of flowers increased.

"I said I withdrew—more correctly, I was evicted. For her, I must have simply dissipated. I stood up and looked at her. Moon-white, pale as a ghost, still as someone sound asleep, she appeared dead to the world. Astonished, I observed that she had hemorrhaged from between her legs. I searched through my trouser pockets, and with the handkerchief

I found, I rubbed away some of the blood. She seemed not to breathe. I detected no pulse. She did, indeed, seem dead. Panicked, I grabbed up my clothes and fled. I thought they—who were *they*, Padre?—would think that I had raped and murdered her. I left her there with God, an ashen corpse in the moonlight.

"The next day, I crept back and discovered that she was gone. Obviously, she had once more passed into a death swoon from which she awakened. No signs betrayed that anything had happened. Had I dreamed all of it, I wondered? But no. There on the ground indeed did lay a sign—the bloodstained handkerchief. Relieved, I grabbed it, as proof of my sanity. And also, yes—a memento. I have kept it near me throughout my life. You understand, Padre. I was not unlike those fiends, who, after her death—*her real death*, that is—disinterred her corpse and tore away chunks of her body. The miracle-working relics of a saint, more precious than sapphires and rubies. I believe that her blood saved my life more than once. In duels with pistols or swords, I wore it beneath my shirt against my heart. After that night we never met again.

"What more can I say, Padre? Recently she has been beatified. Soon she will be canonized. Is this not so?"

"Yes, if no new evidence impugns the recommendation."

"Indeed—and I will have provided part of the reason for that valediction. I am simply astonished. The scene I have recounted was one which she presented in her autobiography. You have read this magnificent book, I presume."

"Yes."

"She omitted the sex, naturally, which my version includes. That affair with the angel . . . you must admit, Padre, how tinted with sexual overtones is her account. A brave woman! How overlapping is the openly carnal and mystical language of ecstasy. Well, after thorough scrutiny, the Inquisition judged my visitation as genuinely divine. She referred to me only as the angel, of course. No one sought my testimony, nor did I volunteer it. If the inquisitors learned what you have heard, Padre, they would dig her up and burn her remains—a jezebel, vile and ignominious. Who am I to challenge her version? Plainly I experienced it all rather differently. But I haven't the courage to contest a saint.

"Was she a saint? Who am I to say? They—those more sapient ones—who decide such issues seem about to conclude in her favor. But where Christ ends and the devil begins, what line delineates, Padre? Maybe the supreme deity constitutes a fusion of these two terrifying extremes. Who knows? Maybe it is from that contentious space we have inserted betwixt them that the saint is born.

"Perhaps it only matters how *she* imagined it—no, no, *not imagined,* she would insist, but viewed in the only way she could—as God meant for one whom he had blessed to view it. I cannot help believing that she largely composed herself, Padre, that she was her own work of art, that she made up what happened. And she—the perfect dreamer—convinced us! And her dream was as real as anything can be. With my puny earthly means I performed as she directed. Maybe that's who saints are anyway, those whose imaginations far outstrip our own, those who take no responsibility, in this regard, but attribute all their imaginings to God. They define the soul's reality, the only reality that ultimately matters, as a reality unattainable for most of us—a reality too grotesque to engage except as a dream. They transform the world, alas, into a place where we cannot live. No wonder we try to destroy them."

"Are you trying to destroy her?"

"I enacted her vision."

"Of course and along the way she just happened to gratify the lusts of an adolescent boy idling through the woods, didn't she?"

"Enchanted woods. Yes, this is so. Destroy her? No. I trust you, Padre—trust you love her. So, was I once an angel? I never viewed myself that way. I pretended. What are we if not players in someone else's drama, far more often than we are in our own?"

"Yes, but over the years she has acted in your drama as well, has she not, señor?"

"Yes, you could say that. Mine the lesser, meaner drama. I do not seek to reduce hers to mine."

"No, because you are glorified, perhaps saved, if elevated to hers."

"Unworthy though I am, I admit that as well, Padre. In this game of salvation, she is the sole card in my hand. I'm playing it now."

"You needn't use her this way. If you have something to repent, I repeat, you need only beseech the Lord."

"If I have something to repent . . . is it her representation of me that stands before God? Our opinion of ourselves counts as only one, and not necessarily the most privileged or worthwhile one at that. She devised the drama that defined who she was, and for a time, defined her angel. Who am I to say who I am? In whose eyes? A thousand different people . . . whoever views me, views me differently. My assessment of myself may do me no justice whatsoever. To have a saint view us . . . well, there we are magnified beyond anything we can comprehend of ourselves. She always argued that anyone who had not been blessed with such visions as hers could not possibly understand the transfigurations that resulted. I believe that too. I am honored that she cast me in such a beatific role, that I could be used in the configuration of a saint. While conquistadors like Magellan and Columbus sailed over the globe, she stood still and turned inward to plumb the depths of the soul. And into the inner sanctum of this woman I sank a flaming shaft."

"An igneous pride lights up this entire chamber, señor."

"Yes, I know that it does. I will not inquire if yours would do otherwise. She gave some meaning to my life, a life otherwise devoid of value. I enjoyed myself, naturally, but all of it far surpassed my own carnal satisfaction, or hers, for that matter. I know that to reduce all of this to the carnal, that ordinary language for which you castigated me, Padre, traduces the sacred, mocks it. The very crime inquisitors themselves perpetrate not infrequently. But this is not my ambition. I was used by a saint. The reality invented in her story contains the last word. It's not the experience that makes the saint, but the saint that makes everything what it can possibly be, *more* than what it can be in the world that exists for the rest of us groundlings. What's more blessed than that? *That* she achieved during our night together. And if a saint declares you an angel, I ask again, who are you to contradict? Am I damned forever because of it?"

"God gave you a will of your own, señor."

"Well, it hasn't always seemed that way. It didn't that night. Having her was the supreme moment of my life; having me—whomever she dreamed I was—was surely one of the supreme moments of hers. No, it's not for me to contest her view of that night; hers was, after all, the higher vision. To such a vision we must all finally defer. Is that not so, Padre? Perhaps that night God touched me a little bit too. Some of all that love must have rubbed off on me, hopefully enough to mitigate the scourges of hell. Perhaps she and I will meet again in another world and she'll talk to me as she once did, revealing all the wonders that she sees. We'll reminisce, and she'll tell me of an event of love that befell her when an angel descended from heaven.

"Again, who can say? I wish her well on her saintly journey into the future. With all my heart, I'm happy if I assisted. Forgive me, Padre, if I have sinned." He quickly covered his mouth with another handkerchief and coughed, and the flowers of blood multiplied.

A month later, Padre Juan Pérez sat in the rectory talking with his visitor, Angela Lomas.

"Thank you, Padre, for confessing Enrique. He was very grateful. He said a heavy burden had been lifted from him. He died the day after your visit."

"Yes, I know. I was terribly sorry to hear. You were close to your brother, were you not, señora?"

"Close to him? Yes, very. He was older than I by three years. I loved him; when we were children, I really worshiped him. And it seemed always important to him that he be loved by me. Close, yes . . . too close, at times. We took some advantages of each other. He took liberties; certain of his desires he satisfied with me that he should not have, if you understand me, Padre. But I never blamed him, never ceased loving him; perhaps it made me love him all the more. That I need not go into. It was all confessed long ago and perhaps sorrowed over some, too. It's a story that makes no difference here, not now."

"Enrique led a remarkable life."

"Yes, he did. Everything to excess, yet nothing ever enough. He fed on life as someone starving. As you say, a remarkable life . . . yes, extravagant, wasteful, full of sin, and I suspect, slight regret. That he chose to confess anything surprised me. Frankly, it mystifies me."

"Who understands anyone completely?"

"Yes, that's true. He lived the life he wished, or nearly lived such a life. No life would have been grand enough. His was one that—how shall I say?—one that to a considerable extent he invented."

"The Lord gave us free will. Do we not largely construct the lives we live?"

"We do, Padre. But I mean he exaggerated what he did. For him no adventure, no matter how grand it literally was, ever proved quite grand enough. In the telling of it, he would always enhance it. Often he merely fabricated, I'm afraid, and one could not separate the truth from the lie. Sometimes I believe he could not himself make that distinction."

"Many things are such that they tolerate different interpretation, señora."

"Frequently that's so. Occasionally, after narrating some grandiose escapade and beguiling everyone gathered around him, he would wink at me and smile and I would shake my head, bemused but captivated by his roguishness. He loved to fabricate. He was reckless, very handsome, and very charming—the perfect liar."

"Why would he do that? The life he lived seemed spectacular."

"I know. But he seemed sometimes to . . . well, value the making up more than anything he did in fact. It was strange. But having grown up with him, I was never that surprised at how much he aggrandized. No, not at all. As a boy, he had a peculiarity that might have predicted something like this."

"May I ask what it was?"

"He used to confess to crimes which he had not committed, from his childhood up to the time when he left home, when he was almost twenty."

"Confessed to crimes he was innocent of—what do you mean, señora?"

"If I did something naughty, to protect me he'd claim he did it. Very chivalrous! I suppose you could say I had the ideal brother, but I'm afraid I often took wicked advantage of him. Perhaps he was one of those persons who feel guilty all the time but never quite know what they're guilty of, so they search for things on which to fix their guilt. Perhaps as a priest you have some experience of such unhappy souls. Why he did this, I have no idea. He wanted me to love him. Maybe that was another thing—an insatiable hunger for love. I loved him all right. But I must say, I did let him rescue me whenever possible. Not that I was ungrateful, as I've already indicated. But the point is that this lying of his continued. He should have written novels like Cervantes or been a poet, although our darling Cervantes would have certainly ridiculed my brother's romantic nature. Perhaps Enrique expected the world to be as appreciative of him as I had been. Maybe it was."

"He confessed to save others?"

"Not always. He would confess to thefts, to assaults . . . once even to rape, once to murder. It seemed to thrill him. Fortunately, everyone eventually realized he did this, so he was never thrown into jail. Sometimes it was laughable; sometimes, for the family, perturbing. Perhaps he was a little insane. I don't know. I've given it much thought, I must say, because I felt somewhat to blame. It seemed he often wished to play out a dual role—the guilty and the exonerated, getting much attention for doing something awful, something dangerous that he never in fact did. Breaking the law and yet not actually breaking it. But I'm guessing. Have I understood Enrique's craziness—inflating a life already overblown? No, not really. It simply never surprised me that he magnified his deeds. He had always done that. I could never hear of his eccentric exploits—even when believing they were mostly true—without amusement. He kept souvenirs."

"Souvenirs?"

"Yes, more childishness. Of all his conquests—letters, a piece of lace, ribbons . . . you know, scented scarves. Why? Proofs, testimonies . . . reminders of his conquests. He saved these things. He'd show me some of them. 'Do you know whose luscious thigh this garter adorned, sweet sister?' A bragging boy to the end. It was as though he needed to convince others of what he couldn't quite believe himself."

"I see. Why have you shared all this with me, señora?"

"You inquired, didn't you? Or because you heard my bother's confession. He knew I liked you very much but it seemed important that someone hear him who knew Teresa de Jesús, our saint—"

"Not yet officially a saint."

"Soon, Padre, there is no doubt."

"No, there is no doubt."

"But you heard his confession, and I suppose I do not wish you to judge him too harshly."

"It is not for me to judge. God is the judge."

"I know, of course, but nonetheless . . . pity him, Padre. And what had Teresa to do with anything? A while ago he mentioned that when he was a student he had chanced upon her strolling in the woods. It surprised me that he had never spoken of this before. I wondered if it were true. Once she had become so famous perhaps he wished to adorn his rakish life with a touch, slight as it may be, of something sanctified. Amused, all I said was, 'Dear brother, you make so little of an encounter with a saint. I guess Teresa truly is unique: the only woman who failed to inflame your imagination.' He grinned and replied, 'What can even I make of a saint? What's left? They make so much of themselves.' A few days later I observed him studying her autobiography. He seemed quite engrossed. Ah well, I suspect he left you as confounded as the rest of us. Oh, and the hour before he died he handed me this package that he wished delivered to you when next we met. I must be going. As always, our visit was a delight. When you are in Madrid, our home is your home. Farewell."

Padre Pérez had not known what to make of Enrique's bizarre confession. In many ways, it had proved disconcerting. It rambled endlessly, in and out of the highlighted body of a woman, or the illusion of such a body, round and round a passionate engagement that vacillated in its outlines and its definition. No matter how he concentrated on the fervent embraces of the lovers, it wasn't always clear or easy to comprehend what was really happening with them, or with the man relating the story . . . or with him, the man listening to it.

The more intently Padre Pérez gazed at the couple—in order to compensate for Enrique's constant discursive thought—the more off-centered became the main event, a disorienting event, which at times seemed to simply fragment, broken again and again by Enrique's commentary. There was a spectacle all right, vivid in every respect, yet it somehow evaded the onlooker's grasp. The more Padre Pérez contemplated it, the more it appeared as a story desperate in the telling, with both pathetic and tragic implications. Remembering it, he would one moment want to cry, the next to laugh, the next to simply stare benumbed at the blazing, bloody bodies of the consumed lovers, each seemingly captivated by a different vision.

He had absolved Enrique of any fornication that he *may* have committed. During much of the confession and afterward, the padre had considered whether he could believe a word of the dying man's story. It was an odd situation. After all, why had he doubted? For a nun to behave promiscuously was not that unusual. But Teresa? How difficult to accept. He didn't wish to believe it. If she—seemingly as devout as a person could be—had succumbed, who then could refrain? And yet, if all Enrique claimed were true, couldn't one nonetheless defend Teresa's vision? Might there not have, indeed, been an angel who possessed Enrique? (Padre Pérez had meditated much on this.)

It was certainly easy enough for everybody to believe how frequently the devil visited women (that snake Enrique discerned winding through their bodies). So—why not an angel? The perfect disguise—which an angel of God could easily assume—would confound anyone. How could you distinguish an exact copy from the original? And an episode as miraculous as that could surely disrupt one's comprehension of everything. Everything that you were doing was being done to you and the meaning of your behavior was something very different from what you understood!

No wonder poor Enrique felt baffled that night about who he was and what he'd done. Did Teresa imagine all this? Did Enrique? Were they both insane? Padre Pérez had lost some sleep over these questions. Moreover, he wondered if he were obliged to do something, to report something. This story probably would, as Enrique had pointedly noted, cast aspersions enough on Teresa to disallow her canonization. Padre Pérez was a good priest, but he loved Teresa, and the thought that he could bring degradation to her memory was too much for him to bear. He believed, as had so many, in Teresa's sainthood. And yet many others had maligned her as a charlatan.

What should he do? As a priest he was enjoined to come forth with any evidence related to heresy and witchcraft. In silence he had always loathed the inquisitors, their cruel methods and the cold-hearted logic they employed to justify their relentless crusade against the enemies of the Church. Perhaps Enrique had not so much desired to save his own soul but to drag another—with eyes as magnificent as his sister's—into hell with him. The padre worried that he might, in fact, be endangering himself. If the inquisitors, who seemed capable of uncovering anything they searched for avidly enough, somehow discovered that he was withholding crucial testimony regarding the canonization of a saint ... what then?

For a while he tormented himself with fear. He felt curiously involved, taken in by something. Certain of Enrique's remarks unsettled him, made him feel somehow guilty, as though he were part of this. *This* what? Conspiracy to hide the lust embedded in the sacred—was that it? The way he had imagined the scene that Enrique described, with all those unnecessary, licentious details—yes, imagined it as though he were indeed part of it, a willing spectator, too aroused to deflect his greedy gaze. Oh yes, how astutely, with a libertine's eye, Enrique had detected this. *We are brothers*... He agonized over this for days, but finally he convinced himself that he need do nothing because, thank God, Enrique's story had been related within the inviolable framework of the confessional. Or if questioned, he could claim that he deemed it all the ravings of a madman, which it may have been.

Padre Juan Pérez picked up the envelope that Angela Lomas had placed on his desk. He inspected it, turned it about, and pressed it. It contained something soft. He opened it cautiously, as though he were a little afraid, as though he already had some dim awareness of its content. Inside he found a bloodstained handkerchief. Immediately he recalled the paroxysms of coughing that had so beset Enrique and the bloody handkerchiefs that he had dropped from his mouth to the floor. But no, he quickly realized that these bloodstains were dark brown, stiff, evidently years old. Padre Pérez frowned and smiled simultaneously. He was momentarily embarrassed but then unexpectedly elated.

If the dead lived on—oh, how unrestful and horrid had been her sleep of death, a nightmare. She had died in Alba de Tormes and had been buried there. Nine months later, her body was disinterred and secretly returned to Ávila where it was reburied. The pope subsequently ordered it returned to Alba. And that too proved a clandestine undertaking. The corpse was again stolen to be returned to Alba and again inhumed. Then it was several times exhumed to check if it continued to emit an odor of perfume, and if it still remained unspoiled by putrefaction—in a word, if it remained the dead body of a living saint.

But in each of these exhumations, the body suffered ever more ravagement and pillaging of its parts. A voracious hunger to possess any part of her drove the crazed to tear away pieces of her clothing and her sacred flesh. They confiscated anything of hers, anything that had belonged to her, because any article of a saint produced miracles. The padre did not condone such acts but he understood the sorrowful human longings that prompted these desecrations. He had himself often wished to have of her some shred of remembrance.

Enrique's insinuations . . . they were rather revolting—yes, and mainly revolting because of the nasty truth they contained. No, Padre Pérez had quite definitely not been indifferent to the beauty of Teresa de Jésus, nor had many others. He had known her when she was older, but even then some of her beauty still lurked in the aging shadows of her face. And her dark eyes—yes, they had pierced and excited his heart. And yes, there had been impure thoughts of which he had confessed and been absolved. He had also dreamed of her—unclean dreams. But these had remained unconfessed.

He stroked the handkerchief and touched it to his lips. Was this some kind of joke? The last laugh of the unrepentant libertine? Was this truly Teresa's blood, virgin blood, blood of the womb, blood of her sex? It could very well be. That was the nature of relics anyway; their authenticity could never be incontestably established. Therefore . . . he would treasure it as genuine. Yes, why not? Suddenly a jolt of anxiety shot through his stomach. He quickly replaced the gift in the envelope and glanced around to confirm that no one had glimpsed the handkerchief—as though it were possible for someone to recognize what it was. He must think of someplace safe to hide this blood of a saint. It pleased him very much to own it.

He looked out the window. Dusk was falling. The form of things had begun to blur. Already he could detect in the darkening sky the moon's pale face. Out of the fading light he could already discern the emerging bodies of the lovers hungrily drawing their form and substance from the oncoming darkness. He saw flames, yellow, orange, and blue . . . and yes, they flamed out like gigantic wings. He imagined that by midnight the exploding conflagration of their passions would be seen hundreds of years away. He shook his head pensively. Was it all true, or not all, but enough? Maybe so. With Enrique now dead, only Padre Juan Pérez knew *this* side of the story. He felt embarrassed by an awareness of the awful power he had been bequeathed. But no, it was power not to be used— no, never again. He was resolved: the story would die with him. It would cast no further aspersions on Teresa's saintliness or the reality of her angel.

Devouring Marilyn

I stood over the subway grating at Lexington and Fifty-second . . . my legs spread wide. Midtown Manhattan, and yet it seemed like a city of castles or cathedrals—gloomy and medieval. Two AM, amid all those thin, towering buildings . . . like the spires of churches, the parapets of castles . . . yes, there at the core of something gothic.

It's hard to explain. Not having slept well for several nights, I was tired and high on too many bennies. So that—uppers nullifying exhaustion—perhaps distorted things.

A crowd had assembled. Hundreds of reporters and photographers and two thousand other onlookers, all beckoned by the incredible promise: *Marilyn would be here.* They had wound through a maze of streets and alleyways to find me, their goddess, or as Mr. Winchell said, the only *world* goddess ever invented by Americans. My white dress gleamed; I glowed like an icon. They had come to worship Marilyn, to feed upon her. I smiled invitingly, ready to perform, awaiting the wind from below to commence. Amazed, they stared, as they would at a visitation, disbelieving that I was *so* there, amazed how easily extended hands could caress me. I waved at them; they waved back. I winked, licked my lips, and blew kisses. They clapped, whistled, and cheered, and sent their own kisses soaring back.

Next to me, the marquee of the Trans-Lux Theater announced *The Creature from the Black Lagoon.*

I spotted my hubby Joe. I hadn't expected him. Deeply pained, he glowered, with that "Yer a fuckin' whore" accusation engraved on his face. Crazy jealous. Winchell, who read everything like a telegram, accompanied him. For some reason Winchell had always despised me. I didn't know anyone else, and pretty soon the two of them disappeared. Either they left or the gathering crowd of anonymous spectators enveloped them or my mind just refused to acknowledge their scolding presence. I'd catch hell later.

I looked at the expectant faces confronting me. Their hunger caused an exhilaration that along with the drugs further disguised my fatigue. I was eager to please. This was, after all, what I did best—*stimulate*, make others desperately desire me . . . *by gazing at Marilyn*. I recognized the avid hunger surrounding me. I'd certainly dealt with lots of that before. I incited it.

As always, such attention imposed enormous demands, but that night I had quickly become aware of it as vaguely menacing . . . too near . . . something . . . I don't know, something not quite explicable. I felt unprotected from all these grinning fans, their bare teeth, obviously starved, like so many werewolves I'd known, for what they'd been promised and had stayed up half the night for. In the chilly air I started to shiver. I was excited—yes, as excited as everyone else there—but a gnawing unease had entered me. Some sort of danger had crept into this comical titillation that Fox's ad men had staged for *The Itch*.

But shadowy threats frequently lurked near me. I was always haunted, something I usually attempted to ignore. Tonight, however, this uneasiness seemed necessary for the drama about to unfold, a grisly drama in which I had, perhaps unwisely, consented to star.

From the beginning it was disconcerting. I couldn't decide whether this was a horror movie or not, a movie in the making or one that I had completed and was now merely watching. Or was this for real? Such distinctions often confused me, probably because make-believe saturated my life. I—but who would that be?—played the part of Marilyn Monroe, both on screen and off. I—Norma Jeane?—had fabricated every inch of her, transplanted every cell of my former being into Marilyn Monroe, a creature of imagination. Actually, the mask I wore had so thoroughly transformed me; I could no longer maintain I played a role.

Then the wind from beneath the subway grating burst forth. It swept my white dress up, exposing my legs and the brown triangle of pussy hair, undyed, the only dark spot in all the shimmering white. For this occasion I had worn no panties. I danced about, pretending to push down my skirt, to resist the breeze, to cover myself, all the while maneuvering to maximize my body's exposure. I pretended to be coquettish, innocent, but of course everyone discerned the pretense. I was only a whore pretending to be a virgin (just as Joe had always insisted, while relishing every inch of me). I beamed when some joe barked out, "Cunt! Cunt!" And a fiendish glint lit his eyes as though he had detected the slut I truly was. "Look! Her bod. There!" he shouted, gleeful. The crowd's eyes feasted upon me as I twisted, a serpent of temptation and damnation . . . a creature from a black lagoon. I seemed lost in myself, borne away by some rushing undercurrent. I was working hard, striving toward some kind of climax, release. The crowd groaned and swayed, laboring with me. It profoundly understood. It had made me; I had made it. *It*—as impersonal as the blood in your veins can be.

I heard the cameras clicking, determined to capture and lock me into their darkroom. Suffocated, I was possessed from within and without. The circle of the crowd gradually tightened, like the binding arms of a lover who meant to engulf me unto death. I wanted to stop them, stop myself—didn't I? I kept smiling, kept tempting them to advance. Mercilessly, foolishly, I kept stoking their desires, foolishly stroking my own anxious excitement. I couldn't stop, couldn't stop them, couldn't resist cultivating our appetite, making us all hunger for Marilyn Monroe— a hunger that grew by what it fed upon.

My dress flew about, a swirl of white. Oh, it will flame out, I imagined, like shining from shook foil. I saw cocks engorging, conjured by my flaming nakedness. (Was Joe's in there somewhere? Was Winchell's?) I noticed women drooling and shamelessly scratching their crotches, groaning bitches in heat.

Cocks and pussies . . . the language of men. I was a story told by men. Of me, there was no other tale to tell . . . I was told.

Amidst all this lust, I gleamed, radiant as an angel, the white of my skirt flaring like the wings of a holy dove in flight, in flight but going nowhere . . . snared wings flailing. I couldn't stop. Couldn't stop. That was the worst of it, where the problem lies, the hideous part. I exerted no control over anything happening, unless some hidden inner demon commanded my conscious will, perhaps a demon to whom I had secretly—or not even so secretly— submitted. Controlled, yes, and running over the same ground, stuck on myself; underground passenger trains sped through me.

Round and round I twisted, wound up like a monstrously beautiful toy, striving vainly to undo some wicked curse by endlessly reenacting it. I kept playing with myself. "Look, her pussy's dripping," some guy exclaimed. He pointed, "Look at it! Her bush is burning." They smacked their lips. "We love you, Marilyn, sweetie!"

Nothing I did embarrassed me. I was frightened but powerless to halt anything that now transpired. Everything kept repeating. I have already confessed that drugs and fatigue may have affected my sense of this bizarre event. Gleaming eyes, dripping fangs, claws extended, cocks throbbing . . . a bedlam ward. Over and over. No, surely all wasn't as I perceived it.

More and more pictures they took, thousands, millions. Somehow I viewed photographs of me scattered all over the world, shots that would freeze for all time this exquisite moment, this feast. They wanted to have me there, within them—in there. For them, I had been so ephemeral, torturously ungraspable . . . although I was on display everywhere. The world's most famous movie star, everywhere, yet beyond reach . . . until now. The blinding eyes of all those sizzling flashbulbs winked flirtatiously. Millions of ravenous eyes gazed upon me—a goddess, whom, even as centuries passed, they couldn't get their fill of. But, oh, they had me now (didn't they?), nailed down in my own "capacious divinity," some Hollywood Rilke once said. Oh, they knew I could never, no matter how exorbitant the cost, let them go. I fed on our hungers—my own and theirs. Unappeased, my own hunger in the mouths of others had returned to murder me. Did I always know it would?

I woke, or fell asleep and dreamed I woke. It hardly mattered because every aspect of my life existed as a dream or a nightmare. Asleep or not, here in the city's gothic heart, I danced and postured, blazing like a white fire fanned by the infernal wind from beneath. Underground passenger trains raced through me. I woke, or didn't wake, or just continued my offering in the nervous space where no one ever slept. Since childhood, I'd been an insomniac. Was this celebration of me observed there, in the stupefying wastelands of insomnia? I turned, a writhing slave girl struggling to untie herself, but ever more entangled by her own grasping hungers. Everything stayed the same, awake or asleep. I was delirious. I drifted back to sleep (or didn't, it didn't matter) and resumed this episode of torturous pleasure, ablaze with the white flames of hell—or was it heaven? I didn't know . . . to me heaven and hell felt so oddly one; the ecstasies of each commingled. Or maybe that kind of mix-up serves as the certain sign that you're in hell. An excruciating pleasure practically exceeding endurance afflicted me. Yet I endured. "That's precisely what hell is—love," another bard declared.

My dress billowed, my pussy burned, my tits squirmed for freedom, roaring trains tunneled beneath my glistening thighs. If Joe were out there, this would kill him, finish our marriage. Probably with this *danse macabre* I meant to end that ridiculous union anyway. But none of that directly affected me right then. I had transcended all those mundane worries. I performed with a strange static movement; I repeated myself, like a child stuttering to find expression. "We got her! Got her!" the photogs cried. "We love you, baby doll," cried the boys and girls. They now had Marilyn Monroe all to themselves. I couldn't liberate myself. They were the life of me. To them, a terrible secret had now been disclosed, as flagrantly as ripping off my clothes. I had been returned to the people, to the dream-body in which I had been conceived.

Didn't I know this gruesome reckoning would arrive, that this was part of the deal? All these years, hadn't they bestowed upon me everything that I had craved—fame, outrageous beauty? Hadn't I been designed according to my own desires, which coincidentally embodied their own? My fans and I—we had invented and partaken of each other, vampires making love to one another. Every desire that gazing could gratify, they had realized with me. Now delivered unto the people, greedily they strove to cash in. I had been a glorious image of memory, of film, gossamer and as insubstantial as fantasy. Now, compelled to touch me, they sought to assure themselves that my flesh was every bit as firm as theirs. My body appeared so juicy, even eatable. They called me "Mother, Mother." *Me—mother*, scarcely more than a child myself. Dear god, hungers so ancient only the blood-milk of Mother can feed. I know. I was half mad half the time. Had they now uncovered in me the phantom of my own mother, whose dementia I always dreaded awaited me? "Mother, feed us, more, more!" Starved appeals out there, in here. Creatures from a black lagoon . . . now showing.

They pressed in upon me, approaching with salivating, gaping jaws. Their moist breath warmed my throat and seeped down the plunging neckline of my dress and singed my tender nipples. They inhaled my skin's intoxicating perfume. Drunk with that odor, dizzy with my incessant motion, my startling accessibility, beseeching, they now rubbed against my legs and pried at my body, seeking a cavity to burrow into, a burning bush to plug their hands into. They wanted more than to gaze at me. But, oh, didn't they understand that I was made *only* to be gazed upon— not to touch, not to marry, not to screw into? Oh, how they longed to consume all that I was to them, was to myself. How they yearned to be part of me, one with me, one whole; not realizing that in doing that, they would demolish me. Long-fingered hands, short stubby paws reached to stroke me, grab me, finger me, strangle me, just so I'd never leave.

Masses seemed now to have converged, rapacious as wolves. Oh, they loved me ardently, just as I had always prayed they would. I fulfilled wishes as primeval as childhood. "Her tits, her tits," I heard the babies crying for my nipples, sucking hard and soft, and long. Unresisting, gratefully, I fed the multitude. It felt wonderfully painful . . . astonishing. And yet, hadn't this gross indulgence characterized Marilyn's whole existence— such indulgence that now had simply grown shockingly evident? Surely this represented the culmination of our life together—the dreamer and the dreamed. Wishes, mine and theirs, had shaped me into a goddess too flawless to be true, too perfect to do anything with other than eat.

But, oh, how truly I satisfied their hungers, as they did mine. I belonged to them, they to me. Finally one body, eating off of itself. The mouth, the apple, one event. They wanted me there with them, exactly as I was, eternally bound . . . a slave. They wanted to pour over me, pour into me, pour over and into themselves. Desire liquefies. I alone embodied heaven: a concoction of their dreams, now safe and sound back inside the belly of the beast where I originated. "No one's safe," I heard a preacher once inveigh against me, "until she's disincarnate." At the time, I thought he was insane. Disincarnate. *No!*—not at the peak of this carnal power. Dear God, keep me whole!

They started to lick me, lovingly at first, warmly, then scaldingly. And then the teeth came savagely into play. "Her mouth, her belly, her cunt, her knees," they named the parts of me as though reclaiming stolen goods that belonged to them. "Yes, it was this mouth—hers—I lost. Give it back! Give it back! I dreamed it first!" At certain moments, I thought I'd die from ecstasy. Hadn't I always longed to die in ecstasy of this kind, the kind that they had prepared for me for years? Hadn't I prepared myself as well for this sacrifice? Although afraid, I seemed unable to oppose them, to cease provoking them. I believed I comprehended the ghastly terms of my reign. Hadn't I always? They tongued away my white dress like cotton candy. I let them. Could I have stopped them? I never tried. I tired. With all the heat, I began to melt. Their many tongues reddened and chafed my skin. Could I have stopped them? I didn't. I felt raw, burned, bleeding, flayed. I began to melt. I tired. Penises, breasts, and eyes had been inserted into all my orifices, climaxing in me. Climaxing me. Words cut into me too and left me panting. I was, after all, a bitch in heat . . . meat to eat. Now, the zenith with nothing left—disincarnate.

The form of me broke down . . . the most famous form in the world— dissipated. Everything gushed and fell apart. Flaming out, fast becoming nothing—a hole where I had been; a lagoon, creatureless. *Me— dissipating! Me!* Millions came into me. Trains. "We've been screwing her for years, a dream at a time," they seemed to say, although none doubted his or her ownership of me, especially not I. "We love you, sweetie pie." Their teeth sank into my shoulders, down to the bone, into my bulging neck veins, into my breasts, into my thighs. Sacred unto death— scared, but undeterred by fear—I succumbed. They tore my burnt flesh away, chewed upon me, savored me . . . goddess, the body of the world. I bled all over them, all over myself, all over the streets of New York, all over Japan, all over France, all over . . . They thirsted upon my blood— ambrosia. I drew them deeper into the whole of me. All of them. (Even nosy Winchell had his snout stuck into the brown triangle, and this was what hubby Joe had really raged all along to do: eat me up, all up—except to do it only by himself. Too bad, too late for that.)

I tired. Everything had worn off, been effaced. Exhausted, nothing of me remained. Marilyn Monroe . . . gone . . . as everywhere now as the air you breathe. Yes, everything merged into one gushing river, and then the river emptied into the hole, a dead lagoon. Little by little, a piece at a time, I departed wholly, a lick of blood, a mouthful of flesh . . . here, there—gone. You wanted me alive forever inside you. Remember—

Maiden's Head

Angel Mae's fifteen, with golden hair, long and luxurious. Usually she ties her hair up in some prepossessing fashion, but when it's unbound it touches the floor. Very lovely she is, and this presents probs for her dad. Every night he locks sweet Angel in her bedroom—to enforce rigorous study habits, he says. But if perchance she has no homework, he locks her up anyway. He worries she has a roving eye and fears she might lose her head over some dude. So Dad forbids her to date.

Actually, he wants her for himself, especially when he drinks a lot, which is frequent. At such times, he'll beat her if she resists his wishes, although that's not often because she never really resists him. She will, however, sometimes pretend to because she suspects that such feigned opposition gets him off. He enjoys this abusive control over her, even when it's unnecessary, but whatever he wants has been pretty much okay with Angel; she's been perfectly obliging. No evident problem there. (This from her diary: *He smacks her mouth, tits, and butt 'til she opens up. She always does. He's lonely; me too. I'm sorry for her, but I couldn't stop watching if I tried.*) Dad's a fairly deranged guy. He swears he'll wring her lovely neck if she ever *seriously* misbehaves.

Angel Mae's behavior is one thing, her thoughts another. She can stand apart and observe herself, look on, from outside the picture, so to speak, like she's viewing herself in a home movie or in a dream. (From that perspective the diary speaks differently: *This isn't happening to me. Take her but leave me here.*) Perhaps she's fairly deranged too. (*She dreamed she'd been hanged by her hair from a bell tower and Daddy was ringing her. Amazing sight! Gruesome. Foretold. I read some of it in a book somewhere. I told her. Look ahead. Look a head. This isn't happening to me. She's over there. I can't stop looking. I feel for her. My guardian angel.*)

Imprisoned, Angel spends many an hour either reading or gazing out of the window. She will comb her hair, draping it over her often nude body, winding and tucking it here and there, exciting herself with its tickling, silken touch. Sometimes she so fills with desire, she imagines that her captivity serves as a kind of hothouse in which her guardian angel is being ripened for some sacrificial fertility rite. *(Naked . . . she feels so dressed, make up, made up, altered—dreaming of herself on an altar, at her throat a blade.)* With all this study time, she is, not surprisingly, a good student. From her diaries, she sounds precocious in some respects. In what she calls her "off time," she reads romance novels and fairy tales, losing herself in exotic adventures. The story of Rapunzel has affected her profoundly; she's read it a hundred times.

Peering down from the window, she occasionally measures the distance to the ground, wondering if she could survive a leap from her bolted chamber. Probably not. She's awfully frail. Once Dad grabbed her by the wrists, flung her nude body around in the air, and dislocated her shoulder. Once he fractured one of her thigh bones when he pried her thighs too far apart. With rapt attention, she had watched him doing this, like watching a video, until the pain shot through her like a bullet and the screen blacked out. *(The physician winks at her, warning against such strenuous gymnastics, all atwinkle with inference.)*

But no, she couldn't survive a leap. And why bother? In the morning he always releases her and she leaves for school. Still . . . just to be able to make that leap . . . *that* means a lot to her. *(To know that if she chooses, she could escape. Like me.)* Sometimes Father handcuffs her to the bedpost, preventing her from even peeking out of the window. The boredom of her confinement then gnaws. She wonders what Rapunzel did with so much time on her hands. Often Angel prays Dad will come to her, with punishments or drunken caresses, it hardly matters—she welcomes any diversion to fill the vast, empty hours. She can't live on reading and dreaming alone; that could drive her crazy . . . maybe it already has. Sometimes she falls asleep with Dad's lips reeking of bourbon inches from her mouth. She zones out a lot in the face of her father. *(She dreamed a snake was coming in her mouth, sliding down her throat, and slithering out the end of her. This isn't happening to me. How many mes are there in anyone?)*

Angel's mom died five years ago, a loss that drove Dad deeper into booze and into his daughter. Not a surprising result because he's always imbibed immoderately, and he's always been excessively affectionate (as well as sometimes harsh) with his comely daughter. Unfortunately (or fortunately), her rapid physical development flowered with temptations too luscious to forego, temptations he never even tried to withstand. He intends to keep her to himself for as long as possible, and locking her up seems a real smart idea—crude but effective. It's important that she not stray far from him, definitely not stray into another male's arms.

But lately Father's not the only stud occupying her. There's Donald Boy, or to some, Don O-Boy, the brawny champ of Fairview's wrestling team. Angel nurses an ever-growing crush on the stud. Don O-Boy's strong and intimidating, stomping down the school halls like a gorilla. He wears T-shirts that show off the nervous ripple of his muscles even in winter. Now Angel is an excellent student. Don's not; he rarely cracks a book. In fact, at times he acts a little stupid.

Recently, in the big state match, an opponent accidentally cuffed Don in the groin. This so infuriated Don O he grabbed the foe by the hair and laid a clamp on him that nearly broke the joker's neck. The school was disqualified for the hair pulling, and consequently lost the championship. Outraged at O-Boy, the coach yelled, "For the damnedest feat of dumbness, they shoulda let ya keep the fucker's head at least!" But classmates like Don 'cause he's tough and regularly pins his rivals to the mat like flies. And Angel can't take her eyes off him, that barrel of a chest and those swollen biceps. (Why, hasn't that body of his appeared in some novels she's read?) Nor can he remove his eyes from her, eyes that she notices usually rivet upon her hair; he seems spellbound by her golden locks, and she digs that. *(They screw and unscrew her. I look. She's all made up. Me too.)*

They screw and unscrew her. This is a favorite expression (albeit obscure), one she periodically repeats in the diaries that were found.

Outside the life with Dad and those quirky diary entries, Angel Mae is markedly reserved. Classmates find her standoffish, difficult to approach, enigmatic. This inaccessibility, combined with her attractiveness, makes her appear to them aloof, a snooty patootie. *(She stays clear . . . they smell Daddy on her. Not me.)* But with Don O-Boy, she's extended herself a bit. Although an outstanding wrestler, Don O's awkward with chicks, and Angel's experience has been . . . well, too tied up for her to afford him much help. So they mostly just gawk and smile at each other—say hi, and blush.

Yes, only that, until one brave day, he's egged on by his jock buddies. "Hey, have at her Don O. She digs ya, man." "Snatch her hair, big guy. Neck lock 'er, man. She's yours, man." "Go on, leg lock the chick, big guy. Go for 'er." "She's vir, man, first crackers. Break 'er." So, Don O-Boy girds his loins, and with iron resolve, ventures forth to nab the snatch.

Seeing him lumbering down the hall toward her, Angel assumes it's a day like any other, nods, and smiles demurely. To her immense surprise, he steps right in front of her. She's shocked. He's so inescapably *there,* a wall erected in her path. *(He's so here up on her always . . . all ways. I'm sorry I can't take her place. I'd die.)* Before *this* wall, however, her cheeks redden; her heart springs like a frenzied bird into her throat, clogging her breath; she begins to quiver.

"Angel . . . hi . . . I was wonderin', I was . . .," he stammers and pauses, as though awaiting a response to something he's not yet expressed. Flabbergasted, she gazes into Big Don's small, watery blue eyes, while his shimmering muscles vibrate in the background of her attention. He in turn stares at her gleaming hair, following its loops as though they were in hypnotic motion. An uneasy silence engulfs them. *There* she is, but Angel Mae also stands apart, and beholds this drama, as though she were reading it in a book. The clumsiness of this exchange makes her feel sorry for Don. Part of her seems older than they are. It's peculiar because taken aback as she is, hasn't she, nonetheless, rather expected that a scene like this would unfold? Her story . . . hasn't it already been told? Didn't she read it somewhere? Sometimes it's unclear how fictional her world is. *(I'm made up; she is too.)*

Finally, she manages to reply, "Yes, wondering, you were wondering . . ."

"Would ya go to the homecoming party with me after the game?"

At this ungraceful but exciting proposal, she again falls silent. *("Part your lips, my child." Make me, she says. He does. She plays with his fire. Something to do with her body.)* Eventually she says the only thing she can: "I can't." She detects how wounded and bereft this leaves him. Air seems to fizzle from his inflated neck. Having no other notion of how to proceed, Angel simply tells the truth, or at least as much of it as she's ever divulged to anyone. "My father locks me in my room at night. I can't escape. I'm a prisoner. I belong to him."

This is difficult for Big Guy to comprehend. Either that or he's too absorbed in the alluring convolutions of her hair, his small eyes gliding around its endless twists and turns. This all seems so familiar to Angel Mae because her own eyes have often circled amid these ringlets. Quite suddenly she becomes aware that she has just disclosed the great secret, yes, but to someone who hasn't a clue as to its meaning or its hugeness. She's betrayed Dad. Not good! *(Foretold. From the tower she hung her golden hair.)* She'll soon be killed. Dad keeps his word. *(Last night: She dreamed he hanged her by her hair. That's her, not this one. I look though. The sight of her's too much not to see. He makes her; I make her.)*

At last, Don O-Boy says, "A prisoner? You mean, a real prisoner?" He appears to be addressing her hair. She can't answer. Really, what else is there to add? Tears well up in her eyes. (Why? Maybe 'cause she fears this'll end the story she's in before it's over.) She's about to walk away, when he reaches and strokes her hair, and she's set aglow with a warmth that surges through her. "Ain't this prison got no window?" he inquires.

"A window?" She frowns, puzzled. (Or not puzzled because, well, hasn't she sort of anticipated all this? A story she's read a hundred times.) "Yes, one window, high above the ground. When I'm not tied to the bed, I look out the window."

"Tied to a bed? You mean, *really* tied to a bed?"

"Yes, you know, like a slave." She sees such remarks confuse Don O-Boy. She realizes he hasn't had the same experiences as she.

"Wow, jesus . . . *yer dad?*" He hesitates, straining to fathom this bizarre situation. Like balls in a slot machine, his eyes roll round the coils of her hair. And then, almost absentmindedly, he asks, "How high's that window from the ground, Angel?" Has any male other than Dad ever called her Angel before? No—or maybe so—it doesn't matter; it's as though she now hears her name for the first time. A man other than Dad voicing her name . . . it has never sounded so magical, so beckoning to something buried within. Oh, how tempted she is to graze her palm over his undulating skin, as she would over the scintillating surface of a summer pond . . . oh, how tempting to—what? How high is the window? Strange question . . . but she knows what he means. This is the rescuer; she's seen him many times . . . story after story.

"Ten feet, I guess. Why?" She's often calculated the distance, of course. Was it for *this* reason? What reason? She knows. It's in her dreams, in her books.

Again he hesitates, brow contracted, immersed in thought, and then, nodding toward her hair, asks, "How long's it?"

"What—my hair?" She knows he means her hair. She witnesses all this as in a dream.

"Yes."

"As long as I am . . . more."

He smiles; his eyes sparkle, evidently with a bright idea.

"What?" she asks.

"Look for me tonight," he answers, somewhat mischievously. "I'll be at yer window after the game."

"No, wait, please . . . you don't understand. I'm a prisoner. Daddy—he . . ." but she speaks to his back, as he clumps away like a giant, seemingly indifferent to her plea.

She moves to her next class like a sleepwalker. All day she's worried. Her heart thumps wildly as though it fully comprehends something below her consciousness. She glides from class to class in a daze. Her teachers are perplexed that she, such a model student, acts so unresponsively. (*This isn't happening to me. I'm not there. It's a part.*)

In one class, *Women's Studies*, they discuss—of all things!—the fairy tale "Rapunzel." Yes, of all days, that this should be the topic. "Here we discover maiden sexuality incarcerated," the teacher observes, "guarded over by a wicked mother figure. Rapunzel's long hair serves to umbilically attach her to this possessive mom, but it also provides the cord whereby her lover reaches her . . . so, what about this, Angel? Angel?" She seems not to even recognize her own name.

"What about what?" Angel at last replies.

"Can Rapunzel's hair both bind and liberate?"

"How would I know?" She pays no attention to the class's muffled laughter. She knows everything there is to know about Rapunzel. Why, asking these questions of Angel Mae is like addressing them to Rapunzel herself. And would Rapunzel answer? No, she wouldn't understand such questions. But Angel Mae does now consider the question, as she strokes her hair. Bind and liberate. *(They screw and unscrew her.)*

As the day passes, the effect of whatever is unfolding begins to stress Angel out. All day her head aches as though it will crack open; at times, she feels dizzy, as though her head is only loosely attached to the rest of her body. *(He slides his finger down the crack of her. We part. Can't stand a part like this.)* Between classes she and Big Don O-Boy pass in the crowded halls. He winks at her and smiles roguishly, and her legs tremble, her knees weaken, and she swoons. Part of her watches all this as she would a home movie. *(This isn't happening. What's happening?)* Once, she thinks he's stroked her hair from behind, and a bolt of lightning seems to strike her, but when she turns with a gasp, she can't see him.

What does Don O intend? She knows. Her mind seems blank, yet she's anxious about something. So, evidently her mind's not blank, is it? Oh, if her dad catches her hanging out the window conversing with another male, he'll kill her. *(Says he'd kill her ass. It's not mine too. I look.)* Sometimes Dad's caught her hanging out the window and he's played with her behind. She plays along. *(He fiddles her with fingers but keeps his thingie out. Not her fault.)* Yes . . . but if he knew another guy were there . . . *down there* . . . yes, he'd kill her. *(My garden child. Plants in me, grows in me.)* She believes her father; his garden obeys.

But what does Don O intend? Her mind shuts off again, because she knows what will occur. She passes through the day in a kind of agitated emptiness, someone walking in the dark but stepping precisely where she's meant to step. After all, in her off time, when Dad's not on her, she's pieced her own tale together from books and dreams. *(Foretold. Let down your golden hair.)*

That evening Father kisses her, and promising to return later to tuck her in, locks her door. *(Lifts her skirt. Searches. Plays her tits, tongues her mouth. "Later, love. Stay put. I'll come.")*

It's about eight o'clock. She calculates: the football game should end around 9:30. Don O could show up by 10:30; her father might have returned by then. No matter what she knows, it doesn't prevent anxiety from flooding her. She lies immobile on the bed, awaiting disaster. She begins to pee her pants. She asks herself, "Dear God, what have I done?" Disobeyed her dad, that's what. He'll kill her. He's always declared he would. Will he? *(Daddy wound her hair three times round her throat and . . . Not happening here. No. No. No.)* Is she really going to die tonight? Locked in, she can't escape this. No . . . yes, but yes she can. When Don O arrives, if indeed he ever does, she'll demand that he leave, yes, or . . . she'll simply not appear at the window. Yes, of course, this is exactly what she will do—not appear. *(She looked in the mirror today. Couldn't see herself. Nothing had been made of her to reflect. Make me, she said. Make me, I said.)* She could say *this isn't me*, but that only works effectively in the castle tower when she and Dad alone are involved. Don O-Boy may have cut that exit off. Maybe some devices only work within the family.

She can smell her warm, acrid urine. She raises her skirt, removes her wet panties, and then the rest of her clothes. She must take a shower, but she won't do that right now. Being naked seems the thing to be. She's not fully aware of everything she's doing. She's merely following some subterranean current aflow within. She's submitting, as she always does. As a maiden condemned, now awaiting execution, an exhilarating terror burns inside her. Her stomach churns, and she feels she might vomit at any moment.

Angel stands, unpins her radiant hair, and lets it cascade to the floor, and then she lies back down on the bed, mindlessly preparing herself for something—something vaguely sacrificial. *(Naked . . . a costume for the altar. I made her up.)* Sure, she's scared. It occurs to her, as a new revelation, that she's been afraid a long while . . . yes, probably since her mom's death; yes, since then, when a protective shield collapsed and left her exposed to Dad's importunities. The witch in Rapunzel's tower kept her safe from such things.

But Angel Mae has loved her father. What's to protect? No, Mother, the trouble's *out there*, out in the world. I can handle Dad. She has, in part, viewed matters that way. Yes, and right now, from somewhere out of the dark, another lover, oh so big and burly (an invader), is heading for her . . . a locomotive charging into the mouth of the tunnel. Yes, even a powerful witch-mother couldn't protect Rapunzel. *(For good luck, Daddy says, "Keep your legs crossed.")* Rapunzel, Rapunzel, let down your golden hair. Maybe even Daddy's love can't keep an angel safe forever.

No, not when she believes she's already cast in a story, not when she believes she found herself already written up, already told.

Angel Mae's hands now slide over the curves of her perspiring body. She imagines her father's hands, his fingers pinching her nipples and screwing into her, squirming about like earthworms. She imagines her hands squeezing him into explosions of lust. It is strange, to her, that he has never inserted his penis into her vagina . . . into her mouth, yes, but not her vagina. No, because he considers *that* incest. *(He stops. "Go in, go in!" "No." Won't go in her there. Daddy's not that kind.)* And construed this way, there *have* been some limits that he, so laudably, hasn't allowed himself to trespass. No, not even when encouraged. *("Go in, go in!" she begs him. No. Me, I'm not that kind.)* Not to consent to anything her father desires simply extends beyond consideration. She doesn't care how he uses her; *that* part of her doesn't, that part enjoys what he does. It's their secret, a secret Dad hopes will all the more bridle her to him. But today some of that secret has wiggled out and let the world slip in.

Only the pale silver-gray moon pouring through the window illumes the room. Angel Mae rocks back and forth, her hands gliding over her fevered body. She feels submissive, directed by someone whispering moist words in her ear. Something wants the current of sex to flow over her and wash away her anxiety. But the anxiety and the sex seem to blend, not cancel. Her hair (is it the cause of everything? Rapunzel, Rapunzel) spreads warmly under and over her, shifting delicately about, a magic carpet. She drifts amid indistinct reveries. It is late September, and acorns from the oak trees now and then fall on the deck. The sound jars her from her trance, as a finger would flick against her forehead. She shivers amid alternating gusts of cold and waves of heat. *(How many mes are there? One here. One there.)*

She's drifting. She pictures Don O-Boy so *there*, as firm as a brick; pictures him gazing at and stroking her restless hair. He wants to wind through her hair, losing himself in it—a man in a forest. And there Dad is too. Maybe it's Dad she pictures stroking her hair, maybe these are his fingers between her legs right now, deep in the forest. Her eyes close; the fingers seem to be rubbing her to sleep, or rubbing her in her sleep. No, she's awake; she sees the moonlight dyeing her flesh gray. Her breasts swell beneath someone's hungry caresses; her body brims with desire. She's drifting, drifting off, drifting back. Stroking her hair. Drifting in her own forest.

Daddy's coming. (Take that me; leave this one.) She's dizzy again; she's been dizzy all day. Something . . . where's something to hold on to? She slips her hand between her thighs (either she or someone else does), and slides her middle finger lightly up and down (she or someone else does). What Daddy holds on to. She stares at the full-faced moon, at its shadowy expression—the face of a mother, a lover, her own face . . . millions of years old. She seems caught in something timeless. Behind a wisp of cloud, the moon seems also adrift, but peacefully . . . but also caught in something timeless. She thinks the moon is like a head without a body, so lonely, unless all the enormity of the sky serves as its body. And that's even lonelier—a body too vast to ever fully behold, to be held. What did Rapunzel think of the moon, her only light in the night?

The face of Angel Mae follows the moon. Her mind wanders. Sometimes she thinks she's fallen asleep, or maybe she floats in a state of wakefulness that's indistinguishable from sleep, or awake in a state of sleep. Time is passing; the moon is moving; the football game's over . . . They are coming for her. Time ticks . . . the moon's still face . . . disembodied . . . millions of years . . . They're coming. She plays a part . . . apart.

She becomes aware that every few seconds something has been tapping against the side of the house. *Your daddy's coming,* a voice (her own?) reminds her. A small acorn flies through the open window and softly alights on her stomach. Oh, dear god in heaven, he's here—Don O-Boy. As though awakened from sleep, she stares, confused, at the acorn on her belly, as though this seed contains some message especially for her. But if it does, she can't decipher it. *Your daddy's coming.* She wants to get up now and go to the window and shoo Don O-Boy away . . . or *not* shoo him away. But she can't budge. She's locked in the story made of her.

The acorn—there in the very center of her—weighs her down like an enormous boulder. Maybe she's not supposed to move; she's supposed to stay put. (*"Hold still, honey." She freezes like hot ice.*) *Your daddy's coming.* No, no, she can't stay here . . . not anymore. No more. *Your daddy's coming.* She strains with all her might against this tiny force that presses like a mountain upon her. There's more tapping against the side of the house as more acorns strike. Don wants her, *really, really* wants her. Another man than Dad wants her. And yes, she wants him too . . . very, very much. Frozen like hot ice.

Slowly, she rises from the bed, as though empowered by some counterpressure even greater than this acorn's. Her own hair drags heavily against her. Her neck strains and arches back against its tug. So much binds her down . . . the story of her life. The air weighs suffocatingly upon her. She gasps. Her hands rake the thick air. She might as well be clawing her way out of a grave. She realizes that she's lying on her hair, that she's tying herself down. She slides about, strains upward, and suddenly she's up and on her feet. She bounds toward the window, leans out, and yes, there's Don O-Boy, his large face grinning as heavenly as the moon.

For five long minutes they gaze at each other, mute. Angel's bare moon-white shoulders brushed with wisps of golden hair show over the window ledge. Don O-Boy can't believe his eyes. She seems to have forgotten her nakedness, or it no longer matters to her, or she's simply unmindful of her appearance, as a sleepwalker would be. Finally, Don O says, "Hi there." Already his penis has hardened and conspicuously elongated. And she notices this even in the semidarkness . . . or she imagines what she's foreseen. *Daddy's coming. (Take that. Leave this.)*

"Hello," she replies, but doesn't say, "You must go. Please, go! Daddy's coming." No, doesn't say that. No, she's too busy simmering in the hot blood boiling through her veins, a liquid fire she's felt before with Dad. She knows only how to consent to its consuming demand. In this lava flow she waits, her body a sacrificial maiden's used to fuel and feed hungers that wash around and through her, through him. Nothing else counts. *You'll be dead soon.* Okay—she's as ready as she'll ever be to die. She knows what she's doing—or she doesn't. Either way, it hardly matters. Only this dark, flooding ecstasy counts, and getting on with the end of your life.

"I'm coming up, darlin'," Don O-Boy informs her, standing like a quaking pillar of Hercules.

"How?" she sighs.

"Drop down yer golden hair." Of course, she knew he'd say that. What else could he say? She's read the story a hundred times. Without a second's deliberation, she gathers the tresses and lowers them slowly to the ground. She's foreseen this. Hasn't all this been rehearsed, in dreams if nowhere else? Dreams are as real as anything. So yes, she knows her part, knows what to do, knows what Don O-Boy's about to do too.

Her breasts inch forth across the windowsill, and Don begins to pant. Swiftly he grabs her thick tresses in his mighty hands and yanks hard to test and secure the firmness of his grip. She chokes; her neck bones pop. Her hands grasp and pull up at her own hair, desperately attempting to relieve the strain of the dreadful force that has throttled her. She gags; she can't even scream. She's about to tumble out the window when she feels her legs furiously seized and lifted. For a bewildering moment she believes that she's about to be dumped from the window. But no, she's held. Her thighs are violently parted and something drills into her vagina. She knows. *Daddy's coming. (Leave me one. That's me over there. Here too.)* He's in her . . . yes, like this for the first time. Yes, for the first time, but hasn't she also rehearsed this, *this* deed so inevitable . . . her truth embedded in a fairy tale. She feels Dad fill her, sees him pounding at her backside, drunk, insane, oblivious of the action at the other end of her that tears off her head. Men at work.

Unable to breathe, she vomits fiery blood. Don O-Boy, champion that he is, climbs her. She sees him pulling himself up, with one fistful of hair and then another, sees herself bending, stretched far out the window, vomiting. She can't fall. Father's holding her; she is nailed to Dad. Wrenching, blood, mucus, cum, shit, spew in and out of her apertures. She feels herself exploding, imploding, a container simultaneously engorged and emptied. She actually hears her neck snap, sees her head snap off, sees Don O-Boy crash, like a bag of iron, to the ground, sees her father copulating with her headless body. It's like a home movie.

The savage sight spellbinds her. She's beside herself. Moonlight gleams indifferently over everything. Don O-Boy lies on his back, stunned. With consternation and disbelief, he gapes at the head that has landed beside him. It stares blindly back at him, its mass of golden hair spread everywhere. Blood has splashed all around. He looks up at the blood spilling from the stub of Angel's neck. Her arms dangle, and for some reason which he cannot discern, sway helplessly. Her torso jerks back and forth, as though pierced and in spastic convulsion. Don O tilts his head because, she—a part of her—surmises, he must hear the groans of Daddy's drunken ecstasy. Blood gushes from her neck and from her once-virgin orifice. Pain electrifies the night.

Angel Mae looks on, sad for herself. (*Take that her over there. Leave me one.*) She has lost her head at both ends, the maiden of ultimate sacrifice. She weeps. (*They screw and unscrew her. Foretold. I told her so.*) How could this have happened—so torn asunder by a dad, by a lover, by her own longings? She knows this is not a dream, that this is *real*, unless . . . everything's a dream and what's real is only a dream of ultimate deceit.

Her drunken father pumps away, evidently ecstatic at having at last surmounted all scruples and committed ultimate incest, perhaps relieved that nothing remains against which he must strain to save his soul. He shivers, climaxes, passes out. She witnesses it all; a regular horror movie, she thinks. Released, she arcs over the windowsill. Sacrificed . . . is she sacrificed? She has dreamed that someday she will be. But sacrificed to what? She'd like to think to love . . . to dreams of love, at least. Look at her. Blood spurts from the gangly stub of neck. Her head among acorns, her once-beautiful hair a tangled bloody mess, rooting in the soil. She's awed by herself.

Before the pain extinguishes every fiber of her being . . . oh, what a sight Angel has of herself! But when exactly is this departing maiden viewing all this? In that instant preceding decapitation, half a breath away from death? After decapitation, with one blink of perception left? How long does it take to see something like this? She has her way of standing apart. So the perspective is one she's pretty thoroughly mastered. Hasn't she rehearsed a lot of this in her head, reading gothic novels, ingesting romantic horror . . . identifying with Rapunzel (*there*, of course, adding her own kinky twist 'cause Rapunzel couldn't let her have it both ways—diddling with Dad and Don O all at once)? All foretold. So, sure she sees in a wink what she's already seen. Makes perfect sense. And sure, maybe it's all a dream. Ultimately, what isn't? There the deepest reality lies.

(I dreamed she made me up.)

At the Circus

Nine-year-old Evelyn Nesbit watched, alternately awestruck and bursting with joy. Now and then a swirl of dizziness sped through her. The circus was almost too much to absorb. She was with Mamie Bonner, her dearest friend, and Mr. Bonner, who had brought the girls to see this—the Greatest Show on Earth. Mr. and Mrs. Bonner had been very kind to Evelyn and her younger brother and her mother since her father died last year. Her bother Howie couldn't join them tonight because he had a cold. He cried and Evie felt sorry for him, despite his sullen anger toward her for going without him.

There, right on the front row, the three of them sat. The moist June night lay hot and heavy inside the big top. Not that the weather weighed down the spirits of the two girls. No, they carried on with zealous emotional displays that delighted Mr. Bonner who, with a beaming smile, occasionally hugged them. The girls found everything breathtaking, as fantastic as a dream.

Fierce lions and tigers—real ones!—leaped through fiery hoops when commanded by a man snapping a whip. "What if they eat him up?" Mamie whispered. Yes, Evie realized the danger too. But no, the man survived, and with that whip, demonstrated his control of everything. Yet, some uneasiness within Evie caused her to think that maybe it was only barely in control. However, for her, at this point anyway, these gray wisps of worry served mostly to enhance the thrills of the circus.

Next, a bellowing bull elephant suspended one front foot over a shrieking woman who had fallen from his back and now lay helpless beneath him. Evie gasped and grabbed Mr. Bonner's hand. But instead of crushing the poor woman, the elephant allowed inches to separate the heavy lowered foot from the cringing body. He even wrapped his trunk gently around the woman's outstretched arms and raised her up. She kissed his trunk, and in response he reared up on his hind legs. The audience emitted a sigh of relief.

The bears also reared up when the silly white-faced clowns with red-ball noses begged them to dance. "What if they eat them up?" Mamie asked again. Yes, Evie knew they *could* do that, but she didn't honestly believe that a bear would. One had visited her in a dream a few nights ago, one who licked her and treated her quite lovingly. He did look a lot like her old teddy bear, Honey, who had never once hurt her. Of course that was a dream, but everything about this marvelous circus seemed to Evie very much like a dream. The clowns made Evie giggle so much her sides ached. Despite Mamie's apprehensions that the performers would be eaten alive by the animals, the clowns made her laugh. These madcap characters in their baggy, torn pants and oversized floppy shoes stumbled, tripped, and staggered about like drunks. You had to laugh.

But they also scared Evie. They seemed a bit too distorted. Their red mouths stretched clear across their faces. Some of them just kept grinning no matter how much abuse they suffered. They seemed to enjoy pain. Others, with long, down-turned mouths and big black teardrops marking their pale cheeks, seemed too sad for anything to ever make them happy. One of these sad figures came limping right up to Evie, and nose to nose, stared at her. "Hello, my pretty one," he said in a rasping low-pitched voice. His gaze stabbed her like a knife. Stunned, her jaw dropped open; powerless, unable to budge, she merely gaped at him. She felt embarrassed. What had she done to provoke such rapt attention? Who was supposed to be looking at whom here? Who was on stage? He had captured her; she had captured him. A distressing exposure of some sort was occurring, but whether of herself or something else she couldn't determine.

He mumbled something practically inaudible to her. Then, quick as a wink, he popped into her mouth a piece of candy. Reflexively she clamped down on it, and instantly a sweet strawberry flavor melted over her tongue. Mamie giggled. But Evie remained frozen, staring, bewildered by the odd expression before her—a frowning face that was also smiling. The clown touched her knee and turned away, his limp even more pronounced than before. Mamie nudged her, and the spell was broken.

"He loves you, Ev," Mamie said, squirming about excitedly. "What'd he say?" With jocular attention, Mr. Bonner leaned forward to catch her response.

"He said, 'Heartbreaker.'"

"You see, you broke his heart, Ev? That's why he walks so funny."

"He walked funny before."

"Yes, yes, you broke his heart even before you met. As soon as he saw you." *What?* Evie was perplexed and certainly a little overwhelmed . . .

but maybe nothing made sense here. She began to suck on the lump of strawberry sugar. It all seemed so unreal.

Suddenly, all the lights in the big tent went out. In the darkness, a murmur rippled through the crowd for a few moments and then faded into a complete silence. Evie held her breath. What was next? She couldn't imagine. A wisp of dizziness swirled through her. The muggy dark enfolded her like a damp blanket. With all this excitement, she had grown somewhat fatigued. For a second, her eyelids drooped and the clown's face made a glancing reappearance.

She was roused by a drum slowly pounding. When her eyes opened, she saw that a dim blue illumination now suffused the ring. Then entered a beautiful young woman astride bareback a cantering blood-bay Arabian stallion. She wore pink tights sparkling with sequins, and her long black hair draped the length of her back. The skin of her arms and long naked legs glistened in the soft blue glow. She had only the bridle and a surcingle, a girth with a handle she could grasp. (Never before had Evie seen a woman so unclothed, except for the time when, browsing through the family's illustrated Bible, she had chanced upon Eve in the garden, chomping a green apple; her only apparel a sleek, handsome snake intimately entwining her thighs.) The drum and the horse's hooves throbbed in perfect rhythm. Evie gazed transfixed as horse and rider circled smoothly round and round.

The dim blue light began to flash on and off, causing the woman and her mount to flicker and their movement to appear slightly discontinuous; they were here . . . then there. It was hypnotic. And then the woman released the reins, swung one leg over the horse's head, spun around, and rode backward. Her hands clasped the surcingle behind her. Her bosom pushed forth; her hair flew wildly in the air. Over the percussion of the drum, you could actually hear her sigh. The crowd applauded. Then she spun again, bent forward, and embraced the animal's neck as though she loved this powerful creature immensely. She groaned. "Oooh!"

Next she bounded to the ground, dashed a few steps, grabbed the horse's mane, and sprang back up. She did that several times, dismounting, remounting, vaulting from side to side. "Oooh, oooh . . ." The eerie flickering light accented the astonishing feat. The crowd roared and applauded each new stunt. Next, gripping the surcingle, she swung her long legs straight up in the air, and like that, upside down, with her black hair flowing over the horse's side, she rode once around the ring. After she had reseated herself, the moan came again—"Oooh, ooh . . ." The crowd clapped and shouted, even whistled. Agile as a rushing brook swerving down a mountainside, everything she did with her beloved animal was riveting. Never had Evie beheld a spectacle so enchanting. Surely, this was a princess out of one of those fairy tales Evie so often read.

The drumbeat then abruptly stopped, and a bright spotlight beamed from the tent top, focused on a man advancing into the ring on a black stallion. The man was thin and attired in black. With eyes like black holes set in a grim white face, he resembled a skeleton. On the horse was a plain black saddle with a silver horn that gleamed between the man's legs. Once the horse and rider were fully into the ring, the spotlight was cut off. The woman commenced riding in large figure eights, at first seemingly unaware of the man now following her. Evie found it creepy.

"What's he going to do, eat her up?" Mamie asked, frightened.

"What?" Evie whispered, also afraid. "I don't know."

The only sound was the thumping hooves of the two horses. The flickering illumination of the arena was now interspersed with longer patches of darkness, so it became increasingly difficult for Evie to anticipate where the riders would appear. There were so many gaps in what Evie saw, or she saw so many gaps.

The woman, startled, soon noticed this stranger trailing her. She began guiding her steed in unpredictable patterns. Sometimes the gaunt stranger shadowed her closely; sometimes their paths crisscrossed, or they traveled in opposite directions. He glared at her; she refused to look directly at him. The spaces of darkness grew greater. By now Evie couldn't tell where the figures would materialize. The scene had become ghostly.

The drumbeat resumed. Ominous, alarming. Something terrible was about to happen. She and Mamie and Mr. Bonner clung together. And then the lights went out for what seemed a long time. The beat of the drum and the horses' hooves ceased. Silence.

Suddenly the woman screamed, "Help me! Please . . . help me!"

Evie's heart surged in panic. What was happening? Was the man murdering the woman? What was anyone—what was Evie—supposed to do? How involved in this awful scene was anyone expected to be? Evie was not on this stage, was she, not part of this? Then it came again: "Oooh . . . no, no!" A groan, deep-throated—summoning. It seemed to compress into the heavy summer breeze, to become palpable, because Evie felt the woman's desperate words stroke her tingling cheek. The thick darkness lingered a moment longer. The lurid blue lighting then eased back on. The blood-bay horse had disappeared. The beautiful woman now sat on the horse with the man in black, facing and embracing him, her hair flung over him, her naked legs wrapped around him. Upon the jogging stallion, they rocked back and forth; they rose up and down, their bodies partially melded together. As the blue light gradually faded, the lovers became evanescent. Then, in utter darkness, the receding sound of the horse's hooves thumped like Evie's excited heart.

Confused, Mamie said, "What's he going to do?"

Evie, dazed and puzzled herself, replied absently, "He's going to eat her."

The crowd applauded, evidently understanding everything and thoroughly satisfied. Evie was clapping frantically along with everybody else, but she was distracted in her comprehension of this tableau. Although she could not have expressed why, she was baffled. How had this gorgeous woman landed in that position—facing that wicked man? And hadn't she hurt herself riding right on the silver horn of the saddle? How had something like this happened in the dark? Had she wanted this? In the blue light she had kissed him! Could that only have happened in that blue light too dim for her to see? Had she not known what she was doing because it was so dark? Had she abandoned her own mount, that magnificent steed she loved so dearly, and crossed over freely, all on her own, into the arms of that dreadful stranger? Or had he taken her over? She had kissed him, the bone face of a skeleton!

(These questions floated about disconnectedly in a place of blurred awareness. Later, when Evelyn Nesbit's own sensational performance—with Stanford White and Harry Thaw—would hold the world spellbound, the questions raised by this scene would resurface, with painful clarity, as appalling images in a mirror. But that's another story.)

Obscure though her comprehension was, Evie had been profoundly affected. None of the circus acts that followed equaled the impact of the woman bareback rider, neither the tightrope walking nor the aerial acrobatics. Afterward, with great animation, Evie—and Mamie and Mr. Bonner too—recounted for her mother the fabulous drama of the circus. Evie furnished abundant details of the woman on the blood-bay horse, although she only briefly mentioned the man who had abducted the woman and forced her to love him. (In fact, in relating the events of the circus, Evie omitted all those aspects of the adventure that had unsettled her. They seemed to have slipped from her memory.) Her mother enjoyed the story and kept repeating, "Oh my, *how* thrilling."

The next day, Evie and Mamie decided to run away from home and join the circus as bareback riders. Unfortunately, they revealed their intentions to Howie, who dashed off and snitched on them. Both mothers now stood careful watch.

"Mommy, please, I want to be like her," Evie sobbed.

"Yes, I know you do, dear. But what about that guy on the black horse?"

"Who?" She had forgotten all about him.

Her mother hesitated and then whispered, as though disclosing a secret, "Mr. Death." Evie stared at her, thunderstruck. *Mr. Death!* A picture flashed into her consciousness of her father's ashen face, smiling up at her from his coffin. *Daddy is smiling in his sleep.* No, darling, Daddy's not sleeping. *What's he doing?* He's not doing anything. No, no—*Daddy!* she screamed, but it was a silent scream, as mute to others as a wail of heartache issuing from within the walls of a castle buried deep in the forest of a dream. Evie gulped as though straining to swallow something. A strawberry taste washed into her mouth. She sucked at it. Her throat constricted. The room spun. Mother reached out quickly, but she was too late. The arena's irresistible darkness had already devoured Evie.

That night, Evie dreamed that while wandering through the chambers of an ancient castle she had discovered a huge dusty mirror. Badly shattered, it reflected a hundred pieces of something so broken up Evie couldn't recognize what it was, no matter how searchingly she peered into it. She thought that maybe she was supposed to ask this mirror something, like—"Who's the fairest of them all?" But what good would that do if she couldn't understand this mirror? The mirror had around it a massive gilded frame that held the pieces together. All the pieces appeared to be there, but trying to decipher them was just too exhausting. In the dream, she decided to close her eyes for a while and she fell asleep. And in that sleep within a sleep, she had no idea where her life had been taken.

The One Great Test

"To each of us," Dennis Griffin's father explained, "*The One Great Test* will come. Some will recognize it, most will not. So you may not recognize whether you've passed or failed it. You may not even know how it's passed or failed."

"I don't understand," the son replied. Dennis liked learning from his dad (who fancied himself a dime-store philosopher), but whenever the subject of the one great test arose, he felt stranded in the dark. Sometimes he even wondered if his dad intended this.

"The one great test is specifically designed for you," his father proceeded, seeming to ignore the boy's confusion. "In fact, in accord with the most devious stratagems, unknowingly, you designed it yourself."

"I don't even know what I've designed myself?"

"Exactly. This conniving self isn't, however, the one that you profess to know. In fact, it is so boundaryless that it can scarcely be considered a self at all. It's an undertow. See?"

"No."

"Once you take the test and fail," his father continued, "your life will be forever altered beyond your means to comprehend. Of course it matters very much *how* you fail. To not take the test, if that is indeed even possible, would prove the very worst sort of failure."

"Dad, you lost me." It just didn't make sense. That it was a genuine conundrum, though, Dennis never doubted. So he fretted over whether merely divining his father's enigmatic message *was* the one great test, and whether, in that regard, he had sure enough flunked. But no—because one day a series of events occurred that convinced him that whatever the one great test was, it had somehow confronted him that day. This was what happened.

When Dennis was a senior in high school, he needed a few grand to flush a coke debt that Dealer Joe had let ride for a couple of months. Although not the worst sort, Joe Lund could be mean, and he was not a man of infinite patience. He'd beaten up three guys in Den's school and left them a sorry sight, which pissed off Den and the guys he hung with. They talked about offing the son of a bitch, but that was all hot air. They weren't the type to resort to such extreme measures, and besides, they were too dependent on Joe, whom they called "The Tit."

Den owed the Tit two Gs. Now, where's a high-schooler gonna tuck that kind of jack? He'd incurred smaller debts before, which with a little leniency from Joe and a little minor theft, he managed to settle. So, once again, with no other recourse, he approached the Tit with hat (and nuts) in hand to plead his case. Joe was a tit you could wring but only to a point. Right off, he suggested Dennis deal for him, run a few bags, wipe the debt. It'd take a week. Den had expected that offer; Joe had made it to others. If the Tit could assist, he would. It was generous, even though it boosted Mother Joe's profits. Kids shit-deep in debt jumped at the deal, "Sure!" quick to mortgage their asses. But to Den, frying his own brain was one thing, burning others' another.

"No, thanks," he told Joe. "Rather you beat the crap outta me."

"Well," Joe nodded, "it *could* come to that."

"Hurting myself's bad enough."

"I respect that—a conscience with a broken leg or two. You don't see it every day."

"Cut me some slack, man."

"Ain't I done that a'ready?"

"A couple more months."

"What's yer collateral, son? Mowin' lawns and shovelin' walks won't git it."

"No . . . then I don't know what to do. Shit, spot me a nickel bag to ease me through."

"A little anesthesia, huh? Look, I ain't here to pain you more, brother. Dig? But extra tick ain't no answer."

"No, but it'll do till I get one."

"That jist might be never. You live in a big house, man. Ain't yer mum hid some mon' in a mattress? Did ya ask her help?"

"She's not my mum—my step."

"That so? Fine-lookin' step. I seen her around. Control must be real hard."

"Control . . . yeah, kinda."

"Kinda? Yeah, well—so, what'd she say?"

"'What do you want that much money for?' I said, 'Nothing. I just need it.' She said, 'In that case, ask your dad.'"

"Ain't he dead?"

"Sure is."

"Shoulda told 'er ya needed dental work."

"My teeth are fine."

"Won't be soon."

"You've got to show some mercy here, Joe."

"Too much mercy's bad for biz, kid. Word leaks, soon ain't a deadbeat ain't jerkin' you off. Ya lose respect. Know what I mean?"

"Fuck!"

"So, Mom ain't layin' out for her boy, huh?"

"Not when she's guessed what for."

"Yeah, I understand. So, no relief there . . . least not thata way."

"Not thata way?"

"Yeah, I got an idea, hon. I like ya, Den. You know I do. On this one, I'm gonna help ya not git hurt nomore. 'Course it's yer call, dude."

"What idea?"

That night, about eight o'clock, Friday, October 31—Halloween. Slumped in a living-room chair, Den brooded over how he—once a pretty good kid, really—had landed into this shit predicament: owing a two-bit drug mother so much he had to pull such a hair-brained caper. What was he doing? He asked himself that a lot lately. Tonight, it meant: What was he doing with *her!* He was obsessed with her, but something was going on tonight that seemed a little freaky, even . . . hazardous. *Hazardous?* What triggered that notion? No. He couldn't believe Joe would go through with it, couldn't believe he would, either. On the surface, it was almost too simple to work. It was even kind of laughable. On the surface? That gave him pause. There isn't any *on the surface*, is there, unless something lies beneath? It amused him to think that his father might have pointed out something like that.

But how had he sunk so low? Well, he did find some causes. When his mom, whom he loved dearly, succumbed to cancer a few years ago, he fell into a funk, and his pot use skyrocketed from casual to intense. A year later, his dad remarried. Was *that* a thunderclap! A bride young enough to be Dad's daughter. It seemed immoral, as though Dad had betrayed Mom. Since Den had also been close to his father, the marriage left the boy feeling even more abandoned.

And—ah yes—it presented another, quite formidable problem (about which in a moment). So he resorted to *more* drugs. Then, a few months later, Dad, a seeming epitome of health, died abruptly of a stroke, of all times, during an act of intercourse! Oh, everything about that death hurt. Dennis saw it happen (about which in a moment)! Afterward, his depression deepened, and to his medicinals he added cocaine. The debt to Joe rapidly snowballed.

As noted, Denny had been close to his dad, who had devoted lots of time to him—fishing, roughhousing, tossing around a football, attending sports events, hunting. They would hunt small game—squirrel and rabbit with a .22 rifle and a 4-gauge shotgun, quail with a 12-gauge. Den was a crack shot, maybe better than Dad. They killed a lot of these small creatures. It was good sport and terrific for father-son bonding.[1] Dad was very fond of handguns; always kept a .22 pistol in the glove compartment "just in case." "Just in case of what, Dad?" Den had inquired. "In case demented banditos try rustling our coach, son. To protect your mom." (*Demented banditos?* Sometimes Dad had a way of phrasing things that could stump his son, make him laugh, really.) His father read voraciously, and together they read newspapers and books, even novels. *Moby Dick* was his father's favorite. One summer, they read aloud every word of that behemoth book. Dennis admired Stubb's spunky way of challenging the implacable Ahab.

"Love the book, Dad. Think I'll stick to goldfish, though. That's too big a dick for me."

"Yeah, who needs a whale of a dick? Too much to handle." They both laughed. Then his father, turning serious, said, "Well, careful what you try to kill, son, 'cause it might be a bigger part of you than you imagined."

He idealized his father. Once he remarked to his mother, "Boy, Dad knows everything." She said, "Oh yes, he's *very* accomplished, take my word for *that*, darling." Her emphasis—"very"—and her broad smile and dreamy eyes at "that" baffled, and inexplicably, embarrassed him.

---

[1]   Later in Dennis' life, though, he will remember the little murders that occurred on these outings as barbaric. He will feel guilty and appalled at his disregard for the sacredness of these small lives, appalled at how unfeeling he was toward these lovely, fascinating occupants of the woods. From the irrefutable viewpoint of these poor creatures, he was a killer. He will be ashamed of his mindless cruelty and the irreparable wrong that he had done, dismayed that there is such a thing as *irreparable* wrong. He will wonder why his father hadn't appreciated all this. Wouldn't a philosopher, dime-store or not, have recoiled at the atrocity of firing a .22 at a heart no bigger than a quarter, at a silver-gray squirrel perched elegantly on a tree limb, upright but hunched slightly forward, with delicate paws tucked neatly into its white, furry-soft chest, resembling a monk in prayer? Couldn't he have protected his son from the worst in himself? Dennis will think—if you can kill such a creature as that, you can kill anything. The mark of Cain, as engraved within us as the veins of our body.

Whatever his mother may have meant, something deep within the boy had imposed its own meaning on her words. In any event, the death of his father had dealt him a crushing blow. The ground dropped from beneath him. From a topnotch student in his senior year, he plummeted like a sleepwalker stepping off a cliff. Actually, he generally felt that way lately—dazed or preoccupied or in free fall.

The distressing loss of his parents was not, however, the formidable problem. *She* was—Ashley, his twenty-six-year-old stepmother. "Son, here's the gal I'm going to wed," his dad had said, introducing them. "I want you to love her as much as I do." Den's heart leaped into his throat, and he could only croak. She was the most beautiful woman he'd ever met. The instant he laid eyes on her, he believed that her breasts were inviting his fingers to stoke them. And now—jesus, what a legacy Dad had bequeathed! He didn't know what to do with her. What to do with her? ("What's beauty worth, son," his dad had once observed, holding up and scrutinizing an exquisite yellow rose, "if you can't figure out how to use it?" As his father leaned forward to smell the rose, Dennis feared that he was about to bite off the head of the gorgeous flower.) But oh, Ashley, Ashley . . . what to do with her! She inflamed the boy as if he were a chunk of dry wood. The night of the day they met, in a dream he saw himself salivating like a rabid dog.

So, Halloween eve, that most cursed of all days, he was remembering his parents; he was vaguely pondering the senselessness of the one great test, and he was worrying whether he'd somehow placed Ashley in any jeopardy. No, he kept reassuring himself, certainly no real danger. But although unable to think of what could go wrong, he did realize that something, of course, always could, because . . . well, it was just the way the world was made. Moreover, he could admit, he sometimes didn't foresee the grave consequences of things.

Therefore, he continued mulling over details, trying to detect possible glitches in the drama he had plotted with the Tit. Damn, he had to chuckle, though. What a hoot if they pulled it off. Still, the cause of some unease appeared to be evading him—a shadowy foreboding. He was nervous, surely more than the situation warranted, especially a situation he was largely convinced wouldn't even occur. In the tangle of his ruminations, he never considered that he might be implicated in a role he either couldn't or wouldn't comprehend. Dennis remembered, with relief, that the Tit had slipped him a few joints. ("On the tab, Den. Mom's good for it.") He deliberated whether now'd be a good time to light up.

He heard her walking down the hall to the living room. His heart jumped; he looked. Beautiful, so beautiful—dressed to kill, Ashley entered the room. She wore a tight short black skirt, the waist snugly belted, a black sweater, black hose, and shiny black high heels. Her long black hair hung straight. A crimson scarf circled her throat. For Halloween, a female vampire, even bloodred lips, all the clichés executed perfectly. Stunning. She began strutting wantonly in front of him. Jesus, it was like a figment from one of his dreams overstepping into reality. Mesmerized and salivating, he waited, wide-eyed; his penis stirred, beginning at once to rise to the occasion. She smiled and looked at him, examining, he felt, the signs of delicious distress she'd excited in him.

"How do I look, love?"

"Would I let you suck me to death? Yes."

"Really? How sweet. No, Den, come on."

"I am coming."

"Ooh, you are? Dear me!"

"You look fine, Ash. Just fine."

"Skirt's not too short?"

"It's short. Too short? Not for me. I'd like it better off."

"Ooh, would you? Such a tease."

"I'm not the tease."

"I think you're right about that, darling. Forgive me."

"Guess worse things could happen to me. Where you going?"

"Out, around. Maybe meet Marge at the club. You know."

"I think I do. What's the hurry?"

"Why, can it be you wanta keep me here for yourself? A little possessive, like your father, aren't you?"

"I could be. Just wondering what you're up to 'sall."

"Oh, I see. That's why those dark eyes wander over me."

"Just checking out the show. No harm."

"No, no harm. You look dejected, sweetheart. The show that depressing?"

"Hardly. I'm just tired."

"What are *you* doin' tonight?"

"Think I'll read *Dracula.*"

"Hmm—sounds fun."

"To jerk off to."

"Oh, I missed those parts. Mark them for me, will you?" She smiled. This sexual bantering she allowed within limits. And beyond the limit, the rabid dog tensed to spring forth and—

When the doorbell rang, he nearly leaped from his skin. Shocked! Was this farce really about to unfold? Jesus, had he known all along that it would—known and yet pretended that no, it wouldn't? These questions had been too unfocused to demand attention.

"Christ, who's that?" she asked. A jolt of panic hit him in the belly. "Expecting someone, darling?"

"Trick-or-treaters," he mumbled.

"Oh yeah. I got a big bag of those little Snickers bars for them in the kitchen." She walked over and opened the door. He heard Joe's voice, or he thought it was his voice, a bit more gravelly though. My god, had he really believed that Joe *wouldn't* do it?

"Step back, bitch. That's cool, nice and easy." Dennis jumped to his feet. "Stay still, punk, 'less ya wanta waste her ass." Ashley stepped backward, her arms outstretched. The Tit was wearing a Halloween mask—a werewolf—and pointing a .38 revolver at her forehead. Once inside the doorway, he halted. His head moved up and down the length of her body, two or three times, checking her out. Dennis had a perverse urge to remark, "Struck a little dumb, are we?" How often had he himself been stung by this petrifying Medusa?

For a breath-holding period, everyone stood speechless, each for different reasons overwhelmed by the situation.

"Well, well now, ain't we the children of the night?" Joe mocked. For a minute, both Dennis and Joe examined Ashley. Nobody budged. Then the wolfman turned to Den, and chuckling, asked, "And who you supposed to be tonight, honey—Dr. Jekyll, Clark Kent, or just Plain Ol' Asshole?" A peculiar, unspoken rejoinder flashed through Dennis's mind, "I'm the Assassin."

Dennis's anxiety soared. The gun, the mask, those harsh commands, the fright on Ashley's face, her gaping mouth—things appeared instantly ominous. Not what he'd expected, was it? (Another question he didn't quite hear.) Things appeared too stark, too real. But it all seemed rather familiar, like a movie he'd seen. Dear god, what *had* he expected? A little spoofing. A game. Well, it still *was* a game, wasn't it? "One twitch, kid, and she blows." Both he and Ash remained frozen. Was this for real? He wanted to laugh to prove just how unserious this was. "Now, let's make this snappy," he heard the mask say. "Git the bread."

"Bread?"

"He wants money, Ash," Den translated.

"Money? What money?" she answered, bewildered.

"All ya got, bitch. Now, if the gratuity's shit, you gonna piss blood on this high-dollar carpet."

"What?"

"Give him what he wants."

"What's he want?"

"Money, Ash. He wants money."

"What money do I have—a hundred in my purse?"

"Ain't big enough. Open, cunt. Write a check."

"*Write a check?*"

"Ain't I *speaking* American?"

She fumbled in her purse and found her checkbook.

"*Write!*"

"What—how much?"

"What's the kitty got?"

"Uh—five thousand and—"

"Fine! Glad I'm here to ease yer burden . . . make it four. I ain't greedy, and we don't want 'em thinkin' yer blowin' town. Make it out to Dennis."

Aw, shit! thought Dennis.

"*Dennis*—you know Denny?"

"That's what ya called 'im, ain't it?" He shoved the gun closer, allowing her no time to reflect. He touched the gun against her temple. With hands shaking, she scribbled out the check, tore it loose, and handed it to him. He inspected it. "The Fidelity Bank . . . about half hour away. Yeah, here ya go, Den. Head out. Ya got—oh let's say, no more'an an hour and half. No time to jerk off, kid. Hurry, or we got a cunt with a bloody hole. Dig?"

Dennis hesitated.

"Go on, honey. I'll be all right," Ashley said.

"Yeah, go on, hon, we're fine."

In the car, Dennis straightway lit up one of the joints and took a drag. A smooth, warm glow melted through him. Ah fuck, things'll be fine, he told himself. Just fine. As he headed off toward the bank, he didn't care that he'd arrived at that consolation by a route of dubious logic. Friday evening . . . the bank open until nine. No rush. Yes, in this traffic, it'd take about thirty minutes to reach; yeah, so over an hour to return home. Seemed like a long time, now that he actually calculated it.

Something wasn't right; no matter how much he deceived himself, he knew that. "Well, yeah, nothing's ever right, is it?" he said aloud. "So does it matter?" *Did what matter?* He found astonishing (because he did notice) the erratic states of denial that he could switch in and out of every other second, denial not altogether effective, however, because his discomfort, ill defined though it was, continued to grow. A strange, sweet anxiety tingled through him, a familiar trepidation, the kind that accompanied forbidden longings. Yes, he knew it well. He sucked the joint like a nipple. "Christ, what the fuck am I doing?" he asked. "Stupid fucking question!" But he didn't quite hear this stupid question as an admonition.

What was the Tit up to right now? Dennis wondered. Yeah, what was he doing right now with Ash? "The mother fucker," Den mumbled. Doing? Oh, just sitting there with a cocked gun. Chatting. Sure, sure—what could they chat about? Kinda hard to chat with Ash all decked out like Vampirella—long, glistening legs . . . breasts pointing at your eyes . . . red, parted lips . . . Yeah, kinda hard. How well he knew that delectable torture.

So what *were* they up to? His imagination started to boil with possibilities as he avidly sucked the weed, letting the erotic apprehension circulate through him. Peculiar, this commingling of apprehension and excitement. Must be, he speculated, what gamblers experienced rolling dice, breathlessly waiting to either be zapped into ruin or to discover all the pussies on earth open to them. Waiting for something in hiding to jump out at you. He was aware of creating something disquieting that he couldn't squarely face. His heart raced. Something—what?—far off, perhaps the distant hoofbeats of a nightmare galloping flat out toward the wall of his chest . . .

Cars had slowed at the intersection of Sabine and Europa, where a weary-looking cop directed the traffic flow. Crawling along, Dennis found himself tempted—but why?—to pull over and relate the whole story. Get some help. How? No, no, that would be foolish, he warned himself. What would he say anyhow? "I'm robbing my mom. A werewolf holds her hostage. But I'm pretty sure it's all a gag. Still, can you arrest somebody? There's a gun in the glove compartment. It's Dad's. He's dead. Something's not right. Arrest *somebody!* What? No, I can't explain why my dick's so out there."

Senseless. He didn't quite grasp this story himself. Something was missing, or invisibly there. Wasn't this like a dream where you view everything except yourself, everything except the person doing the dreaming, the creator, the master mind? Yeah, sort of.

Everything moved in slow motion, including the cars. A tingling gray aroma filled the car; everything advanced through a haze. For some reason, he remembered the hunter's moon he had seen that month. A moon huge and bright orange, spectacular, set low in the eastern sky. And in the west, he could see Venus, glowing in her own stellar splendor. Standing there gazing in awe, he felt pulled by both these heavenly powers and held in place by their equal forces. Yes, and he felt that right now—the prowling hunter aroused by a goddess.

Less and less he fathomed the elementary drama that he had composed with the Tit. It had barely registered that there was anything *to* fathom, to delve down into. It dawned on him, however (again, as though for the first time, everything seemed to be only now dawning on him, as though he'd been napping) that he really didn't know this creep, the Tit, at all. No, not really. Hadn't the sleaze logged a year in the state reformatory . . . wasn't it for B and E? Yeah, oh yeah, but only now did he remember this.

"How do you forget something like that, asshole?" And—Shit! Den recalled, as though someone had just whispered in his ear, something about a rape. Hadn't Joe baby been accused of raping some chick . . . yeah, and been acquitted . . . or not acquitted? How long ago—a couple of years? "Maybe not, but shit, maybe so!" Hmm . . . hard to say. "Forget about it," Den ordered himself. "Forget about it. It's done."

The sun was setting. What time was it? He glanced at the phosphorescent face of his watch, glowing in the dark like something alive, but didn't bother to read the time. What day was it? Time was playing tricks on him. He couldn't even recollect the events of that morning. The morning? Ah yes—he had confronted the Tit . . . about something. What? He sucked the joint for clues. He felt like a helium balloon aimlessly aloft, dangerously close to the knife tips of pine trees, a fire of some kind inflating his thoughts just enough to maintain altitude. He passed the cop, who glanced briefly into his bleary eyes, as he waved him on. Sure, rat on the Tit . . . lose that mother . . . and ain't no dope no more. Yeah, button yur lip, Den. Dennis grinned at the cop, aware of carrying a big secret that he somehow hadn't entirely disclosed even to himself.

For a while Dennis lost the content of his thoughts, as though he had traveled through an utterly empty space. He was certain he couldn't have blacked out, because he was still on Sabine traveling to wherever he was going. Ah yes, Fidelity Bank . . . heading there for some reason. But that didn't matter. No, he tried rather to harken back to what had recently been exciting him. "Get *that* back!" he demanded. "What—oh yeah, raping her, eating her—vampires, werewolves. Horror movies. Me— Mr. Hyde . . ." How readily his drug fantasies enlarged into melodramas. Halloween . . . christ, had the stars and a hunter's moon aligned against him?

Wait! My god, in what kind of peril had he placed Ashley—*his* Ashley? *What was he doing?* Again, that question that either he couldn't or didn't want to address. Had he imagined this fiasco would be as easy as snatching candy from a baby? "Well, yeah, and so far hasn't it been?" He grimaced and then frowned, realizing that this could go wrong, so terribly wrong. What a fucking fool he'd been! But, hey, once Joe, or whoever that was, had gotten in the house, aiming that .38, what could he have done differently?

A fair question. By that point . . . yeah, once in the house, he couldn't have done a damn thing. Nothing. 'Fessing up might've worked: "Hey, Joe, cut the crap. Ash, it's a gag!" No. That might've made things a hell of a lot worse. But that course of action hadn't even occurred to him. The asinine error (which, oh, he fully owned at last!) was that he'd planned this friggin' heist with some fart he scarcely knew. Had he been brain dead?

In his present befogged meanderings, why, he actually seemed to be realizing quite a lot. Yeah, well, great—but too late! Hindsight. His dad used to claim, "Butt-sight's a waste, son." Right, because wasn't he already wondering what it was he'd just realized? Damn, lost it! Yes, well, he wasn't unacquainted with this sort of edification, certainly. "Pot enlightenment" a lit. prof at school termed it.

He continued on a current of excited worry. He now saw the fiend inserting his gleaming gun barrel into Ashley's salivating mouth, compelling her to "Suck this!" And she did it! He blamed her. Christ, was she ready to swallow bullets for the fuck? "Why did you open your mouth, Ash?" Dennis scolded, his eyes feasting on the conjured image of her white face and gaping mouth. Den sucked the joint, straining to magnify every lurid detail of Ashley's defilement.

By the time he arrived at the bank, he had to force himself to recall his purpose. To withdraw some money . . . it made no sense at all. Another blank space intervened. In a drug fog, he entered the bank and cashed the check, but apparently like a somnambulist, because when he "awoke" he was surprised to find himself now returning home. Four thousand bucks in his pocket. A mindless transaction. Easy as pie, yes, but by now oddly insignificant. He had even forgotten what the money was for. He remembered a brief exchange with his dad:

"Money's a red herring, Den."

"Hard to think of it that way, Dad."

Weren't *they* red herrings, too—the maiden and the werewolf? Wasn't he just too busy envisioning their activity to attend to business? What business? Well, that was certainly unclear, but he was incapable of averting his riveted eyes from the carnal sights that seemed to materialize so very clearly in the smoke haze of the car's interior. He remained vaguely mindful of, and even fascinated by, the way a certain quality of anguish continued to escalate his desire—the remarkable way jealousy always does. Feeling inclined to exacerbate such arousing torments, it now occurred to him that he couldn't even be positive that the masked man who had barged in tonight *was* dealer Joe. No—for all he knew, it could have been a genuine werewolf.

"Yeah, some shit disguised as precisely what he was!" Den muttered. This idea did help scare him some more, helped excite him a little more too. He lit another joint. His mind began to reel with dreadful yet ever more engrossing imaginings. What if this sadist were hurting her, battering her into submission, violating her, or worse, seducing her? Stimulating her into consent, making her succumb, making her kiss the fucking rod, making her beg for a good fucking, down like a bitch in heat. Yeah, begging him to sink envenomed fangs into the hot, bulging neck vein of her lust, poisoning her will. Yeah, what if? Shit fire, maybe this werewolf *underneath* was a vampire, as shrewd in the ways of lechery as Dracula himself. By god, Den would drive a stake through the heart of the fucking fiend. Harpoon the mother fucker. "Ah, man—" he whimpered. He reached down and stroked himself between the legs. These thrilling worries had given him what felt like an erection three miles high. Harpoon the fucker! He drove as in a dream, threading through—what his father once said of Poe—a maze of gothic cerebration.

He entertained the thought that Ashley might just qualify as *the* prefect prey for Drac's rapacious quest. Knowing her as he did, was this inconceivable? *Knowing her as he did*—did he mean as his image of her behaved, that phantom locked in that cellar of lust which his imagination had concocted? Maybe, in fact, he didn't know her all that well, he told himself. After all, from the beginning hadn't his desires played with his fabrication of her? He tried but couldn't quite recall right now what it was that his lit. teacher had said the other day about innocence and pricks.

(What the teacher had said was: "From the hothouse of adolescence some pricks will seek out a fairytale princess composed of as many platitudes as possible of defileable innocence. Virgin-whores ideally depict the contradictory desires of such pricks." Had Dennis now retrieved this wisdom, he might have admitted that, yes, his was such a prick. But was she such a princess? This would have given him pause.)

Did he know her? Not really. He had mostly made her up. (Yeah, and hadn't that same teacher pointed out that when your needs are desperate enough—hell—your fantasies can make anything out of anybody?) Yes, he feared Ashley might prove the perfect gal for Drac! "Jesus, jesus, what am I doing with that," he now wondered, "blaming *her*?" Shit, how well did he even know himself? Not very. Look at this ridiculous mess he'd waded into—and for what, this wad in his jeans, a red herring in his pocket? To keep Joe Lund from kicking the crap out of him? Hell, maybe he needed a damn good trouncing.

Dennis glanced in the rearview mirror and grimaced. Halloween. His own face now even appeared monstrous, bestial, a griffin—one half animal, the other half animal. He grinned. My god, the spell of Halloween was cast over everything. Maybe there were evil spirits afoot this night, possessing and hurrying those souls along that were already halfway down the road to perdition. That sure would explain a lot, wouldn't it? he thought.

He snapped on the headlights. How very much clearer his road suddenly seemed; it was as though there really had been a fog in these streets he was driving through, a fog *out there.* On pot, he sometimes wasn't sure where the fog was.

Nearly every time he got high, his head burst with visions of making passionate love to Ashley. Drugs lent an extravagance to this erotica. But then again, everything seemed to: the dementia of adolescence powering forth a penis that blossomed willfully in the space Dad had so precipitously vacated. He was a wreck in her presence (a presence either real or imagined). He knew that, and she plainly perceived the wreckage too. At every opportunity he had spied on her, watched her in the shower, watched her dressing and undressing. He was always glancing up her skirt or peeking at her cleavage, praying her tits would pop out of her bathing suit.

His meager attempts to conceal such probing proved ludicrous. She so frequently caught him in these surreptitious sightings that they became comical. How often had she flashed at him that warm-as-blood smile, with eyes agleam, when she trapped him ogling her like a drooling maniac? Sometimes they'd both burst into laughter. (She once said, "You're awfully good at laughing at yourself, hon, got to give you that." It pleased him that she credited him with a virtue.)

But this spy business he pursued earnestly. In the wall separating his closet from her bedroom, he had drilled a pinhole, thoroughly camouflaged by the pattern of the wallpaper on her side. This delicate penetration he'd carried out before his father died, so he had often observed them making love. Once, while watching them, he had been so energetically jacking his dick, he managed to consume all the oxygen in the closet and fainted. He awoke to find he'd been placed in his bed. All his father ever said was, "Out awhaling, were ya, son? Well, how's the ol' harpoon afeelin', Mr. Stubb?"

It was from this hideout that he had witnessed Dad's demise. His father was pumping Ash with such gusto that it came as no surprise that his cerebellum ruptured. And while Dad pumped her, Den pumped himself with equal vigor. Naturally, Dennis leashed the impulse to bash through the wall and abduct her for his own smoldering purpose. During these tumultuous embraces with his father, Ashley was always very outspoken—lots of noisy "Fuck me, fuck me!"[2] And for this deadly finale, she had emitted many such exclamations, even adding a terminal scream.

So emotionally overwrought by this lustful commotion, Den may have preposterously muddled things, because at the instant of that scream, he'd not only "shot myself," so to speak, but his father had also ceased. Too much converged. During that eruptive episode, the connotations of love and death may have crisscrossed in the onlooker's psyche. (When, later, Ashley tearfully informed him that his father had died peacefully in his sleep, the boy, with a secret little grin, let the lie, lie.)

After Dad had departed, Dennis devoted many hours to straining his eyeballs at that tiny aperture in the closet wall, waiting for her to disrobe for bed or bath. Although from that cramped location the breathless enjoyment of her was a trifle suffocating, it was worth it, because she would often strut her nudity, posing either before the mirror across the room or right in front of his coffinlike enclosure. Sometimes this posturing appeared so performed she seemed alert to his tireless gaze upon her; either that, or she was actively responding to someone else whom she imagined was watching. Sexually playful, even inviting she was, and yet an invisible line had been drawn between them, either by her or him or both, that forbade trespassing. Theirs was certainly a sexual game, but one with a few inviolable rules of conduct. To Den it was often rather disquieting, but always oh so luscious. In her presence—outside the closet—he willingly endured a frequent affliction of blue balls.

All these recollections enveloped him as he drove home. Sitting in the car was like sitting inside his own mind; he'd created quite a theater. He sucked on the joint—was it the second or third one?—as he concentrated all his vision on his cinematic inventions. Yes, there, right in front of him, he now pictured the vampire king, masquerading as a Halloween wolf, fucking to death his beloved Ashley, and she there masquerading as the entranced bride of Dracula. Of course such a bride was also a vampire. Christ, his mind was basically a horror movie, the theater of a pothead. Everything appeared eerie, uncanny, spellbinding. But hadn't he witnessed such performances a hundred times before, with his dad as the beast in reality, and himself as the beast in fantasy? As he sped home, a determination rose in him to nab these two bloodsuckers in this act of blatant betrayal. *Blatant betrayal?* He'd worked himself into a pathetic state. A peculiar

---

[2]   In an English paper, Dennis had quoted this as an example of an expletive, and the teacher had given him a B+, not an A, because he had neglected to cite the source of a direct quote. *Plagiarism*—confiscating something and then passing it off as your own.

arousal, a swirl of crazed horror and jealous lust swept him down a flooding blood-river. Unquestionably, some mysterious current, which he still refused to plumb, helped hasten him along. *Betrayal?*

"How's this shit gonna end?" How did he want it to end? *"What? How do I want it to end!"* Another question that blindsided him, like the unexpected left hook his father would tap him with when they boxed together.

He discovered himself parking the car a block from the house. He punched off the lights, and with barely a thought of intent, popped open the glove compartment, and drew out Dad's .22 pistol. His hand folded so comfortably around the butt, he felt relieved, as though finally confirmed in his mission . . . whatever exactly that mission was. He cut through a side street and headed down the alley behind his house, half running in a rush to catch them. *Catch them*—then what? He failed to see how far the plot had veered from its original storyline: the repayment of a debt. The ostensible storyline, because perhaps this—this into which the plot was now rapidly evolving—had somehow been the story's destination all along. *"What am I doing?"* from somewhere far off in his head the question came and the answer did as well, *"I don't know."* His dad, the philosopher, could have enlightened him. "You're following a maze of gothic cerebration, my son."

A light glowed in the living room, but Dennis knew—oh, how absolutely he knew—they were not in the living room. Perhaps it was the present—what, what was it?—*derangement* within him that knew so absolutely. Quietly, he entered through the back porch, stole upstairs, slunk down the dark hallway, ducked into his bedroom, and then into the closet. He smiled, thinking absently . . . *Mr. Hyde.* Sure, why not—if the mask becomes you . . . besides, he thought, ain't everyone evil in this play? He could hear moaning before he even reached the peephole; before he looked, he knew what he would see. And sure enough, there they were, fuckers! Only a dim table lamp shone, but oh how vividly they radiated. For a fleeting second, he sought to recall (from the lit. class again) whether it was angels or the damned whom some poet claimed blazed like torches when they loved.

How faithfully these fuckers reenacted any number of his drug-conjured visions, but now the starring role had been usurped by Joe the Tit, or by this vampire costumed as a werewolf. The closet heated up immediately. In his oven abode, Dennis stared gluttonously; his blood boiled. From an opening the size of a speck, it was as though he were witnessing the primal event of the world. "Ooh," the evil animal moaned and howled, a wolf through and through, the light of the full moon pouring over him as his flesh smacked violently against (ooh, Den imagined it) her blood-gushing slit. She uttered no sound, save a grunt when the beast knocked the breath out of her. No other sound, but Den heard her well enough—*"Fuck me, fuck me!"*—as clearly as though she were whispering these explosive words in his own ear. Expletives . . . confiscating something . . . yes, again . . . and again, and then passing it off as your own . . . yes, yes, he must remember—cite the source. The whole day had been a plagiarism.

Dennis's hard-on throbbed mightily. Indomitable, it had thus far stuck with him throughout this entire escapade tonight. Off and on he had been unconsciously stroking it, as though it served as the touchstone for the—what?—reality of things. He stroked it now. And *this* was confirmed: everything had the unquestionable reality that only in a dream it can have.

Then . . .

Silently, he slipped from his airless cubicle and stole to the doorway of their bedroom (*their* bedroom?). Absorbed in themselves, they remained oblivious to him. This was familiar too, his great aloneness in the presence of someone else's passion. His arm, as he lifted it, felt heavy. As though synchronized with his leaden limb, the vampire-wolf upraised himself, with her legs wrapped, clinging round his hairy neck. Dennis saw the beast strike her hard, then strike her again, harder. He had seen his father do that once, too. No, none of this was new, none of it except Dennis's own raised arm, and the weight it now held.

She groaned in evident agony. He had knocked her unconscious . . . or almost unconscious. The son of a bitch! Dennis cocked and aimed the pistol at the beast's howling head. The shot would be an easy one. Strangely, he remembered a silver-gray squirrel he'd shot one cold January day. It looked like a monk engaged in prayer, the exact opposite of this fiend. Yes, this up-reared wolf, so tumescent with lust, presented an easy target. "How will I explain this?" Dennis asked himself. "Simple," he answered. "I was saving Mom from this demented rapist." (Demented banditos robbing the stage.) In a brief second of lucidity, he actually composed the complete tale he'd tell.

He fired.

"Ooh!"

Had matters concluded right there, that alone would have been a harrowing day for Dennis Griffin. He had intrigued against and stolen from his father's wife. For this much, he could have forgiven himself. He only meant to snatch a little fun, not to harm anyone. Minor, innocent wrongdoing, like smoking pot or cheating on your income taxes . . . nothing any sane person would consider criminal. Besides, he'd intended to repay the four grand eventually. No, no problem there. It was a loan, unendorsed, but a loan nonetheless. Hadn't he imagined it all as quite benign—stupid, unthinking—all right, juvenile, but still quite innocuous? Of course events hadn't played out as anticipated (at least not as anticipated *that way*). Poor Ash had been beaten and raped by a two-bit thug, and Den had iced the bastard, vampire or no. It had all become tragically complicated.

When Ashley finally awoke, she recounted the narrative she knew— a simple recounting that, as expected, rendered Dennis inculpable. Even had she known how implemented he was in the robbery, he doubted that she would have altered her story. No—she would have pardoned him for everything, stuck to her story, and protected him from the scrutiny of the law and the severely different assessment that justice, no doubt, would have delivered. At the perfunctory inquest, the judge had not only exonerated but also complimented him on his courage, which he called "calculating courage." The judge even implied that society was better off with Joe Lund dead. Or maybe he hadn't extended his condonement that far (*calculating* courage?). In any case, it seemed that all of this—the theft, Joe's sexual assault, the homicide—proved infractions of which the court and Ashley absolved him. A good thing, too. Despite all Den's self-justification, he actually needed more than this official absolution because other aspects of that night troubled his conscience more than anyone could have suspected, because besides himself and maybe, just maybe Ashley as well, no one knew of them.

Meaning what? Well, what's been related so far was not quite all that had transpired that evening; no, and perhaps not the worst of it, either.

After shooting the wolf, Dennis gazed disbelievingly at the ghastly tableau. *What had he done?* Had *he* done this? The fuckers lay lifeless. The snarling beast had fallen backward, with his penis still stuck in her; they were Siamese twins coupled at the groin. Dennis sympathized with the wolf's reluctance to disengage from her. After all, that was the way that he himself would wish to pass into the afterlife. It was curious how unangry Den was toward this abuser of the woman on whom he focused all his desire. Why? Perhaps because to the creature whom Dennis Griffin had killed he owed a huge debt of gratitude, gratitude for this opportunity here now before him to fulfill a dream; perhaps also because this dead beast could carry (if Den's conscience should ever require it) the responsibility for what was about to occur. After all, hadn't this drug-mother set all this in motion? "I got an idea, hon. I like ya, Den. I'm gonna help ya not git hurt no more."

His father's gun dropped hard to the floor. He stared at the couple, as though trying to decipher the purpose of some ancient, unburied statuary. Again, the sight seemed familiar—his father and Ashley sleeping. So much that day had a *déjà vu* taint about it. How long did he gaze at them—a minute, an hour? He lost track. All day time had been beguiling him.

Motionless, he stared, somehow not entirely involved; again, as that spectator in a dream, he viewed everything except himself. He looked at Ashley's face; her expression seemed so remote, the face of someone he didn't know at all. Having watched her fuck the beast, fuck him, yes, but with a kind of lethargy, Dennis had realized that she was out of it, yet he was surprised that she now seemed *so* unconscious. My god, had *he* killed her? *He*—the beast or Dennis himself?

But no . . . ever so faintly she breathed; her lips quivered. The two locked bodies resembled a piece of wet, flesh-colored stone. The wolfman, with a red dot of a hole in his forehead, as arched as a ballet dancer, stuck in the cleft of her upraised thighs. It amazed Dennis—the tenacity of desire. He studied that tiny bullet hole, awed that something so small could make such a huge difference—to the Tit, of course, it made all the difference in the world.

Carefully, he pulled the beast out of her hole, rolled him off her, and let the corpse fall with a thud to the floor. The monster stared blindly at the ceiling, his erection still upon him, still responding, even in the hereafter, no doubt to an irrepressible memory of her. Dennis could again empathize with such frozen heat . . . helpless, dispatched into eternity with a hard-on . . . the only way worth going if you gotta go. But then, Dennis mused, these evildoers always return, don't they, movie after movie? They're impossible to annihilate. Death's a game to them. Dennis's attention then turned to Ashley, and he totally forgot about the dead animal beside him, whom he'd cast out of the picture.

Transfixed, he gazed at Ashley's nude body—after all this, strangely iridescent. She lay unconscious or semiconscious because she was moaning like someone in a dream, either wounded or in yearning. His own erection trembled with eagerness. Miraculously, it had (like the beast's) been sustained through all this turmoil. Yes, and again with some amazement, it occurred to Den that tonight his prick had never for an instant wavered—a lodestar. He marveled at this feat: the world falls to pieces and the prick remains upright, steadfastly committed to the object of its desire. It confounded Den, but only briefly.

Oh, Ashley. Could she forgive him, he wondered, for staring like this at her, displayed so utterly? Well, was this that different from the day-to-day voyeurism in which he'd already so heavily indulged? Yes, because here she lay completely helpless, wounded, and he was taking advantage of *that*. Could she forgive him for not pouring sympathy over her battered body and immediately ministering—*somehow*—to her distress? (Christ, he sympathized more with the dolorous condition of the beast's prick—so rudely dissevered as it had been from its felicity!—than he did with this woman whom he ardently craved and professed to love.) Could she forgive him—"Please, Ash, forgive me!" he pleaded, bowing his head in what looked like supplication. Forgive him for removing his clothes and—

Somewhere in his mind, yes, he thought: Forgive me, Ash. But what would be the grounds for that forgiveness? I was a kid, spaced out, overexcited, beside myself (as Mr. Hyde would be), confronted with you so starkly you; *you* the object of my most fervent dreams—*you*, disarmed, spread out, free for the taking, with no one watching except my poor self. No one would ever know, but even if they did, even if *you* did, to me it would be worth all the shame, even be worth dying for. My lit. teacher would call it the do-or-die romanticism of adolescence. Okay, call it that. I know the true romantic would have licked your wounds. (Maybe not all of them. Byron would have done what I did.) I ask myself, "Was this exposure of you *the one great test?*" If so, so be it. Fuck—what would any male do differently?

He'd have put that satanic query to anybody, or at least to any male alive on the planet, and rested his case. However, the hesitation required for such deliberations as these couldn't last long that night; no, not in such a situation as he was then in, they couldn't. No, Dennis Griffin did what he had to do.

His prick slipped into her wet, surrounding warmth. *She has readied herself for me*, he thought, so easily forgetting the fucking wolf's ground-breaking role. Then, astonished, he heard her whisper, "Love in me in love me love." She was talking unintelligibly in her half sleep. But to whom? Damn, it was unnerving. Again, he carefully perused her face, red and bruised; even in the faint light, he could discern that. The brute had beaten her unmercifully, but surely not into this nearly comatose state.

No, he suspected she had been drugged heavily, with heroin, probably. That was sad. Look at her. He would not have wished it to happen this way. No, but what was done was done. He had her now; his prick had her—at last! It was as though he'd stumbled into the chamber of Sleeping Beauty. If he passed this up, for *that* he would be unable to ever forgive himself.

Through the rest of the long night he kissed and embraced her, both gently and roughly, fucking her in every position into which he could forcibly mold her inert body—unresisting but hard as any corpse to wrestle about. *Mostly* inert, because sometimes she returned the caresses, groaning in answer to his handling of her. She was so there, and yet so far away, sighing, sighing, but whether in pain or ecstasy or both, he couldn't distinguish. He didn't know whether he was pumping life into her or extracting it. He hoped she was lost in a euphoria that reached beyond or transformed pain, or even required pain for its very continuance. Maybe even that didn't matter; maybe only his own pleasure ultimately mattered.

She kept muttering to herself or to him or to someone else or to no one. Can you talk to no one? Listening to her, he tried for a moment to imagine that: talking to no one, that *he* was no one. "What's the matter?" He heard her murmur. "Nothing love went wrong in me 'sall. Who's coming in are you not expecting are you?" He stuck his tongue in her mouth. Whether to quiet her or to enter deeper into her meaningless mumbling—he couldn't have said.

For a long while she bit down hard on his tongue and sucked. It was painful, but it only intensified the excitement that pulsated through him. For hours he screwed her—her bleeding cunt, her bleeding asshole. With his prick for a knife, he stabbed her from every angle. He screwed her dangerous but bleeding mouth, screwed her garbled messages back down into her gagging throat. She moaned and hummed continually; sometimes she even sang incoherent lyrics.

And she talked and talked, a language that grew increasingly strange because her utterances seemed addressed to someone else. "See I cry," she whispered. "Whatever's love's okay here." "I'm not me are you?" "I live under this, too." And so on, a haunting, troubling speech that kept mentioning love. "A love cut cut." "Are you him love he? Oh no love." He wasn't even sure how to punctuate some of this, other than to thrust his dick between her words. She drifted in a dream, and at times he felt that he probably did as well. For Dennis, nothing mattered except his involvement with her right then. It neither mattered what had led up to it, nor what would follow. Right now, his whole existence amounted to her. She embodied everything.

Her facial expressions changed repeatedly, from terror to pain to rapture to bruised blankness—a countenance as ashen as death. Her eyes mostly remained shut, but sometimes she opened them, seeming usually to stare at nothing, or at scenes located in another universe. Blind man's bluff, he thought. Did she recognize him? He was fairly sure she didn't. He was making a blind woman. So? What did she need to see? After all, this was his apparition, not hers. (If this *was* the one great test that Denny had to fail—at some point amid that failure, he imagined that he heard his father saying—"Then for christ's sake, let the kid have his day. He's alone, anyway. Who cares? She doesn't. Go at it, Stubb. What's a harpoon for?")

And yet, occasionally, she did look directly at him, and he felt she beheld him, beheld everything about him—clear to the roots of his soul—everything that God himself could see. Insensible to the world, did she in fact comprehend so deeply? Surely not. For her everything must be revolving around werewolves and vampires; if she perceived him at all, it must be as a wavering illusion emanating from obscure gothic realms . . . everything passing before her as evanescent as moon shadows. Of course—everything a wavering illusion.

But at the time, he hardly cared at all what she experienced. It mattered only that she was there—the incarnation of his own fantasia. Yes, whatever nether region she may have been inhabiting, this was—from his perspective anyway—his dream, and for its enactment he would have paid any price. If it meant her ruin or his own . . . well, so be it. The cost was now of no concern. He had killed for her.

He came and rested and came again, hour after hour—paroxysms too perfectly compounded of desires ancient and strange to ever again fire that profusely. But eventually he exhausted himself; his life, he felt, had finally spilled from him. This beautiful vampire had drunk him dry. Barely moving, he hugged her limp, now totally silent, body, both of them seemingly lifeless. He thought: Three dead bodies in the room. He listened to her breathing in his ear. He knew that nothing would ever equal this moment's fulfillment.

As the profligate son, he had gladly squandered his fortune. He smiled—actually smiled—at this macabre accomplishment. Dastardly it was, but he knew he loved her. "I love you, Ash. I love you," he told her silent, dormant flesh. Of course it was a little creepy. In possessing this body, stung as it had been, into a coma, perhaps he was enacting some sort of necrophilia, kissing the deadly, but no less dead, lips of a vampire. No, she wasn't dead, no, but as paralyzed as she was and as unable to wake, she certainly appeared more than halfway there. Anyway, whatever love was to anyone else, that moment was what it meant to him. Adolescence is lubricious (did his dad say that?), and he was, moreover, a male who had been given a free hand. So, between fucking and love he made no clear distinction. Lubricious—what did that even mean? Well, whatever . . . right now he was convinced that the immensity of that mysterious emotion—which he called love—sanctioned everything. It did; somehow, it just did. He fell asleep and then heard a distant pounding that he first interpreted as his own heartbeat. But, no, it was a

knocking at the living-room door. He knew . . . *he knew* the werewolf had
come. Fear jolted him out of sleep.

Upon awakening, his head had entirely cleared. He saw Ashley at
first with a moment of surprise. Everything now appeared so clear, so
completely unrelated to the fantastic events of the night before. My god—
what had happened? Yes, oh yes, he quickly recalled it all. He embraced
Ashley's torpid body. She was again moaning, now struggling to revive.
He glanced over the side of the bed at the corpse stretched out on the
floor. Still, there playing dead—unrisen. Its dull eyes looked through
the eyeholes of a mask into nowhere; its now deflated penis slopped
restfully. Den gazed at him, a dead man in disguise, and thought that
like Ahab, he, Den, had struck through the mask . . . yes, but here the
mask remained. How clear everything appeared in the morning sunlight,
but who *were* all the people in this room? My god—more incredible
than a dream it had all been!

His perplexity lasted ten seconds. No, the werewolf wasn't playing
possum . . . Den bolted up and hurriedly dressed. He didn't want Ash to
recognize him right this second, no, not until he better recognized
himself and had a little time to sort through some of this madness. Gently,
he kissed her forehead and covered her body, and with scarcely a second
thought, he walked into the kitchen and phoned the police.

Sitting at the kitchen table, waiting, he noticed the bag of Snickers
bars that Ashley had bought for the trick-or-treaters. It was open. Denny
stared at it. Why was it open? Had some kids shown up and been given
this candy? Jesus, had kids—made-up werewolves—interrupted whatever
the Tit and Ash were doing? Trick or treat! "Here ya go, kids, grab a
Snickers and scram." "No, give us the candy yur givin' him, lady." "Sure,
sure, come back in a few years." Not much older than these Halloweeners,
Denny knew well the hungers of these little monsters. With fledgling
peckers (maybe sorely titillated by *Vampirella* comic books), they had
demanded some of that sweetmeat Ash was dishing out to the Tit. Ah
yes, kids seeking treats in the month of the hunter's moon, with Venus
tugging at their fledgling loins. Oh yeah, Denny understood. He grinned
and shook his head. "Pretty damn weird," he whispered. Then he
unwrapped a candy bar and bit into it.

Shortly, two officers arrived. He led them into the bedroom. Ashley
was still woozy and uncommunicative. The boldness of her beauty somehow
accused him. He hadn't expected to feel like a guilty criminal. So, yeah,
what was he, a juvenile delinquent, doing here with this gorgeous woman?
It was, perhaps, not that evident to the police that he was now a man
(after all, he was barely old enough to drive). Alarm swept though him.

What if they instantly detected every single thing that had happened? What if they could smell a black, lusting heart? In their line of work, his sort wasn't all that uncommon. He was perspiring; he could smell himself.

Of course he told them an expurgated version of events: This lunatic broke in at gunpoint, held my mom hostage, sent me to the bank to cash a check—uh . . . and how much was that for? Can't recall. Lots. It's in my pocket somewhere. I returned, snuck into the house, caught the fuck banging Mom, and plugged the bastard. One of the officers, Den sensed, scrutinized him with some bemusement, while the other gawked at poor Ashley, whose arms had suddenly flung forth, uncovering a breast, white as the face of the moon. An extraordinary distraction! Dennis thought, "My god, what timing! Did she intend that?" Damn, sex surfaces from under everything. He would have laughed had his jealous resentment not checked that response. But what should he do—re-cover her? No, he decided not to tamper with her any further.

"Did ya know this guy?" the officer asked politely, as he pulled off the mask. (And yes, it was Joe Lund!)

"Did I know him? No, I didn't know him." (He supposed he really didn't. In fact, seeing him now like this, unmasked and limp—murdered—was jarring. Joe was so much smaller than the monster he'd played when alive.)

"Where'd ya get the gun?"

"It was Dad's. He always kept it in the glove compartment. It's registered."

"But not to you, right? Yeah, well, never mind. Good thing it was there, right?"

"Damn right."

"Where's your dad?"

"He's dead."

"How'd you know he was raping her?"

"Dad?" Immediately, heat oozed up the back of Dennis's neck, as he realized how very nervous he must be to have replied so stupidly. "Oh—him—how'd I know? What do you mean by that?"

"Well, couldn't they've . . . No, 'course not. Sorry, kid, the job breeds a suspicious mind. Got a couple needle pops on her arm, right here, looks like. He juiced her with the horse, 's'my guess. Yeah, anyhow, she'll tell her side in a sec. That's what counts—right?" He smirked.

"Yes, sir, officer, that's right."

"How she doin', Sam?" he asked his partner, who seemed not to hear, with his eyes so tightly glued on the rise and fall of Ashley's breasts. "Sam?"

"Is this yer mom, kid?" Sam finally spoke. "Jesus christ!" Dennis now felt sorry for her—all the men who had mauled and used her, who had destroyed her will. Sleeping Beauty . . . every guy had gotten past the thorns and into the castle, but no one's kiss had woken her. And all she had wanted to do last night was vamp a few guys. Well, Dennis supposed that she had indeed done that.

Finally, Ashley woke to tell the definitive rendition of the tale—at least the one that everyone bought. Of course, it too was foreshortened.

What a day of crime: drugs, robbery, assault, rape, incest, murder, to say nothing of moral turpitude. In all that, Dennis at some point wondered, was there only one great test here? Should this whole day count as *only* one?

Well, that was that—*almost*...

Things eventually took another unexpected turn. At first, as mother and son, they consoled each other, mostly by endlessly recounting the adventure—at least as much of it as Ashley seemed to know. The sex he'd had with her went unmentioned. Did she know? Strange, but about that Dennis nursed ambivalent feelings. On the one hand, he'd gotten away with something, an act of love that, in itself, he believed, had hurt no one. Whatever physical damage Ash had suffered had already been inflicted upon her before he returned from the bank. Yes, he fucked her *then, afterward,* but that certainly caused her no added physical harm. The most he could accuse himself of was the grossest sort of insensitivity, and well, yes, a moral lapse.

That aspect of things did trouble him ... somewhat. And there was the rub. Naturally, he liked to regard himself as not callous. But not to have fucked her? Please! Afterward, he'd assert it a hundred times: Only a saint could have withstood such temptation. Actually, he gloated over his achievement ... whether ignoble or not. If granted an opportunity to undo the deed, he would have refused. Yes, he'd rather have died and gone to hell than return that stolen gem. A big part of him wanted to proclaim that she belonged to him, to tell her how she belonged to him and *why*. He wanted to share his victory, have a little celebration of himself. It was a deed that for its enhancement begged to be exposed to the victim. But he refrained, afraid of her response. He wanted her to forgive him, yes, of course, but even more he wanted her to rejoice that fate had forced the issue, rejoice that he, brave man, had forced the issue ... yes, and then to hear her declare, "I belong to you, lover. I always have. We belong to each other now forever. How it happened, that's incidental."

But that didn't happen.

After a couple of months passed, one day, appearing very downcast, she said, "Denny, I've something I must tell you." She sat in the same living-room chair in which he had sat that fateful night, waiting for the masquerade to begin. Her long, shapely legs were crossed. As usual, he had been gawking at them.

Then looking up at her face, he said, "What's wrong, Ash?" She looked pale, as though she might be ill. He knew what she was about to say the instant before she spoke.

"I'm pregnant."

"You are?" A thin smile, nearly imperceptible, creased his lips. She peered at him for a long while, silently, studying his reaction. Their eyes locked, he believed, in full disclosure. He concluded then that she knew much more than he'd allowed himself to suspect, more than he'd feared, more than he'd secretly wished. But how much more? Everything? Yes, wholeheartedly, he now hoped everything. He realized how deeply he'd been hoping for that from his first blissful entrance into her dreaming body. He recalled her undead eyes gazing through a drug-haze at everything happening, perhaps catching eerie silhouettes of this son of hers through the mists of Transylvania.

"Could this baby be yours, my love?" she asked. He paused to decipher the oddly ambiguous phrasing: Would he accept the child as though it were his own, or as truly his own? Well, maybe this baby was his, or maybe it was a wolf-child. Her intent gaze told him that she saw the truth, that truth which he now desperately wanted revealed. She swayed her leg hypnotically, up and down. He heard the soft, hypnotic rub of her nylon hose. As always, arousing. As always, his penis began to stir. He couldn't help it; he just couldn't help it, and evidently neither could she. The undertow.

She, who had that night been a blind witness to the making of his manhood, now testified to its culmination. Oh, could this baby be his? A giddy elation filled him as he answered, "Yes." She nodded slowly, smiling, and her eyes gleamed upon him with what he felt was the radiance of love.

Did Dennis Griffin pass the one great test?

In fact, my son, in accord with the most devious stratagems, you designed it yourself.

Making the Seen

"**Y**ou wanna write it?"

"Do *I?*"
"Do *we?*"
"Together?"
"It's about us."
"Okay. You start."
"Okay. Boot the computer and scoot the keyboard over."
"There. Hit it."

"Watch it!" Jane barked.

"Dogs bark."
"An intimation of what's to come."
"Oh yeah—'barked' . . . of course, that's good."

Jane barked, grabbing Jake's elbow to keep the glass door from smacking him straight in the face. He gasped, disbelieving what had nearly happened. That was always amusing; she'd witnessed comparable scenes dozens of times before. He hardly ever immediately believed the unexpected, and since so many unexpected events befell him, he often discovered himself paused in an attitude of disbelief. How impossible— that door, it almost bashed him.
"Impossible," he said.
"No, it isn't," she said.

"How's that sound?"
"For a rough draft, pretty good. I like it. Change the tense."
"Change the tense?"
"Present. Try it."

This is the commencement of the evening they have resolved to forsake their virginity. They have been lovers in everything but the ultimate deed, but they have finally convinced each other to add the irrevocable finishing touch. With the near bang of this door, however, things threaten to start off with a whimper. Still, who can read all life's warning signs, especially when young, in love, and overheated?

"Hm, I don't know."

"What?"

"Virginity . . . origins . . . loss . . . nostalgia . . . I don't know. It's *passé*."

"You think so?"

"Warning signs you can't see that smack you in the face . . . nothing's what it seems—"

"Or never getting to the point."

"Or not recognizing it if you do."

"Yeah—postmodern."

"Yeah, maybe so. Go on with it awhile. We've got a plot, don't we?"

"Yeah, eventually. But who's gonna wanna read this?"

"Who? Our friends."

"Great—you read it; I read it. Who else?"

"Anyone interested in the misfortunes of young lovers who are nearly murdered attempting to consummate their love."

"Jack and Jill . . . it's been done a million times before."

"Not this way. Quit stalling."

Luckily for Jake, Jane always endeavors to guard him against such mishaps. The previous week, he bumped himself with a heavy coffee mug and caused a nose bleed. True, his nose does tend to bleed at the slightest provocation, but that collision typified his general inclination to knock or stumble into things.

"Are you going to put yourself down?"

"A little. It's the truth."

"*Truth!* Please! You're so old-fashioned. We invent truth."

"That's true."

"Go on, darling."

Since their first date a couple of years earlier, Jane has been striving, but with only a modicum of success, to safeguard him against misadventures potentially actualizable

"'Actualizable'?"

actualizable by his farsightedness.

"Okay. First draft. Everything's permissible."

Refusing to wear his glasses for other than reading, he avoids entirely conceding the extent of his defective vision.

"So, *that* was the reason! It's really sorta touching."
"Yes, it was . . . is."
"So get on with it, love."

On their first date, they are strolling along Fourth Avenue in the Village, visiting the few surviving used-book shops. (They both read avidly.) They are mildly stoned.

"Mary Wanna and us—*ménage à trois, n'est-ce pas?*"

At one point, they are discussing book bargains they have just picked up browsing amid the eight miles of books the Strand advertises it houses. It is early evening, still fairly light, so even though occupied with their conversation

"Some intriguing topic . . . feminism's contradictory attitudes toward pornography, I think it was."
"Sounds right."
"Or the legalization of pot for persons between the ages of five and ten."
"That sounds right too."

Jane has glimpsed that brown little mound half a block away. She merely notes its presence as anyone would, so naturally she assumes Jake also will.

"But what did she know?"

When they reach it, he steps smack into the rust-colored mush of fresh dog shit.
"What the—," *he exclaims, stopping for a second and frowning, totally perplexed.*
"What?" *Jane pretends not to know what has occurred.*
"Oh . . . nothing . . . nothing."

"'Nothing'! I love it!"

Well, it's awkward. However, they continue, feigning ignorance of the incident despite the stink that clings to every footfall. They chat on about philosophy

"Plato's account of Aristophanes' theory of the bifurcation of the autonomous body of commingled lovers. Had we gotten any further than that?"

and women's rights.

"How'd it go? If, for a woman, every act of intercourse with a man is rape, then what if—"
"Please, I can't concentrate. You're trying the reader's patience."

As they do their "ignoring," eventually the foul odor dissipates into the all-inclusive atmosphere of the East Village.

"Oh well, shit happens, I reminded myself."

They are not only going round and round in their debates but circling the block as well. As a wicked fate would have it, upon again arriving at that cursed spot, he executes precisely the same fatal step.
"What the—"

"Here, let me write this part."

So dumbfounded am I at the precision of it, I wonder for a fleeting moment whether he, in fact, has perfect vision and the blackest sense of humor I've ever encountered. Has he staged all this? Alas, after encountering in the days that follow several similar misadventures, I will realize that such disingenuousness was not the case here. He simply can't see things close at hand. Pretty endearing, really. But auspicious beginnings these are, indeed.

"There!"
"You switched to the first person. And you're beating around the bush, hun. Skip the dog-shit intro."
"Sorry. Cut back to the movie."

Jane grabs his arm and barks his name. He stands and stares incredulously at the glass door.

"Or rather, I now suspect, you stared through it as though it were invisible and had violated the requisite substantiality for material things."

"Wow! Heavy!"

"How in the world did that get . . ." He hesitates.

"It's been there since they built the place, darling." She sighs, takes his hand, and ushers him out.

"What did you think of that?" he says. "Jesus, god in heaven!"

"You would have thought a meteorite had exploded in the middle of Washington Square."

"That's my Jake," she observes, kissing his hand, and then drawing him on. They have to get going. After all, for this night they have planned their destiny.

"'Planned their destiny' . . . christ—what a joke!"

"Will you stop interrupting?"

"Sorry."

First, they had planned to catch a movie. They have done that—The Maid and the Minotaur.

"An R-rated titillater, but the sort of boost neither of us, as I recall, required at that point."

"X-rated. There was insertion. Creatures, half animal, half man—*men*, in other words—copulate freely with innocent cowgirls."

"Oh yeah . . . and it frightened me to observe what I had to measure up to."

Next, they are to head for the park where Jane fully intends to succumb to the manly importunities of Jake, her Romeo.

"My turn, again. Hand over the keys."

"Go to it, baby."

He likes being called Jake. Not so much because that happens to be his name, but because of its connotations—strength, virility, hard, lean, sharp as a knife, a lover and layer of women.

"A lover and layer of only one woman."

"You swear?"

"Damn right."

These virilities are not, unfortunately overtly manifest

"Self-pity disguised as self-depredation. Readers will pity you, all right—but for your style, not because you possessed an organ that lacked courage."

"'An organ that lacked courage'! Enough to bring tears to a stone. Think I'll keep it."

not manifest, although frequently they had found full-blown embodiment in his dreams. What a contrast.

"'They had'? What tense are we in here? Be conscientious."

These dreams depict a view opposite both to the persona he presents to the world and the one he holds of himself. Or not expressly the opposite, because we regard this puissant Jake (let's describe him)

"'Puissant'? A trifle pretentious for our little chronicle, ain't it?"

regard this puissant Jake toward whom he aspires in dreams, as somehow portraying an authentic, if unlived-out, aspect of himself. After all, must not such dream characters constitute part of the repertory of whoever we genuinely are?

"That's good."

We thought so.

"First person again. Past tense. Okay, do it that way awhile. No, let me."

We had once sagaciously deduced this after analyzing a dream of mine about a seeing-eye dog with shaggy little golden bangs flopping over its blue eyes like the blonde bangs I myself sported at the time. We determined that I was that seeing-eye dog guiding the blind around.

"Who the blind was, I refrained from speculating."
"Kind!"

*We extrapolated. Therefore—*mutatis mutandis, *as my Latin teacher would preface all generalities—according to his dreams, Jake he was, in more than name merely. These Jakes were poised to impale my sweet maidenhood.*

"What sort of fiend would impale a sweet maidenhood?"

"Any male."

"True, especially if it's the sweet maidenhood of a seeing-eye dog."

We had just graduated from high school. We loved each other deeply. We were a shy, bookish couple, perhaps average-looking, mutually dependent, I suppose, and protective.

"*I'm* average-looking; *you're* beautiful!"

"Aw! I love you."

I protected him, as indicated, from the crap on New York streets, from mistiming the swing of see-through doors, from spilling more drinks than he would have spilled on his own, from misjudging the distance of our lips when he closed in for a kiss . . . from enlarging the scope of the unforeseen.

"What's that mean?"

"Should I delete it?"

"No."

And does he protect me? He likes to think he does.

"You abuse your writer's privilege here."

Although here (with my devious assistance), he was imperfectly consistent. He "protected" me from the rude importunities of the Jake-Within, whose lascivious exploits included barbaric molestations of me, binding me, stripped naked, with ropes and chains, enslaving me to do his lustful bidding—all of which he dramatized in dreams.

"And still do."

These rape dreams truly displayed the full, albeit discordant picture of my Jake—on the one side, the tumescent perpetrator plunged like Genghis Kahn, the warlord, into my subjugated maidenhead. And on the other side, the tumescent spectator standing by, rubbing his eyes in incredulity at such audacious mishandling of me. No doubt it was the tumescence that resolved any apparent discordance, and betrayed the single-minded man behind the two performers—Jake-of-Day, Jake-of-Night.

"No doubt."

*And yes, I did indeed take some responsibility for enkindling that tumescence . . .
often so undisguisedly affirmed in the crotch of his jeans.*

"Yes—in fact, I feel that characteristic feature affirmably enkindled
right now."
"I see what you mean."

*When he first confessed these ribald, sometimes savage, dream escapades,
I gasped, covered my mouth demurely, as though totally dismayed.
Ashamed, he apologized profusely and swore he'd never again presume
to dream of me thus.*

"'Thus'—yes, well, never trust a promise an erection makes."

*I smiled, raised my hands to my blushing face, and ever so slowly my
fingertips parted my yellow bangs. My eyes must have gleamed like bright
blue light bulbs.*

"Hm, yes, I do believe they did."

*Virgin though I was, the intensifying lust of our amorous play had been seeping
through the pores of my inconsistent resistance, a lick here and a tongue poke there,
a hand moiling around all over the place, a finger or two inserted in and out and
about, worrying my privates. My juices, I'm afraid, flowed obligingly and a trifle
too profusely for virtue to hold the fort.*

"Hey! Keep those paws to yourself, buster!"
"How 'bout—"
"Later."
"But my tumescence—"

*He pressured me evermore mercilessly; I permitted and even led him
along a little as necessary and befitting.*

"'As necessary and befitting'? Great! Now it comes out."

*Allowing, I guess, that Jake-o'-dreams a chance to strut his stuff. And rise to
the occasions he did. So, after several months of deeper and evermore fervent
sessions of petting with the continual propinquity of his erection,*

"'Propinquity'?"

after many hours of soul-searching dialogues throughout the winter and into the springtime, after all this, we did at last decide that after The Maiden and the Minotaur, *I would spread my legs, unreservedly acquiescing to Jake's by now overpowering prods.*

As mentioned, we headed for the park,

"Ah yes—we called it 'The Garden of Earthly Delights.'"
"You want to pick it up here?"
"No, I want to see how a maiden handles this."
"Handles what?"
"The loss of her netherhead."
"Netherhead. Cute. What do men lose on these occasions?"
"Well, on this occasion I did nearly lose my head. But no, we men lose nothing as mythic and poetic as a maidenhead. So go on. Let's see how it went."
"*How the Maidenhead Went . . .* good title."
"Maybe so, but go on. We headed for the park."

there to perform the ultimate, the deed or deeds, beneath the sprawling limbs of the old secluded maple tree under which we had so repeatedly lain with sweet Mary Wanna that summer, reciting poetry to each other that we'd composed. Usually we debated the permissibility of premarital sex before twisting up in dramatic enactments of the subject matter in question. We did everything that could be called penultimate.

"That's it—right at the door, like Onan, my seed spills on the ground."
"As did mine, figuratively speaking. Anyway—"

It was a lovely time: talking interminably and toking Mary Wanna to death and deciphering the mystery of our soulful love through its physical revelations, physical revelations of everything but.

"'Everything *but*'—stuck at a coordinate conjunction!"

Yes, this park, this tree—a special site.

"Nice. *But . . .* but shouldn't you mention the killer on the loose?"
"What killer?"
"The one that slashed up three NYU coeds in the Village that month."
"Oh yeah. Why's he important?"

"Who's gonna understand our jumpy behavior in this scene without knowing he's lurking somewhere in the background?"

"Yeah. Maybe you're right. Who was he? Did they catch him? Hum . . . let's call him the *Mad-Dog Killer*."

"By the time the reader gets the point of that, the story'll be over."

"Let's forget the Mad-Dog Killer. We've got action enough coming up. Besides, I don't know what to say about the creep. Do you?"

"No, guess not. So skip him, then."

"Just forget motivation. This is postmodern, honey, so ultimately, we can only parody ourselves."

"'Parody ourselves'? Hand me Webster's dic. Yeah, wait . . . hold on a sec. Here . . . *parody*: 'A feeble or ridiculous imitation'—now that would be of ourselves. Great! So, back to our Tree of Knowledge."

Late at night, screened by the venerable tree's massive trunk, canopied by its sprawling leafy arms, we had sometimes listened, straining every auditory receptor, to the ardent tonalities of other lovers who were, alas, more advanced than we in the down-to-earth handling of carnal pursuits, diffident young souls though we were.

"*Then!*"
"And still are."
"*Really?* Christ, to think we haven't grown a bit."

We did twice undertake to peer through the dark, and spy upon the tangled, agitated shadows that emitted those arousing rhapsodies, often panting, groaning, grunting, sobbing, and generally carrying on, sounding as though they were assaulting each other.

"Funny, how much love can sound like murder."

Sometimes the luscious sensations evoked by those shadow-sounds seemed interminable because they were like a gust of hot wind blown from a thousand miles through an open window that while fast asleep you breathe into your dreams, and because the shadows of bodies pushed by this ancient invisible force rock you in a feverish embrace, the salacious inspirations of which you wish could abide forever.

"Wow! How exactly is that sentence punctuated? Jesus, you take my breath away. It was like that for you, wasn't it?"

In the dark we never espied anything in graphic detail, but those few clandestine encroachments, indefinite as they proved to be, nonetheless further incited us toward our hard-won decision to finally go the distance.

We reach the park and make straight for the tree.

"Watch those tense shifts, hon. Use your blinkers."

Intoxicated with expectation, our veins pulsate with excitement. And the pot we'd been ingesting vivifies everything.

"Do you *ingest* pot?"

The night is hot and unusually dark. For some reason, none of the park lamps are lit, but we haven't fully realized this because we have been guided to our tree by instinct. Now that we have arrived, however, we can scarcely see each other. And that scares me.

"Say 'scares us.'"

The customary pale hue of these late hours is absent tonight. Unseeing, motionless, gawking at the umbra of each other's faces, we clutch hands like abandoned children. Struck with confusion, we seem to have forgotten what it was that we came here so completely resolved to do, as though within such meager light, we have mistaken our pathway. We stand silent, and the minutes that pass seem like hours to me, to him as well, I'm sure. My heart beats fast; so does his, I'm sure.

"Yeah, you bet. Feel free to speak for me."

The palms of our hands became damp. It's quiet enough

"'It's'—have we been using contractions?"

It is quiet enough to overhear someone whispering on the moon. Maybe the marijuana is thoroughly infusing our senses.

"Too bad Poe or De Quincey can't take over here."
"You're doing fine. Go on."

And then, suddenly, as though someone had tossed a bomb into the air, a woman screams. Startled, we both jerk.

"We're scared shitless 'cause the Mad-Dog Killer could be cutting up another coed. Note this, otherwise—"
"Okay, in the revisions we'll splice him in. A Poe touch."

Jake steps forward to clutch and shield me, but our foreheads bash together. We vault backward, and as luck would have it, poor Jake trips over a large exposed tree root, and I go tumbling after. We are so awkwardly struggling to regain our feet that we fail to detect that the screaming woman has now modulated her tone to that sort of moaning and purring which I should have myself been emitting by now. Vertiginously

"'Vertiginously'? Cut that."

and like beaten puppies tucking their tails between their legs, we scamper away, down the unlit park lanes, like bats guided by radar, winding our course among the trees, miraculously avoiding collisions.

"Puppies, bats, and lost children? Hm . . . much to ponder."

Too embarrassed and humiliated to utter a word, with downcast heads, Mary Wanna unable to elevate us, we trudge along the street—Adam and Eve expelled from the Garden of Earthly Delights.

"But still virgin! Pathetic, really."
"We were kids, sweetheart."

Both of us

"How sadly touching to recall."
"Well, yes, it is."

now and then shakes our heads

"'*Our heads*'? '*Shakes our heads*'? That can't be right. 'Both' is plural."
"Shakes *his* can't be either."
"But it is."

as though saying "No, no." It is as though we are traversing the landscape of a terrible dream. But bad as it appears,

"It's sagging."

"What is?"
"Our tale. Change something."
"Change something?"

the overheated night has not yet finished with you two unconsummated lovers, who have unsuspectingly transgressed the border into a disconcerting reality through which you are now being hurried like bedazed children tumbling down a steep incline.

"Second person. That might work. Go on with it a bit."

Amid your continuing befuddlement

"'Befuddlement'—that's just too—"

bewilderment, you have journeyed into a side street off Bleecker, somewhere in the West Village. Although the streetlights burn, they are spaced far apart and scarcely illuminate some areas at all. But confounded still by the disheartening aftereffects of your bungled concupiscence

"'Concupiscence'? Who knows what that means? Do you?"
"Not precisely."
"Yeah, well, okay. It's cute. Leave it."

bungled concupiscence, you simply fail again to heed how very ill-lit sections of your surroundings have become, and how the neighborhood has turned shabby. Moreover, no one has passed by you for at least five minutes.
Eventually, you realize that something is strangely amiss. You don't quite recognize where you are—not quite, that is, because you do know your general location in the sense that you can (can't you?) get out of here. After all, you still detect the distant lights and muffled noise of horns emanating from Seventh Avenue, although those references do seem rather remote, like the images of recollection. But while you can return, you don't know exactly where it is you have arrived. You stop and stare at each other for the first time since you entered the park, so passionately expecting to wrap your eager limbs together like the limbs and roots of the tree that was to hide and watch over you. How dejected you have become. All you did was fall.

"'All you did was fall' . . . as remote as 'images of recollection' . . . cryptic, gives an appearance of depth."

"Can depth have an appearance?"
"Hm . . ."

But although that fall now seems like centuries ago, it still brings you down.

"That's enough of *that!* Back to *you.*"

Bad as it appears, I can see Jake's troubled expression. He stares blankly at me, our faces too near for him to see how equally distraught I am. He lifts his eyes and gazes absently over my shoulder. I see him squint and push his head slightly forward.
"What are they doing?" he whispers, more to himself, perhaps, than to me.
"Who?" I ask, turning toward where he points. His attention has been arrested by a doorway about fifteen feet away, over which an entrance lamp glows. At first I inspect it mindlessly as you do when drug-induced memories cast a thin film over everything.
"What are they doing?" he repeats.

"Weren't we a bit more spaced out than you're allowing, dear?"
"More than I'm allowing?"
"Yeah. Things get a tad surreal now, don't they?"
"Yeah. So?"
"Motivation, dear. Prepare the reader. Who's gonna believe the awful thing that befalls us?"
"We are. Hey, baby, this is postmod stuff. Get with it. Trust me. Everything works."
"Horse shit!"
"Exactly—especially that."

Then I make out the curious, but from this distance, not quite distinguishable markings on the door. We step closer. On the thick wood door we discern the carved figures of a man and a woman locked in an obscene embrace. Amazed, we advance even closer. Despite this dim illumination, we can nonetheless see the sharp, deeply carved details. A voluptuous woman is bent forward on hands and knees, doglike, thighs stretched wide apart, her rump arched up to receive the huge phallus of—of a muscle-bulging bull! Or a man whose lower half is the hind section of a bull. Out the sides of the man's head protrude a set of long, sharp horns that have gashed the woman's back. The nearer we approach, the more accurately we perceive the fantastic workmanship. Soon we are within a few inches. For Jake, such proximity causes the scene to blur and swim a bit, as though the lovers actually simulate motion.

"How would you have known it was producing that effect on me?"
"Was it?"
"Yeah, but—"

It is very peculiar, but the scene is giving me the same optical impression.
"What are they doing?" *Jake asks. Even though he must know perfectly well, he still can't quite believe what he's seeing because now he sees only a kind of undulation.* "What are they doing?" *he repeats.*
"Fucking," *I say.*

"A powerful revelation, indeed . . . there in plain sight, right in Puritan America. But 'fucking'—by using such a word do we gain or lose readers?"
"It's the most potent word in the English language."
"Right, and there's no perfect synonym for it, either. Besides, it's in *Webster's Ninth New Collegiate Dictionary.*"
"It is? You checked that?"
"It's why I bought the dictionary."
"Wow! I'm impressed."
"But instead of 'fucking,' call attention here by using a word no one knows the meaning of. That they'll forgive."
"Like what?"
"I don't know . . . say 'fructifying.'"

"Fucking," I say.
I feel sharp pangs in my belly as my blood begins to stir. We both have now begun rubbing our hands over the copulating bodies of the doorway, running our fingertips along the grooves, retracing the artist's designs, copying for ourselves the delicate definition of these caressing forms. Across the swollen, vibrating muscles of the man's bending back and down into the crease of his bull-buttock we slide, over the mold of the pair's quivering thighs, their gaping mouths, around the pressured fullness of her swaying, bursting breasts, and tightened nipples. We feel the tongues in their dripping mouths, the wetness of their organs. Over and over we stroke this shuddering pattern, until within our imaginations we are touching and inserting our fingers into corners and orifices not actually exposed by the artist.

"Our minds are working over their bodies, copying, revising, augmenting—*making them*. Is this clear to the reader? Show, don't tell."

"All authors tell immensely more than they show."

"Well, okay."

It has become blissful, dreamy. Grunting and whimpering and gasping sighs issue from them—or do they issue from us, or from memories?

"'Memories'? Memories of what?"

"Fingering in the Garden of Earthly Delights."

"Fingerfucking. Say it!"

"Later."

Jake and I are breathing heavily, perspiring, unaware of where we are. We seem not to have noticed that we have also begun fondling each other, forgetting to discriminate the shapes of our own figures from those carved into the door. We mirror the work of art; it mirrors us. A fire begins to flame within, a fire that could burst inside our own bodies, as it must have burst forth within the imagination of the artist who molded these entwining configurations on this entryway, imparting his passion to his creations, and through them infusing us, who now consume all of which our adolescent sensibilities can partake.

"What a mouthful. But yes—"

Yes.

"Yes, and I'm up in you at last; jacking in and out, in and out, in and out, slowly, then fast as a jackrabbit. Your legs are wrapped around me. I can't believe I've made it. Up, up. Oh, christ, yes. And you are murmuring in my ear words that sound strange and obscure and melodious. Your voice hums through my nerves, and an ecstasy surges through me that even in my dreams I've never experienced. And if I could die right now and preserve the memory of this moment eternally, I would—I'd die."

"Wow! Remember that, we'll add it."

"Yeah, the insertion in the revision. So go on, go on."

Yes, and an animal something springs loose from within us. Life, oh, life imitating art. Art imitating art imitating art. Wild, wild. Our hearts pound, as though we have been racing away from something that we now race madly toward. We have apparently recovered for ourselves the precious event that we had lost sight of when, back there in the park, the scream of an impassioned woman frightened us half to

*death. Quite possibly. Quite possibly we would have preferred to stay enthralled in
this fantastic scene forever.*

"I would have. Would you?"
"Yes. Oh yes. The supreme moment of my life."

*But sadly, misfortune again assails us. For some unaccountable reason,
Jake imprudently taps his fist against the head of the man-beast screwing
the gal and—of all things!—Jake's nose starts to bleed.*

"Christ, I really couldn't distinguish myself from that satyr, could I?"

*Now matters rapidly worsen. The knock on the man's head awakens the
dog that has—who would have suspected?—apparently either been
napping soundly or listening quietly on the other side of the door. It
begins barking ferociously. Rooted, limbs entangled, we freeze like
petrified trees—alto-rilievo for a door—*

"We, *alto-rilievo,* just imagine! But isn't this where the Eaglet says to
the Dodo, 'Speak English!'?"

*with Jake's shaft rammed up to the hilt in me. In two seconds the door
bursts open and a man and a woman stand before us, stark naked, wide-
eyed, the man expansive, enlarged with rage. Dizzy in a beehive of
confusion are Jake and I. Six inches of Jake, in a flash, shrinks out of
me.*

"It's closer to seven."
"How do you know?"
"Measured it once with a yardstick."

*Six inches or so shrivels out of me. And unsupported, I plop down like a
dropped bag of potatoes.*

"'Bag of—'"

We are aghast. Things explode.
"What the hell's goin' on!" *the man yells.*
"They were peekin' in, the bastards were!" *the woman yells.*
"What the hell's goin' on?" *the man repeats.*
The dog too is outraged, barking like he's demonically possessed.
"The bastards watched us! They watched us!"

"What the hell."

"Sick 'em, Rex!" the woman hisses.

Suddenly, Rex bolts like lightning into violent action, ripping at my new sexy dress, his jaws holding on with a grip of iron, tearing it back and forth, and yanking me about like a rag doll. Frantic with terror, I kick out and land the toe of my shoe squarely in his hindquarters, instinctively repeating a method I once had perfected to kick off the head of a toadstool when I was three.

"What?"

And bingo! Bull's-eye! And I think I glimpse the mad dog's genitals go whizzing down the sidewalk like the head of a toadstool.

"Jesus christ!"

Rex yelps and rolls, and drags his bloody butt down the sidewalk like a slit-open sack of red paint.

"Paint in a sack? No, try 'sack of bloody tomatoes,' rhymes with potatoes (above). Keep those *o*'s rolling."

I'm free. I spin swiftly around to assist my lover.

The woman is shrieking like someone in a bedlam ward. "Kill him! Kill him! Wring the bastard's neck!"

The man, hairy and sweaty, clamps his hands 'round Jake's skinny throat, and squeezing, hauls him stiff with fear, like a manikin, toward the entrance. The crazed man growls like Rex growled only moments ago (castrated Rex, who now, however, wails pathetically at the indifferent moon).

"Slam the fuckin' door!" the woman shouts. "Chop off his head! Chop it off! Quick! Quick!" The edge of the door hits hard, and Jake's skull is squeezed in the door jam. He gasps, strangled, his breath cut off.

"It's as though I'm unconscious. I'm dead. I'm dreaming. I'm dreaming I'm dead. Unable to budge, I'm being lifted, erected. I'm an erection elevating into the dark wet womb of total night. I'm a hanged man. I feel I'm going to climax with a totality that will define my entire being, my infinity. God's now granting the wish I made only a minute ago: an unending climax. I'm losing my head. I think I'm in you, my dear, true love. It's all unfolding inside you."

"In me as you have always been—my heart, my womb, my blood."

"Another insertion for later. But now—*hurry, go on, go on!*"

Suffocated, Jake begins to gag. This beastly assassin is about to murder him. The woman has stepped outside, and she is jumping about, now and then swinging her fists and leaping back. I am scratching and screaming at the murderous brute who's killing Jake, and throwing wild, aimless roundhouses at the bitch whenever she ventures within reach. Finally, I catch her in the jaw; she staggers and keels forward as though she's stone dead. In the process she nearly manages to bury me beneath her.

"Did you mention she weighed three hundred pounds?"

With an act of will never before exercised in waking life, Jake summons every ounce of strength that remains to him.

"No, you—your dear terrified voice screaming in desperation summoned me back from death's door, and yes, back from my demented state of ecstasy as well. You woke me, revived me. Every part of me heard you and converged into one explosive power ball."

Jake the mighty of dreams at last explodes into action. He breaks the killer's grip like Superman and lunges forth into the street, gigantic in stature.

"Yes! Puissant, in every one of those seven inch."

He grabs my hand, and in a wild frenzy, we bolt down the sidewalk, racing toward the far lights and crowds and clamor of Seventh Avenue. The hubbub of the avenue begins to overpower the uproar swiftly receding behind us: the screams from the two naked maniacs, and the howling of Rex in agony. The blood from Jake's nose has stained his face and shirt. I can see the red splotches of it as we flash along under the streetlights. My beautiful dress, mostly in tatters, is also bespotted with blood, not only from the slight wounds Rex inflicted but from the immolation of my hymen, my deflowerment—gangbanged by Jake-One and Jake-Two. For dear life, we dash on, clutching hands, lovers exiting from this nightmare, together in one piece, fulfilled beyond our wildest dreams.

"Bravo!"
"We made it!"

Bonnie

That morning:
    "Oh, what lovely, lovely June weather, darling, perfect for your wedding. God be praised!" Mother had exclaimed. "Do you have to go to Kansas City?"

"Yes."

"Why?"

"To get some decent luggage. I told you."

"Luggage? Luggage in St. Joe isn't decent enough? Okay, darling, whatever you want. It's your wedding. Just don't be late for the rehearsal. Promise Mother that."

"I'll be there."

"Promise?"

"I'll be there."

"Bonnie—"

"What?"

"Act happy."

"I will."

"You're not."

"I will."

Her father chimed in. "That's great, Bon. Now go on over there and give Mom a big hug."

"I will . . . later."

That afternoon, she didn't entirely agree with what she was doing, speeding north out of Kansas City on I-29, heading back to St. Joe, trying not to be too late for the rehearsal. But she was already twenty minutes late with still another thirty miles to go. She just had to do that last-minute shopping in KC. Just get away. Well, she had purchased three fine pieces of luggage—Tumi, leather. But damn! She had promised everyone, especially Mom and Andy (Andrew Perth), her fiancé, that she'd arrive on time—that is, two hours early.

"Unexpected details will require attention, darling," Mother had stressed.

"I'll be there, Mom."

"No miniskirts. Sends the wrong message, dear."

"What message?"

"You know very well. You're beautiful enough as is. Don't make problems."

"Count on me."

Andy's such a nice boy, a good family. "And he really loves you," Mother had noted probably a hundred and fifty times. *Nice boy* meant he was polite, made good grades, never scuffed his shoes, and willingly attended Mass every Sunday. *Good family* meant fairly well-off, and because of that, fairly snobbish. They owned half a dozen successful laundries around town, and more than a little pretentious, they were into appearances. One of the reasons Bonnie suspected they, well, wanted her for their Andy: she was pretty. ("You're a better-lookin' gal than he is a guy," her best friend Nell had once observed.) That had to be it, because Bonnie's parents were grade-school teachers: Mom taught remedial reading; Dad, seventh-grade math. That must have been hard for the Perths to overlook. But evidently, Bonnie was pretty enough. Pretentious, yes. It had been a one-generation bounce-up because old Granpa Perth had been cut from the same blue-collar cloth as a garbage collector.

Anyway, after Andy and Bonnie became engaged (a year ago, right after high school), the Perths requested, and not so delicately either, that Bonnie quit her job as assistant to the librarian of the St. Joe Public Library.

"Well, darling, of course," Mother explained. "You're almost a Perth, and *that* job's unfit for the likes of you now."

"But I love *that* job. I love to read." She finished off a crime novel every other day. She imagined herself the only woman in the world reading this stuff. But those lawbreakers fascinated her, and moreover, she couldn't take her eyes off the down-and-dirty dames who circled them like moths around a candle. Wonderful, lazy work . . .

"Quit the library! Oh, Mother knows you love it, but these are better times now. The Perths are right. You must act who you are."

"*Act who I am?*"

"Do as Mom advises, sweetheart. Quit the job. Besides, you don't have to read *in* a library, dear."

No, but it was easier. Whenever Mom discovered her reading one of those trashy novels, like *Dillinger's Lugubrious Moll,* she'd sigh and sigh again until Bonnie was obliged to respond. "*What?* Mom, for god's sakes, St. Joe's where Jesse James got shot. I'm a child of the town!"

"Don't say for god's sakes, please. And it's not Jesse James you're marrying." Then Mother would shake her head in disappointment, perhaps even evidencing a little heartbreak.

"What is it, Mom?"

"Oh, nothing, dear, nothing at all. Just silly ol' Mom being silly, 'sall. Be a proper wife, Bon."

"Yes, Mom, I will."

As for loving her . . . well, yes, Bonnie supposed Andy did, but in a fashion almost too insipid to detect. There wasn't a spark in him anywhere, and he seemed to sleep a lot. He liked to be called Andrew; Bonnie sometimes called him An. But he was a good guy and a conscientious student. He offended no one and was well liked. During his senior year, he had been elected president of the high school in a remarkable victory. Over the speaker system, the principal announced that out of two thousand students, only one dissenting vote had been cast. Nell had teased her, asking if, by any chance, that one vote had been hers. She denied the truth and said no.

Bonnie's problem was she couldn't bear to disappoint anyone, especially Mom. When hurt, Mother was capable of shedding big rolling tears that she wouldn't wipe away. No, she'd sometimes even indicate that she wished Bonnie—the cause of the pain—to pluck a Kleenex and dab from her cheeks the signs of her heartache. Dad was another matter . . . Bonnie loved him more than anything in the world, and he felt the same about her. He was gentle as a piece of fur, caring as a sickbed nurse, and wimpy to the bone. He hated conflict. More than anything he wanted his wife and his daughter to be perpetually happy. As the easiest and surest way of accomplishing that, he encouraged Bonnie to see things Mom's way.

"After all, Mom loves you," he'd say, "and she wants nothing but your happiness, sweetie. Never forget that. She's right. Andy's a nice boy. He'll make a fine hubby. Now, give Mom a kiss and dry those baby blues. Everybody loves ya, hon."

Any tension between mother and daughter plunged him into deep despair. Occasionally, from a lugubrious mood, hints of suicide would shadow forth. "Maybe everybody'd be better off without me."

"Without you, Dad?"

He'd hold up a lighted cigarette (one from the two packs he smoked daily) and stare at it morosely. "Maybe I do have cancer."

"What!"

"Yeah, just maybe with me not interfering, everybody'd show more love."

"Hang on, Dad. My god, I'll hug Mom."

"Please don't swear, darling."

Mother possessed lots of power, but Bonnie knew that Mom did love her, exactly as Dad, with a sad, sad smile, maintained. And Bonnie did love Mom, yes—very, very much. For a wimp, Dad had lots of power, too.

Sure, she liked Andy, but oh, dear lord, he bored her senseless. He wanted to smooch with her all the time—just kiss, that was it. No sex. What century was he living in? Once his tongue inadvertently poked into her mouth, and you would have thought he'd frenched his grandmother, so full he was of guilt and apology. "Sorry, sorry, I'll never do anything like that again. I won't spoil our wedding night." To Bonnie— honestly?—these scruples seemed to represent virtue engendered by fear.

"I'll never hurt you," he said, with an expression the seriousness of which was beyond description. It was an expression that frequently appeared on his face, and Bonnie's jaw would sometimes drop in sheer amazement at how he achieved such a look. Humorless as a dead pussy (as Dillinger once remarked about some Johnny Law). Often she simply despised Andy Perth. Once she dreamed someone who resembled her enough to be her twin took off her clothes and lowered her body over his wide-eyed, terror-stricken face, smothering him to death. Certainly an appalling thing for that person to do, but Bonnie had to laugh because that was exactly the way he'd look if she herself stripped in front of him.

Anyway, that was the awful dilemma. Or here was no dilemma, not one anyway with enough power to stop her in her tracks, because here she was, in fact, racing down the highway to this disastrous rendezvous. A fate worse than death—marrying someone who bored her body into numbness, and her mind into a blank white wall. But this would please Mom, and as a consequence of that, please Dad as well. Jesus—buried alive!

Perhaps because speeding along and shortening the distance to her premature burial had created a readiness within her, a sudden realization dawned on Bonnie: *she was very compliant.* Yes—rather like her father, and in that respect, rather like Andy too. How embarrassingly obvious! She recalled an obscure remark she had once read: Sometimes things are so vast, *so everywhere,* no outline distinguishes them; shapeless, they are impossible to see. She now understood what that meant. Gad—cold comfort!

Just as this insight struck like a harsh burst of morning sunlight, the car began to lose acceleration. The motor lost its hum. After a moment of confusion, she realized that the car had simply died. She was coasting. She edged over to the shoulder, and the car slowed to a halt.

Wow! She sat there, somewhat dazed, staring straight ahead. She found herself shaking her head in disbelief and actually grinning. No, she couldn't believe it. It was as though God's finger had shut down the engine, had just in time prevented her from doing something really stupid . . . or if not prevented, at least postponed the tragedy. Okay, better than nothing. Why, yes, every hour delayed would be an hour added to her life. She inhaled deeply and gave a long grateful sigh of relief. Traffic whizzed by, evidently mindless of the miracle that had just transpired.

All right—now what? Mother would soon be calling on the cell phone. After all, they hadn't spoken for ten minutes. Bonnie didn't know what to do. She wanted to do nothing except savor these precious moments. She gazed at the spectacular fire-orange sun beginning to decline in the west. She wondered whether she would be here all night. Hmm . . . wouldn't that be wonderful? The cell phone lay in the passenger seat like a time bomb. She glanced at it with growing apprehension.

What do women do when their car breaks down? Hadn't she heard that you lock the doors and wait for the police? But she had never seen a woman locked in her car. Everyone she'd seen had gotten out, opened the hood, and gawked at the engine. Besides, it was still daylight. She was pretty good-looking, so she probably wouldn't have to wait too long before a guy would stop and lend some aid. Besides, she knew how to cope with men well enough; even working in a library teaches you a few things along those lines. Besides, something interesting might happen. *And what exactly do you mean by that thought?*—from someplace deep inside her she could hear Mother bray.

The phone rang. "Where are you, dear?"

"Stuck in traffic." She was amazed. Was that the first lie she had ever told Mom?

"We're all waiting. Father O'Brien's getting impatient. All your friends are here . . . waiting. Everything's sooo beautiful. Andy . . . he looks sooo handsome. Nervous as a kitten, though."

"Oh yeah?"

"Yes, he is. Hurry."

"I will."

"Daddy's here. Wanna say hi?"

"No."

"Hi, sweetie."

"Hi, Daddy."

"We love you, sweetie. Mom's gonna cry."

"I know."

"Hurry along."

"Okay, I will."

"We're all waiting."

"Okay." She hung up and felt nauseous. Dear lord, how long would they wait? It seemed to her that everyone had gathered for a feast and that she was the sacrificial lamb. What was there to rehearse anyway? How much practice did you need to walk down a church aisle and repeat what old Father O'Brien sternly commanded you to repeat? Couldn't she wing it? Oh please, would someone, please, rescue her from this extinction?

She sprang the hood release, opened the door, and swung her legs out. She paused, amused at how intentionally she was displaying her legs (great legs, she knew), allowing, even manipulating, her skirt to ride halfway up her thigh. She smiled at this exposure that she held ever so briefly. Darling, please don't wear such short dresses. I won't. You always do. You're not that kind of girl. Don't embarrass the Perths. Nasty rumors get around. My, my, was she that kind of girl after all? Deep in the truth chamber of her heart, she suspected that she probably was. Oh well, no harm. Who's looking? Who knows? God's looking, dear. She got out, lifted the hood, and stared at the motor. Sure enough, it wasn't doing anything. With gratitude she stared at its inertness. This machine had just stopped. What a simple idea! It mesmerized her. A machine had done what she couldn't.

"Hi. Need a hand, hon?" Startled, she glanced up and saw a man grinning mischievously and walking, with a bit of a swagger, toward her. She hadn't even noticed his car pulling over. He was lean and young, perhaps a year or two older than she. Kinda cute, not much taller than she was in high heels. It took about five seconds for her to decide that she liked him, and she sensed immediately that he seemed to like himself.

"Oh thank you," she replied. "It just died."

"Got a mind of her own, eh?"

"Sure does."

"Probably ain't as dead as she's actin', though." *Ain't?* This was not an educated man, she noted with mild but inexplicable appreciation. "Dressed up . . . looks like you was goin' somewheres."

"Well, it's good I'm not anymore."

"Oh yeah? You'd kinda rather wouldn't, huh?"

"Afraid so."

"Want me to take a look at yer dead friend?" He now stood near her. She paused for a moment and studied the small eyes, black and beady as raisins, that were darting over her face, like someone trying to connect the dots. She thought that there was something . . . well, desirous in his efforts. These were flashing, fast-flickering eyes, like a bird's or a rattlesnake's; vigilant eyes that would always guard her, or cause her endless trouble. Action-hunting eyes. Creepy. She had to admit, she liked them. "Well, do ya?" he asked, his head gesturing toward the car.

"Hm—I guess so."

"Got yer doubts, don't ya? But okay, let's check the damage. Git in. Try to crank 'er. Maybe she just needed a snooze." She did what he said and nothing happened. She heard him fiddling around, and then he said, "Okay, goose 'er again." She did. Nothing. "It ain't gonna pop. Ya got a mess o' oil all over the place. Somethin' overheated." He came to the door she'd left open and asked, "Want me t' drive ya up the road a piece? Find a garage or somethin'. Platte City's close." He was staring at her legs, which somehow had once again become considerably exposed.

"That would really be so kind. Do you mind?" *What am I doing letting an absolute stranger pick me up?* she asked herself. *That's right! You're not that kind of girl, sweetie,* the voices inside asserted.

"No problem. Glad to help."

She gathered her purse and the cell phone. "You need any decent luggage?" she asked. "It's Tumi . . . leather."

"To *you,* leather?" This confused him. "Decent luggage? Well, no, don't think I do. I ain't got nothin' that good to pack."

She reached for the keys, hesitated, and changing her mind, left them in the ignition. She left the door wide open too. She wasn't fully aware of what she was doing (which seemed to have been the state she had been in all day), but right now it sure felt right. In fact, as soon as they set off down the road, she felt more elated than she had ever been.

His car was a total mess. Junk scattered everywhere: Coke cans, beer bottles, clothes, tools, a couple of *Penthouse* magazines, trash tossed about. It looked like a dumpster. She glanced at him and saw him smirking. She smiled, and said, "You sure look awfully pleased with yourself, mister."

"Well, I like helpin' out."

She continued inspecting the clutter. "You live here?"

"Lotta times I do." A ray of the dying red sun struck the edge of something silvery in the backseat.

She gaped and said, "What's that?"

"What?"

She pointed.

"Oh, that. Well, what's it look like to you?"

"A gun."

"That's right. Ain't never seen one?"

Her eyes widened and gleamed. "It's a magnum . . . . 357—right?" she said.

"Right! Damn, where'd ya learn that?"

"I read. Live next door to Jesse James."

"St. Joe gal, huh?"

"Yeah. Used to be a librarian."

"A librarian? Ya don't look like one."

"What's a librarian look like?"

"Well, I only know'd one, and yeah, yer right—she looks jis like you. But, damn, ya coulda fooled me."

"Guess I fooled a lotta folks today. What do you do with that big shooter?"

"Gas stations, 7-Elevens, yesterday I knocked off a bakery, you know."

"Geez! You're kidding."

"Nope. I ain't."

"*A bakery!*" She started to giggle. "What'd they cough up—a couple hundred donuts?"

He laughed too. "Jist about. Ya wanna try somethin' . . . maybe tomorrow?" The phone rang. "What ya got there—a phone? Hope ya ain't gonna snitch on me." She listened to the phone, each ring causing her blood to surge with new resolve. *Act who you are. Do it Now!*

"Is this the window button?" she asked.

"That's it."

She lowered the window, kissed the phone, and flung it out of the car.

"Guess ya ain't home."

"No, for once I ain't." She couldn't remember ever before having said *ain't*. "Gas stations and 7-Elevens? How 'bout laundries?"

"Laundries? Well, I don't know. Well, hell yeah, why not? Hey—what's yer name, darlin'?"

"Bonnie . . . and yours?" Why did she know instantly what he'd say? Had she read it all in a book somewhere, seen it in a movie, what? She laughed before he said,

"Clyde."

The Unveiling

It is as painful perhaps to be awakened from a vision as to be born.
                                                              —James Joyce

T he six-year-old child steps from her bath, dripping wet. Drying herself off, from the second-story window she watches the performance with growing excitement. In the square of this little frontier village, people have congregated around a magician executing fabulous deceptions. Numerous horses are tied at hitching posts; buggies and buckboard wagons clog the dirt road running straight through the country town. The atmosphere is festive. Music blares gaily—a drum, fiddle, and harmonica. Now and then some drunken cowboy fires a gun at the sunny sky.

What an exhilarating day. Earlier this morning, a man who raped a woman and stole a horse had been hanged for horse thievery. Naturally, this public punishment has been much enjoyed. Such ghastly events, even though frequent, always provide invigorating entertainment for all—for all except, of course, the star attraction himself. A couple of hundred yards away, near the church and the graveyard, the culprit, openly exhibited, dangles by his broken neck from the outstretched limb of the old gallows tree. A warning. The villagers consider these displays rather decorative. The corpse, however, is no longer the main event; the deceiver is.

The girl lives above the general store her parents own. Although her window furnishes an excellent panorama of the show, she rushes to join the crowd below. While she towels herself, she sees the magician jab his index finger up into the air and twirl it about. His finger glitters in the sun like a rod of gold. A young man and a young woman standing near him grab each other roughly and start dancing like maniacs. Or they do not really dance, but merely spin as fast as a wagon wheel. Soon their bodies blur together, and to the girl, seem even to fuse. The fiddle and the drum play. The crowd stomps its feet, shouts, and cheers the couple on.

After about a minute of this, the magic man claps his hands once and the frenzied dancing desists. When they stop swirling, however, they cannot release one another; they are attached, like Siamese twins, at their midsections. No matter how fiercely they exert themselves, and even fight, they are unable to disengage. People shout obscenities at them, guffaw mercilessly, and make lewd imitative gestures. The woman strikes the man solidly in the face because, having abandoned the futile struggle to release himself, he has instead decided to kiss her on the mouth. His nose is bleeding, but finally he overpowers her and does kiss her long and hard. When the woman fully succumbs, loudly and shamelessly emitting guttural moans, the harmonica cries out with her.

The heat of the lovers melts them evermore securely together, and the little girl can barely distinguish one from the other. She giggles at this as she rubs the towel over her tantalized body. She is quite breathless herself, as though she too has been jumping about. She knows that the magician has only glued the couple together, as she herself had recently done with a boy doll and a girl doll that her parents gave her for her birthday, or glued them like the two dogs that yesterday somebody mean had somehow hitched together, with one dog riding and rapidly bumping the other's behind. It was so funny at first, but eventually the dog on top had to kill the other to get free. Apparently, the girl's attention drifted from the lovers because she notices that they have somehow just vanished into the crowd, doubtless still embracing, fastened belly to belly.

The playacting titillates her, stirring new sensations that both delight and mildly menace her. The magician is very handsome, like her father. He wears a long black cape and a black wide-brimmed hat; a brilliant red scarf winds around his throat. A thick black beard masks half his face. He is the tallest and strongest man she has ever seen, maybe even grander than her father. In her aroused state, she believes he has caught a glimpse of her rubbing herself and that he has even beckoned her forth with a smile, a wink, and a slight tilting of his head. She can hardly release her eyes from this visitor who enacts these beguiling ceremonies. But she forces herself to tear her gaze from him, and she dashes from her room, down the stairs, and out into the street, thoroughly mindless of her nakedness.

She wedges her small, supple body through the dense assembly, prying people aside with her little arms, like a desperate swimmer endeavoring mightily to attain the shore. Almost every resident of her village and the surrounding farms is present, entranced by the clever illusions of this stranger who has so recently arrived from some unknown place. Colorful posters had advertised the coming of *The Master of Illusion,* but although everyone anxiously awaited him, no one was sufficiently prepared for his enchantments. Apparently, the master illusionist can induce anyone to believe anything.

Panting, the child manages to push and elbow forward to the front of the crowd. A rooster, carrying a strand of straw in his beak, struts to and fro within the crowd-encircled space; his red cockscomb bouncing pridefully, his blue-green and rust feathers shining in the sun. The people—local farmers and town shopkeepers mostly—gape in awe at this most commonplace sight. But what these spectators in fact behold, the girl eventually establishes from bits of conversation, from exclamations of astonishment, and from a little of her own logic, is that this fowl balances with its puny beak a huge oak barn beam ten feet long, weighing at least a hundred pounds. Even her dearest playmate (to whom one day she shall be engaged) gapes, transfixed—he who could see through every card trick she had ever tried to play on him! And there also stand her dear parents, also wonderstruck, completely unmindful of their daughter's presence. Across from her too stands the blind man of the village—that is his name, *Blind Man*—and for a moment she notices that his dead gray eyes point at her particularly, and he appears to be grinning. It's peculiar. But she can't dwell on him because she's worried about whether she can trust her own eyes.

All these neighbors . . . all of them such silly fools! Can it be true? In the dream she had last night, she was playing with herself by a river that she had never seen in real life, when an infamous outlaw, as stern looking as her father could be, galloped up to her on a fiery steed, aimed his gleaming six-shooter at her, and compelled her, mostly against her will, to fork over her living heart to him. It was difficult to comply with his demand, but she figured out a way. Her heart plopped from between her legs as though she had laid an egg. And then instead of mounting her up beside him, he galloped off, leaving her abandoned and heartless. The relinquishment was bloody and scary, but upon waking she did find her heart still beating—as fast as it is right now—in its usual place, and she recognized at once that she had been duped. So now she easily fathoms that all these folks here in her town are, by this handsome outsider, also being duped. With a flash of total comprehension, she deduces that she alone, in all the world, remains undeceived, and so, as any dauntless savior would do who discerns such a liberating truth, she screams at the top of her lungs:

"It's a piece of straw! Jest a piece of straw! Look!"

She senses she has done something audacious, as though she has flung a stone through the one stained-glass window of the only church in town. The entire scene shatters. The people, rudely jarred, abruptly refocus their vision, as though they have been roused from the depths of a dream-filled sleep, and from their beds transported into the dusty commotion of the street. In the wink of an eye, the child's brash revelation has diminished the giant beam to an ordinary yellow strand of straw. She grasps at once the devastating effect she's produced. The spectators now gawk at the inane fowl. Everybody grumbles indignantly, embarrassed—everybody but the little girl, of course. In her supple nakedness and her exultant pride, with her hands set on her hips, she poses in the noon sunlight as a disenchantress. At that miraculous meridian, the marvelous magician approaches her.

"Well, hello, my pretty," he intones unctuously as he bends down and smiles near her face. The crowd has begun to disperse. "So ya want all to behold ya, do ya? Okay with me, but it'll cost ya, my pretty." The child stares into his riveting black eyes, the eyes of a ferret that roam leeringly over her, and she doesn't know whether this frightens her or— and even more—excites her. This occurrence is too overfull for her to comprehend the hunger showing through his searching inspection of her. She senses though that he seems to be licking her naked body as a dog had done recently, licking her up and down—long slobbering tongue strokes, thirsting after all the salty juices he could eke out of her sweaty pores.

In her own utterly seduced predicament, she also imagines that she has actually mesmerized this extraordinary illusionist. His large bearded countenance leans so near, she espies her own face mirrored in his pupils. She is uncertain whether she is staring at him or at herself. In a few seconds, she feels encompassed by him. She is so attracted she extends her arms toward him. Immediately, he wraps his cloak snugly around her eager but trembling body, and lifts her up against his chest.

Neither utters a word. He carries her closely, privately, silently through the congested street. No one even seems aware of her. He holds his strong hand between her legs, stroking and squeezing her there, as though coercing her to deliver her heart to him. So secreted away is she that it is almost as though she flies invisibly amongst all these old acquaintances. Her little boyfriend races by, and he too never even pauses. Her parents glance away when the magician with their child brushes against them. Only the blind man's lifeless eyes follow the route of her brief abduction down the center road of the village.

At the door of the general store, the magician lowers her. She feels as though she has emerged from within his body, that she has been bathed in the source of his dramatic power.

"There! Yer baptized. Now, remember what ya did today, my pretty one, so ya'll understand what'll later afall ya. Goodbye, my pretty." And he steps away from her.

"No. No, don't go!" She rushes after him. He bends down to her.

"We'll meet once more, I promise ya that. Remember what ya did. Remember." He whispers these words, and his tongue pokes into her ear's small aperture. He rises and then turns, and after two or three paces, he simply disappears.

"What'd I do?" she shouts after him, as though she has already forgotten. "Don't go. What'd I do? Don't go, please." She thinks she hears him reply over the tumult of the street, "Ya been baptized, my pretty. Go! Live up to it. Don't fret. I ain't leaving ya. Not ever." But he's nowhere she can see. Instead, in the pathway of her vision, suspended above the crowd, is the rigid body of the offender; its peculiarly cocked head seems to stare at her with popped-out eyes. And she thinks how very much she loves to swing from the limbs of trees.

Surprisingly, the curious escapades of this day fade almost instantly from her conscious recollection, and they remain buried, until . . .

A decade later, she awakes. It is a glorious June morning. She lies quietly. Something undefined troubles her, teases her almost uncomfortably, a voice murmuring from afar—something exciting or menacing. Has she forgotten something? The realization dawns that today is her wedding day. Happiness wells and mixes inharmoniously with her peculiar mood of unease. She stretches out her arms and spreads her legs. Slowly she begins sliding her hands around her full, shapely body, fondling herself as she has done practically every morning of her life for as long as she can recall. In the palms of her hands, her breasts are full, the rosy nipples erect and ripe. Her fingertips work up and down the soft, oily crease between her legs. Today, at this sacred intersection of her thighs, the groom will enter to steal her oh so willing heart. How avidly he has yearned for it. He claims that every night he takes her in his dreams. She smiles; nearly everyone in town does that. She is now sixteen, and as she well knows, stunningly beautiful.

She muses over her beauty, envisioning herself now as clearly as she would her image in a mirror—her long yellow hair, blue eyes, high cheekbones, pouting lips, and tall, perfectly curving body. She has always been beautiful, even as a child. She has furnished a feast for the eyes of everyone in the village. The mere awareness of such a luscious blessing, as her own beauty certainly is, now causes her heated blood to race even more. Today—oh, the sheer pageantry of her; oh, such a soaring expectation.

Her memory wanders, as it frequently does when she is gratifying herself like this, over those myriad eyes, the bold ones and the shy ones, that have stared so desirously at her throughout the years. Even her own father relished watching her bathing or dressing or simply prancing about nude. He'd say, "Ya yank my hungman t' life, sweet meat," and he'd up and flash her a peek of what he meant. Mother would reproach her with, "Ya gotta stop workin' yer paw thata way. He's anailin' me raw. Gimme a rest. Let 'im hang, ya wicked child." But, oh, what could she do? God made her as he wanted her. Not do what God wanted? Impossible.

Yes, a long, long history of sensual beauty she has been—displayed, beheld, reached for, and withheld. Withheld . . . mostly. Yes, even as a child, men, and many women too, have dreamed of her. This she knows because they have openly confessed these dreams in church. In fact, so many men have done so—is it *all* the men in the village?—that it no longer alarms anyone, so common an occurrence has it become. At times the dramas of these divulged dreams have been so shamelessly licentious that children have been ushered from the church, indeed, as she has been herself on several occasions . . . she, too, forbidden to hear these dreams of her.

She strokes her smooth skin into a warm, tingling arousal. She shuts her eyes and pictures herself. She cups her hand firmly between her thighs, plants her heels solidly, exerts her leg muscles and arches her back. It is as though a powerful hand that is not her own pulls her up from the mattress by her vagina. She seems to ascend into the air, to levitate, her physical beauty elevated. It is so very physical, she imagines it a beauty not entirely of this earth. She breathes heavily, enraptured, but her desire continues to mingle with some elusive inquietude. It exhilarates, yet sometimes also scares her, to experience desire indomitable enough to so literally elevate her. But oh my god, she thinks, what the world wouldn't give to behold her now hanging in the air.

This is a very special day, she reminds herself—a *very* special day. Yet some foreboding echo resounds within her. ("A very special day it will be, indeed, but not precisely as you foresee, my pretty one"—words barely heard, seemingly whispered from nowhere.)

She continues for a while, luxuriating in these intoxicating self-images, still agitated by a restive subcurrent of anxiety. This room above the general store is quiet. Of course the store is closed today; so are all the other stores in town, because everyone has been invited to the celebration. Her parents have departed early in the buckboard, leaving her the white mare to ride. The wedding is to be in the next village, where the groom lives.

She has overslept. No doubt her parents, preoccupied with last-minute arrangements, forgot to wake her. She imagines herself prancing on the white mare through the town; what a beauteous sight this will be! Her father said, "It'd be enough ta bone-up a blind man." Mother replied, "Stop yer mouth-vomit, hon." Father said, "Truth, ain't it?" and they both chuckled, because it surely was. But upon viewing this splendid day, she now decides to walk. Everyone will be waiting, with the groom—"world's luckiest man" as they all call him—waiting in a spirit of exhilaration for the bride's arrival. And here she will come, striding across the swaying green summer fields, advancing amidst the waving flowers, a vision resplendent with heavenly beauty, the embodiment of a shared dream of desire. Oh, the sight of her!

Within these reveries of what has been and what is to come, she attains the peak of her excitement, a glow-burst within her belly. Moments pass, and then she lowers her body, or it feels rather as though her body is lowered and then released. Her mind is mostly blank now. But wasn't she, scarcely a minute ago, seeking to recollect something else, something nebulous scratching at the thin inner lining of her heart? Well . . . it's eluded her for now. No matter—whatever it was, she persuades herself, it will undoubtedly return. After all, it does abide someplace inside her. And a murmur reaches her: "Yes, it does abide."

She must hurry now. She has a way to go. Quickly, she slips into a skimpy, nearly transparent summer dress and departs. The journey to the other village will require a couple of hours. It is such a glorious day. The placid breeze strokes her, and the folds of her light dress wave around her legs. She strides down the road leading out of the village. She passes the saloon that is certainly quieter than it has ever been, passes the horse and cattle corrals where animals, so tranquil they seem to be dozing, glare dumbly at her, passes the silent stables of the blacksmith, and passes the sheriff's office and the half-dozen now-empty jail cells.

The town appears abandoned. But no, not quite. Down the road she sees a woman "on the hanging tree," as folks would describe it. She had roused a Bible salesman, but when he went to assault her, she licked him on the ear, exactly three strokes with her black, venomous tongue, and as he testified, made his member go useless as a cow's tail. The judge concluded that her sorcery could make fools of other men as well, and it was this bit of enlightenment that determined her doom.

The two women now look at each other, each unfathomable to the other. It is a little disconcerting that on such a very lovely day, the buzzards pluck so at the sorceress's naked flesh. How awful! Remove her skin and she's not at all as she had appeared to everybody . . .

But this dead woman is not the only presence here.

When the bride arrives at the village outskirts and passes the graveyard behind the church, she observes the blind man seated on a bench beneath a gnarled cypress tree. He is motionless as the gravestones. The blind man knows her well, certainly differently than others do. She stops and looks at him. He turns directly toward her. Positive that he is aware of her presence, her heartbeat quickens slightly, and she remembers . . .

When she was younger, she would sometimes, late at night, steal out of her bed and walk down to this graveyard. No one ever saw her. At night she was invisible because, she has always surmised, God intended the spectacle of her to materialize only in the full light of day. So she meandered through the graveyard, magically shrouded by the dark, absolutely safe, it seemed. Sometimes she would even lie down on one of the graves and fall asleep, and the next morning, her parents or some neighbor would discover her. In the cemetery, she would rove among the headstones and the shadows. Sometimes she witnessed lovers embracing, sometimes drunken men baying at the moon like wolves. Sometimes she would stumble over men or women who were either dead or had been wounded in bloody fights with guns or knives or fists; sometimes she swung and fondled the corpses on the hanging tree. Sometimes she saw ghosts; sometimes the blind man. Whenever he happened to be here, she would watch him as he stared at the moon, at the graves, or at her.

The folks of the town attributed preternatural powers to him. He could, for instance, locate underground water, divining the site for the sinking of a well-shaft with such unerring precision that people believed he had even redirected the course of underground streams to flow where he pleased. He could foresee the future too. It was rumored that as a young man his sight had been perfect—he read books; he was a scholar. But one day he chanced to lay eyes on a woman whose irresistible beauty consumed his imagination, so much so that she appeared to him in a dream, disguised as the blazing sun. Because he was powerless to avert his eyes from her, he woke up blind. His eyes had been burned out by her. Often, the girl has pondered whether her beauty is as annihilating as the woman's who had accomplished this.

Once, on a bright moonlit evening, she had passed this very spot and discovered him sitting exactly where he is now. It was not an uncommon encounter. On that occasion, however, she had marched up to him (this had been premeditated) and had removed all her clothes. He remained mute, though he certainly knew that she stood close in front of him. He breathed his breath on her bare stomach. She reached forth and clasped his hands and laid them on her breasts, and when he drew back slightly, she held his hands in place. "Look at me," she whispered, and nudged his hands, which began to search over the treasures of her bountiful body.

For a long while, she had wanted him to see her in the only manner he could, and to desire her as all others had, and to realize, as all others had, that he could never completely possess her. No, not the way all the lovers whom she had spied upon among the graves possessed each other. In tantalizing him this way, she never intended to be cruel—heartless, as men would later lament—no, rather the opposite. It comprised part of her earliest and deepest understanding of herself that she was designed as a spectacle, and no spectacle could ever be entirely possessed without forfeiting its capacity to unbalance complacencies.

The blind man's large hands, at first awkward and hesitant, soon assumed a graceful ease and slid over every inch of her moon-pale skin as smoothly as streaming waters. Unexpectedly, she felt a current of warmth, and a thrilling sensation pulsed through her, the surge of which quickly intensified and quite suddenly flooded over her. Gently he inserted his fingers into all the orifices of her youthful, and until then, inviolate body. He spread her legs wide; his strong arms braced her, and a sharp pain knifed up into her as a huge hardness cut into the tender nerves of her center. She groaned with a painful pleasure beyond her means to either comprehend or assimilate. He burned in her like a lighted torch, and her blood poured over the flame of him. She felt something burst, and instantly she guessed that her heart had broken loose. The moonlight went out, and she lost consciousness.

She was awakened by the jolting movement of her father carrying her home. When he placed her down, she saw wet bloodstains on the front of his shirt. Dull pain forked through her belly, and glancing down, she discovered blood trickling down her inner thighs. Shock and disbelief struck her. "Got the curse laid on 'er," her father remarked. "Rag 'er up 'fore a cur's snout spots 'er good." And mother replied, "Plug yer muddy mouth, hon."

That was then. Now too the blind man turns toward her, and she asks, "Ain't ya coming to my weddin', Blind Man?"

"I been a'ready."

"How's that?"

"In a dream."

"Ya dreamed o' me?"

"Yes."

"Like the others have?"

"I don't know. Everything's a dream to me. Is it to them?"

"Was I good to ya in your dream? Did I strip and force ya to feel my naked body, just like once before, right here, where we are now? Did ya want me? Did ya have me again? Did ya fill me with yerself, like then?"

"Maybe it was here. Anywhere's the same."

"But what happened? Was I a blazin' light of beauty?"

"A revelation."

"I was?"

"The dream of you."

"How—a revelation, Blind Man?"

"The blind made to see."

"To see what?"

"More illusions."

"Of what?"

"Desire."

"Illusions of desire?"

"Yes."

"On my weddin' day?"

"Today."

"I don't understand."

"It doesn't matter. You can't escape the dreams you been adreamed into."

"I'm in everybody's dream."

"Yes, you are."

"I'm glad."

"Yes, I know you are. Be careful how they wake."

"I belong to one now."

"Yes, you do, indeed. But sumpin' other than you know."

"Ya said today the blind'll see. Then—today I'll wake 'em?"

"Yes, you will, but only to another dream."

"Of me?"

"Their other dream of you. Yes."

"I don't understand."

"The dream they can't forgive, the dream you wake them up to."

"Am I to blame for that?"

"You are blamed."

"Sometimes ya talk so crazy."

"Yes. Go. You're late already. Everyone's waitin' for sight of you. Show them. I've seen." He turns toward the corpse of the woman hanging from the tree.

With this, the bride proceeds on her way. She suspects the blind man is intoxicated, but she has no time to waste deciphering anything he says. She must hasten now. Exuberant with life and all the urgent anticipations of maidenhood, she decides to venture a shortcut across the summer-painted fields, a pathway she recalls having once traveled as a child with her little boyfriend, the very person she now hurries forth to wed.

Shortly, she is dancing along through a wide, green meadow, dotted colorfully everywhere with the swaying heads of flowers and the fluttering of white and yellow butterflies. But this blossoming landscape rapidly becomes totally unrecognizable. She is amazed because, she estimates, she could scarcely have covered a mile. Hadn't she, at one time or another, traversed every inch of this homeland? And yet nothing appears familiar. Nonetheless, she maintains confidence that she knows well enough the general direction she must pursue. Yes, something deep within her knows how to get to where she's going.

Imagining her wedding inflates her heart with a kind of impatient ecstasy, and this glorious balmy day envelopes her as sweetly as a miracle would. It is true that she mostly pictures herself; others appear to her only as mesmerized by the radiance of her unreachable beauty. A mild, fragrant wind lifts her easily along, light as a feather, through this verdant scenery of wildflowers. Dazzling red poppies and yellow daisies spread out everywhere around her, and the outreaching arms of trees seem so embracing. It is as though the magnificence of the day were solely created to enhance this display of her. But quite suddenly, from out of nowhere, a few gray clouds have now ushered in and drift above. They seem a trifle misplaced. But no matter. She feels as joyful as she had when a child, dashing across the farm fields, her heart thumping adventurously.

She strains to revive those distant, careless days, to resurrect some specific occurrence of those departed joys. She remembers that whenever she roamed through pastures or plowed fields, she'd watch farmhands gawk at her until she disappeared from their captivated sight. If she happened to return the next day, there they would be, petrified in identical postures, as though all night not a single muscle had flinched as they awaited her reappearance. She wonders if they're still there. Thus, she glides along amid these joyful reveries, her spirits elevated ever higher into the azure sky of this her wedding day.

Presently, however, she notes with some dismay that the bright sunlight begins to wane. How much time has passed? Merely asking that question suggests a surprising possibility. Perhaps hours have lapsed! The afternoon has turned uncomfortably warm, and her body and dress now feel a little damp. She stops and surveys her location, still baffled at how unacquainted she is with this region. Is she truly lost? An excitement seeps into her awareness that resembles the feeling she awoke with this morning, mixed as it is with a slight apprehension. She now steps along perplexed, even confused. Where precisely have her inclinations delivered her? How strange. And up there, isn't that the hanging tree that belongs to her village?

An even more unexpected sight now confronts her. There before her flows a glistening river. It is startling. No river that she knows of exists so near her home. It's impossible! Good heavens! How far *has* she strayed? As confounded as she is, she nonetheless remains, for some reason inexplicable to her, convinced that the direction she has been pursuing leads straight to her destination. But halted at the bank of this mysterious river, how isolated she now feels.

She stares at the quivering water slipping past; actually, it appears nearly motionless. She must reach the other side. She stares across the flickering surface. How lovely it is, how graceful. How very cooling it would be. How inviting. The water is neither too deep, nor the riverbed too wide. She raises her dress over her head and steps naked from the river's edge into the coolness. She has thoughtlessly tossed her dress on the ground; what she will do on the other side without it is a question that never even occurs to her.

She commences wading across with languorous purpose. The water rises halfway up her thighs. A tingling titillation streaks through her as the chilly water rolls around her upper thighs. Her nipples stiffen, as dark red as ripe cherries. Sensuous desire begins to pulsate inside her. Midway across, she pauses—just as she has so often been before—in wonderment at the magnificence of her nudity. The sun is fading; the clouds have thickened. Perhaps even the clouds have gathered to look upon her. And this most exquisitely beautiful exposure, which she now so fully allows, draws her seductively into a self-caressing rapture. She moans, arching her cherry-tipped breasts skyward as an offering to some thirsty deity. And yes, she detects grinning faces in the clouds and large gray eyes gazing down.

Surrendering to this delirious infusion of pleasure, she shuts her eyes, remembering all the desirous men (and women too) who, over the years, have been enthralled by the sight of her. She remembers the delicate movement of the blind man's hands tracing over her curves, remembers the pressure of his fingers as he worked them into the tight holes of her body, and the excruciating pain as he implanted his seed deep up into the core of her. He alone had penetrated her, broken her mirror. How long has she believed that his seeds lay dormant within her, and that one day she'll give birth to some manifestation of his blindness? Anyway, being had by the blind doesn't count. Everything about her is a spectacle; nothing blind can ever possess her. As far as she's concerned, she remains a virgin.

.The shadow of some far-off memory wavers faintly within her, a troubling memory—someone's voice, something not wishing her well. It is not unfamiliar, no, but it has always been too obscure to bother her, like a fly buzzing in the dark when she's trying to sleep. But its volume now starts to rise; words are almost audible.

The river murmurs around her. On the borders of her dreamy consciousness, as though from across a vast distance, she finally begins to hear a voice that has, until now, been whispering too inaudibly to her. "Hello, my pretty. No, my darlin' . . . no river flows here. It's all within ya . . ." She realizes now that this voice has been whispering to her, beyond her full awareness, all day long. No . . . much longer even than that.

Suddenly, raucous laughter assaults her ears. Her eyes pop open. She is stunned, bewildered. There they stand, in the fast-faltering, cloud-darkened light of the late afternoon, the entire wedding party, bedecked in their finest clothes, erupting with scurrilous shouts of outrage at her vile posturing. "Kill the filthy bitch!" someone roars. In chorus the throng repeats these harsh words of judgment. "Kill the bitch!" What do they mean? She glances around, as jeering condemnations burst forth. "Kill the witch!" "String the cunt up!" "She tricked us!" "The whore tricked us!"

The river has evaporated. Paralyzed in her nude pose, rooted in this unprotecting meadow, her eyes lock in disbelief upon her wedding guests. Several, but especially two—a particularly obnoxious man and a woman—ogle her, their mouths slobber as they mimic the gestures that she so self-lovingly performed a brief moment ago. And her bridegroom gazes upon her, seemingly frozen, even in all this summer heat. His fist is raised as though it grasps an invisible dagger. "Lynch the bitch!" "She blinded us!" "Noose the cunt!" She sees two ghastly faces, bloodstained beyond recognition, obviously wounded by some appalling sight. Someone is swirling a lariat over his head. They are all mounting their horses.

"It's time," a voice whispers from lips that actually seem to graze her ear.

Flooded with terror and shame, she turns and flees panic-stricken across the broad fields. She senses the madness within the mob that chases her, a madness ringing down damnation upon her. The thudding horses' hooves and cries of the villagers merge and roar forth as from one gigantic figure racing after her. The hanging tree looms ahead, reaching out its arms like a deadly lover. If she can only reach that embrace in time, give her body to that tree, be lifted above all this screaming pursuit, and with her spellbinding beauty freeze this madness into stone. She has been, hasn't she, all that they have ever lusted after, all that they have dreamed of? All of them—publicly, they have confessed these dreams. Yes, but outside their dreams such flagrant exposure—hers— proves more than they can tolerate. Only a witch would refuse to confine such outrageous temptation to dreams. She deceives.

"Kill her! Kill her!"

Amid her own derangement, she strains to recollect whether, back there, she had glimpsed her parents witnessing her absorption in her own physical splendor—in their eyes an indecency. Were those two bloody faces theirs—theirs the disbelieving eyes ripped from the sockets? The thickened clouds cast a mantle of darkness over her vision. It's getting dark; night must be coming on from somewhere out of the light. Suffocating, she runs, runs faster than she ever has in life; her shapely legs, strong and swift, but neither as strong nor as swift as the horses that bear down on her, horses oddly indifferent to the enticement of her legs.

Their other dream of you . . . the dream they can't forgive. Voices speak within her trying to explain, but nothing can make sense to her.

Her heart kicks, fighting to burst free; her lungs burn, gasping to inhale the burning air ignited by this fury of commotion. Lunging on, she strives to escape the hungry hands groping after her. She stumbles, exhausted, hits the hard, unyielding ground, and sharp rocks bite painfully into her flesh, and her blood gushes. The limb of the giant tree extends above her, a long black shadow. Its horror now a blissful, proffered comfort.

"It's jest a piece of straw. What are ya cryin' for?"

A rope encircles and cuts into her neck. It's yanked, and she chokes and topples backward.

"Oh, jest that," a voice says, either mocking or consoling.

She's yanked up—up. Her body jerks nakedly. She still believes that her beauty has driven them insane, that they are stringing her up like this merely to achieve the fullest possible view of her. They cut her up the middle like a slaughtered pig, nonetheless. They close their eyes, she believes, because her voluptuous breasts tempt them too severely. But, nonetheless, they rip her heart out of her chest (or—she thinks—her heart springs free all by itself).

"Oh, jest that. Ain't nothin', ya see—piece of straw in the beak of a bird."

Why is she resisting? After all, she knows that this has all been foretold—knows, but can't recall when. Isn't this her very own ultimate fulfillment, screaming though she is against it?

"Ah, let 'em have ya; it's yer weddin' day, my pretty one," a voice either well-meaning or mocking advises her. "All of 'em, they're the bridegroom. Ain't nothin'—a piece of straw, jest."

Blinded with tears, she imagines herself dropped from the limb of the tree. Imagines herself consenting. Imagines herself rolling in the grass onto her back. Imagines herself stretching out her arms, splaying her long legs, and readying herself to be partaken of. Imagines herself opening her burning, trembling body for everyone to have a piece of at the wedding feast . . . oh *this* the most luscious cake of all.

Dear god, have they *really* destroyed her beauty?

"Jest takin' it in," the voice replies.

Will they really eat her alive?

"Oh, it ain't so bad. They been eatin' ya alive every day. Ain't nothin' really. What's yer beauty for, my pretty? Ain't it all a trick—a piece o' straw?"

Oh, if only she had the breath to speak, she'd bring them to their senses. She wonders: Without her, into what embodiment will their desire flow? How will they sleep without her? Dreamlessly—dead. In their dreams, it is into her their pleasure pours. Her death is theirs as well. Can't they see that her beauty has blinded them?

Unable to tell whether she hangs in the tree or lies on the ground— an ascension or a fall—she now becomes insensible. The rain begins to fall, cleansing the blood of her beauty off the folks of her village.

It is now he gathers her up, swirling his black cape around her. "As I promised ya, my pretty one, I'm here." His arms upraise her into the falling night of this her wedding day. And the master of illusion veils her in the everlasting darkness that finally possesses all beauty.

Mare

The sun sinks out of sight, but night has not yet fallen, so the sea is still blue and also the sky. He closes his eyes and holds her hand and lets himself be led like a child. Naked, they walk slowly along the ocean's edge, and tongues of water lick their bare feet. It is peaceful, and they are alone—alone, except for a single figure so far down the shoreline that it appears only as a protruding black dot, miswoven into a tapestry. The early evening is quiet. Although the surf whispers against the sand, it whispers so continuously they seem not to hear it. A gray cloud-body has gathered in the distance, but they pay no attention. Somewhere behind them a faint drumming sound thumps against the wet sand—another continuous, monotonous rhythm that has remained unnoticed until now—but they can see nothing when they turn around. Like a rumbling issuing from the middle of the earth, it seems enormous.

"It sounds like hoofbeats," she says, as she squeezes his hand and then lifts it to kiss with glistening lips that she has painted, as she always does, blood red—always, because she wants her lips to remind him of a wound. A breeze swirls through her weightless hair, threading her into the surrounding twilight. And when the tips of her hair touch his leathered face, he imagines the softness of her hair stroking him as an artist's brush. He smiles beneath the mask and opens his eyes. He knows that she dreams that they will remain lovers forever—until he's forced to murder her. Forever, then, is not long until tonight.

At this stage, they're calm; because they've been through all this many times, they seem inured. At this stage, the rumbling in the background is barely worthy of observation. Yet . . .

"Yes, it sounds like a horse," he replies, as though he were an echo.

They stop, and she gazes at him wondering, he suspects, what his real—no, she'd say his *other*—expression is, because, of course, she cannot see through his mask. That the mask itself smiles means nothing necessarily; perhaps he is not smiling, and yet, what it expresses counts for a great deal to her. She has designed it this way. On the surface, he always smiles *at* her, *for* her.

"I like to believe you are smiling at me every moment," she says.

"Yes, I know you do," he says.

She slides her fingernail—sharp, it seems to him—along the outline of his lips, tracing the delicately molded configurations of the stained leather. Her brown eyes narrow; they almost shut, as she inspects every detail of the workmanship—the fine texture of the leather skin, its perfect tints of tanned skin, its exacting slopes and angles imitating the lineaments of what she has conceived as his handsome face. It is a face, she claims, which once she had beheld, she would never again have to worry about its reality, so flawlessly has her art captured it. As she so often does, she long and lovingly adores the accomplishment of her craft. He has forgotten what he looks like.

"You look like this," she'd say, holding up in the palm of her hand a small mirror.

"I see I'm hidden."

"Yes, and revealed." Though he gazed at length into the shining O of her hand, he failed to recognize himself. He appeared so small. To both, only what she desires to see matters—only what she desires matters.

"Never remove this face. Promise me," she says, almost beseechingly. She says this every time desire begins to stir within her. He feels the heat radiate from her body and notices how rapidly she has started to breathe. She seems to have absorbed the warmth of the dying sun.

"No—why would I do that?"

"No, I know you never would," she says, reassured, and they begin again to stroll.

Why has he permitted her to fix this face upon him, to control this impersonation, to cast him in this soon-to-be tragic plot? To please her? That would have been enough. To please her in any way is his supreme happiness. He is the instrument she can play as she wills. Yes, to please her is enough, but it isn't everything. As he is being concealed from her, maintained by her—an oval reflection in her palm—so is he concealed from himself; in some sense, maintained from himself. But however that is, it falls beyond his comprehension at the moment.

As they stroll in slow motion, as people may in movies or dreams, he hears her ardent breathing mix with a rhythmic rumbling that resembles the rolling of distant thunder. That slight vibration of hoofbeats pounds the ground, causing their feet to tremble. He glances at the sky. It leans closer to them now, and because they have lost a little more light, its blue has deepened. It still looks clear, though, except for the recent materialization of a few shadowy cumulus clouds that seem to have appeared from out of nowhere. So carefully and unobtrusively have the clouds drifted into place, the lovers fail to notice them. And what is that projecting from the sand that's been there all along? The lovers are too busy with their own dream to pay any heed to such a remote projection.

She releases his hand and begins dashing ahead of him. He watches her nude body racing away, watches her brown hair whip wildly in the summer wind's warm fingers. It excites her to be observed, and observing her excites him. She is exerting her heart, forcing her blood to rush ever faster. "I want my heart attacked." She has told him that every time he has entered her. As her passion increases now, so does his own—as she now means for it to. So unpredictably evocative are her sensuous flights, he senses some buried vision of his life aching to reappear.

She runs with great speed and elegance. He stares at her. The wind is moaning, or she is—"Oooh." "Oooh," it vibrates through him. As always she hypnotizes him, tears away his resistance, as she would the lid of a coffin; and resurrects him, as she would the dead. Her body, as rhythmic as a snake, as stunning as the paralyzing enchantment of Medusa, transforms him into a throbbing pillar of desire awaiting her command. She confounds the distinction between her will and his own.

Who is wishing this to happen—to happen again? Who stages this recurrent spectacle? "Are you blood hungry?" she asked during that time of the month. What monstrous intentions are coalescing within us today—again today? he asks himself. He shivers, already unconsciously responsive to the ghastly intimations answering him. Some erotic vision of terror has been revived and is working its way to the surface, or is *working out* the surface, duplicating itself. He begins to fear that he will burst if he fails to let the vision use him; yes, if he resists her purposes the least bit, he will burst. It astonishes him sometimes how he lets her manipulate him like a child, how he prays she will. Other times, it's not astonishing at all, because how much more than a child is he, anyway? He can hardly lift his feet now, so terrified is he by her desires and by his own as well, since his have become so merged with hers.

"Shove it clear up in me . . . your desire. O, fill me. O, fulfill me. O, break me open like a walnut. Gore. Bleed me. Let me die for you, by you. Bring me off with you. Make the O. Oh yes!" she said or he said . . . when? . . . in a dream . . . maybe last night . . . or maybe not yet, maybe not yet voiced beyond his own anticipations.

"Can't you see what's plainly not there?" she asked.

Confused, he asked, "What do you mean?"

"See. See? Nothing—the knife's gone out in the dark. O."

"I'm too concealed by you to see."

"O."

And what *was* that down the shore line, which still he could not make out, which kept catching his eye . . . that unrelenting distraction? He is by now well related to it. They occupy the same reverberating ground. He knows that—as things in dreams that make no sense are known. Something wild is running down the strand or under it, as in one vast dream field.

He steps after her, a few strenuous inches at a time, a man disabled, or strangely enabled beyond his means to impersonate, to live up to the part into which he's been cast by some long-forgotten misperception of himself and the world—a boy who once dreamed of himself as a deadly superhero. A hundred yards away, she turns and strides back toward him, closing in on her stunned prey, her pace as methodical as a stalking lion's. Her firm breasts bounce full and ripe; her large nipples jut out, leaking a sticky golden-brown honey that even in this faded gray twilight glistens. He can taste her thick sweetness already trickling down his throat.

With a slight, down-pointing motion of her hand, she directs him, as her minion, to focus now on the triangle of dark brown hair, an inverted triangle, crowning the lithe movement of her strong thighs. He follows these physical outlines of her desire, understanding that soon she will want his erection to ram her open, to savage her body here on this primordial floor of vibrating sand. She commands where he's to look— what he's to see through his leather face.

Mesmerized by her body, he is all eyes for her, as well as a knife raised up by her hands, poised to be thrust where she wills. Thunder murmurs from afar. Secretly, the clouds have further thickened. She is coming for him as a ravenous animal would. Barely able to move, he stops. Her long legs reach forth with such celerity, any intention to flee from her now is out of the question.

A few feet from him, she stops. She is panting. Her lustrous eyes glow; her teeth gleam. She is so full of extravagant promise, lust, and threat, she could be a vampire. He feels schemed against, as though all his life he has been plotted against by something within himself, minacious, beyond his understanding, but which she understands perfectly. He has always been quite certain that she comprehends far better than he the alarming drama that he is dreaming to play out at her behest. She is at the core. Or is he at the core of her? In the O of her, she'd maintain. "In my absence."

"Can you hear the hoofbeats now?" she asks.

Oh yes, of course he can, especially once she's realerted his attention. Now he hears what he has always been hearing—the encroachment of a beast, still far away, but whose presence looms too huge to face.

"It could be all the hearts in the world beating."

"No, only yours and only mine. Open mine and see," she says and beckons him with a slight wave of her arm.

He resumes his arduous advance toward her; she waits, quivering hot and radiant as a pillar of fire. Over her shoulders he can finally detect the shape that they have been steadily approaching. Although, in fact, it seems no nearer to them. It seems not defined by space alone, but by time as well; it seems years away, and yet it now appears much more distinct, enlarged—but years away. It is the figure of a young boy or girl kneeling in the warm moist sand, watching them. He supposes the child is unaware that he is looking back. The dark, growling clouds continue to amass, soaking up the pale remaining light. From this distance, or from so long ago, it amazes him how clearly he perceives this silhouette, immobile, except that now it lifts the right arm and with the thumb and index finger makes a circle, an O, that is held against the right eye as the left eye simply closes. An imaginary telescope, he supposes . . . yes, now peering through a hole, or into a hole, at them.

Once again he halts, hesitates, and looks at his love and then at the kneeling child and then at his love and then at the kneeling child and then at her. *Déjà vu:* Has he not already seen what's going to occur? Has *who* already seen? Being watched as the overheated blood courses through their veins, shaping every ripple of movement, will inflame her desires even further, possibly—he fears—beyond sanity. Within this space nothing appears completely sane. The hoofbeats are sounding nearer, yet he is not wholly conscious of their increasing cadence. She catches the uneasy shift in his concentration and glances over her shoulder. He blinks, and she is back at him in the bat of an eye, shaking her head and grinning with malicious delight at what she has seen that he sees. It is as though that is the single detail, that lone spectator, which she has been waiting either for him to find or to put in place— the viewpoint by which they are sustained. He believes that everything was put in place long ago without him, that he only plays the part of himself.

The wind has increased, as has the silent and darkening cloud cover. Her hair whips frantically, inflamed. She loves being spied on, looked at from the outside, as though *there* is where she's real, not where she's standing, but *over there* is where she actually is—in the eye of the beholder. It's how she wishes to die—or rather to "expire," she's told

him more than once—in an execution of lust . . . being watched, pried
into by starving eyes, ravenous but unable to eat their fill.

He actually feels if that child would turn away from them, they would
disappear, as a child's reflection of a self outgrown, or a mirage seen
through, like the reflection on a windowpane. The child is father to the
man. Yes, he believes that if the child turns away, his mask will peel off.
He will become nothing, swept away by the wind; and her burning body
will incinerate in the thundering rain of fire that's coming, with charging
hoofbeats, to rectify this passion. But no, the child is not about to avert
his stare. The scrutiny is merciless—predetermined by the plot, one
recurrent plot forging the spectator's designs, as a tenacious memory
played out in a lifetime of dreams. No, whatever is happening, once
made it is rerun unto death.

"No one escapes the undertow of the dream that invents his life,"
she once observed. "Death is the sole deliverance. Do you dream of death?"

"No."

"*No?* O. Yes, that's exactly how it appears—a dream of nothing."

The foamy water at the sea's perimeter laps against their ankles. He
stands motionless, absorbed by the relentless designs surely bedreamed
by a demon and implanted into her mind. His heart pounds as though
he has been running half blind from all that he has struggled to avoid
from behind the expression she has fixed on him and made him wear
for her—all that he has struggled to avoid seeing before they ever met.
He can't even recall what he looks like. Looks like when? And what did
she say? "Don't worry, my darling, beneath this mask lies another. You
look the way you look." The ground quakes more thunderously; the
hoofbeats now boom like the percussion of a drum. Something that has
broken free and bounds across the years is about to overtake them, as
they had always dreamed it eventually would.

"Cram my fecund holes with all the germs of your salacious
imagination," she commanded once (but when?), and later, again and
again.

"What do you mean?"

"Infect my entrances with your dreams, I mean. Stop me up. Suffocate
me with your breathless dreams. See this? Oh! Can't you see what's absent?
Ooh! Make a death that lives." She said that to him . . . when? . . . the
last time . . . Then one said, "*O.*" That was all—*O.* But when was that?
Any time it could have been. She often spoke to him like that, like a
crazy person; and he listened to her like a crazy person.

They step into the sea, up to their knees. There is a loud clap of
thunder; a flash of lightning tears the blackening sky. The rain begins.

The stage setting is perfect enough for this rerun dream to become reality again. He lifts her; her legs wrap and lock around his waist. He jabs his erection into her gap, and starts to cut his way to her pulsating heart, thrusting, thrusting—a maniac beside himself. She is riding him, being ridden by him—horses and riders. They act as though they have only a few moments to reach the climax of this drama. And they do. All in the wink of an eye. But who is watching them? In full view they are— but of whom?

Her eyes roll; her mouth gapes. She gags on her own sudden inhalations. Lightning flashes, and he glimpses the whites of her rolling eyes. She is insurged with ecstasy. Some dispassionate portion of him tries to examine what's going on, but his mind is too possessed for that kind of attention. Struck by the overpowering sight of her, he's mostly blind to anything else.

Her hair lashes against his stiff, sustained smile. The mask covers his expression. Who, then, is this the expression of? The unfaceable, she'd contend. Can't you see? O . . . oh, how many times has he savored this display of her intemperance and his own lustful compliance? Often, but never, never so extreme as this. "You say that every time." Who said that? Even now he can't believe his eyes—the ecstatic postures of the woman he loves, as she is being fiercely stabbed to death by him—he, even now, the instrument of a will greater than he knows. Unfaceable.

Look! Oh! She twists around him, straining and squeezing with all the might of her wet limbs, like a sea serpent fighting for its life or strangling him out of his. He is seized, and so is she. Oh! He stares at her, cutting away at her. My god, he realizes, she must be bleeding badly. Oh! Without altering the rhythm of his thrusts, he imagines her upended, legs straight up and splayed, like the blades of a scissor. He sees between her legs—oh!—the gushing hemorrhage he has caused. The wounding effects of that wound upon him, upon her, can never heal because the wounding is recurrent. "The violence of love allows no other way." Did she assert that? "But who can bear such bloodshed?" Did he ask that? His memories are confused, gapping, awash with bloodstained spaces.

Exhausted, breathless, overcome by her unrestrained, homicidal determination, he still can't release his eyes from her wrenching exertions. She is pumping him too, pumping him full of the flooding sight of her, draining out his life—a succubus, feeding him on her crimson mouth while sucking out every drop of life-juice in front of this poor, fixated child, casting him forever into scenes too blinding to see his part in, and thereby . . . oh, thereby unable to recall once and for all.

Tomorrow morning, perhaps, this child, tracking the hoofprints of a gigantic horse along the empty beach, will find his bloated, consummated corpse drowned in a surfeit of pleasure and awe, smiling meaninglessly at a white sky devoid of aspect, or at a watery underworld. If he ventures forth into the deep water, perhaps the dead woman's insatiable arms and legs will entangle him just as they did her lover, and he will lose his innocence in her timeless embrace, just as her lover did. Or maybe the sun will not rise tomorrow, and he will simply be stuck in the blind spot of his entire existence redreaming himself.

The rain pours in torrents. The ocean actually seems to swell, to enwrap them evermore profoundly. They could be buried alive here if they're not careful; but they're elsewhere, unmindful of any surrounding larger than the embodiment of their two hearts. He feels the sweet, viscous honey of her leaking nipples slide thickly down his throat. He pictures their surging bodies . . . yes, there they are, on display in the dark day, out in sight, mounting each other, making up a spectacle, all on their own (but for one other)—an embodiment—all ashow. She craves to suicide, to force him to stab her, to knife her into an ecstatic death. Death at the heart. Oh! And (one other) the child from afar witnesses all—or all his green understanding enables him to see through the hole he's concocted. He imagines that this could be her precious blood redoubling the volume of the sea, not the rain . . . yes, her blood awash over him. It drives her mad to know that someone watches her being copulated, perhaps to death, that she's dying in total sight, beheld so, all ashow.

He wonders fleetingly if the child grasps all this, if the child is terrified, if the child comprehends anything, if his handmade telescope also envisions this as the future being constructed for him, invented right now, before his very eyes, by two lovers whose truculent contortions and pain-sounding suspirations appear insane. He wonders if the child sees all this . . . sees *this* way. The child's viewpoint seems compelling, repeatedly disruptive of his consecration. He forgets for a second his mission.

She loses herself, infused by passions driving her ultimately to death, driving him ultimately there as well. She desires not simply to die, but to be murdered; and not simply murdered, but murdered by her true love before this aroused onlooker. Who in the world sees this? Thoroughly concupiscent, she works hard to give the child down there eyeing them with that makeshift spyglass the total comprehension he requires to dream and redream this scene for the rest of his life. Yes, redream it into his manhood, when a man in his dreams will see as the child he was (and in part, must remain) this bloody scene of his own conception.

She is about to ejaculate him, to end them. It's all her doing. Even now some part of him needs to view himself as a guileless child, as a tool of her lust run amuck. Blame *her* desires. Yet he desires her desiring more than anything. Yes, even now a part of him knows he wishes to appear blameless for the deeds of his own contradictory, prohibited lusts. But no—whatever he and she are doing, they both are. Does it show? Who can tell? Make the child a part; keep the child apart, all ashow, asleep.

He worries the mask will slip, overheat, melt. An excitement is about to rupture him, and he's aware of its inescapable deadliness. Exhausted, he exerts himself in a series of final, killing thrusts. Up, up with the knife. Oh! Death to the heart. Paroxysms shake her, as though she's being electrocuted by a lightning bolt. Her heart is pricked; life gushes forth. She screams and screams and screams until, breathless, she folds forward, an actress bowing, and they sink beneath her dead weight into the depths of the sea.

The sea, like a curtain, blankets the surface of their depth. Their depth goes on, in a kind of undersight that the perfect eye of a dream alone can see. They cling to each other, fantastic acrobats, slowly revolving, disencumbered of the gravity of air, somersaulting beneath the sea's skin, released from surface constraints.

Who will recall us? he asks. That far-off figure? That child . . . a *boy*—yes, a *boy* . . . hasn't he always known that?—a boy spying on them, spying on them now, even in this pitch-black compression of the sea. "The child and I see through each other's eyes," he informs himself as he and she sink deeper, spiraling deeper, as though they were unwinding. Unconducted now by her living designs upon him, his perspective becomes disoriented; the angle of perception becomes obscured. He's acting, that's for sure, but he has no idea whose play he's playing in now. He's enacted. He's going round and round, dizzy in a world of his own, his imagination trapped in a single plot, damned inside a world with only a single plot. His own making. At least she holds him still. In this utter darkness, locked together with her forever, he imagines her scarlet mouth, her beautiful hair waving rootless, her red blood effusing round them as inky black as everything else.

They descend ever deeper into the depths of this bottomless sea, configuring themselves. Endless empty circles. And he wonders whether they still are being reconfigured as the phantasms of a child's bizarre understandings, making sense that only a dream can portray. The beholder's eye fashions all; yes, and then diurnally resees its creations. "How many more times must we enact this child's bewilderments?" he wants to bellow out, but at depths as hermetic as these, his thoughts remain unutterable.

She has dug her sharp nails into the numb flesh and bone of his illusions; he holds her dead remains. Life after life. Caroming downward they go, evermore insentient. Life after life. "Can I ever wake from this? How far can we fall?" he asks, and reasons that, eventually, they must burst out the world's other side—reimagined phantasms, real as they can be. Yes—but in the meantime, they're merely lying dormant awhile in their oneiric domicile. Light as a feather they fall, compressed by a universe of black water, like twins afloat in utero. Real as souls can be, all adream. He wonders if he, too, is dead, oh, but tonight it's too dark to see anything other than dreams. He smiles. He could live with this serenity, sleep indefinitely under the storm, away from the track of a fiendish horse out to trample them. But this is never where it ends.

Again—

Suddenly, the rapid rumbling of those irrepressible hoofbeats, and the unseen horse appears—glistening, jet-black—racing past the site of the ultimate spectacle, past the drowning lovers who now perform silently, invisibly, past the years, straight at the spectator's made-up eye. Lightning cracks the sky like a black egg. In the electrified night, the child now beholds, in dazzling stroboscopic frames, the successive leap and lunge of the horrifyingly beautiful beast of the ferocious storm.

Thunder displodes. The rain is virtually total, the atmosphere saturated. The child is inundated. The black mare soars into the child's telescopic vision, massively, charging at him with a savagery too resolute to rein. There is but a moment to plead innocence. *"I saw nothing! Nothing! I'm sleeping. They did it, not I,"* the child yells, terrified, knowing that this illogical disavowal has never once deflected the monstrous creature's trampling hooves. The child drops the made-up hole through which he's been spying. Now, as usual, everything's near enough for his naked eye. The surging mare towers upward, overreaching the child's imagination; she looms too colossal to contain, exceeding the totality of his vision. His own raw, unfathomable desires become indistinguishable from this equine transfiguration of unremitting dread—his own. No! No! I saw nothing! She's only an O.

Nothing's there. I saw nothing! I saw the nothing there is to see.

The mare—it is as though she is an issuance of the sea, a thalassic apparition coeval with the flooding arousals of night . . . after night, after night, after night. Liquescent, she is the eye of the torrential storm. She arcs, tremendous, majestic, rearing up, and dropping down through the rain-filled dark. Hers is a terrifying beauty, too shocking to behold, to hold. She is, again tonight, the dark, all it's made of; without her, no darkness exists. Without her, the darkness is creatureless—featureless. She is again tonight a gleaming, discontinuous progression of blinding lightning gashes scarring the heavy sheet of rain, a knife cutting open the sea. The bloody knife, the bloody wound. The unhealed. The site. Oh!

Terrified, the child again falls on his back, as he has done on all the other nights, and shuts his burning eyes—of all things, feigning sleep— but he lifts and jabs out with his puny limbs, speeding them up and down like spikes driven by an astonishing might augmented by terror too ancient for his life alone to explain. Frantically, he seeks to burst open this outrageous creature's belly, to strike a telling blow, low down, transpierce the vulnerable entranceway to her furious heart. But oh so quickly he—as always (he never learns!)—works himself to exhaustion.

"But what is all this futile exertion anyway," the voices of lovers whisper from the fathomless, watery dark. "What else, other than a worn-out disguise, a disingenuous means of submission? Give it up. It's something only a man now reimagining himself as he might have been as a boy would dream up. Don't you see? Yes, give it up, our child." "*I can't! See!*" the child screams.

The mare's black body now soars everywhere; her upraised body's everywhere. She is too much to see. So again the exposure proves too profound. Her unbearable gigantic weight comes crashing down upon the child's chest. He believes he has impaled her because he's pumping his fist back and forth inside her thick liquid loins; she's heaving and gasping as though she's about to die.

The hope that he's now fatally spiked her vital part lasts less than a second. Again, tonight, in consternation, he realizes she's not dying at all—wounded to death but not dying. Immobilized, atop his torso, he feels her unrestrainable quivering, tastes her mouth-foam pour over his face (a blood-salt sea vomit), feels the heat waves of her grunting exhalations as though the storm of her lust continues to juice a thousand volts into her undead corpse. Engulfed by the dreadful affliction of her beautiful body hemorrhaging all around him, he sinks into the depths of her wound as he would into a soundless sea, held as profoundly as he can ever be. Only an O—disavowed. Again he feels her mane fall so profusely across his eyes and mouth he cannot open them to tell what has befallen him. Again masked in time. Nothing. Then again—

Do You Mind Hanging Up
That Fucking Phone?

As he did practically every Sunday at 8 AM, Walter Bailey boarded the bus in Atlantic City for Manhattan. Having spent all night and all day shooting craps and playing cards, he was tired and damned depressed too because he'd lost twelve hundred bucks. His system hadn't worked. Of course, off-days afflicted even the best gambling systems . . . but still—twelve hundred bucks! Shit—and this on a teacher's salary. Oh well, upsy/downsy. At least he won a tad more often than not. He once added up all the days he'd logged in at the gambling tables—all his winnings, losses, and expenses—and estimated that over the years he had averaged about thirty-five cents an hour for his labors. What the hell, he enjoyed it—entertainment minus the hassle of personal relationships. Not that he disliked personal engagements, not as long as they were circumscribed and fleeting.

He'd intended to head home earlier, but he'd hit a winning streak at blackjack that prevented him from giving up hope on the losing streak that followed. He felt grungy tonight because he'd neglected to shower this morning. A pungent whiff of his own BO stung his nostrils. No big deal. He'd dry out soon enough once he got seated. He didn't look forward to the two-hour ride back to New York. Ah well, he could use the rest. His body found the Greyhound's continuous hum soothing; moreover, he could either get in a little reading or grade some of those boring-unto-death comp. papers from his students in English 102, a task which he had, as usual, delayed for as long as possible.

His briefcase tugged at his arm. He was definitely lugging around a lot of weight. Oh, yeah—and lately he'd become aware of growing older, accumulating years (christ, was he really sixty?), and of having put on a few extra pounds that he sure as hell didn't need. Getting on the bus, he told himself, "Enough! Chill out. Mind over matter. Read that book, relax, doze, fuck those papers."

The bus was crowded and dimly lit. He walked slowly along the aisle, searching for an empty seat. As always, plenty of blacks, Latinos, Asians— the downtrodden flushed from the City of Broken Dreams. Was he the only white person? In surroundings like this, his paranoia liked to frolic a bit. What if something sparked the pent-up rage of all these colored folks? Yeah, great—and there Professor Bailey would be, Mr. Whitie, ready at hand. Time to compensate, honey. Well, here he was among them, and he supposed, they were among him—menacingly so. Recently, discussing with his students Poe's story, "Premature Burial," a sassy black chick remarked, "I'm the you ya buried, hon." This proclamation, spiced with a teaspoon of sex, unnerved him. He pondered a moment, and replied, "So, you're the part of me I'm unable to live, is that it?" A fairly lame rejoinder, he thought. She answered, "Yeah, the black, dirty part. Call me up sometime." The class snickered. When he reddened with chagrin, Mike Turbo, a jock smart-ass, blurted out, "Ding-a-ling—she got your number, dude."

He knew he could occasionally go slightly paranoid. Frankly, he kind of enjoyed it. It lent an edge to life, kept you vigilant and on your toes, helped uncover meanings and patterns in a world where none existed, helped forge a system to beat a dealer who ultimately couldn't be beaten. But since Walter perceived this aspect of his personality, he figured that meant he wasn't really paranoid, because the real paranoids never knew it. Mirrors didn't work for paranoids. Anyway, if you weren't a touch paranoid living in the Big Apple, you had to be crazy.

A wave of unease swept through Walter: What if all the seats were taken? A hundred and twenty miles, strap-hanging in the aisle, the sacrificial lamb . . . But no, near the back, one seat remained, near the window, next to a white guy, of all things. Pretty funny, the two outcasts consigned to the rear of the bus.

"You mind?" Walter asked for some reason. Maybe because the guy's head leaned to the side, as though his neck were broken.

"No, no, of course not," the man said. As Walter sat down, he heard, "Of course not. I'll meet you at the SoHo Bar and Grill on Greene off Prince. Nine, tomorrow night. No . . . hey, come on, I'm not mad. Are you? Okay, good, fine, see you then—'bye."

Jesus, this asshole was on a cell phone. Walter detested these damn things. Nowadays, they sprang out of everyone's pocket or purse and barged into your personal space, imposing upon your attention a strange discontinuous text. And this could happen anywhere. Sacred zones of peace and tranquility were rapidly vanishing. Jesus—and just try to find a spot to hide!

The guy with the phone wore a well-tailored dark blue suit. Dapper, nice-looking, about forty-five, Walter guessed. Stockbroker, professional gambler, con-man type. That cell phone and the sharp contrast in their appearances encouraged Walter's immediate antipathy toward him.

Walter switched on the overhead reading light and drew forth the book he now planned to read, but as the bus began to pull away from the terminal, he glanced out the window and spotted a bedraggled middle-aged woman waving her arms wildly, trying desperately to flag down the departing bus. The driver probably saw this but chose to ignore her plea. Tough luck. Had she been more attractive, Walter believed, her efforts would doubtless have met with greater success. She dropped her arms as the bus accelerated. A minute late . . . too bad—Walter sympathized with her. Chance—one turn of the card . . . *bam!*

Then Walter noticed, reflected in the window, the face of the man seated next to him. He observed with a start that his neighbor was staring at him, or rather staring at his reflection. It was a trifle disconcerting— that unexpected eye contact with a stranger who had been peering at you, for who knew how long, peering in a sneaky fashion. Mildly embarrassed, Walter smiled at the mirrored face. The other man did not respond. Although his eyes pointed at Walter, he seemed oblivious of him, evidently preoccupied.

"A minute late . . . a buck short," Walter chortled, referring to the poor woman abandoned on the bus platform. If the man had intended to reply, he had no time because at that instant his cell phone rang. Shrill, piercing, abrupt, it startled Walter, zinging a bolt of anger through his gut.

"Hi. Ned speaking. Yeah, I'm here. Where else would I be? What took you so long?" Ned (good to have the guy's name) must have been expecting the call. He was speaking rather loudly, as people on cell phones invariably did. Christ, anyone on the bus could overhear if they wanted to. "Did I say that? No, I didn't say that. When? If you want me to say I'm sorry—forget it. No, I understand . . . I just disagree. So drop it. I said drop it. What are you crying about now?"

Walter was uncertain what to do. He had an impulse to cover his ears, more or less mocking the situation in which he'd been placed. He was still gazing at the man's reflection in the window, and the man was still looking at him with that same blank unacknowledgment, as though he hadn't yet realized Walter's presence. "We can't meet tonight. I just can't. I'm not accountable to you. No . . . stop crying."

Walter glowered, incensed at this presumptuous bastard staring absently at him in the window. The bastard seemed to be conversing with a woman whom he'd upset. Naturally, Walter couldn't piece it all together. He wanted to order the jerk to hang his dirty laundry elsewhere. Ned was telling the woman, "I don't want to deal with any more of this bullshit." You don't want to deal with any more of this bullshit, Walter found himself echoing internally. Oddly, Walter felt an urge to defend this unknown woman from this con-man. Like . . . just punch the fucker in the mouth. How do you not eavesdrop on this, how do you avoid being drawn in? Didn't the bastard even care? What was he—some kind of pervert, an exhibitionist . . . flashing that cell phone . . . a closet whiney wager?

"No, I haven't done anything to you. You bring this pain on yourself, honey," Ned said. Of course you do, honey, Walter thought. This creep's not about to own any responsibility. Walter could hear this stockbroker correcting a client: "No, it wasn't my fault I lost your money in the market." Christ—the poor bitch on that phone who had to contend with him.

Other than Ned's racket, the passengers seemed awfully hushed. Maybe everyone was listening in. The guy's voice certainly carried throughout the bus. A captured audience. Walter wondered, did it bother anybody else? Surely, it did. But hell, maybe not. All these foreign psyches—the repressed . . . who could say? People valued privacy damn little these days. After all, wasn't that why this bastard was getting away with this shit? Of course everybody was stressed out and frazzled, hunting for a glimmer of diversion. Maybe they loved listening in; maybe this was a bus load of perverts—voyeurs.

In the glare of the glass, Walter Bailey detected his own glare. The image was arresting—glaring at himself, seeing himself so full of rage, a rage that in this position appeared leveled at himself. How peculiar. Walter played with the conceit: the glaring yet transparent reflection also permitted you to see through yourself. Was this the first time he'd ever caught this sight of his self-directed anger? Did it reveal anything about the way he felt toward himself? Distracted by Ned's chatter, Walter let the question slip away unanswered.

"I'm hanging up now. Call me back when you come to your senses. 'Bye. No, I don't want to talk anymore. 'Bye." Walter heard a birdlike chirp when the bastard pressed the hang-up button. Ned shifted away from the window and faced forward. Taken aback, Walter did the same. He couldn't decide what to do. Miffed, churned up he clearly was, but also somewhat guilty that he had, indeed, been listening in, peeking in the window. Angry, yes, that his own privacy had been invaded, but also because he had been compelled to eavesdrop. Should he confront the issue or just let it pass? He contemplated the matter. What would he gain by confronting the man? He wasn't likely to reform the insensitive clod. And after all, the phone call *was* over. And who could say, maybe the call was important? It sounded like it was. Why aggravate your aggravations? Hey, live and let live. Walter allowed that maybe he had overreacted. He was tired. He had suffered some money loss; he felt nagged at by those comp. papers. Yeah, he just wanted to veg out, read a little. Okay, so do that, he advised himself. From the corner of his eye, Walter marked how motionless Ned sat . . . a bit too motionless, as though composed of stone.

After the wave of anger had in fact subsided, with an audible sigh of relief, Walter Bailey opened his book and commenced reading. The book, entitled *Primal Scenes*, Walter had picked up at the Strand on Twelfth Street for a couple of dollars. It contained some pretty lurid stuff. The author seemed to regard the world as some sort of poetic nightmare. But exhausted, Walter's concentration wavered, and after about fifteen minutes, he closed the book, switched off the overhead lamp, leaned back, and shut his eyes.

How very quiet the coach was, quiet as a graveyard. He could have been riding a ghost train. His neighbor with the phone certainly resembled a ghost. And all these other dead souls packed around him . . . yeah, a mausoleum on wheels.

His mind drifted. I'm the you ya buried, hon, the black, dirty part. The soil, you mean?

Walter briefly entertained the possibility that he might have ventured into the *Twilight Zone*. He had always found it curious how his mind, when fatigued, would meander into such eerie terrains. As expected, though, the vibration and the hum of the bus massaged away any remaining irritations. It was like being carried in the powerful embrace of a giant mother—yes, but transported where? He fell asleep and saw himself as a child running through Central Park. At first he was dashing across the rolling green summer lawn; then he was dashing with frantic urgency, as though in response to a ringing in his ears, a ringing summoning him, as though he must . . . *Answer the phone!*

Walter woke, alarmed and gasping, trying to place the voice that was speaking to him. "What took you so long?" the voice asked. But no, the man on the cell phone wasn't addressing Walter. "No, I'm not mad, are you? No? Good. What? Well, what do you do on a friggin' bus? Hold your breath. Know what I mean? You're bored. What's to do? Now, if you were here, sweetheart . . . well, we'd talk turkey." Talk turkey? Jolted from sleep, that phrase served to focus Walter's attention. Talk turkey—what did that mean? Walter knew, but he couldn't quite recall. Who was this con-man next to him, speaking this corny lingo?

Walter felt prickles of heat in the back of his neck as his rage resurfaced. He then turned and stared directly at the bastard. Ned, however, absorbed in his little tête-à-tête, appeared not to remark this. "A long day, baby. I'm beat."

"I'm beat, too," Walter abruptly declared and quickly flicked back on the reading lamp. Get a little light on the subject. Although he surprised himself with the comment, Ned ignored it.

"What?" Ned said to the caller.

"I'm beat, too," Walter repeated, adding extra volume. "So beat."

"Wait . . . hold a sec," Ned said into the phone, then turning and frowning, said, "Sorry . . . are you speaking to me?"

"Would you mind hanging up your cell phone?" Walter asked, in a tone of fake repose, which betrayed bridled rage. His heart pounded like a fist.

"Hang up the phone?"

"Uh-huh," Walter said.

The man chuckled, as though he had heard a joke, then turned from Walter, and resumed his conversation. "Hi . . . I'm back. It's nothing."

"It's nothing!" Walter mocked angrily. "Hang it up."

"Wait . . . hold on," Ned spoke into the phone, then said to Walter, "What's the problem, friend?"

"The problem is *you* on the phone, friend."

"Me on the phone?" Ned's countenance somehow managed to combine a scowl with a smirk.

"Oh yeah," Walter answered, "you on the phone." With furrowed brows, the two stared at each other for a long moment—one bemused, one enraged.

And then returning to his phone, Ned said, "Look, Kim, I gotta call you back. I'll explain later. I said, I will explain later. 'Bye." He jabbed the off-button, and again simply sat stone still.

"You're pretty unaware, aren't you, Ned?" Walter observed.

"Am I bothering you?"

"Does Kimberly know our circumstances here?" Walter asked, glad the woman's name had finally emerged. Names betokened substance. Although for Walter, Kim possessed no substance at all—disembodied, voiceless, inferred, just another invisible presence he had to watch out for to escape getting blindsided. All these wireless connections.

"Excuse me . . .," Ned returned, sounding even more bewildered. "What has Kimberly to do with you?"

"You and Kim are embezzling all my space."

"You mean, talking on the phone?"

"I do."

"It doesn't seem to bother anybody except you."

"Well, I don't know . . . *them*, you'd have to ask. But speaking for myself, it's rude. Do you really not know that?"

"That sign up front says 'No smoking/No radios.'" Ned was indignant. "Cell phones aren't against the law, bud. It's a free country."

"And to make matters worse, Ned—you talk so loud. Is that 'cause Kim can't hear too well?"

"You want to say something to me, do it without the insults. And don't mention Kim again. I mean it."

"But you see, I feel *you've* insulted me. That's the part you're slow to grasp."

At that second, the phone rang again. The eyes of the two men locked. Walter noted how very physically near this man was to him. Something was astir within him that couldn't entirely be ascribed to anger. It wasn't fear. Ned was too dapper to resort to violence.

"Don't answer it," Walter whispered in a tone that astonished him because it hinted at something almost intimate. The phone rang again. In the pause, Walter whispered, "Let Kim wait, Ned," and pushed his chin forward, closing the distance between them by about an inch. The phone rang again.

"You gotta be nuts, fella," Ned declared, also in a whisper, as he punched the answer-button. "Look, can't talk now. Everything's fine. Tell you later. Kim . . . no, later. 'Bye." He shut off the phone. "Now, stop bugging me," Ned barked. Then he raked his fingers through his exquisitely combed hair.

"You bugged me first," was Walter's retort, delivered as a bark of his own. Noticing Ned glancing past his shoulder, Walter turned and observed that everyone on the bus seemed to be staring at them. Walter couldn't help but grin at all these dark, silent faces. (The you ya buried, hon.) What were these spectators thinking of these two combatants? Walter imagined that perhaps they viewed him as their champion, the man who speaks up against inequities. Returning to Ned, Walter attempted to carry on the conversation. "Do you want to talk?"

"Not with you," Ned replied. "I'd like you to leave me the fuck alone. Understand?"

"Leave *you* alone?" Walter exclaimed. "We seem not to inhabit the same universe of discourse." It occurred to Walter that this fellow actually had failed to get his point. What do we have here? Walter wondered, as a measure of calmness resettled within him. This scuffle,

Walter could now recognize, did not result from a genuine disagreement. No—two people can hardly be viewed as disagreeing if each is responding *to something different.* And that was happening here. Apples and oranges. No, they were reacting differently—but not to the *same* thing.

How to get the same thing on the table? An idea struck Walter. He opened *Primal Scenes,* which had been lying in his lap, and facing the ear of his antagonist, began reading aloud sentences and passages that he selected at random. He wasn't sure why he had chosen this desultory method. Perhaps it vaguely resembled the gaps and blind spots that he had encountered while overhearing one side of Ned's phone dialogues. He read:

"Everything comes to you by way of indirection. Oh, Amanda. With your eyes so inscrutably closed now, what do you see?"

He flipped randomly to another page:

"Their lips press firmly against each other's, but clearly the feeling of that kiss must be considerably deadened by the shrouds that drape around their heads. Did you ever kiss a broad in a shroud, Phil? No? I'll tell you about it sometime."

With a grimace, Ned gaped at Walter, while the latter turned to another page and continued to read:

"You married a woman named Agnes Thatcher Lake, a carnival queen, dancer, tightrope walker, bareback rider, and lion tamer. Now there was a package! The ideal catch for ya, Bill."

Another page at random:

"She dreamed she stood naked before a full-length mirror, swaying from side to side, wondering at her body. Some engrossing paradox troubled her. A voice told her, 'Figure this out—then eat.'"

"What's this all about?" Ned demanded.

"Don't worry . . . forget plot. Plot counts for nothing nowadays. Postmodern. Insert anything anywhere. Juxtapose. Throw in the kitchen sink . . . phone calls . . . Kim, Ned, me—burps and farts, any junk'll do. À la John Cage—get it? Any thump on the eardrum's music. Every card in the deck's a wild card. Boundaries . . . for the birds."

"What do you think you're doing?"

"Reading. What do you think I'm doing?"

"Well, read to yourself."

"Why? There's no law against it, is there?" Noticing that Ned seemed again to be checking out the bus people, Walter looked and discovered them still looking at Ned and him. Walter gestured widely with his arms, apparently wishing to encompass everyone on the bus. Then he shouted, "Okay—you folks wanna hear more? Okay, you got it." And raising his voice, he resumed reading:

"'This,' he whispered, pausing between each word, 'this . . . is . . . the . . . only . . . scar . . . I . . . bear.'"

He chose another passage:

"*Quickly he sank. Total blackness. He realized that his eyes must be closed, but he knew with certainty the sea was red; so evidently he saw nothing, except what his imagination engendered in this crimson darkness.*"

"Enough!" Ned shouted. Walter heard the people on the bus grumble. He felt the restless undercurrent of the natives. The soil was trembling. Vibrating, humming, the bus sped on.

"No, no, listen. You'll like this part, Ned," Walter said and then continued:

"*'You're not supposed to see me; you're not supposed to call me. You're supposed to leave us the fuck alone. See?'*"

Walter paged quickly through the book.

The phone rang.

"Hello," Ned growled. "Damn it, I said I can't talk right now." He hung up.

"Kim? Yes . . . here—listen to this, Ned," Walter said, feigning passion:

"*Terrified, yes, but something other, very definitely, also arose within her that day that intermixed with the terror.*"

"Hey, Kimberly might just love this stuff," Walter suggested. "Ring her up, drag that crybaby in here. Talk turkey—bang her in the open . . . local street theater. Everything's a drama, but no big narratives, mind you—home-cooked neighborhood crap. Something folks just bump into. You know, nonsense we're coerced into deciphering. Get us all in there. Poor Kim, gang-bang her. Everybody here's game. Why not? Shove that fuckin' cell phone up our asses; make us like it. Hey, Ned—for your dick, honey, every orifice a free ride . . . cum in any ear you like. Ring-a-ding. Rouse the dead. Use it or lose it, baby. Here, listen, let me know what you think." He read:

"*Desire—a dark, turbulent undercurrent, flooding the walls of her will. It was this precise concoction of emotions that would later revisit her at the summits of intercourse and knock her out—*"

"*Stop,* unless you wanta belt in the fuckin' mouth."

"Cold-cock me, will ya, Ned. Well, I guess we've reached the summit of our intercourse," Walter said and exhaled heavily. All of Walter Bailey's wrath had dissipated. He was surprised—surprised at himself—unsure of exactly what had happened. Something buried had burst or blossomed. "Okay, we fought it out. It's a tie. Clean break," Walter said, now beaming at Ned. He felt like some kind of Buddha, self-enlightened, smiling beneficently upon his former foe. The smile was profound, unrelenting, embracing, quite irresistible. Beneath the force of its appeal, Ned succumbed, shook his head, and let his own lips also spread into a smile, bountiful—Walter believed—in the generosity of concession.

"Here," Ned said. "Keep it as a souvenir, buddy." And he handed the cell phone to Walter, who—though quite surprised—accepted it with a gracious nod. "You know you're a wacko," Ned noted, elbowing Walter's arm gently.

"I gotta grant you that," Walter confessed. A ripple of suspicion crossed Walter's mind. Was Ned playing a joker here, trying to trump him, to snatch a little of the moral high ground for himself? Sure, Walter could read it that way—as a plot maliciously redirected. If that had, indeed, occurred . . . well—Walter could admit—it was impressive.

"Now, I don't want us to get started again," Ned said, with a low, amiable chuckle, "but given all we've been through, shouldn't I at least mention that BO of yours I've had to tolerate since the moment you sat down?"

Well, he'd be damned! There it was—out of the blue, the sucker punch. An O. Henry ending. "Okay, Ned, you tagged me with that one. I didn't realize it till I boarded the bus. Pretty gross. I'm embarrassed. I apologize. Nothing I can do about it now."

"Yeah, well, forget about it. No big deal," Ned said and laughed.

"We gotta stomach each other, right?"

"Two New Yorkers? You bet." They both laughed.

Then Walter turned and once again surveyed the bus people. They were still frozen in hypnotic attention. Looking back at them, he was keenly aware that there was so much about them that he couldn't see. Underground. The dead—perhaps ultimately unforgiving, but looking on nonetheless. Invisibly there. Dangerous. He'd have to keep a sharp eye peeled. You're standing on the soil, bud. Call me up. He smiled at himself. Yeah, he was a wacko. Any plot was preferable to nonsense. But upon all those assembled here, Walter Bailey also smiled, giving them to understand that the performance had now concluded. Several of them nodded, Walter judged, with approval. Perhaps it was a moment of mutual gratitude: he and Ned had amused them, and they had spared the white men the murderous consequences of their latent wrath—for a while, anyhow. I'm the you ya buried, hon. Call me up. Triumphant, Walter raised the cell phone aloft, as one would a trophy. And grinning—Walter Bailey presumed, with favor—the dark-faced, indulgent races turned away to mind their own business.

The Voyeuse

The Photograph

The young woman scrutinizes the photograph with all the elements of her heart and her imagination suspended. It is of a man and a woman either making passionate love or simply fucking intensely without the love. Either some third person had taken the picture or the camera had been preset for an automatic time release. They are both probably in their early thirties. The woman's eyes are closed, and her mouth gapes. Obviously she is panting, enraptured. The man stares at her face, much of which is encircled with the woman's luxurious black hair. The arrangement of their bodies and the position of the camera intend to stress as flagrantly as possible exactly what is happening. The woman stretches her long legs as wide apart as she can so the man's erection can be seen halfway inserted into her vagina. Her pubic hair glistens, as does the man's hard penis, so the vagina must be very wet. Their bodies also glisten. The genitals occupy the precise center of the picture. The woman clasps her hands behind her head. Her back arches strikingly in what must be an almost painful curve. Thick pillows have been intentionally pushed under the small of her back to force that high degree of angling. The man's hands squeeze the woman's breasts so tightly that it seems her red nipples have popped out under great pressure. Maybe the man is staring at her nipples and not at the woman's face. It is difficult to be sure. The woman's right leg aims like an arrow off the bed, straight and firm. It points to the camera or to the person taking the picture or to the person looking at the picture. You are meant to follow the length of the leg up to the genitals, but also to keep sliding your eyes up and down its lovely lines. The man's left foot pushes against the floor, not only to secure his balance but also to enhance the power of his penetration as much as possible. Physically, he looks very strong. His muscles are sharply defined. Apparently, the lovers have been at this a

long while. Although the somewhat artificial pose has to have been staged,
the posturing fails to affect their ardent involvement with each other.
Perhaps it even increases the ardor. They are both very beautiful. The
young woman, the spectator, conjectures (because she recognizes the
floral pattern of the bedspread strewn on the floor) that she must have
been about twelve years old when this photograph was taken—six years
ago. The scene pictured before her is so shocking she seems to be gazing
at two strangers. And yet, except for her mother, these are the two people
whom she has loved more than anyone else in the world. Until this
moment, she has believed that she knew them as well as she knew herself.
This is a picture of her father and her aunt.

The Aunt

"So you discovered that picture, did you, darling? Sometimes I worried
that you might, though maybe it's good you did. Who can say? I guess
that one was taken about . . . oh, I don't know . . . about ten years ago."

"That long?"

"Maybe not. I like it. It's very theatrical. The colors . . . quite vivid,
aren't they? A touch unreal. Possibly too much light. A bit overstated. I
remember it like yesterday. I am very sorry if it brings you pain, my child.
Evidently, it does. Does it?"

"I feel like killing myself."

"Why?"

"I'm confused, Auntie. Please, you must tell me the truth."

"The truth? Oh, that. You sound like your father. You mean mine,
my truth, don't you? Of course you do. I haven't any other."

"Since the car accident . . . since mother's and father's deaths last
year . . . yours is the only truth there is."

"Your father used to assert that all truth is only part of a story that we
make up. He said that all the time. As an academic, a true philosopher,
he should have known, I suppose."

"Please, Auntie, help me through this."

"Where did you find this picture, my precious?"

"In the bottom of mother's jewelry case. I guess it was meant to be a
secret drawer. There were others there too—all like this one."

"Ah yes, of course, it would happen that way, wouldn't it? Even as a
little girl my sister would conceal things where they would be easily found.
Even when she played hide and seek, she'd hide next to your elbow. She
couldn't bear being excluded."

"You're not hiding things here so well yourself, are you, Auntie?"

"No. Is this what overexposure is?"

"You're very beautiful. You always were. You still are. It's hard to take my eyes off you. It's easy to see what father saw in you."

"What did he see?"

"Beauty."

"Your mother had plenty of that."

"Yes, but a different kind. You were always very sensuous. They spoke about that often. They called you lusty and luscious."

"Did they? Well, yes, they would. He certainly made much of that aspect of me. So did I. So did your mother . . . All right. What am I required to say about this photograph? You look very anguished."

"The wool was pulled over my eyes."

"Shouldn't it have been?"

"What can I believe in?"

"Make-believe."

"Did my father love you?"

"Yes, I'd say he did—in a way. He loved your mother too—probably more. Mostly, my dear, he wanted to . . . well . . . fuck me. May I speak so crudely?"

"I hoped you would."

"Would an aunt address her niece this way?"

"Most of them probably wouldn't. But would you, for my sake?"

"He insisted on calling what we did 'fucking.' Sometimes that just *is* the proper word. Well, fucking, that was fine with me. He said he was trying to preserve his immortal soul from too much of my . . . 'embodiment,' he called it. That was both amusing and perfectly true. But never mind."

"No, tell me, what do you mean?"

"He needed for sex to be earthy, dirty, even debasing at times. And I can't say that being debased *some* never appealed to me; it did, a little. Having that side of ourselves affirmed frees us. But your father had no intentions of leaving your mother, nor would I ever have wanted him to. That, let me assure you, was never in the cards."

"When did you begin this, Auntie?"

"Begin what?"

"Fucking my father."

"Oh . . . even before your parents wed, we—as your dear father phrased it—jumped each other like rabbits in spring time. I'm the one who introduced your parents, as you know. They wanted a child, I didn't. Thank god they raised you, my darling one."

"My mother was not enough for my father?"

"No, nor was he enough for her. He was always very guilty about everything, you know. Guilt generated those interminable philosophical obsessions of his. He could thrash himself into the most fantastic erections by simply puzzling over high-minded abstractions. Yes, it's true. Just as you can see there for yourself, all captured in living color."

"I don't know what you mean."

"Just look at his gorgeous muscles shining, a body working at me tirelessly, but with a brain that never shut off. Dear me . . . he must have been cogitating deeply right here, at the precise moment the camera snapped us. Ah yes, I recall he was . . . the difference between appearance and reality. Always a bedeviling concern. Yes . . . I'm sure that's what he's working on here. I'm afraid you caught us in a philosophical act, sweetheart. Learning that should attenuate the shock. No, don't imagine for an instant that that absorption in your father's gaze is fully occupied with me. It never was. He would have been too ashamed to reveal such total craving for me. But he revealed enough. You must admit—I do have our Plato hooked in pretty good, don't I?"

"You think this is funny."

"In a way . . . but not really."

"You always had such a strange sense of humor, Auntie. But nothing's funny to me. Not now. Who can I trust? Who are you? I have no idea of where in the world I am."

"That's why you're here now, isn't it? My lost child."

"I've lost my balance, Auntie."

"My fallen child too."

"What have I stumbled on? Can't you lift me up and get me out of this?"

"Lift you up . . . oh yes—if you let me. But I can't very well undo the fall that you've taken—the nasty fall, as you see it—or remake us all so that you would never have been lost in the first place. I can't give you back what's now lost to you and to me, as well, forever. You want me to rewrite this story?"

"No."

"Yes, you do."

"That can never be."

"It's done all the time."

"I don't understand."

"Only imagination can save us from the hell our imaginations created. Your father said that. That would be his advice to you."

"What? Everything's becoming more confusing."

"That's what being lifted up's about."

"I'm bewildered. My god, is this *really* my father and my aunt?"

"Is it? Or two masked imposters, you wonder. Or merely my aunt and my father nakedly wearing disguises other than those they've always worn? Obviously, things are not as overstated as I thought."

"Don't laugh at me, Auntie, please."

"Forgive me. I don't really know what to say."

"What's going on, Auntie? Please."

"Odd, isn't it, how we can never make anything clear? We always lose the focus."

"I thought this picture was clear."

"No, you didn't, or you wouldn't be confronting me."

"I need you to tell me what I'm seeing, that's all."

"That's all . . . hmm . . . all right. I'm trying. Where was I? Your father's guilt over fucking me, and even more than that, guilt over his love for me that derived from that fucking, made guilt—for him, but not for me—the very essence of our affair. With your mother, he felt desire for other women. With other women, no desire at all, and he longed only for your mother."

"But here he is with you, Auntie."

"Yes. Well, I proved the exception. As your mother's sister, I embodied something of your mother, we could say, and yet I was another woman. Such ambiguities boost the sex stuff immensely. It's all rather tangled— as desire invariably is. A maze. Someday you'll find out."

"Someday! What else?"

"What else? Well, let me think . . ."

"Tell me, please."

"Your father used to beg me to whip him—how 'bout that?"

"Whip him? No!"

"Or he would enforce some kind of bondage on me. In fact—unless I misremember—in this very snapshot, leather straps tie my hands behind my head. Oh, don't be so shocked. Please. It's done all the time."

"All the time?"

"No, but frequently. Naturally, he neither received nor asked for such—such what?—kinky entertainment from your mother. Not until . . . anyway . . ."

"What do you mean?"

"I'll get to that—maybe. Anyway . . . he needed your mother pure as snow, perhaps also as cold as snow, somewhat withholding sexually, yes, as long as she remained—and she did—in every other way understanding and indulgent. He wanted a virgin and a whore. Is there a man who isn't a Dr. Jekyll and Mr. Hyde? Hm, some, I suppose, are just Mr. Hyde. But sex is oddly concocted for everyone. Your mother loved the way everything between us had come to be so complexly devised. She and I *knowingly*, let us say, played our parts. Your poor father, however, unknowingly played his, in this regard."

"What regard?"

"She and I were quite perfectly suited for him—even more perfectly than he realized. May I speak this bluntly to you, my darling one?"

"Yes . . . please . . . bluntly. I said I wanted you to. More than he realized?"

"Pretty soon your father had to divulge our wickedness to your mother. A cumbersome confession it proved, too, even though he spent an agonizing year rehearsing it. Your mother, with feigned magnanimity, forgave him and then added, a few days later, to his total consternation, that . . . well, maybe . . . after some honest soul searching on her side—maybe it was really fine with her. What an actress!"

"What was fine with her?"

"That he could, if he and I so chose, continue right on. That was rather cruel of her—and also of me. You see—all along, from day one, I had been graphically relating to your mother every single juicy detail of this steamy romance. And why not? Hadn't she and I shared everything since childhood? Well, we had. She relished our sexual shows, like watching x-rated movies, she claimed."

"Pornography? Is that what this is?"

"Only when you focus too immoderately, my dear, rather as we're doing now . . . Enough?"

"No—finish it, Auntie. You must."

"Finish it? I don't know how to do that. But very well, my love. Your mother felt very much included—'insinuated,' she said. She cherished your father's mind and his guilty way of being in the world—we both did."

"His guilty way?"

"Not that guilt interrupted the flow of the River Sex, mind you. No, guilt often intensified it in strange ways. Only things wrong and dirty interest this family. You're fast becoming a chip off our old blocks. Anyway, sex was something your mother mostly appreciated from a slight distance; that is, she was an unabashed voyeuse, bless her heart. Peeping Judy, she named herself. Are you a Peeping Judy?"

"Am I?"

"Seems so. But back to Mom, Dad, and Auntie. Your father—with his head forever stuck in clouds of metaphysics, while his swollen organ forever plunged my inner depths—no, he never had a clue about this conspiracy until after his grand confession and your mother's seeming beneficence. No, not till after that, when she *then* became an even more . . . well, highly featured spectator, should we say . . . But what has any more of this to do with you, my wounded pussy cat?"

"What a question!"

"Yes."

"Auntie, it means everything."

"You're making it everything."

"It's not funny for me, Auntie. I could die from this."

"You could—being, as you've always been, humorless as a stone—you could, if you work at it hard enough and let it seep thoroughly enough into your bloodstream. But maybe all you need to know is that your mother and father loved you deeply and that you felt their love, and the way they loved you, you felt was the right way for you. That's all that finally counts. And I love you too, and you very well know that. What else, tell me, really matters?"

"I don't know."

"You'll find out."

"Why did you take these despicable pictures?"

"Are they despicable? To us, they weren't. But why? Hm . . . probably because our guilt and our pride insisted we preserve incriminating evidence."

"I don't know what that means."

"Neither do I, perhaps."

"Please hold me, Auntie."

"Oh yes, my darling. Come here."

"I can't tell where I am, Auntie."

"You're here."

"Where?"

"In the scene you've found."

"What do you mean?"

"What you've seen you've entered into."

"Into what?"

"Into the whole of us."

"I've been killed. A world of lies. I wasn't ready for this"

"Who ever is?"

"To think, I saw nothing. I've been dead all my life. Oh, Auntie, how'd I get here? Can I ever get out?"

"Not through the door by which you entered."

The Memory

My parents had taken me along with them to visit Auntie, who had recently moved to another area of the city. I must have been about six years old. My aunt introduced me to half a dozen neighborhood children with whom I went off to play hide and seek.

It was spring, early evening, and somewhat cool outside. Because I was a new kid, when my turn came to hide, they decided to allow me a little extra time—which meant they would count to one hundred, not fifty, and very slowly. They began to count, and I went dashing off at full speed. A couple of blocks away, I darted into a building, the front doors of which stood open. Breathless, I rapidly ascended a flight of stairs and turned down a corridor and then down another and then climbed another set of stairs and cut into a large room that connected to several other rooms of varying sizes, one of which exposed another network of hallways that forked off in various directions. Down one of these inviting passages I raced, shot around one corner and then another and then bolted up another staircase and then maybe another and another, and once again streaked in and out of a series of rooms. Now and then I'd hit a blind alley, and I'd reverse and aimlessly choose another course.

Eventually, beginning to tire, I noticed a coat closet. I entered it, crouched down, and partially closed the door. Out of breath and pumped full of excitement, I thought that I had uncovered the consummate hiding place. I peered into the gray, empty room. At this most exalted moment, I suddenly realized the emptiness of all these rooms. This large old building that I had been racing through was completely abandoned. At first, this merely enhanced my pride in having discovered such an ideal hideout. In my elated state, I waited and I listened, imagining the terrible befuddlement of my new friends and the admiration they must now hold for my unsurpassed skill at locating a spot to hide where I could never be found.

There I sat, my arms folded around my raised legs, my chin resting on my knees, not quite comprehending yet that I was now more absolutely alone than I had ever been in my life. Time passed. The daylight had begun to fade. I opened the closet door and stared into the vacant, commodious room. I waited and waited for what began to feel like a long time. I grew very tired. I am not certain, but I think I must have even fallen asleep and dreamed because—this could not have happened—I remember a chandelier falling and shattering to pieces, and crystals of glass scattering on the floor, glittering like gems in a jewelry box.

Perhaps only an hour passed. I don't know. I was becoming a little chilly. I rose and stepped quietly over to the window, expecting to spy my friends scurrying wildly about, searching for me, perhaps worrying about me. But the street appeared totally deserted, no signs of life, no cars even. It was then I became frightened. What if no one would ever be able to find me—having too successfully ferreted out this inviolable hiding place? What if everyone had deserted me—fooled me—and had been playing a game other than the one that I assumed we were playing? In running away—and so expertly too—I had permitted *them* to hide from me. Had I been fiendishly deceived? And from out of nowhere, a horrible thought arose: What if everybody in the world had absconded, died even?

These dreadful possibilities scared me so, I began to sob. I had to get back home. And again, a flash of panic: What if this hideout of mine proved so impeccable that even I couldn't find my way out of it? I attempted to open a window—I think I wanted to scream—but it was sealed shut and so were others that I tried. I started racing through the deserted rooms again, up and down and around through the long halls and steep winding stairways. My footsteps echoed sharply in the silence of what I now understand to have been a vast arrangement of interconnected buildings. Disoriented, I scurried from one floor level to another, bumping into dead ends or locked doors. I crisscrossed rooms that seemed familiar, as well as others that I knew I was entering for the first time. I opened a dozen closet doors; I wanted to find *something*, anything besides more and more emptiness.

All the windows offered diverse views of the outside world, but sometimes a view from the same window, when I would happen upon it again, seemed quite changed, maybe because of the waning light or evening shadows or my increasing fatigue or the blur caused by tears—or fear. Everything was always the same and yet always altering.

From many different windows, I observed, affixed to the side of an adjacent brick building, a colorful billboard collage publicizing circus spectacles. The artist had depicted a ferocious tiger, bright orange with black stripes and splayed claws, midway in its leap through a flaming circle of fire, a snakelike whip striking its powerful back. There was also a voluptuous woman scantily clad, spread-eagled, upside down, her arms and legs tightly bound to a rotating wheel, and daggers, thrown by a wicked-looking man in a black cape, stuck out all along the outline of her exposed body. Next to these scenes stood a clown dressed as a hobo, totally forlorn, white faced, with a fat red down-turned bottom lip and heavy-lidded eyes that shed giant teardrops but seemed concentrated on nothing. He slumped over against the stanchion of a street lantern like a lifeless doll. Everything about this disquieting poster threatened me. I must have reencountered it twenty times. As the most constant feature in this labyrinth, the exhibits displayed on the poster should have served as a fixed point of orientation, but mostly they only succeeded in magnifying my confusion, because none of my perspectives of them remained constant. I should have been relieved, grateful that I had found at least these renditions of life. But no, these figures on the billboard unnerved me: a wild beast, a half-naked woman with knives thrown at her, a painted face of exaggerated despair. Each reappearance of these pictures further aggravated my fears that out of all this emptiness something terrible might materialize, or perhaps worse, nothing at all would materialize and I would be lost forever, frantically searching for an exit from this nightmare into which I had ventured all by myself.

At some point, I actually began to hear human sounds—a woman and a man, sighing and crying out, sometimes as though in pain. It was horrifying. Although frozen in dread, I strained to hear. I felt assailed by utterances, strange and sometimes agonized. The sounds seemed emitted from the interior of the walls that enclosed me. I did not comprehend then that the heating and air vents served to conduct this disturbing commotion. I listened to the voices that came echoing through. "Oh my god!" a woman sobbed. "Oh no, harder! I love you! I love you! Harder! Harder! Hold me. Hold me. Hold me. I'm yours, yours," she screamed, choked with sobs. "Everything's yours. Forever . . . ever . . . ever. Can't you see? Love . . . love . . . love . . ."

I resumed my rushing about—hectically attempting to flee this envelopment of whispering and panting and screaming pain, and yet at the same time, I endeavored fitfully to seek its source, hoping for help from *someone*, anyone to get me out of whatever this place was I was in.

A couple of hours must have lapsed, and I must have covered several miles in my anxious, exhausting wanderings. Dusk had now descended, leaving some of the rooms and other areas almost entirely dark. Other places, however, were dimly lit by high-ceiling lights that had been, apparently, automatically switched on. Also, through certain windows, a full moon cast a pallid blue tint on the blank walls and interminable floors. I had been crying and rushing about so much in such agitation that I had worked myself into a fever and a chill. I wasn't even sure what floor level I occupied because I kept ascending and descending, struggling to find the doorway through which I had entered this desolate building. Although I do believe that I was so utterly caught up in the futility of my enterprise that had I been standing directly in front of that door, it would not necessarily have occurred to me to walk out through it. For some reason, the door *in* was no longer the door *out.*

In my muddled efforts to relocate that door of egress, I somehow managed to climb continually higher in the building until I ended up at the very top in a spacious attic. Here there were no openings into other rooms, no further passageways, no doors other than one to go in and out of. And aside from a rectangular window that extended the entire width of the end of the room, there were no windows. Bewildered, frightened, and exhausted, I stared at the enormous window. The moon's soft wan light flooded through it, painting a large, pale blue square on the floor. In the middle of this patch of lunar light, I discerned a dark silhouette.

To my fatigued perceptions, the scene resembled a huge photograph. I walked slowly forward. I stopped, startled. Now within a few feet of this scene, I could distinguish the shape of a reclining man and a woman, their arms wrapped around each other—sleeping . . . or dead. But no, they moved slightly. After a few moments, irresistibly attracted, I stepped cautiously closer. It looked like there was a mattress under them, with rags and cardboard and rumpled blankets scattered about, along with lots of empty wine and beer bottles. The faces of the two people rested so close together they could have been kissing each other in their sleep. Their bodies lay clothed only by the blue moonlight. No doubt, theirs were the voices, carried through the building's vents, those that had engulfed me so disturbingly. After all my frantic zigzagging seeking to escape the trap in which I had so ingeniously concealed myself, this, *this* then, was what I had found: two drunk, sequestered lovers.

For some reason, I suddenly felt comforted. I moved nearer. The floorboards creaked. The man woke. He lifted his head. He saw me. His eyes gleamed in the moonbeams. We stared at each other for a rather long while, like figures encountering each other in a kind of dreamland. He then smiled, raised his hand slightly, and waved at me. I waved back. He motioned me to the bed and then lowered his head and immediately sank back into sleep. I heard them both breathing heavily. I smelled the alcohol. It was as though I felt the warmth of their breath heating the cold fever of my trembling body. After a few seconds, I tiptoed over and lay down next to the woman. Neither of them moved nor said a word. I scooted over and snuggled closely against her warm, damp back, and placed my arm around her. I touched the man's open hand, and he closed it softly around my fingers. I fell asleep inside the warm sound of their deep breathing.

The Dream

She dreams that she is at a carnival, that she is about sixteen years old. It is a hot, sultry summer evening. In a large city square, a band plays. A dense crowd of masqueraders dance and interweave under lanterns that cast the dancers in eerie patches of multicolored hues. She sees harlequins and demons and domino figures, jugglers and clowns. And close to her, she sees two disheveled tramps, a man and a woman, whom she realizes are not in costumes. They alone are exactly what they appear to be, but she is probably the only person who notices this. They are intoxicated, but so is almost everyone else.

A general merrymaking envelops the young woman, the dreamer, and yet something slightly sinister evokes unease within her. Around the square's more shadowy perimeter, couples only partially clothed, intimately embrace in postures that seem calculated in their lewd details not only to capture her attention, but to confuse and frighten her as well. She observes that other masked figures are either continually emerging from or stealing secretly away into the narrow streets that lead out of the square and go twisting endlessly off into a darkness embedded with alluring obscurities.

Like a sleepwalker, she begins to thread slowly among the commingling throng. Men and women smile invitingly at her, their lips and fingertips touching gently whatever part of her body they can reach. She lets them do anything they wish. With each of these strokes, a smooth, warm current of desire slips tingling beneath the surface of her skin. It is as though she has no clothes on, no resistance at all. She recalls having put on the black satin mask that now covers the top half of her face. But she refrains from glancing down at herself lest she discover what everyone else beholds so clearly and so obviously hungers for—her own nakedness.

Other than those two inebriated tramps—who linger rather intimately near her like useless guardians—she cannot be sure she really knows any of these people who are taking such liberties with her body, arousing her however they please. All whom she passes, with their playful obscenities and lustful liberties, act as though she knows them very well . . . at least they know who she is. When she catches the gleam in their eyes or feels their lips on hers, yes, it does sometimes seem as though she has felt these particular kisses before, although now they are wet, and the tongues that slide into her willing mouth carry too much temptation for her to even bother to understand or try to prevent from soaking into her body's moist pores. Now and then, she hears voices, yes, vaguely familiar, murmuring close to her ear, "We love you, we love you, we love you, we love you."

A grinning harlequin, in a costume of red and black diamonds, offers to blow his breath across her burning breasts to cool her down. His breath is inebriating, like incense. She says, oh no, she cannot possibly permit that because her mother and father are watching, and she starts searching for them so she can prove that she is telling the truth and that she is not afraid of such crude advances. "But everyone is wearing a mask," he notes. "How can you ever know who anyone really is?" he asks her, and she feels the heat of his sweet breath on her throat.

She sees a man and two women standing, gazing up at a huge billboard attached to an old abandoned building. It is an advertisement for the festival. She walks over to them. One of the women carefully inspects her, then smiles, and tenderly caresses her cheek. "Ah yes, there you are. Showing yourself off at last. You are very beautiful. You look like your mother, my darling. Don't be frightened. Love is all that matters here, isn't it? It will be all right. You'll see." The woman takes the man in her arms as though she sought to demonstrate something. He deliberately evades directly confronting any view of the exposed young woman (who happens to be dreaming all this), and unlike almost everyone else, he restrains himself from touching her. Although his face is veiled entirely with a black silk scarf, she knows that he can, and that he has, nonetheless, seen her. He lowers his head as though ashamed. The woman remarks in a kindly tone that he is very intelligent but too cowardly to ever honestly face himself. "Why, he wouldn't even recognize his own face in a mirror," she says and smiles, as though she means not to really offend or embarrass him too much.

Now the young woman, the dreamer, turns to the other woman who aims a camera at the billboard. When the camera clicks, the dreamer finally looks up at the display and discovers there a man and a woman making passionate love, both are wearing masks. The shadows and shape of genitals at the center of the picture are ingeniously configured in such a manner that they seem to represent a mask. The young woman reads what is written beneath the lovers: Make the Mask that Makes You Up. Or do the words say "Wakes You Up"? It is a little blurry, but it somehow appears to be a very important message. She turns, hoping she can now recognize all the different people who have guided her to what she takes to be a grand revelation. But everyone has vanished, even the man who was a coward and the woman who allowed him to hide in her embrace and the other woman who stood right in front of the lovers and boldly photographed them, a beautiful woman who looked like her mother. The dreamer can no longer even find herself. Everybody has disappeared except the inanimate lovers hanging so hugely exposed behind their masks.

The Monologue

Auntie, this could be the death of me. Yes—but what could be the death of us isn't always easy to foretell, my lovely one. Fragile as a flower. Watch where you look. You remember all the pussies curiosity killed. No, not when I should have, not when I slid open the secret drawer where mother hid her jewels more or less in plain sight and I uncovered, as I could scarcely help but do, all the telling photographs of you and father that she—I believe *she*—had taken and kept for who else but me. I thought that I would die then. *Then* and *now*, it seems, my precious. Oh, the rabbit hole you've fallen down. Everything I had been told was a lie. Lust under the skin of everything. About all *that*, no one told you anything, did they? No. They displayed it. Monstrously. "Fuck" is sometimes the perfect word. I'm going to kill myself, plunge an ice pick in my heart. Then what? Nothing. Stop gazing at your reflection. Reflection? Now you sound like Echo. Oh. You're misconceiving yourself, darling. I'm naked now. And believe me—beautifully so, my child. Newly made. I cannot be consoled. Not now. Humorless as stone. Still . . . so exposed, Auntie. Like you, like Father. Two saints fornicating. Such touching self-pity becomes you. Becomes *you*. Was I hiding or being hidden from? What does it matter? Aren't you naked and alone either way? I'm amazed. A maze. I once dreamed beside the bodies of two sleeping souls of love that my unclothed body was part of a festival wherein I was partaken of. Yes. And wasn't the blood of your beauty aroused then? As myself, I saw nothing of myself. I see myself only among fantasia—photographs, dreams, and mirrors . . . a face in the eyes of others. By indirection, let's say. You're either in the picture or snapping it. What's it to be? Either way, you're in it, of it. What I discover is not what I am led to believe I'll find. I know. Amazing, isn't it? We all discover that to be the case. But I can't bear it. I've been beguiled to death. Adulterated. Sometimes "fucked" is the perfect word. I'm going to kill myself . . . unless I'm dead already. Am I, Auntie? We are make-believe. Be one of us. There's nothing besides. For you, love's here too. Yes, but woven out of fabrication. Sometimes it is, and very beautifully, too. Sometimes. I've been misled. Sometimes. Often. Sometimes. Enough. My Aunt and Father fucked before the eyes of Mother and me. So? So—I'm murdered. But the game is called "Misleading." Things are never what they seem. This game is called "Things Are Never What They Seem." Sermons and clichés. Finally—yes. Lies . . . smoke and mirrors. Invitations to imagination. It's all imagined. Yes—imagine that. I blame the adult world. Of course you do. But why? Who are we adults, other than the fantasias of infancy? You dreamed us up long ago. Who's making up who, then? You sound like your father. I found two derelicts copulating on the floor and went to bed with them. Yes. In the morning they carried you home. We were stunned and so relieved I think we started believing in God again. I don't know what any of this means ultimately. Ultimately, no. Nothing. Keep chasing your own tail and you'll fornicate yourself to death. No tale I mean. I recall that even as a child you never laughed. Not once. Anyway, what you're waiting for, you've already made to occur. And you can only weep for the self you see made up and hanging in the sky like a crucified lover in a dream. Is that it, my sweet little pussy in a mask she can't remove? Auntie, take my hand. Yes, of course. I've held you since the day of your birth. Many have. Contradictions and madness. All. Not all. But enough. Who conceived me? You did. And you did too. I'm growing on the ground of deceptions. Where all of us lie. Fragile as an egg. Humpty Dumpty. Auntie, say you're sorry. I'm sorry. Auntie, say you're sorry. I am—and sorry, too, that you must continue to find yourself so damaged. Dead. I'm dead. I can't be as unfeeling as you need for me to be. I was killed to begin with. See? I do. Too much light. You're such a wound licker. A child knocking at Death's door. Say you're sorry. The earth's too old, too full of what none of us will ever have time to learn. Love's whatever it is, oh, so many contradictory things lie there. Anything can be called *love*. So, there. Look at Daddy up me. That's me, all right, no matter who you may have thought I was before you caught your father in me. If you can't see that well—listen, then. The heating vents talk. I'm sorry. Harder, harder . . . take me . . . forever and ever and ever. And what would you do if you found me all aswoon, yes, and bleeding right here on the cold ground, injured mortally? I'd call you "my child." And all of us would circle love round you, spread wide our dripping thighs, and reach our strong arms down and draw you up inside the center of us. Who'll be there with you for that? All those who have already shown up. Everyone till then who's been invisible to you except as you claim to have only viewed them in dreams or moonlight or pictures hidden in Mother's jewelry box. Then call me "my child"—now—again. My child. It's over. No, no more. It's over. I'm left hanging. A hole in my heart in plain sight.

At the Gravesite

Sperm Travels

Dori was as innocent as they come. And in those I'm-not-that-kind-of-girl days, that's saying something. Not that I knew much more. We were sixteen; it was August, the hottest month of the year. It was 1956, in St. Joe, Missouri. What could you expect? She made so much out of nothing, but the nothing *did* turn out to be a big deal: the poor rabbit died, her Transylvania family arbitrated, and I nearly lost the ding. "Randy"—she sobbed—"you gotta do the right thing." I did. I married her with . . . well, *persuasions*, shall we say. I don't know, maybe she wasn't as innocent as I supposed. Here's the story: it's a cautionary tale with a kink.

After my dastardly deed (hold a sec for that), she was superscared. Her grandma (a witch, endowed with the face of a hyena and the body of a gorilla) had told her that sperm travels. *Sperm travels.* Huh? Well, yes, but . . . So, we (mainly I) had done the worst thing . . . maybe ruined our lives—hers especially. That was what she thought. Pretty extreme. I had trouble reading it exactly that way, but with all her screeching and a bit of pounding of me (and herself too) with her fists . . . well, such hysterics convinced me that it *was* possible. (Hey, naive or not, what's not possible? About that, you'll see what I mean.)

She cried profusely, imagining the horrors to come. (Certain other horrors for myself, I hadn't a glimmer of. Hold a sec for that.) Her mom would be appalled; her dad, speechless with shock and rage. Now, this dad you wouldn't want to enrage. He slaughtered beef in a packinghouse and looked as powerful and ferocious as a bull. (For that matter, you wouldn't want to mess with Mom either, or Dori's older brother, Boor, or Grandma . . . hell, everyone in the family had the build of a professional wrestler.)

Anyway, Dori envisioned the family having to move out of town, and for shame hide somewhere in the Ozarks. (Mind you, this family had moved *to* St. Joe *from* the Ozarks.) Moreover, when word leaked out, everyone in our high school would view her as a slut. She sobbed that she might as well just go ahead and embroider a scarlet *A* on her breast. (Wouldn't you know, we'd both just read that Hawthorne novel on the sneak, a book the '50s thought had a lot of sex in it. Jeez.) And me . . . she prophesied, I'd be acclaimed some big stud . . . at her expense. Such theatrics. Still, the distress seemed real enough.

"How could you have done this?" she screamed at me. (A berserk streak ran through her at times.) "How could I have let you?"—she screamed that at me too. "We loved each other," she said. I said, "That's why, Dor, because we love each other." She countered with, "Well, I hate you now." But she begged me never to leave her, to help her. "Randy—do something!" Huge tears rolled down her cheeks.

This was not—I hate to say it—a mind well composed. But it broke my heart to see this. Here before me, the one I loved, knocking me about the head, but beautiful as an angel no matter what—she, filled with suffering caused by me, and I could do nothing. Over and over, I said I was sorry, promised I'd do whatever she wanted. "Oh great," she said, "the horse is already out of the barn"—which seemed like a funny way of putting it. I said that if she were late with her period, we'd have to call a doc and find out what to do. She said she'd rather die than call a doctor. This was a small gossipy town—everyone would know in five minutes; her shame would go public. (This also was possible.)

Her complexion already glowed like a red apple. At one point, she declared we'd have to marry. I hemmed and hawed and made it clear that—yes, absolutely, I'd do anything she wished except that! She said (almost as an aside), well, her family wouldn't like that. (Oh, the things you just don't quite hear. Her family wouldn't like that . . . Wait a sec.)

This agony continued for a while. Then she turned from me and stared off into space; her jaw dropped, as though a bright idea had struck. "Maybe that *would* be best," she said. "What?" I asked. "If I just died," she replied. (How did I know she would say that?) Yes, she said, she would pray to God for forgiveness and then swallow all her mom's sleeping pills. (Sleeping pills—now, those wouldn't be prescription, you see. No, they'd be some concoction of weeds, roots, and flowers, a teaspoon of rat's blood. Witches' brew.) Poor Dor. I'd never seen anyone so tormented. And yes, it did seem that my ding (she called it "the ding") had done this.

I held her, tried to soothe her, wept a few scalding tears myself. We were both Catholics; guilt flowed as freely as blood through our veins. It looked bad (if Grandma were right, and hers was a grandma incapable of error, so endowed with ancient wisdom was she . . . and did I mention, really mean-looking too). But Dori could be so immoderate in her reactions, and moreover, she was superstitious; her whole family was out of the Dark

Ages. (Once, eating at their house, I accidentally knocked over a shaker of salt. Everyone—Mom, Dad, Dori, and brother, Boor—made the sign of the cross, and with heads bowed, all mumbled a few prayerful words. Even the cat, a foul-smelling brat, made a funny little gesture, folding her paw inward. The cat wiggled her whiskers, and then, for ten long seconds, the tribunal stared at me, an emissary of Satan. To me, her mom, dad, and brother looked like a trio of assassins. Crazy . . . utterly humorless. In hindsight, had I an ounce of sense I would have cupped the ding with both hands and fled. You'll see what I mean in a sec.)

Okay, so . . . what did I do to upset Dori? The ding popped out of my pants—a will of its own. Yeah, so, you'd think—no big deal. It had pulled this trick a couple of times before, always hard as a marble statue. And as always, Dori—beautiful as an angel of God—stared at it in fascination, as though she too had petrified into stone. That night (the night that caused the upset), Dori touched the ding . . . quickly, lightly, as she would a slimy toad (mind you, only this much after months of coaxing!). Fierce with anticipation, naturally the ding shot off in a flash.

That's it. No big deal, you say. (Actually it was. It was the first time. Actually it was for other, graver reasons soon forthcoming.) But in the deed itself, where's the crime? You'd never guess. I shot off a veritable hose, a fountain, right. I said it was the first time. Mouth agape and wide-eyed, she had seen it coming. She ducked, as one would from a hail of bullets, and covered herself *down there*. Okay, so? So, a drop hit her exposed thigh. So? So her grandma, fount of arcane wisdom, had, as I said, told her, *sperm travels*. Like I said, the Dark Ages. Sure, I'd heard that too . . . somewhere (no sex ed classes in those days). But since I wasn't perfectly certain what it meant, I deferred; I let her spook me.

"What if it traveled right up and into me?" she asked again and again, as worried as if she'd swallowed a drink laced with arsenic. "Right up and into you?" I echoed. "How do you know it traveled into you, Dor?" "That stuff knows where it's going, doesn't it?" "I guess so, yes," was my studied response.

Good Catholic girl, pretty good Catholic boy—hey, genitals were things you didn't mess with. Her grandma had warned her, "Never—*never*, do you hear?—touch yourself *down there*"—except when bathing, and even then recite the Hail Mary—"'cause God will turn your hands fiery red so everyone will know what you've been up to, evil child." And I'll be damned if it wasn't true. One morning, Dor awoke and discovered a radiant red rash on the fingers and palm of her left hand (the devil's hand). She had to own that, unbeknown to her, that hand must have strayed into her pajama bottoms and fiddled around.

That left hand, Grandmother had cautioned, was the hand to watch. "But that's hard to do when I'm sleeping, Grammy," she'd protested. "No," Grammy insisted. "You're yourself when you're sleeping too." "But, Grammy, what if it itches?" "Then you've had nasty thoughts, child. Pray—don't scratch." Dori told me (why, I don't know) that her brother, Boor, had caught sight of the offending hand glowing in the dark and offered to chop it off. (A family of barbaric but effective methods.) She declined Boor's offer, although—honestly?—it wouldn't have surprised me had she accepted. This was one bizarre family, I kid you not.

But for me (homely-as-a-hound-dog me) Dori's beauty was compelling, blinding. It totally distracted my attention, as in a nightmare a gorgeous naked woman would be standing amidst a gang of ghouls. Anyway, to conceal the rash, she wore gloves for a month. Luckily, it was January, and she told everyone her hands were cold. Everyone laughed. She knew nobody believed her. It was pretty awful. God might even stain her tongue black for lying. How would she explain that? A black tongue could have only one meaning. (Or it could be worse. Lie to us, you lose your tongue—Mom, Dad, and Grammy threatened, and they weren't joking.) You get the picture.

Back to the traveling spermatazoa. Okay, okay—I had to concede: so, say the sperm hit home. What then? She finally decided against suicide because that too would hurt her parents, perhaps even more than the shame induced by her sexual misconduct and its possibly dire effects. (*Hurt her parents?* It sounded odd, difficult to imagine, really. It might infuriate them, make them want to kill you . . . but hurt them—no, I didn't think so.) "Besides, my family would blame you," she said. "Blame me?" "Yes, they'd kill you." "Kill me?" (Ha, ha. I sorta just laughed that right off, as any fool would.) Back to what to do. Call the doctor. She said she wouldn't, couldn't . . . no, *I* must. "Randy, be the man, make the call, honey pie." Don't mention her name, she pleaded, don't use my own either. Protect her, protect us. (Lie . . . sure and risk *my* tongue turning black!)

"Call the doctor right now, Randy." "Shouldn't we wait to see if your period's late?" "No, it's going to be late." "How can you be sure!" "I am. I already feel funny in my tummy." "But it only happened an hour ago." "Oh, Randy—don't make this harder for me. Look what you've done already. Please." "Okay—but—okay." It wasn't easy, but I did call, stammering and stuttering. I told Dori they needed a urine sample. What for? I don't know, I admitted. What do I put it in? They hadn't said, but I said they said put it in a jar. How much? I said I didn't know. Fill it.

Okay. That night she stole out to the trash and retrieved a half-gallon prune juice jar her mom had discarded that afternoon (after brewing some vile potion to poison a few mice that, despite that spooky cat, had infested the house). Secretly, she cleaned and polished the jar like a piece of precious china. All week long, every time she peed she added a little to the jar. Daily, she showed it to me (why, I didn't know), and I smiled approvingly. (What else could I do?)

When it was full, I carried the jar in to the clinic. Puzzled, the nurse asked, "What's this?" "For a pregnancy test," I nervously informed her. She chuckled and shook her head sympathetically. "Oh, honey . . . oh, well, never mind." I gave a false name—Larry Longshot, my best friend— said I didn't have a phone, and that I'd call later for the results. She smiled, and said, "Sure, fine, Mr. Longshot. The results of the rabbit test would take three days." *The rabbit test*, what was that? I wanted to ask but didn't because the nurse's tone seemed to suggest it was something I should know, common knowledge. (Amazing, isn't it, the things we pretend to know about sex?)

For three days Dori went to Mass. Every day she said ten personally composed prayers, ten Hail Marys, and half a dozen rosaries. She told me (why, I didn't know) that her prayers mainly consisted of—"Please, God, don't let any wickedness have traveled up into me. I'll never do again what I'm so sorry I let Randy do." It didn't make me look good. I prayed too, although not quite as much. Prayed for the rabbit, prayed he wouldn't bring bad news.

Dori couldn't sleep. She was nauseous; she vomited frequently. Every hour, her belly seemed a bit more enlarged. Like she said, something funny in her tummy. At this rate the baby would arrive in a few days. Grammy gazed suspiciously at her with squinted, x-ray eyes. Dori's anxiety was dreadful and damn contagious too. I had to exert all my remaining influence to prevent her from blurting out a confession. She wanted to confess (that is, tell what I had done to her), prostrate herself at the feet of her family, and implore forgiveness, submitting gladly to any penance. (*Confess to her family!* That certainly placed the idea of suicide—hers *and* mine—in a more appealing light.) She felt the inevitability of doom. She longed desperately for something . . . *anything* to relieve the unbearable strain of waiting for the ax to fall.

And it fell. When I called, the nurse notified me that the rabbit had died. "You mean, she's pregnant?" Bemused, she replied, "Yes, congratulations, Mr. Longshot!" (*Congratulations?* You've committed murder, son, and now you're sentenced to death. Congratulations!) I asked if there could be any mistake. "About the rabbit? No—it died. But, yes, false positives occur. We can repeat the test if you wish. Bring in some more urine," she said, and added, "A small-bottle's worth will be fine."

Flooded with despair, I waited two hours before phoning Dori. I pictured her hovering by the phone, a nervous wreck. Her mother answered. "Why, no, Dori isn't home." A long pause, and then in an icy tone, "Isn't she with you?" "No, not with me"—scared as hell but sounding upbeat. "Well, I guess she went shopping, Randy"—this said with angry suspicion. "Hello . . . are you there?" she asked, and I felt her rage crawl through the phone line. I was mute, dumbfounded, and stunned even more, when after another long pause, I heard her utter a nasty little expletive before she slammed down the receiver. Dear god, what was happening? Where was Dori? She, beautiful she, wandering the earth, alone, bereft, fleeing that sicko home of hers and her good-for-nothing lover, her belly inching outward, full of our sin.

In her state, I couldn't imagine where she would go. I hunted for her everywhere I thought she could possibly be. I checked out some of the stores downtown, just in case she might be shopping. No luck. Of course not. *Shopping!*—for that she'd have to have gone completely batty. I called all her friends. Nothing. That afternoon, I called her home again. Her mother said, "Why, no, she hasn't returned yet." There was a sharp edge in her voice. Was it that her concern was growing, as mine had been all day? Her concern? No . . . more likely her hatred for something (me?). But where was my precious Dori? What was going on? I was baffled, speechless. Her mother asked me (told me) to come over *right now.* "We want to talk to you, Randy—right now. Do you understand?" I felt summoned by a voice ancient and commanding. Oh sure, what about? *Right now!* Jesus! Okay, sure. We want to talk to you. *We?*

I took my time, in no rush to face the inquisition I foresaw.

My god, where was she, my Dori? Surely she hadn't reconsidered . . . no, impossible, not suicide. She wasn't *that* depressed. Yes—yes, maybe she was. And whenever I found her, I had the official bad news. She hadn't somehow found out about the rabbit, had she? I was shaken, really shaken. Confronting Dori's distraught parents right now was the last thing in the world I needed. (*Distraught?* No, there again such terms couldn't easily be applied to these folks. Trust me. Would Dracula's kin be distraught?)

But I did as I was bidden. It was a sunny afternoon, but inside that house it was dark and as somber as a tomb. They greeted me calmly, coldly, and never even asked me to sit down. There was Dori's hulking dad and her hulking brother; never had I seen so much brute force assembled in so confined a space. And for the first time I noticed that her mom packed a lot of muscle too, and damn, so did Grammy. (Even the cat, with steroid eyes, bulked up.)

I could detect a smoldering anger discoloring their bloated, dream-distorted faces. And (here was the real freak-out) they all (except the cat) wore long, black leathery aprons—slaughterhouse aprons! A thought sped through my mind: I've been convicted. These wackos intend to murder me. Irrational? Maybe; nonetheless this house was not the place to be. Weak-kneed, dizzy, I felt faint. Dori, my Dor, love of my life, in this hour of dire need, where wert thou?

Ol' Dad didn't waste a minute. He motioned, with a quick no-nonsense head-hand gesture, for me to follow him into the kitchen. I did, accompanied by everyone. The cat, having bolted ahead, already sat hunched on the countertop, grinning at me as I entered. Creepy. But not as creepy as the table covered with a black tablecloth, and the gleaming butcher knife placed so tellingly in the center. Dad said, "You must submit to the lie detector test. Strip." *What!* "At once!" he commanded (another voice, ancient and implacable). I stood trembling, mortified, disbelieving. Did I hear what he had plainly directed me to do? I did.

I cannot describe the panic that surged though me. These people were insane; they really were insane! You ask, didn't I know this? Of course I did. After all, Dori was crazy, wasn't she? (She was just too gorgeous for a minor detail like *insane family* to matter.) *Where was she?* Was she part of this? This what? This gruesome game. The deranged thought struck me that she was the cat! Clearly, terrified as I was, I had myself gone slightly bonkers. I do not wish to dwell upon the ghastly particulars of what followed. I'm not one of those pathetic bastards who must return to the scene of past traumas to rub their wounds raw again. Not my style. (And yet—you note—you *are* recounting this weird tale, aren't you? In a way, reliving it. All right.)

After I was stripped by the clan and spread on the table, Mom grabbed one ankle, Grammy the other, and Boor held my two arms back over my head. Bands of steel. With these apes affixed to my limbs, I soon realized the futility of resisting. Talk about humiliation, and the horrible got worse. When I was spread-eagled atop the table, Dad raised the butcher knife above the ding, and with that voice from the bowels of hell, asked, "What did you do with Dori?" That was the question. This wasn't funny. His eyes were the flat gray eyes of a madman with ice water in his veins.

My mind raced about and crashed into blank walls. *What?* What did I do with her? What did that mean: Where had I abducted her to, or what had the ding done? I felt I was going to piss, but no, the ding wasn't

working right now. I said, "I don't know where she is, I swear to God."
Foolishly, I stuck out my tongue so all could behold how unblack it was.
This seemed to bewilder my onlookers, but only for a second. Dad further
elevated the knife. There, right above me, I saw the countenance of
Death. Not a joyful sight. And what were all my hosts gazing at? With
laser rays, all eyes converged upon the ding. Poor ding, had he retreated
any farther, I wouldn't have had to fret his loss. Shrunken as much as
could be, he was, alas, so pitifully trying to hide in plain sight.

"What did you do to Dori?" Dad growled. Ah, *to* Dori! That clarified
matters some. It was the ding's doings that were on trial. They knew
where their daughter was. Of course they did. Yeah, and what had she
told them? What had she confessed all on her own, or what had they
tortured out of her aflame-with-guilt soul? Just how hideous was all this?
I couldn't tell. Naturally, lying there hog-tied with the ding in peril, every
lucid thought had flown off.

Better believe I confessed! What did you expect? I betrayed the ding
to save him. Part for the whole, the whole for the part. I told them he
jumped out of my pants unbidden. I couldn't help it. I stood firmly upon
my innocence. I told them the devil had gotten into me—(I specified)
into the ding. I could see their eyes firmly grasp the very object of my
emphasis. All of you know how that can happen, I said. One unguarded
moment, Satan's in. Possessed I had been. Amen, amen, yes, they had
surmised as much. I heard Grammy moan (a hyena, sure enough); then
Mom and Dad moaned. You would have thought the knife hung above
their private parts, not mine. It was a ghastly thing. And the cat purred
in obscene commiseration. (Not too bad for a befuddled youth—eh?)
What a nightmare. Everyone's bananas, yourself included. Still, I thought,
I'm a goner. Kill the body, save the soul.

"*Kill! Kill!*" Boor shouted, a lunatic pure and simple. "But . . . no!"
Mom exclaimed, amid a sudden burst of tears. Amid tears, yes, but she
asserted herself as forcefully as an oncoming freight train: "*You will wed.*"
I will wed? What! My mind had not entirely taken flight. *Only that,* I
thought, with a sigh of relief that resembled a deflating inner tube. Yes,
ma'am. My intentions. How did you know? My very intentions. I've been
searching all day to find Dori to wed. "*Tomorrow,*" Mom declared, tearful
but still prepared to flip back into kill mode if one of my eyes blinked
wrongly. Tomorrow? Yes, tomorrow's not soon enough for me, Mom. I
love Dori.

"*Sweet boy. Sweet boy.*" I can't say for sure who whispered those lovely,
consoling words. I was delirious, you see. They sounded purring, as
though they issued from the cat. Hell, in those circumstances anything

was possible, right? They unbound me. I rose, as one back from the dead, and stood upright on the kitchen floor—wobbling, but still a man. Without a drop of emotion, they embraced my naked, trembling body; the cat licked my toes. Free as a bird, I was ready to wed.

Dori returned, miraculously, that very evening. Where she'd been, I never even asked—not then, not later. No more was said about anything that had happened, not about the sperm that travels, the dead rabbit, Dori's mysterious disappearance (and—*voila!*—reappearance), not about my humiliating ordeal. Nothing, not a word. And nothing about the total insanity of the family. (An insanity that I was to find, surprisingly, I would fit into rather comfortably.) No, not one word; questioning anything might have landed me back on the slab. You understand. (After being slabbed, you're not the man you once were, believe me, not the man you might have someday become. No, sometimes you're cut down in such a way, you just can't grow back up.)

Anyway, the next day, as planned, we wed. Just the family and the cat—real intimate, as intimate as all these cold fish could be. I don't mean Dori was cold. She was as happy as a child who had won a carnival prize.

Hey, was it all a ruse? Had I been conned, manipulated, shotgunned into wedlock? Abused (as we say nowadays)? Get a man at any cost? In the '50s, in St. Joe, Missouri, women hadn't yet changed much. It depressed me then (and would as well today) to search too deeply into that question. I've given it little consideration. I was (am) afraid to. I think of those black aprons, of that malicious cat, of sperm sneaking into Dori's body, of nearly bidding the ding adieu, and . . . well, I cringe; my mind whites out like a TV screen after the programs shut off in the wee hours.

What's left to tell? Not much. After an event such as that, the rest is, well, detumescent, we could say.

You ask, would I have wed the beautiful Dori without all this fuss? Frankly? No. I was a kind of ordinary-looking guy, homely even—and in high school that's not a good thing—so in snagging Dori, I felt lucky as hell. But beautiful as Dori was (still is), I believe her family's craziness eventually would have scared me off. The family's understanding of the world was crude, as I've noted, medieval. But I have to admit, sometimes crude's the way to go. It worked with me. You adjust. Besides, I can't say I've regretted the results. Worse things could have befallen me, as we well know. Dori and I, we've had our little ups and downs, but whenever she mentions sharing with her family any bone of contention between us, well, that settles the matter instantly. Terror streaks like lightning through my nervous system, and I concede in a flash.

What else? Oh, the baby the dead rabbit foretold never did show up. Small detail. Probably not a great surprise if you weren't convinced that sperm travels the way Grammy claimed it did. So, the rabbit lied; no doubt the rascal's tongue turned black as coal. What else? As you can imagine, I've had my nightmares—knives gleaming above my groin, cats screaming in my ear, "sweet boy, sweet boy." Nightmares of Larry Longshot, disguised as a demon, accusing me of betraying our friendship and vowing to cast me someday into hell. Pretty terrorizing, let me tell you. I can't claim my mind was left unscarred.

Dori has longed desperately for a child, but my sperm have not chosen to travel up that gully. In fact, that river acts quite dried up. I sure hope they don't drag me back to the slab on that account. You know, alarm the ding again. No wonder nothing travels forth from him anymore. To Dor, on that score, I might as well be dingless.

No hard feelings. The ding has a mind of his own. Some things it refuses to stand for. Thank god I'm blameless. Although, I do keep expecting Dori to invite the clan to take a hand in the matter. Maybe she already has; maybe they think the devil's in the ding—indeed, never vacated the ding—and they're afraid to monkey with him again. Oh well . . . still, Dori and I . . . well, we've been happy enough. What the hell. Like I said, I loved Dori (still do). Yeah, sure, but, well, it was a package deal—Mom, Dad, Boor, the cat (still alive!), and Grammy (still alive—no doubt forever!). Everything comes in a package. Okay . . . let's say—lesson learned?

The Cliff-Hanger

Naked, I hang down a hundred feet over the precipice, the rope tied firmly around my middle, held at the other end in the strong hands of the boss, my father. My only weapon, a bowie knife hooked on the rope at my waist. The dark purple ocean moils below, waiting. I see its vastness, hear the roar of the incoming waves, see and hear them crash against the jagged teeth of the rocks. From the bright blue sky, the midday sun burns down upon me. After many days, my flesh has blistered and cooked. I can't recall when last it rained. I lost track of time long ago, so I have no reliable idea of how long I've been in this agonizing state of suspension. The rope squeezes, and my gut pains excruciatingly. If it's not one pain, it's another. Pain is constant. I piss and shit when necessary. I am, in this respect at least, free as these vulturous birds that besiege me. Not infrequently, I vomit. I suffer from vertigo. I have always feared heights; they upset my stomach. Dad knows this, of course.

This can't go on forever. No . . . but why not? you ask. The boss himself says so, says he's getting older, claims he's weakening (although of this I detect no signs), says he's old and soon he'll die. Maybe I don't believe that either. Old, yes, but undying. I believe my father will never let me down. Even so, what a miserable spot to be in, dangling over a cliff.

Sometimes birds, buzzards mostly, pluck hungrily at my roasted flesh, tearing away strips of it. Flayed . . . pain beyond imagining. There seems to be something inside me they want—liver, heart, spine, the works. Although I've given up a few chunks of myself (what a bloody mess am I!), with my knife I do fend them off fairly well; even in my sleep I'm chopping off their savage heads. Whatever it is they're really after—the inside stuff—still belongs to me. During the day, hourly, they attack my genitals, but I hold firmly to the family jewels. I'm proud of this; maybe the boss is as well. Certainly I feel a little foolish hanging here, dangling down from Dad like an appendage of some kind, fighting for my life, but Dad . . . well, he wants to make a point. He's my loving father, and naturally I trust him with my life. I always have. Yeah, and he's the boss.

Dad's rich and powerful, generous, and in his way, loving . . . indulgent, he'd say. Okay, indulgent . . . but everything does have to go his way. Forget about choice with him. He says, *Do!*—you do. He thinks I'm spoiled rotten. Maybe so. All my life he's impressed me, awed me, really. Of course he's taught me what to be impressed with. Money— that's the big item, let me tell you. He convinced me that the almighty buck solves all problems because any problem can be transcribed into money language for its solution. He sold me; I bought it . . . okay! But here I am, hanging, baking in the merciless sun, like a pig on a spit, barfing up my lunch, my boiling blood dripping into a sea hundreds of feet below, unable to buy my way out, 'cause the boss holds the reins. Holy cow—I might as well be penniless.

Don't get me wrong. I've got plenty of money (although according to Dad, there's never enough). I'm what you'd call a rich kid. It's money Dad's given. He stresses *given*, because he maintains that I've never actually worked a day in my life. To him, I'm an idler, a daydreamer, a scribbler of ridiculous verse. All those private tutors he hired for me, he thinks only filled my noggin with unprofitable nonsense. Maybe so, because the real business, Dad's business, is what I paid the most attention to. "And you didn't learn anything there, either," he has many times informed me.

But I've worked for him since I was seven. Yeah, he took me right into the business, a business he built from scratch. He's a self-made man. Once upon a time, as he will repeatedly note, he didn't have a pot to piss in. Hard to imagine. Well, with all my dough—I'm a big cheese in Dad's company—now I haven't a pot to piss in, literally. Is this the point he wants to get across? He wants me to understand his origins? He made himself, made me, made the world we live in. Okay, I get it. Maybe he thinks with me he's failed, that I'm—well, imperfect, a blemish on his perfection. I have to puke.

Well, not having a pot to piss in's not the problem here. No, as I've said, I freely piss and shit just as any bonafide animal does. The sea's my pot. I suppose that's the fun part of all this. (Black as it is, I keep my sense of humor.) Eating's a little awkward but manageable. Daily, Dad lowers a pail with water and food (usually pretty choice . . . what you'd expect). He's a caretaker. Sometimes he throws in a cool can of beer. I'm sure the point is not to starve me into understanding what going hungry's like—no. Besides, he needs me alive and alert, ready to learn, to apply what I've learned, to suffer correction. So yes, he feeds me, always has. Am I to feed myself? Geez—is that it? Just tell me what you want me to know, boss. Cut to the chase. He says he has and nothing's gotten through. Okay, if he says so. Smirking, he will observe that someone as dumb as I has to be very intelligent to be this dumb. Is that a compliment? That's the way he talks sometimes: obscure.

Every minute of the day, I keep a sharp eye peeled for those fiendish vultures. In the daylight I can't risk napping. They circle tirelessly. I espy a dozen congregating for an assault right now, wheeling around. It takes them awhile to figure out a plan. They're stupid. It's always the same with them—head on, dive-bomber tactics. Stupid, yes, but it sure wears you down, a piece at a time.

The boss assures me that this "outing" (as he terms it) is for my own good and that the suffering that it entails distresses him far more than me. Okay, if he says so. But as far as I can tell, birds aren't snapping at his gonads, and he's not leaking blood from every pore. ("Oh, and the blood I've pissed for you, my ungrateful son," a refrain he oft reiterates.) While sometimes difficult, I do believe his every word. Remember, he's always been supremely successful at moneymaking. He rolls in dough. The Midas touch. Who can argue with a being of such achievement? Who can challenge the methods, ruthless or not, of such a being? The ends justify the means, and money's the end. Perfect logic. But will hanging me over a cliff help anyone make more money? Finally, it occurs to me to pose this question to the boss. Because unless this shit and blood of mine that drops into the sea is changing into gold, I ain't worth a damn dime.

I'm not even sure I actually ask the question. At times, conversations with Dad exist solely in my mind, but spoken or not, he answers. "Making more money's not my objective here, son." Shocked, I struggle to look up and catch his facial expression. (His is a stern countenance, unyielding as granite. As a boy, I used to wet myself when he glowered at me.) I have to rotate myself upside down. The acrobatics are fairly easy but crucifying, literally gut wrenching, because the rope twists tighter and cuts sharply into my tender, sun-fried abdomen. So, ass up, I try to glimpse the boss's face, snatch a clue to the meaning of that most uncharacteristic remark. Standing on my head in midair, I must look like a circus clown to him. Maybe only in certain unnatural positions can you hear things you've never heard before. Is this the point of this?

I cry out, "How 'bout some elaboration, boss." Unfortunately, because the sun happens to be behind Dad's head, a glare prevents a view of him. Dad appears as a ball of white fire—blinding. This is disconcerting. I can't see my father, my own father. I have been assuming all along that this is a lesson of some sort in moneymaking, an initiation, the imparting of sacred wisdom from father to son. Maybe it is, indeed, the imparting of wisdom, just not money wisdom. Blinded thus by father's brilliance, more confusion assails me. Frightened, I feel an attack of diarrhea. Quickly I spin right side up and let loose. This is always a chancy business because the stink titillates these killer birds.

But Dad ignores my request. A man of few words, he's all action. (To teach me how to swim, when I was four, he tossed me in our swimming pool. I fainted, nearly drowned. Bored with what he later called my hysterics, the boss turned his back, and when he did, one of the servants dragged me out. I still can't swim. The boss would say, "Right—something else you can't do." And here I am now, arms and legs flailing about, a clown swimming in midair.) I try again, "Boss, why are you wasting time on teaching me something if it won't turn a dollar?" Silence. Silence is golden . . . is that it?

Hours pass, days, months. I'm a pendulum that's lost all sense of time. It's no use. "Dad, it's no use," I scream in pain, or act as though I do; my voice sometimes goes but not the pain. Voiceless screaming. But he can read my mind—*that* he made clear long ago. (As a child, I would frequently play with myself—you know what I mean—as all kids do. He always knew, yes, even when he was in another country, as if through telepathy. And he'd pour acid on my hands, not enough to permanently damage but enough to prevent me from fingering anything for days. He believes playing with yourself is a waste of time. Time's money. Hanging here, however, I do occasionally yank off, mostly after dark, and he says nothing. Why's it okay now? Is this to show me what my life's come to: jerking off in barren space, still a worthless child? Is this it: I'm a metaphor of my own life? He'll say, "Poppycock," so I don't ask. Anyway, I've heard that hanged men shoot off. So the boss probably understands that in this situation it's almost involuntary.)

Dad's been like God to me, all giving, all punishing; I've worshiped him. I used to stare for hours at him as he sat behind his desk, as though on a throne, making mounds of money hand over fist, a wizard conjuring it out of the empty air. The spectacle took my breath away. He never forbade my worshiping him, but maybe he's grown weary of such sycophantic idolatry.

You're thinking, "Where's your mom in all this, son? Shouldn't you be adoring Mom?" Well, lately—oh, I guess, for several days—I've been trying to blame Mom for my predicament. Why? Because she's always amounted to nothing. That's why. To the boss she's never mattered. He considers her "only an oven to bake goods in." But she's a beauty, let me tell you. She's always nude. Dad said, "Be nude," and that's how she goes about. And she's an eyeful. There was a time I would have liked to bake some goods in her myself! There *was* a time, yes . . . but the boss doesn't value beauty, no, not unless he can sell it.

Actually, Dad once implied that's how he got the seed money for his initial business undertaking. Yeah, sold her out. So it seems she proved good for something more than merely baking a kid in (that's me—baked goods!). I think he used her beauty to make a point (I mean, a point other than the one I often found myself making around her). He wanted to demonstrate the vanity of such carnal temptation. I watched him over and over again ignore her, treat her as though she were invisible; if not a means to money, then she counted for nothing. She was the direction toward which I was *eventually* taught not to point my desire.

Yes, so eventually I came to look solely at Dad. Her—her what?— *significance* just faded; she virtually disappeared. Naked and beautiful, no matter. Undesired, she gradually grew thin, and finally she had (we noticed sometime or other) just disappeared. In fact, I'm not even sure I any longer have a mother (except perhaps in dreams and recollections). So I guess nothing's there to blame. She's not an obvious part of this. Unless, transfigured, she's the sea beneath me, at one moment as gleaming and rippling as an infinite sheet of silver or gold, at another as wrathful as a dragon. But I have no idea what I mean by this. I suppose— bleeding, parched, in pain from head to toe—I've lost my mind.

Oh shit—the birds are back! I grab the bowie. Huge wing spans, bloodthirsty, open beaks, furious beady eyes . . . *swish, swish!* Two crazed heads pop off. Then a few more. I swing wildly, round and round, like the blade of a fan, decapitating, scoring left and right. Damn, there is some delight in this when you're winning. *Oh no!* I smack at one big bastard, miss, and it bites off the little finger of my left hand. In agony, I thrash about so violently, I finally succeed in scaring all of them away . . . or maybe the delight of their little theft satisfied them enough, at least temporarily. Squawking, laughing, they do always seem so pleased when they rip off some chunk of my delicious flesh. Sometimes when I am quite delirious, I wonder: Do these dreadful carnivores belong to the boss, work for him? Is it at his bidding they mutilate me? Insane thoughts, I know, but in my state, you can hardly expect sanity. I gaze at the bleeding stump of my finger in astonishment (just as I did when they snapped off three or four of my toes). A part of me just gone—*wack!*—just like that.

But enough. Enough.

"Dad! Dad! Enough! Save me! Save me! Whatever wrong I've done, I'm sorry. I'm a poet, harmless, good for nothing. Okay—I'm not the perfect and the upright man."

"That's true."

"So, okay—*I'm your son. I'm sorry.* Okay?"

Exasperated, he shouts, "This is not a punishment." Not a punishment? This is unsettling because, I confess, I had begun to consider it a bit that way.

I no longer trust my perceptions of anything. The bird battles have exhausted me. I stare at my mangled finger and wonder how much more I can take. Things blur. I seem absorbed in a deep, silent absence. I seem to have closed my eyes because now I notice all the bright sunlight has vanished. Sometime or other, thick dark clouds collected . . . without my even having noticed. How could this have happened? Did I fall asleep? In broad daylight! . . . with those lunatic birds . . . risking life and limb? Yes . . . yes, I did. Vaguely I recall dreaming something. Dad has always insisted I tell him my dreams so he can keep an eye on me and have a good laugh.

"Dad, I dreamed."

"Oh yeah. Always the foolishness. Okay, let's hear it. I need a laugh."

"I dreamed I watched you slowly and tenderly running your hands over Mom's body, inch by inch. And every part of her you touched turned to gold. This greatly excited both of you, excited me as well. Eventually, she changed, petrified into a gleaming statue of gold. You stared at her, mesmerized by what you had made; she seemed to stare tauntingly back at you, fully conscious of her spellbinding beauty. Perfectly motionless, you both seethed with desires that you were utterly unable to act on. It was very exciting, Dad, and yet somehow terrible. I wanted to flee this scene of frozen love, but I couldn't budge. That's all."

He laughs boisterously. "It's hilarious. *Me* seething for your mom! You're a comedian. A dream of alchemy. It sounds like you, son. Everybody's stuck."

"Gold spoiled everything, Dad." I realize that I happen to have just said something blasphemous.

"Wrong answer again. That dream shows a dummy who doesn't know how to use gold."

"Is this my lesson, then?"

Long, long pause. I drift off; I dream the same dream again. Captivated, I gape at the glistening body of my mother. I see the shimmering ocean's golden skin extending far enough to fill all my vision. I wake. I feel my liver gouged at and torn. Swiftly I decapitate a couple more of these flying cannibals.

Then a long, dead silence. My mind drifts amid my pain and the vastness of the sky; my eyes, with a dizzying vigilance, circle with the birds. (This may have lasted days.) Suddenly, the boss shouts at me, "This is not a punishment." His booming voice startles and rouses me from my absent awareness. "Pull yourself up by your bootstraps, son." Again, I twist about, contort my flayed body in another supreme endeavor to behold my father's countenance. Again, no luck. His head rises above the thick clouds; it's as though a huge black hood has draped over him.

"What do you mean, Father? I'm to fend for myself—is that it?"

"You are too stupid, my son, ever to know anything for certain."

"Then help me, Father. You're too inscrutable. I'm dying. Raise me up; bring me back to life. Show mercy."

"Save yourself for a change." Save myself for a change . . . *for a change.* My heart sinks. So he refuses to rescue me. So that's how it is. Now what am I supposed to do?

"Father, will I hang here until I perish? I'm nearly dead, you know. The birds eat me alive."

"Is that your choice?"

"Choice?" I hesitate. I've never thought I had a choice in anything. But, dear god, what's he implying? "What! Would you let me die, Dad?"

"Yes. I'm sick and tired of carrying you. You just don't get it. All this time wasted. How long we been out here—a year or so? Frankly, son, you're not worth a plugged nickel." Ooh, that hurts, really hurts. He's never said *that* before. All right, but what's he expect me to do, weak as I am, climb the rope all by myself? He speaks again, "I love you, son, you know I do—so enough said about that—but looking at you I must conclude, what rotten luck! If every powerful man walks with a limp, as they say, then you're the thorn in my heel."

"Dad, that hurts. You've never said such hurtful things before."

"Of course I have—daily. You forget . . . every day, you forget. Pathetic."

"Is this why you're inflicting this outrage upon your son—so that I'll remember the hurtful things you say? Lift me up, Father. I'll practice remembering, I promise. The rope is cutting me in half."

"So be it." This he speaks with a finality that bites into my heart like the beaks of a thousand birds.

Suddenly, a despair with an intensity I have never before experienced overwhelms me. This isn't funny; some things you just can't laugh off. *Boom!*—like a hammer, it hit me in the heart. I gasp . . . then slump. It's as though all my blood's been drained; I hang limp as a rag. I feel that my life as I have known it is concluded. Something has died, or something that I have always recognized as my self is dead. I have to let go of Dad. He wants to let go of me, but he won't do that—who knows why not? Or maybe he will, maybe he's about to do precisely that; maybe in another minute or two he'll simply open his mighty hands and release me. Maybe he will do that for himself, for me.

I begin swinging back and forth—at first slowly, as lethargic as someone waking up. I then strain to increase momentum, for something, for some critical enactment. Yes, I have to swing out far enough to avoid the rocks jutting up at the base of the cliff. At this point, I'm not altogether clear what I have in mind. The wind's velocity abruptly accelerates, as though all nature is part of this upheaval. I crane my neck to find my father's face still shrouded with black storm clouds. All I see is his brawny body, his huge muscles bulging under what must be by now even for him a tremendous labor. His arms form a V as his fists clasp together clinging to the rope, and I hang like a pendant from Dad's groin. Surely he must soon either drop or lift me up.

But suddenly (is it suddenly?) it no longer matters what he does because with this engulfing despair has also arrived the realization that I can set myself free. I can do this myself, and I *must* do this! Why? I ask myself. I swing with urgency, kicking furiously off the cliff's stone face, building the momentum to fling myself someplace, to fly out, out there to the other end of the earth. In my condition, anything's possible or nothing is. *Anything* and *nothing* seem oddly synonymous. And all the while I'm thinking, asking myself questions. Am I doing *this* (whatever exactly it is) because the boss wants me to? Maybe so. Who cares? It may be what he wants, but it is definitely what I want. What's that? What's that? I want freedom, freedom at any cost . . . freedom from torture. Any dad who'd let his son die, who'd kill his own son—my god! (Abraham—Isaac . . . how 'bout swapping your son for a ram snagged in a thicket, Dad?)

Perhaps a despair that I can no longer deny impels me toward this decision; impels me toward some desperate deed which I only dimly comprehend. I glance down at the raging billows, dizzy with fear, terrified of my own irrevocable resolve, frenzied with excitement. Somehow I feel this is the only real choice that I have ever made. Horrifying . . . the first will be the last. Oh, the appalling terms of this exhilarating freedom; I know this, or maybe I don't. I'm bewildered. Down there the raging sea waits, now impatiently. Is it really my mother, stretched out, twisting her lovely limbs about, waiting? She—the nada outside all desire—death? Death and freedom: from here, how identical they seem. Anything and nothing.

Swinging now in the widest possible arc, I draw out my faithful bowie knife, and with all my remaining strength, I begin sawing the rope. The wind blows fiercely; a cold rain begins to fall. My burning flesh rapidly cools; I feel blood, sweat, and dirt caked on my skin being washed away. Cleansed. The sea roars like a famished beast, its black mane flaring ecstatically. I feel my desolation blown away by the gale, passing as quickly as it had come. All my anguish is miraculously transformed, replaced by a surging ecstasy that races through my ruined body. I saw at the rope madly, excitedly. I swing like an ape—out, in, out, in . . . panting, swinging madly . . . out, in. The sea is growling, starving, naked, a wrathful mother reaching up to repossess her forsaken son. The storm rages; the wind throws me back and forth, a rubber ball against a rock wall. The rain drenches me. All the daylight is fading fast; you'd think it's the end of the world.

I look up one last time. Yes, yes, I behold my father's face, luminous, heavenly, hellish. Through the thick black storm, unaffected by the roiling blackness, it glows like a pot of gold. He looks down upon me. He frowns. Oh, that horrendous frown, a frown that has, through my life, killed me over and over. He's angry, terribly angry.

"What are you doing?" he shouts.

Not for a second do I interrupt my feverish work or the rhythm of my arc. He's surprised. Amazing! I've done something that surprises the boss. I grin with some satisfaction too profound to comprehend. "I'm leaving you, Father."

"My son, my son, no, *don't*—don't move!" he yells. Even above the howling storm, I hear his every word, deafening, as though his lips are close enough to bite off my ear. I feel him rapidly towing in the rope, a fisherman frantic to reel in his catch. The rope quickly shortens, limiting the extent of my swing. I know I must hurry. But . . . what? *What?* Is this fear I detect in Father's voice, a note of pleading? "No, son! Don't move! Don't move!" What! Can this be? My god—*he wants me back?* This, then, is not what he intended? He never intended to lose me? Or not to lose me this way, with me cutting myself loose? Or is this gruesome struggle between us exactly how he expects this to end?

For one brief moment, I stare into his implacable eyes. Is there a flicker of admiration there? Yes? No? You tell me; I'm too busy. I've got to get out of here. There's an eye-lock. Me!—staring Dad down. He's determined; so am I. Swinging (but with less and less sweep), cutting insanely . . . up, up I go . . . slashed by wind and rain . . . ascending, still hooked. Fast . . . he's reeling me in, a fish fighting desperately for its life. Now I'm hardly swinging at all. I'll never land beyond the rocks. It doesn't matter—I can't swim anyway. Hurry, hurry! I'm nearly within his grasp. One of his hands opens to grab me. A second more and I'm a goner. Only a few strands of rope remain. I cut.

Mother's Tale

I never knew my fabulous father. He vanished before my birth. I learned of him only through a single story my mother, the teacher, told to me when I was a boy. Because I was a rather nervous child, this story upset me. Mother loved me dearly, so she probably never intended such a disturbance, although she could be rather peculiar. It wasn't only the scary sexual stuff, it was the way she delivered it, everything she mixed in with it. I present this now to extricate myself from its clutches. Of what I was told, I am the teller.

When I was eight or nine, I asked Mother who my father was and why he had gone away. I was lying in bed, and she was about to read me to sleep, as she did almost every night. She paused and stared into space. She then set the book aside and switched off the light, leaving the room colored with an eerie blue-gray moon glow. She commenced in a whisper, as though divulging a secret.

"He may have first been a boy, like you, my darling, until one day maybe while playing with himself, a god or a devil—let's say a devil—altered him into a raven." In the moonlight, I saw her smile and glance at me with gleaming eyes, perhaps to assess the effectiveness of this beginning.

"A boy like me . . . who became a raven, a bird?" I asked, confused. (To this day, I well recall how warily I avoided repeating the reason for this alteration: Dad playing with himself. Each time Mom caught me in such indulgence, she chided, "Oh, playing with yourself's so lonely.")

She continued. "Yes, a bird, and oh so much else besides. A particular bird, a raven, dashingly handsome, sleek, black as night. And a very unusual raven. Tell you why in a sec. His name was Raven, so that's our last name, you see."

At this point, Mom decided to climb into bed, which she sometimes did, especially when the dark frightened me (afraid, I suppose, that some beast would carry me away from her). Quickly she undressed. "Scoot over, hon, let Mummy get comfy." Placing her arm beneath my neck, she drew me to her. In the warm room we lay unclothed. Hypnotized, I gazed at her body and her pale face. In the light of the bright full moon, she resembled a ghost; I scarcely recognized her. Whenever she smiled, her teeth gleamed like razor blades. My heart was already pounding. It always excited me to look at her naked, but something more than that was now at play, or something else fused uncomfortably with that.

"Okay, here's the only tale your father ever shared with me. On a hot summer evening, like this one, Raven's gliding low in the sky, floating in lazy circles, searching for windows to peer into. He's sneaky, loves perching in trees near windows, often chancing upon the most extraordinary sights—some real turn-ons. You can imagine . . . or maybe you can't." (But yes, I could. At the age of eight I'd already engaged in much after-dark neighborhood snooping. And yes, I too had chanced upon these turn-ons. Nothing's more educational. Of course, at that prying age, everything is intriguing. How it delighted me that I took after my lost father.)

"That night Raven had been soaring over a seemingly uninhabited forest. However, after a while, he spots the yellow light of lanterns—no electricity out here—emitting from a cabin deep in the woods. He swoops down and alights on the branch of an old elm tree slumping near a bedroom window. He looks in and spies a young woman in a sheer white nightgown standing before a mirror, gracefully combing her hair, long hair as black and shiny as his own glossy feathers."

Sheer white . . . meaning see-through? Well, although I fixed avidly on that detail, I spoke about another. "Was her hair black as yours, Mom?"

"As black as mine used to be, sweetie, yes. Raven told me that she was the most beautiful woman he had ever beheld."

"Beautiful as you, Mom?"

"Do you think Mummy's beautiful, darling?" She continued to whisper; occasionally her damp lips grazed my ear.

"Yes, the most beautiful in the world," I said and hugged her.

"Oh my, thank you, honey. So do you wanta hear this story?"

"Yes, tell me about Dad . . . everything."

"Okay. He watches the woman comb her hair, and suddenly the bathroom door opens and a naked man staggers into the room, a powerful giant, ten feet tall, hairy as an ape. Awkward in his movements, he seems intoxicated or stupid. Everything about him's so enlarged . . . so swollen. It's two feet long—you know. You'd obviously think the woman's aroused him. But no, this attribute's perpetually him, throws him off balance, I guess. It glares red, like a phosphorescent tube of light. Hideous. Hairy as King Kong. You can picture him, I'm sure." Oh yes, yes, I could. She hesitated a moment and cuddled me closer. "Exciting, isn't it? You like this story, sweetie?"

Yes, I did, without yet fully comprehending all the reasons why. A murky fear seemed, from the start, to compound my excitement. A monster-man sporting a luminous two-foot boner . . . creepy. And I believed her; kids believe in the monstrous—at least this impressionable one did.

"What does Daddy do?" I focused on Dad, on the bird.

"Waits and watches. The woman—let's call her *Beautiful Woman*, shall we?—she freezes and stares at the bloated man's mirrored reflection. The giant—let's call him *Giant-Thing*—he then slides from beneath the bed a large trunk. Opens it and gawks inside. Sharp-eyed, Raven detects that it contains nothing, but Giant-Thing gawks for a couple of minutes. Raven suspects that he's rather obtuse—"

"Obtoos?"

"Dumb as a shoe," Mother, the teacher, explained. "The Giant-Thing then commands the woman to fetch him a bucket of salt water. She complies *tout de suite.*"

"Too sweet?"

"Quick." She snaps her fingers. "Raven notices that she trembles, evidently frightened. Giant-Thing growls, yanks the pail from her, and shoves her so forcefully away; she trips and begins to cry. Let me tell you, she cries *all* the time. He yells at her to shut up, then hoists her up, and flings her across the room as though she weighs nothing. She crashes against the wall and collapses, unconscious. Her flimsy nightgown whisks up, fully exposing her abdomen and shapely legs recklessly sprawled. Raven, hardly a creature to pass judgment, with his own behavior frequently less than admirable, still abhors the misuse of such an exquisite woman. Of course, he doesn't know that Giant-Thing knocks her out a lot, that he likes to. Raven, naturally, ogles her revealed flesh . . . naturally, as any healthy male would and—"

I gingerly picked an item to respond to, not that display of flesh, not that fluorescent boner, not even that horrible violence, and not how Mother knew Beautiful Woman was knocked out *all* the time, no, none of these, but rather—"Why doesn't Dad help her?"

"Well, he does consider interceding. He's very clever and he might have managed something. But no, he elects not to. If avoidable, such a gargantuan—"

"Garganchoo-what?"

"Giant as this you wouldn't hasten to confront in any fashion. And with all his manhood upstanding, shimmering—know what I mean? Why meddle in domestic affairs? Raven isn't that involved—not yet. Besides, he's awfully curious about that trunk, the bucket of salt water, and just what this Neanderthal's up to—"

"Kneeunderall?" Another mouthful.

"Monstrosity . . . bone for brains. Stay with me, love. You needn't know *every* word. Enjoy!"

"What does Daddy do?"

"At first, just takes in the show. Wouldn't you? Put yourself in Dad's place."

Put myself in Dad's place . . . I didn't know why, but that also disturbed me. Under the circumstances, a kind of creepy invitation. As I've disclosed, as a kid, I was overwrought.

"Okay, next the hairy hulk, elevated as a flaming telephone pole, gulps down the entire bucket of brine. Jesus—can you believe it? The guy's a pig. Then what? You wanta know? Then he pukes, violently upchucks every drop, plus some, 'cause the garbage's all crimson with the jerk's own blood. Vomits part of himself!

"Raven's right: He is stupid. Even though this messy performance revolts Raven, as it would you too, he's gotta laugh—quietly, quietly of course. It just seems so absurd, so idiotic. Raven wonders if it's some freaky pagan ritual, you know, some peculiar act to appease God or coax him into giving you presents . . . or to appease the devil—yuk, who knows? Some of that junk's superfreaky. Say your prayers, honey; God'll find that's good enough.

"Then Giant-Thing does something else really weird—but with Raven, you've already noticed, weird's kinda normal. Giant-Thing takes a fishing pole from the closet, then—get this—tears a small chunk of flesh from his forearm and baits the fishing hook; *baits it with his own flesh!* Disgusting, isn't it? Then into the trunk filled with puke he casts the fishing line. Can you believe this craziness?" Trouble was . . . I did believe this craziness. A very gullible child!

"Raven can barely suppress bursts of laughter." I didn't get what was so funny. (That was part of my problem: after dark, my sense of humor vanished.) "And all the while, mind you, the Giant-Thing stays all brightly swollen like he's real horny. Know what I mean?" *Yes, Mother; yes, Mother, go on!* (The very things she demurely avoided saying, she said so loudly. The teacher knew that of course. She loved teasing. There was, I see now, a bit of mockery in all this.) Her knee nudged my leg. Teasing, which is fine if you're not overwhelmed—but I already was by this grotesque intro to my dad. She had now ceased whispering, and I stared at her ivory face as she gazed impassively at the ceiling. I thought for a second—a terrifying second—that I lay beside a corpse.

I broke the long, few moments of silence with my familiar refrain, "So what does Dad do?"

"Just chuckles to himself . . . possibly scratches his head with the claw of one foot. I don't know. What's to do?" Mother shook my shoulders gently, maybe as reassurance, because she felt me shivering—she had to—yet she remarked nothing about that. Yes, shivering in all that heat. Even though naked, the warm, moist air in the room—almost too thick to breathe—pressed heavily upon us. (Perhaps I should mention that family members traipsing about in the buff constituted part of our child-rearing philosophy in those days—unashamed nudity its goal. None of that anxious tiptoeing backward to eschew peeping on a parent snoozing in the nude. No, Shem and Japheth as with daddy Noah. No, gawk your fill! Naked bodies weren't supposed to mean anything, at least not in a family context. A naked body was like a naked tree. Not for a minute did it ever work that way with me.)

"Now what happens?" she continued. "Raven's as nosy as you are right now. Well, at this point, Beautiful Woman, whom Giant-Thing had kayoed, bestirs herself. And what d'ya think? *Wham!* The slack in Thing's line zings straight out. Yes . . . a bite. Something . . . what? He jerks up on his pole. *Boing!* And there flapping frantically from the hook is a juicy, jumbo salmon. Honest! Trust Mom. Sure dumbfounds Raven, your dad. How 'bout you, you dumbfounded?"

With so many things occurring, I could scarcely respond. Like a broken record, I kept reverting to Dad. Maybe I also sensed I shouldn't look too closely, too openly at certain matters, no matter how naked Mother and I were. Before the Tree of Knowledge, stand with your eyes squinted.

"What'd Dad do?" Troubling as the figure of Dad himself was, he served as partial mooring amid all the agitated undercurrents of that story rushing in upon my green and floundering psyche. And strangely, through all these undercurrents, my own hard-on served as a kind of mooring as well. "What'd Dad do?"

"Nothing. Don't worry, Dad's acomin' soon. I'll hurry to that part. Giant-Thing slams the fish brutally against his knee and kills it. He then grabs Beautiful Woman's thick hair and yanks her up from the floor. She strives not to scream, 'cause he'll beat her. He's beaten her nearly to death at times."

"I'd like to kill him!"

"Would you? Well, she used to think that, think of stabbing him while he slept, but she was always too petrified to try. Eventually such wishes drowned in a deepening hopelessness. Anyway . . . now he orders her to fry the fish for his dinner. She obeys instantly—a slave, submissive to the core. You probably pity her. Remembering all this now, I certainly do—lots. I can tell you, she had long passed that stage of self-pity, though." Oh yes, I did pity her. God, was ever a damsel fraught with such distress. But selfishly, I fancied all the sugar kisses she'd surely bestow on the boy who rescued her . . .

I said, "Dad should've done somethin'."

"Well, he does do something. Okay, okay, I'll get him in here. Be patient, love, I want this story to make sense. Everything's senseless, hon, till it's part of a story. See? We *make* sense of things; that's the only sense they have, the sense we *make* of things. They haven't any sense at all on their own. See?" the teacher said.

"I'm not part of any story," I said.

"Sure you are. You're part of this one. Anything only makes sense in stories; in fact, anything only comes into existence within stories. Understand?" No, I really didn't understand that, then. Although I suppose by now I do. I gather Mom meant that we largely invent the worlds we inhabit. A scary idea, but liberating . . . I guess.

But Mother—I now realize I could have said—if the story itself is senseless, what then? Making stories, Mom—is it like pulling a salmon out of a pail full of your own bloody vomit on a hook baited with your own flesh? Could have said it, but didn't. Instead I clung to her, to the world she was making, holding on to every word, struggling to stay afloat, clinging to what was sinking me, like clinging to an anchor as it plunged its way to the floor of the sea.

"Does Dad just keep peeking? Does he ever jump in?"

"Dad's comin'. Hold your horses," she said and gave me another firm hug. "After the naked monster completes his feeding, he rips the nightgown off Beautiful Woman, and then . . . well, it's just atrocious what follows. As always—believe me—blood and pain 'sall she gets. His lust—well, never mind, my darling. You'll read between the lines, I'm sure. When you're older maybe—"

"I can imagine, Mom."

"Oh, can you? My goodness, aren't you the little man." I wasn't merely imagining. As I've owned, I'd myself done plenty of window work, so I had a fair idea what Giant-Thing did to Beautiful Woman. As my mother told the story of my father, the spooky portions spread out gangly fingers inside me, but I begged her to resume. I couldn't let go.

"I gotta hear everything."

"Everything? Well, maybe you got a right to know. After all, it's only one story and—"

"And it's about my dad, Mom. Come on, please, I got a right to know."

"All right, maybe you do. All right. So after Thing's sated, he decides to journey to a far-off island to hunt down women he can steal their teeth. He needs their teeth for rituals. Always fresh teeth too—you can't reuse the same old teeth."

Stealing women's teeth! That was too shocking to acknowledge even having heard. I said, "Rituals?"

But Mother, the teacher, chose not to improve vocabulary here but to stick with the grisly. "I can't remember why he needs those teeth. Something to do with . . . hmm . . . yes, with warding off evil spirits, females, probably—yes, females who might bite off his—oh, you guess which part. Nuts, isn't it?" I laughed and then so did she. "Luckily, Beautiful Woman still possesses her teeth. Anyway, he says he'll be gone for a month or . . . forever. Sometimes he returns immediately because he simply forgets why he left or even that he meant to go anywhere. But however long he's away, she's his chattel—"

"Cattle?"

"Exactly—cattle. She must stay put. He used to lock her in the outhouse. But he soon saw that was unnecessary 'cause her fear of him prevented escape. Besides, where could she flee? This isolated forest is all the world she knows. That men elsewhere, for instance, behave differently, of this she has no clue."

"Where are her mom and dad?"

"She doesn't know she has parents. The Giant-Thing kidnapped her when she was a babe. To her, his beastly treatment's normal; remember, it's all she's ever known. Isolated in the backwoods, everything crude and ignorant. A place, someplace not even on the map . . . as far away as the deepest part of you. Not like the fine, modern home you have here, sweetie. Too bad for her. Pathetic, isn't it?"

"Did Dad tell you all this?"

"All what?"

"About her mom and dad."

"He didn't have to. Anyway, Giant-Thing loads his backpack, and even though it's midnight, heads off into the wilderness to yank a few teeth. She lies bloodied in bed, drained by his vicious engorgement, limp as a rag."

"Engorgement—yes! Do it!" I had no idea what I was saying. It was then I fell in love with big words, which have always meant to me something dirty and forbidden.

"Okay, okay, here we go. Enter Dad."

"I can't believe Dad just sat there."

"What would you have done, sweetie? Think about it. Say you're peeking through this window here, as the moon now is, and you see Mummy being—"

"Engorgement!" Yes, my god, I was a trifle overwrought. She smiled and her teeth glistened.

"Well, let's get into Dad's head now, shall we? Okay, remember, this isn't any ordinary bird perching mindlessly in a tree. No. A raven's a carrion that devours practically anything, not a fussy creature. And he's exceedingly lecherous himself."

"Lecherous?" Evidently having grown thoroughly impatient with my limited vocabulary, or with the nervous use I made of it, Teacher again ignored my question.

"Witnessing the scenes in the house, unsurprisingly, whets Raven's own appetites. Have they whetted yours, honey bun? Yes, indeed, he wants a little salmon and a little . . . well, first the salmon, then we'll see. So he resolves to imitate Giant-Thing, to be him."

"Be him? What's that mean, Mom?"

"Okay, now you learn about your Dad. He was a shape-shifter."

"*A what!*—like Plastic Man?"

"No, he could do more than tie himself in knots and stretch a mile. He could transform himself into almost anything he wished, anything that he could strongly enough imagine, or intensely concentrate on. Incredible, isn't it? Do what you do in dreams, let's say, or in fantasies. You've imagined being—who?—Superman, haven't you? Or dreamed of yourself as a handsome prince who marries a gorgeous princess? Ever dream of being the Invisible Man, love?"

"The Invisible Man?"

"Someone who sees everything without being seen, who manifests no appearance at all. Never mind. Anyway, so Raven dives down, alights on the front porch, and instantly transfigures himself into a replica of Giant-Thing—naked, hulking, erect. Although a perfect disguise, inside he remains who he is. See? Pretty tricky, eh?"

"Wow, my dad could do that? How?"

"Who knows? Who knows what change is?" said the teacher. "Anyhow, he opens the door and struts right in, easy as pie. There's Beautiful Woman bleeding in bed. What a sight! Woozy, still recovering from her ordeal. You understand, or maybe you don't." *I do! I do! Jeez!* "No matter. She's probably dreaming of a prince who'll rescue her. No, forget that. She never heard of Prince Charming, or of rescue either—not yet.

"Startled by Raven, she springs up, wide-eyed, stunned by the unexpected reappearance of her tormentor. Did he forget he meant to take a trip? She dreads that he's returned, doubtless to abuse her again. To tie her with ropes, for instance, hang her from rafters, stick pins in her flesh, and lick her blood, a sadist relishing her screams. An absolute savage. I could tell you more, but won't. Someday, maybe.

"Raven examines her pallid, terrified beauty and licks his new-formed lips exactly as he's seen Giant-Thing do when satisfying his hungers. Her mouth and nose still trickle blood. She bleeds in other places, too, but never mind about that. Some details, my son, I prefer not to emphasize."

Of course with all those intimations and hints as broad as highways and those tickling little body strokes she now and then conferred, my god, what more emphasis could the teacher give! How intensely these highlighted gaps increased my anxiety, compelling my imagination to enter places beyond my means to safely conceive.

"No, Mom, please. I gotta know everything that happened. Please, it's my dad! I deserve to know."

"Deserve? Where'd you get that word? Well, some things, my love, kindle too many fires and that's not nice to do to kids. But maybe this once, just this once—no—well, we'll see. So Raven asks Beautiful Woman to please fetch the bucket of brine. *Please?* This sounds odd to her. *Please?* She dare not, however, pause to ponder its significance. No, frightened, she rushes to serve her master. He then drinks as Giant-Thing had done, vomits, baits the hook with his own flesh and tosses the line into the swill. Sure enough he snags a salmon. And then he asks Beautiful Woman if she would please cook the salmon for him. He asks, doesn't order her, says *please.* Yes, it sounds very odd to her. Puzzled, she nonetheless dashes to gratify his wish.

"Raven swiftly devours the meal. Never having tasted fried fish, he finds it succulent. Fearfully, Beautiful Woman watches him. Although a marvelous copycat, he nonetheless wonders how convincing his performance is. Of many details, he's unsure. For instance, he can't recall whether Giant-Thing's right—or left-handed. But from her distressed countenance, he assumes he's managing well enough. Beautiful Woman does perceive that something's a bit off, but this perception, mainly unconscious, combined with the supervigilance of fear, misfocuses the picture, causing her to misread some telltale signs—like the quirky way Raven lurches at his food, as birds do, abruptly lowering and raising his head, pecking, or the way his eyes dart. But something soft characterizes his manner, and that does make a beguiling impression on her. And— *he smiles at her!*—something Giant-Thing has never done, not once. Yet, in a million years, she couldn't have doubted that this exact look-alike is anyone other than her torturer."

"Dad's foolin' her. He ain't who he is," I said.

"*Isn't* who he is. No, not entirely. Good thinking, dear. Well, after Raven's eaten, he reaches out and strokes her hand. She flinches, because once, sitting at this table, Giant-Thing had, in a flash, stabbed her in this same hand with a fork. Nailed her to the table. But Raven persists, stroking her gently. *Never* has she been gently stroked. Never, as the bruises all over her body testify. Confused, uncertain what to do, she does nothing. Of course she suspects that this is all a fiendish trick, that at any second he'll start beating and raping her, behaviors he relishes. Yet it seems something quite different's unfolding here."

"Is her hand all right?" I asked, worried. Picturing that hand nailed down made me sick. Mother raised her hand up in the moonlight and spread her fingers.

"Yes, good as new. See? Now, Raven itches big-time for this gorgeous woman. Bloody and bruised, she's still *so* naked, *so* ravishing. He's male, horny as a March Hare, his animal nature—yes, him too, all of you. Know what I mean, sweet cakes? A chance like this, Raven can't let slip." Mother's fingers roved lightly over my stomach and downward. I admit, she had caused an erection, or maintained it, but that was all right. With Mother, naturally, I never did anything with it. That I wouldn't, we both clearly understood. "Watch where you point that thing," she'd sometimes joke. (Again, the advanced child-rearing philosophy: Nothing wrong with a little erection, natural as a sunrise.) She resumed her story.

"Raven begins kissing her on the lips, on her ear and on her neck. An unfamiliar heat seeps through her; set afire, her skin feels like glowing embers. She quivers, not from fear, or not fear only, no, because the fear is dissolving, blending with this strange, fiery tingling that she craves. And it does increase, as though some incinerating potion has infused her blood. Next, he leads her tenderly back into the bedroom. *Tenderly!* My god, what *is* this? As one bewitched, she follows. Softly, he lowers her onto the bed. Her arms open; her legs simply spread. Oh so softly he licks the blood from her open wounds, and her wounds heal, her scars fade . . . free of scars as I am here because of him. She feels her will dissipate, or rather his will and hers mingle, as the hungers of each consume the other."

Here Mother began to sigh and squirm. Her voice again became murmurous, and her lips and the tip of her tongue would now and then play upon my ear. My scorched ear! I couldn't help it; it was both arousing and frightening. I tried to pretend that this part wasn't happening, the arousal, even though we both fully knew it was. I tried not to draw attention to the obvious, but my erection undermined all such efforts. I listened to her with my entire being. The erection affected my hearing; it enhanced my listening. Perhaps I foolishly imagined it protected me against a yawling torrent of threats issuing from all of them, from Beautiful Woman, Mom, Dad, Giant-Thing.

"Actually, Beautiful Woman doesn't even understand," Mother whispered, "that *this* is desire she's experiencing, never having experienced it before. She's as spellbound and bewildered as a child. Nothing's being imposed on her, certainly nothing that any portion of her resents or secretly opposes. Oh, Raven's a hoodwinker, a seducer, all right. The rogue! But so what? He whispers to her how beautiful she is, how captivating, how hotly he desires her. His hands stroke her moist, yearning body. Absolutely tongue-tied, she's powerless to utter a single word. She merely groans like a damaged animal. For once, in the pain of bliss."

As Mother's hand grazed over my body, I honestly wasn't sure she remembered with whom she was in bed. She seemed transported by her own story. I listened with all the nerves of my being, electrified by every scene set before me.

"Raven asks if he may have her. *He asks!*—asks *her* permission. What she wants matters! It's not merely his own lust that counts. No. For the first time in her buried life, she's happy, and she longs to make this stranger happy. Oh yes, she now apprehends that she *is* with a stranger, or anyway with something certainly alien. A metamorphosis too bizarre to—"

"Metafosis?"

"Giant-Thing's changed so much," the teacher answered, "morphed beyond her comprehension. And she is, to herself, even greater cause for amazement. She recognizes neither his behavior nor her own feelings. Even her dreams could not have concocted this drama."

"Morfed . . . con-cocked? No, I get it. Don't stop."

"That's the worst, my love, when we can't even dream our happiness." Here Mother's whispering desisted and her roving fingers ceased their titillation, leaving me a bit of a Giant-Thing myself. Morphasized. I trembled slightly, mainly because of all the strange, unfathomable interactions racing round in the framework of my arousal . . . My father—someone other than totally himself, a forgery, imitating a monster, but actually in more ways than merely appearance. The three of them: a fiend, a tricky dick-bird, and a woman, beaten by one and screwed bloody by both. All this recounted by Mom, nude and fingering my flamethrower, keeping poised for action against the demons of hell. Pretty comical. These demons thrived on fire, especially fire derived from that source, the sort of source and the sort of fire that they themselves had created.

"Oh, my tumescent *you!*" The remark was distant, anomalous. Although it could have, indeed, applied to me, it seemed not to.

Scarcely capable of speech, I replied, "Too messy?" I didn't know the word but I sensed what she meant. Filled to the brim. Too sweet. Too sweet.

"Dear me . . . sorry, love. Who knows who's responsible for the effects of a story?" She giggled. "Well, of course Beautiful Woman gives herself to Dad, because his kindness entrances her *and* because she fears her Giant-Thing's wrath—after all, this does appear to be Giant-Thing, although in some uncanny way, it certainly doesn't. Yes, under all the newfound bliss that boils like lava though her veins, misgivings and lurking trepidation still threaten her. She's incapable of accepting at face value, so to speak, that someone's truly loving her so gently, someone who appears to be her beastly overlord. At any moment she still expects him to strike her or yank her limbs into contorted postures to accommodate some barbarous lechery. When you've been treated so vilely, it's hard not to expect it again. And yet, after a while, the surging rapture does mostly prevail and sweep her further into this enchantment. She feels what we'd call love, but since she's never felt love before, she can't even recognize it as such. It feels wonderful—that she knows. Oh, she's being had by the trickster. Conned. But hey, who knows from whence rapture springs? This blissful upsurge will overtake you someday too, darling. Just wait," Teacher said.

This blissful upsurge . . . was that something even more than what I was then experiencing, a phantom skulking at the edge of imagination? My distraught mind grabbed desperately at a technicality. "Wow, Mom—but should Dad've been doing that? She's married."

"Yes, yes, he should have. Oh yes. Don't be silly. Remember—as an infant, when she was maybe three years old . . . yes, say three or four, this monster abducted her and hid her away in an obscure forest for maybe . . . oh say, eleven years. She was maybe fifteen or so when your dad discovered her and awoke within her passions she'd never even dreamed of. Certainly, he should have done what he did. My goodness, wouldn't you? Would you have just flown off? Besides, she was irresistible, and irresistible temptations, sweetie, are irresistible. Period. Something someday you'll appreciate, trust Mom." She paused.

I already appreciated that point. Oh the pictures Mother's tale drew in my mind. My heart throbbed. Again, I knew not how to reply. The pictures mother's tale drew in my mind . . . Confusion assailed from many directions, from different depths; things I saw, I somehow sensed, I wasn't supposed to see. The emperor's new clothes. (*Or see,* but have enough sense to act as though you don't.) In that heavy summer heat of gray moonlight, I just waited and listened, and tumescent, stared mesmerized at Mother's ghostly appearance. Was this my mother, or some imposter, the haunting configuration of some shape-shifter? Was my real mother elsewhere? Was anything ever only what it seemed?

Her voice startled me. "But maybe he should've withstood that temptation more stubbornly, 'cause guess what happens. While Raven and Beautiful Woman embrace, each preoccupied with the other, who should enter the room? That's right—Giant-Thing! They're so engrossed, the lovers fail to hear him. He walks in and halts. *Huh!* Flabbergasted, his mind boggles at the sight that confronts him: two entwined bodies, glistening yellow in the lantern light, moaning and rocking back and forth, up and down. Picture it. It doesn't seem to quite sink in. Finally— although it does take a full minute—he recognizes Beautiful Woman, her eyes glazed, rolled back in rapture, her mouth foaming, gasping for air, grunting for *'More! More!'* Writhing, farting even—yeah, sorry, it happens—her arms and legs encircling and clinging for dear life to her paramour—"

"Paramour?"

"Not a version of her Giant-Thing's ever inspired. No, sir! His tiny brain reels. But no, this can't be she—not his slave. Impossible—beyond belief! She who dreads him more than the Grim Reaper—"

"The Grim Reaper?"

"She who fears the Thing even in his absence, fears he'll discover whatever she's done against his wishes and will punish her severely. For something as egregious as *this,* of course, he will simply kill her."

I stumbled over "egregious" and repeated, "Paramour." Maybe the word's velvet softness lent me a place to hide.

"Never would she, his groveling slave, defy him so, never commit such an audacious outrage as this. Betray him! *Never!* And yet, here she is, plundered by another before his bulging eyeballs, before the might of all his swollen bulk. She—plundered and loving it!"

Paramour. Paramour . . . everything seemed to swarm around that word, like bees in a hive. I seemed stuck . . . paramour . . . stalling for time to absorb this swarm of everything. The swollen bulk of all his might . . . oh, Mother, tear me away. I'm rooted (and still am, in a way, but I'm writing to deracinate myself . . . big, dirty words . . .).

"Glowering, blathering, beside himself with rage, Giant-Thing raises his fist like a ballpeen hammer to strike this marauder a murderous crack in the back of the skull. Suddenly, the paramour turns, and Giant-Thing's again shocked, stymied; an even greater disbelief stuns him. Agog, he glares at a mirrorlike image of himself. It's too much to absorb. Face-to-face with himself, he thinks he's dreaming. Feeling her lover withdraw, Beautiful Woman's vision readjusts, and she spots the Giant-Thing towering above, white with rage, a statue of Hercules. Huh! Giant-Thing's both here in her arms and there!

"She bolts up, perplexed, breathless. She, too, thinks she's dreaming. Raven knows he's not dreaming. Your dad at once begins to reconvert himself into the bird that he was—is—so he can scat the hell outta there. The conversion requires only three seconds, but the instant that it's complete, Giant-Thing grasps the situation. He's not all that swift, but his brain clicks just enough here. *A shape-shifter!* What else could it be? He swings with all his might at poor Raven, the hammer fist sending him whizzing like a cannonball across the room to splatter against the wall and slide inert to the floor, a bloody mass. From here things speed up."

No, no, I wanted to scream. *Don't speed things up!* Paramour . . . paramour. Too sweet. Too sweet. Please—no more! I'm a child. Stop me from seeing what I can't, won't, remove from my sight. Tear me loose. Too sweet. Too sweet. Ghosts in the stark moonlight, gleaming teeth, my father pounded to a bloody pulp, my mother not all here . . . my desire and fear crisscrossing, running haywire . . . a hard-on holding out, a vigilant guard dog before the mouth of hell. No more. Go on, go on.

"Giant-Thing belts Beautiful Woman in the face hard enough to knock her cold. Perhaps because he—astute as a shoe—did nonetheless discern that a shape-shifter had finagled her, he postpones killing her. Can't be certain of that. Sometimes he's too dumb to fathom. I bet the dumb ape's flummoxed—flummoxed, that's the right word here, hon—yeah, probably can't shake that image of his double from his noggin. Who knows? It unsettles him; he's superstitious, see; it's as though he slaughtered himself . . . maybe. Yes, maybe he's too befuddled to remember he intends to kill her; maybe he'll merely yank out her teeth. Whatever.

"Anyway, he knows that the only sure way to destroy a shape-shifter is to cremate . . . burn, burn him to ashes, but after scrutinizing the mutilated bird, even poking and stirring the mess with his finger, he determines it's quite dead enough. So he scoops up the smashed carcass in his hands, carries it dripping to the outhouse, and dumps it down the shaft—this part we have to imagine, because who's there to witness it?

"When he returns, Beautiful Woman's revived. She's a survivor. Briefly, her face turns to him, beseeching and desperate. Then, pitifully, she quickly curls into a ball to protect herself. That doesn't work. He batters her extra good, then rapes her, practically impaling her with that gory, long-as-your-arm protuberance, and then he batters her again. Her blood stains the sheets. Insensible, she sinks into a bewildered unconsciousness while he drifts into a peaceful sleep, having forgotten to murder her."

How do you forget to murder somebody? I felt washed far out to sea, drowning in confusion. I was listening, listening, but a roaring in the depths of my ears deafened any clear understanding. Hanging on to an anchor that is sinking.

"Around midnight, Beautiful Woman wakes," Mother was proceeding, "her assaulted body in anguish. Not to wake the fiend, quietly she slides from bed. She is nauseous and she badly needs to relieve herself. Naked, sore, she falters toward the outhouse. The moonlight's radiant, as it is here with us, darling. She enters, squats down, places her elbows on her knees, rests her swollen, aching head in her hands, and begins to weep. Things are awful (they've always been), but today something incredible has, indeed, befallen her, something genuinely miraculous, although—dear god!—she's been nearly beaten to death."

Dithering. Deluged. A roaring in the depths of my ears, smothering . . . swirling. Speechless. Quaking. Excited with . . . by terror—a thrilling rollercoaster, death a thin rail away . . . a horror movie, vampire fangs screwing you in the throat . . . My erection hung on. Why? A fool's sword. Go on, go on, tell me the rest. I can't stop listening. Are you even talking to me? Am I merely listening in? An invisible man? Yes, almost all of everyone's unseen. It was as though she no longer entirely lived here, as though she'd been abducted . . . away somewhere else, maybe in another's arms. Living in her own story. I saw her smile reveal the moon glint of teeth. I stared, transfixed, as she continued.

"Some angel had made love to her, and now she actually hates the maniac with whom she's lived in torment. Yes, she can hate him now not only because of his horrible abuse of her but also because now she has a glimmer of all that he deprives her of. Oh yes, if she could kill him now, she would. But right now, she hurts too much to consider that any further. Where, oh where, is her true love? Slaughtered by this perverted ogre. She feels her bowels stir excruciatingly as the large waste drops from her, splashing in the deep hole. Racking pain rakes her intestines as she strains to release her load, struggling to dump all the bile of her wasted life. Excrement falls freely from her, splattering and echoing in the chamber. Her abdomen contracts; she resembles a woman giving birth. She breathes in the sickening, malodorous air. When she's empty, she remains seated, crouched over, sobbing but at least physically relieved."

Mother, I'm still here. Remember me. I can't breathe any more. The malodorous air. I'm covered, six feet under a shitload of words. Go on, bury me in your stinking tale. The awfulness . . . stories of adults, the story I'm now telling, trying to tell my way out of it . . . a fish out of vomit.

"Stay awake, dearest. The end's near. Or go ahead and sleep, sleepyhead, if you're sleepy." I wasn't sleepy; I was mesmerized. "So after a time, Beautiful Woman's sobbing ceases, and she sits there in the dark, hot silence of the stinky latrine, rocking, endeavoring to soothe herself, recollecting the oh so gentle strokes of her departed lover. She longs for his return, even as a ghost . . . oh, that would be fine, even as a ghost. Then she hears a gurgling below her and feels her fanny warmed by a billowing heat. She's surprised but unafraid. After this extraordinary day, what can frighten her? Not even death . . . only a solace that would be. The upsurge of warmth feels good, so she keeps motionless, alert, awaiting something momentous. She senses another miracle in the vicinity. Why not? This has, most assuredly, been a day of amazements. She waits and listens, unaware that she's smiling."

"Did Dad tell you all of this?"

"No. Yes . . . something's churning underneath, something fomented by her own excrement."

"Fomented?" Did I say that? Probably not. I'd quit using my ignorance to snatch at words as shields. Besides, this tactic the teacher had refused to humor any longer.

"Yes. Excited, her bottom grows increasingly toasted. She smiles; I recall it. She recognizes this heat because it's now inside of her too; it's the same heat, the heat he stokes in her."

Stokes. I didn't repeat that; she did, not to explain anything but rather to emphasize the not-understanding, the not-to-be-understood that infiltrates the sense that stories make of the worlds they make up. In the allegory, absurdity and meaning clasp as lovers eternal. A salmon out of vomit.

She repeated, "Stokes, stokes, yes. Oh, something beneath is definitely afoot. Dare she hope? Well, dare she?"

"What is it, Mom? Can't be Dad. Is it?" Would a drowning kid ask that? Not likely. I was talking to myself, either then or maybe only now.

"Something scratches softly against her pudenda. Oooh, it tickles her, tickles like crazy, divine, god-crazy. You know what pudenda are, sweetie? Here." She placed my unresisting hand between her thighs and rubbed my fingers around a couple of seconds, then removed it. "There, now you know."

"Oh," I said or didn't say.

"Nothing like hands-on schooling." The teacher chuckled.

No. Don't . . . keep it up. Keep it up.

"Okay . . . the tickling becomes persistent. Hmm, humm . . . feels so very, very good, believe me, reignites her inner fire—trust Mother—thumps her heart *bam, bam* against her swelling chest. Feel." She placed my compliant hand on one of her breasts for a moment, then slid it away. Yes, I felt her thumping heart all right. "Oh, no . . . can it be . . . ooh, can it be—he, once annihilated, now reincarnated? Dare she hope? A sudden fanning, a wind gust, more fervent heat. She's mad with expectation. Something warm and solid pushes gently into her, high . . . oh my god—high up into her, two feet. She bends forward to accommodate her revived lover's intent.

"Gradually, with much sloshing about, he ascends fully formed out of her stool. She lifts herself farther to assist his whole ascension. She's spiked, hit as with a bolt of lightning and filled, refilled with gold. It hurts, but ooh blissfully so. She swoons as a martyr would on the way to heaven, with a god risen within her.

"Yes, oh yes, he's back—back in her! God in heaven! She leans far forward, wholly compliant. Yes, he's back . . . and in up to the shank! Awkwardly, she staggers out the door, pressed upon but held firmly by his embracing weight, held amid a powerful flurry of feathers. Claws close sharply around her bursting breasts, a beak forcefully clamps the nape of her neck, punctures the skin a bit, I recall. She bleeds. She shrieks with raw ecstasy. Wings alternately whip and squeeze her torso. Anyone watching would think she's being murdered. Her pleasure has long ago learned to affix itself to pain; there's been no other pathway—women get the knack of it. Sure it hurts, like it always has, but now Beautiful Woman's in love, and that makes all the difference. She knows tenderness is somewhere in there too; she remembers it. Yes, at first he's a bird, a raven, huge—much enlarged . . . he's a tricky fellow, all right.

"Resplendent is he in the silver moonlight. His wings envelop her within the sphere of his magic. Out of her own excrement he's reconstituted himself. She—*she* resurrected him, fertilized him, her bird of love. Out of a cesspool of despair—*this!*"

"No, no, I don't believe it!"

"Yes, no doubt. *It is he!* In and out, in and out. She's raw—a woman—bleeding with a burning, sensuous pain. Raw, sweetie, from a hard day's use, by two men and one fantastic bird, animals all. Now, again, blissful ravishment returns—believe me. God almighty—to be had by a bird! A dirty bird, at that. This sort of bliss, you probably will never encounter, love. Rare it is but not unheard of—Leda and her swan.

"Afterward—finally . . . oh, it seems to have gone on and on, for hours—he releases her exhausted body and lowers her to the ground. Damn, what a day she's put in! And hey, what an eyeload for you it's been, right? Well, why not, it's about your dad! Dazed—she's been dazed most of the day—Beautiful Woman gazes up at her beloved, blind with love, and sees the Giant-Thing looming above her like a mountain."

My god, she just couldn't rid herself of him. Giant-Thing, in one guise or another, inevitably ends up in her. "What happened to Dad?" Did I say that?

"Not to worry. This *is* your dad, sweetie. Don't be fooled. Men—dads—look like monsters at times. But he's just masquerading again, spoofing. He digs a kinky joke; he's a prankster. By now I catch on quickly. I know who he is, or rather who he isn't. He lifts me from the ground, gallant, a knight of old."

"Lifts *you?*" She paid no attention to my question, if indeed I asked that. As I've noted, she actually seemed not always fully present, but neither was I, for that matter. She was with Raven. Where was I? Underneath it all—buried, my penis sprouting up, one living flower. Lifts *me* . . . *me*—maybe that's what I had been hearing all along, pronouns eliding all the way along. Was everything she was telling me a mockery, even of herself? Trust Mother.

"I knew what he . . . what *we* were going to do, baby. Some things you just know. A wish that's been dangling around forever can sense its long-awaited fulfillment hovering in the air. We stroll back into the house, giggling like two giddy kids, like you giggle when you're doin' somethin' mischievous. Oh my, what a day! And now, another transcendent moment nearly arrived.

"The lamps are still lit. Raven takes a butcher knife from the kitchen drawer. It flashes with threat in the yellow light. Giggle, giggle. What fun. She hasn't known what fun is either. Don't be scared, honey pie. A happy ending's coming." She felt me shivering, with cold heat—a fever.

"We steal into the bedroom. I can scarcely contain my laughter. Now's the time of ultimate revenge. He's behind me, gently goosing me forth. We glare down at the sleeping body of Giant-Thing, big, ballooning moonward, not necessarily in response to some gruesome sex dream 'cause, like I said, he's always poked up like that. Glowing like a rod of molten iron.

"Raven hands me the knife and nods, grinning as though both granting permission and sharing responsibility for this most portentous deed—portentous, don't ask! Stay with me, honey—I grin back, snatch the knife. I glare at the huge protuberance emitting light from the middle of Thing's legs. I clack my teeth. I'm sorely tempted, but no, not that. He wouldn't be the same, and it's him, nothing less that I must exterminate. Without a second of further hesitation, I plunge the blade up to the hilt into the black heart. Of all things, the eyes pop open."

"*No, Mother, no more!*" I screamed silently, as from the depth of the sea.

"He stares at us both in stark consternation . . ."

"Consternation . . . please—no more." Did I say this? It wouldn't have mattered.

"Stares first at me, then at his double. Stupid to the end, he probably thinks he's killed himself. Obviously, it's all too much for the ape to figure out. Stupid to the end. With a booming, choking cough, the Giant-Thing disgorges a tremendous fountain of blood. He vibrates wildly, like someone electrocuted. It's spectacular, really! We watch, amused, for several minutes, until the scarlet geyser finally fizzles out. We're splattered. Who cares? Motionless as stone, he's still gaping—wants to see the show to the end, damn it. I glance down to check, and sure enough, it's still there, elevated as ever, pointing moonward. Unfazed, jutting from a bushy profusion of hair, scarlet, fluorescent. Turned on! Oh, you men!

"I hear Raven laughing and feel him goosing me. I just can't forgo this. No way! With every inch of mouth and throat I've got, I engorge the Thing, gagging, but overjoyed. If it meant the death of me, so be it. It evened the score. But mistaking my purpose, the goon actually grins. Jesus, men! Then with the jaw muscles of a lion, I bite fiercely, shake my head, tug with all my might, and eventually chomp off at least a mouth and throat full. Sweet revenge. What an encore, huh? I chew it like a delicate morsel. His big grin fades fast as he sees himself eaten alive.

"We watch, because again he's hosing us, this time with the tubing that's left. What a blood shower—sensational—and this with a hole in his heart. I chew. It's rubbery, like a big bar of licorice. I swallow. I actually wonder, 'Is the dark inside of me now all alight?' Honestly, who can account for the foolishness that dashes into your mind at such moments? I thought of all those fangs he'd ripped from the mouths of women . . . women who'd now rejoice.

"At last the shower sputters, and with a cute little bubble wink or two, shuts off. I see that finally he's truly dead, although with eyes still bulging, not to miss a thing. Who knows what the dead are able to see? Lightheaded with a sense of real accomplishment and with gladness for the first time in my life, I turn to face my paramour."

Who *are* you, Mother? I know I never asked that; I would have been afraid she'd answer. I could handle no more enlightenment.

"Suddenly, the magnificent form of a raven bursts again into existence, a ball of blazing firelight. Before my bedazzled eyes, all I behold is the flashing sweep of his glorious plumage. Iridescent . . . everywhere . . . speed, strength, gushing air. There's a powerful pressure of burning wind. Wings, a blur of glistening blackness. Ascension. I'm blinded. Then—*poof!*—he's gone. Quite an exit! I faint."

And then she added—or maybe she didn't, "And then I wake . . . and years later—let's skip the intervening time, that's another story— years later, here I am in bed with you, my darling, both of us glowing in the dark with heaven-sent light."

And maybe I asked, or maybe didn't—I was far out by then—"Where'd Dad go?"

"Don't know," she might have responded. "Sooner or later, a raven's gotta fly, hon; it's his nature."

Confused, I saw words fly at me like wild birds: obtuse, paramour, chattel, morphed, uncanny, lechery, bedazzled, flummoxed, that's the right word here, hon . . . my lord, did I understand a word of anything she'd said? I was profoundly exhausted; maybe I had lapsed into some half-dream state. Crazy questions arose. Who was she? *What?* Did I really ask that about my own mother . . . my own mother, the foundation of the universe? Who was anyone, anyway? *What?* Well, maybe Dad had changed himself into Mom, or into me, into anyone or everyone I knew. No one was, for certain, who they seemed; everyone was possessed or a copy of something they'd rather die than admit they imitated.

I was astonished that my own watchdog erection had withstood the gleaming teeth of Mother's tale. Watchdog, flamethrower, whatever, good to have around. Who knows, maybe I sort of understood why Giant-Thing maintained his perpetual light, though in the end it did no good; Mom put it out. Everything about this tale of Mom's scared me, and yes, shot me through and through with desire. Desire is always embedded in terror—sometimes very obscurely—triumphing over terror by secretly embracing it, a triumphant surrender against the world's onslaught . . . masochism (when'd I learn that exotic term?), masochism . . . our last-ditch stand, pleasure at any cost. How would Teacher have answered? Crazy questions. For many long years, I've searched for a moral to Mother's tale, like making out shapes in the shifting fog.

It wasn't quite over.

"Oh, Mom, I can't believe this." Did I say that? *I can't believe this.* Sounds so tepid, but maybe the question of belief does reside at the heart of this: that we can never completely disbelieve the fantastic . . . *this* the core of all our woes—the fantastic is true. (No, this conclusion, I suspect, is too ludicrous to apply to anyone other than myself.) No moral. Yes, eventually, I gave up hunting. No moral lies hidden here, none, I'm afraid, made of anything other than illusion. But that's okay. Whatever you think you find's fair. Keeps the senseless at bay—for a while. Would the teacher agree?

Immersed in total belief, shuddering, I said, "I can't believe this."

She answered, "You can't? It's proof you want? Well, from the events of that astonishing day, *you*, my darling one, came to be."

I came to be. I guessed as much.

We lay unmoving, silent as gravestones. I gazed at her, at the moon-white embodiment of this tale, a beautiful woman still. But that was enough. Spent, we slept together, two Ravens enfolding somewhere within the wavering boundaries of the child-rearing philosophy of the day. I dreamed that I was soaring, with wide-stretched sable wings, into the recesses of a dark forest, searching for a glowing yellow window to peer into. A place, someplace not even on the map, as far away as the deepest part of me.

After that night, we never again spoke to each other about any of this. We couldn't. I've waited until now—after Mother's death—to retell the tale. The cause is the cure. A salmon out of vomit.

The Damnation of Tommy Henderson

About my bosom buddy, Tommy Henderson . . .
Oh, if I could pray for him now, I would—long and fervently too—but my influence with heavenly powers is too meager to matter. I feel bad about him; more than normal, I mean—guilty bad, you know. Why? I can't really say. Probably not for any logical reason, but maybe because of the mother I had, or the father I didn't. If I can't pray, I can remember, and who knows, that might be worth something to him; it is to me. As long as a part of you is recalled, surely that fragment remains alive—*re-called*, summoned figuratively forth, if not literally back. If this story rings like a confession in places, well, perhaps that's all it is.

Tommy. I idolized him immediately. What a striking personality he was. Athletic—strong as a Brahma bull, coordinated, fast, handsome as Burt Lancaster in *Trapeze*. Rough-guy type. A three-inch pink scar lined his left cheek. Fascinating. From a knife fight with a gang o' hoods he claimed he quelled in Brooklyn. In Brooklyn—jesus!—where all the armies of night hole up. He was smart enough too. Sure, not what you'd call scholar smart, but street quick; and, man, would the chicks peck outta his proffered hand—I mean, *any*time!

Valentino. Yeah, Lancaster and Valentino—picture that. (In those days, movies, old and new, provided templates into which I crammed much of my desultory experience.) Mother, however, viewed him differently. After she first cast her critical eye over him, she suggested to me that he should audition for monster movies, *The Hulk*, or something equally hideous and overblown. Well, he could clobber the crap outta any asshole in the seventh grade (the year he transferred to my school), and nearly every guy in the eighth stepped aside as well. They were all scared shitless of 'im. Practically overnight he became a superstar, a force with which to reckon. The guys feared and trembled and tucked in their dicks; the chicks oohed and aahed and flashed their beavers. He made explicit what most of us had already surmised: Two categories comprise the world—muscle and beaver.

His family had some dough, expensive cars, riding horses. Nice boost. If he liked you, from the relegated to the elevated you sprang—*boing*! When he hit the scene, I was scarcely more than your ordinary nerd. Naturally, I wanted to buckle to him quick. And I did, as soon as I saw him bloody Benny Magoon's big nose 'cause bully-boy Benny goosed pretty-as-a-peach Mary Mae Bell when she wagged her delectable ass too irresistibly in his hound-dog face. And I swear I saw with my own bulged eyeballs how Mary Mae oiled her snowy white panties in a blink for Tommy, 'cause o' that gentlemanly deed performed for 'er. "My god! *Wow!* Thanks!" she gasped, with that big-eyed Marilyn Monroe innocence. "Ain't nothin'," he muttered and did a crooked little James Dean smirk, with Benny barfin' blood for background. Imagine how that sort o' rumble cranks up the hormonal seepage of pubescent kids. He glanced at me, winked, and nodded—friendly; guess he straightaway dug how impressed I was.

I told Mother. Why? 'Cause I told her everything. She just shook her head with what resembled worldly wisdom and declared that Tommy needed his noggin cracked in two 'cause that cunt Mary Mae only wanted Benny to ram his snout up her butt a foot or so, and everything would've been fine and dandy. Mom minced no words. If I'd had a dad around, I think he would have tempered her some. Maybe not. But a dad not being there made a difference, left a hole to fill, if nothing else. "Who's my dad?" I interrogated and received as reply, "John Doe, dear. A one-night bang who blew town, leaving behind the seed of you in Mommy. That's who."

So, best friends Tommy and I became. Chemistry, I suppose. He bullied me plenty. But hey, what'd it matter? Yeah, I ended up knocked about a bit. We wrestled. Bloody lip, scuffed knee, a bruise here and there I always got. Not too bad. If ya can't deal, split. Once he kneed me in the groin to demonstrate a sure-fire technique in self-defense. I turned green. It took a week to walk upright again. But hey, fuck it! Mom—enraged over the abuse bestowed upon my battered genitals—decreed that he should have his balls snipped off with her pruning shears. Like I said, she minced no words.

But what was the big deal? I survived our roughhousing, didn't I? And besides, he liked me. In those early teen years of fragile self-esteem, nothing counts more than being valued by your peers, with imitation serving as the highest form of flattery. Undoubtedly, he liked me partly 'cause he could lord it over me whenever he damn well pleased. I probably got off on that mistreatment in some obscure way that I didn't then—nor do I now—care to closely inspect or admit. Yeah, he lapped up my high admiration and flattery, I could tell. In any case, he was kind of big brotherly toward me. He enjoyed tutoring me in baseball, boxing, and wrestling—manly jock stuff. A lotta go-till-you-drop calisthenics, I recollect.

But because of him I did, eventually, improve athletically. He also gave me a few "pointers" on jerking off; and whatever I learned about girls in those days, he mostly taught me. Was he adept at unsettling "twats"! What twats were good for, I learned from him. Moreover, he augmented my gutter mouth immensely (not that my own mother hadn't, as well, contributed sizably to this accomplishment). He was certainly good-looking, but more important, he displayed greater maturity than the other guys. After seeing *Samson and Delilah*, I sometimes called him Victor Mature. Mother remarked, "Oh yeah, he's as mature as the head of a prick ever is." (Mother's language—well, it certainly drew attention to itself; it had always been colorful, sometimes a little crazy, and to me, often unnerving. I couldn't put two and two together at the time, but her vulgarity increased strikingly with Tommy's arrival.)

Well, prick-head or no, he knew ways to titillate the budding concupiscence of the gals. Right off, he helped me master the fine art of peeking up their skirts, and "accidentally" touching them, "boob snatching" he termed it. I got clobbered a few times 'cause the twats didn't always smile when I pulled such stunts. Still, now and then I did succeed. If I boob-snatched 'em helping 'em off with their coat, they might just roll their eyes skyward and sigh in fake ecstasy, "Oh, thank you, thank you." And then add, *"DORK!"* He'd laugh, thereby making such humiliations worthwhile. But with him, it seemed the girls themselves usually staged the squeeze. Elvis Presley appeal—he had it, by god! Then there was the snatch itself I learned of—the *real* pot o' gold.

"Who ain't givin' snatch ain't worth havin'." Casanova himself could not have addressed me with authority more elevated.

"Why's that, Tom?" I inquired.

"'Cause it ain't free. Nothin' that precious's worth payin' for. Get it, dude?" No, I didn't, quite. Neither did Mom—or she got it perfectly. When Tommy died, she prophesied, as a sorceress would, that female devils would "snatch" his precious nuts and toss them free of charge into a scalding fire. "Count on it, son." What's the retort to such a pronouncement? I had none. I recognized well enough that mother's life contained an abundance of ills that nourished her negativity. Not infrequently, her comments sounded senseless; at least on the surface, they did. But they troubled me nonetheless, and on occasion, when I laughed at her, she saw just how heavily her strange assertions unsettled me. Why she allowed my relationship with Tommy to grow, I haven't a clue. Maybe she pitied how needful I was of a friend; maybe she needed a scapegoat upon which to target the rage that attended all her bad memories, something to jab her voodoo pins into. And—mamma's boy that I guess I was—I kept delivering him over, a dumb gladiator, to the tiger claws of her vehement condemnations.

I said he taught me. More talented than I at every physical feat, he instructed me in the aforementioned sexual "arts." But as far as school work was concerned, I think he exerted himself to avoid learning anything. That, of course, was also impressive because for preadolescents, book-smarts was for nerds, or worse, fairies. But Mother insisted on the books. In her poor used-to-the-bone life, she had read few, and she probably imagined they possessed some kind of magic. Once, I quoted Tommy on the worthlessness of study time, and Mom informed me that someday my dear but so misguided friend would require his mind for something other than pussy punching and he wouldn't have the brains to realize that he had lost it overplaying his head. *What?* She staggered my comprehension, but I think I finally got that one. Another dire warning against diddling my nether parts. Or maybe that wasn't what she meant. Sometimes the convolution of her rage twisted in upon itself like a nest of snakes. Not knowing what to reply, I said, "Oh, *Mom—jesus . . .*" and felt a little sick in my gut.

With Tommy, I pretended studying was stupid; I scoffed but continued excelling as a student—a contradiction he perceived but let slide. Why? 'cause either he cribbed my homework, or I simply did his for him. Did I care? Not really. Other more venturesome, more manly undertakings occupied him and—I must have reasoned thus—the menial school tasks served as my contribution to these loftier pursuits, for which he was, alas, the more befitting instrument.

Like: We're over at his house. I'm upstairs pondering an essay contrasting ancient Athens and Sparta; he's in the rec room downstairs sucking Sally Sue Hornet's maximally developed tits. Rock 'n roll blares smack into my learned involvement, but even over Presley ("You can do anything but lay off my blue suede shoes") I now and then overhear Sally squeal, "Don't! You stop that! Now don't, really! To*mmy!* C'mon. I mean it! Ohhh . . ." *Ohhhh!* What would a Spartan do? I might have asked my horny self. Push-ups.

Frankly, it was a pretty fair deal 'cause, like movies, Tommy's deeds afforded a vicarious component to my not-always-directly-discharged lust. His were not adventures kept selfishly or discreetly secret. No, he always narrated his sexual conquests in generous, succulent detail—every sigh, slurp, and slush of Sally's, or how he sucked a cup o' juice from Jill's jugs, and "coulda gone right on and porked Pam, but she's doin' the jockey," as he put it.

"What?"

"Ridin' the rag."

"What?"

"The rag. The bloody horse. For christ's sake!"

"Really?"

"Didn't I say so, kid?" To me, whatever he said was gospel.

He flicked his middle finger up in front of my nose.

"What's this bloody fucker look like?" I stared, confused, thinking that for no reason he had merely flipped me the bird.

"No, shit!"

"Believe it, kid." Yes! There I beheld, jutting upward before my astonishment, the wicked implement of Sally Sue's impalement—the crimson taint barely, but still, discernible to true believers.

Mother laughed, took another swig of whiskey, and assured me that after Tommy's death he'd suffer a state of torturous thirst because he would be forbidden to suckle from all the succulent, brimming tits of meretricious (but pissed-off) women flying around. (Meretricious—Mom occasionally came up with an obscure word that had a frightening sound about it.) Not infrequently, Mother envisioned women as also damned—just not as excruciatingly damned as men. Mother was insane, not that I could admit that then, not even fully now. (To call a mother full of pain "insane" seems somehow to shamefully misconstrue the heart of the matter.)

But how firmly she imbedded in me her stinging disparagements, like a wasp implanting its eggs in a hapless host. I was about twelve or thirteen years old, highly impressionable, and admittedly, overly attached to her. Not good! Wouldn't I sometimes raise a boner when she combed my hair, stroked my cheek, or caressed the back of my neck? "Watch where you flex that love muscle, sweet," she'd say before giving me a quick little kiss and lick on the lips. Around the time of the Sally Sue Hornet escapade, Mom stuck her tongue in my mouth, and for damn near half a minute, squirmed it around. Did I move away? Afraid not. When she stepped back, she asked, "Do you think your pal would eat that up?" She was a bit tipsy. I glowed with scarlet embarrassment. My *pal?* Not always swift to comprehend, I first assumed she meant my penis. But the question sounded peculiar, even for Mom. The next day it dawned on me that perchance my *pal* was Tommy. That, however, made even less sense, given her relentless castigation of him. But sometimes she made no sense. Yet, as I've conceded, many remarks I deemed senseless did, nonetheless, strongly affect me.

Her castigations could be relentless, and I did provide her with much material. I told her practically everything about Tommy, as she had conditioned me. "Never, *never*, lie to Mother. Now, tell me exactly what happened, sweetheart." Yes—a wuss. (Probably why I continue ratting on everybody—as I'm doing now.)

Once, after school, a couple of delinquents itchin' for a scrap attacked me and would certainly have pounded me to a pulp had my pal not intervened and hammered their ugly mugs, chasin' 'em off wailing like babies. Stallone in the flesh—a Rocky/Rambo guardian angel! When I dutifully recounted this valor to Mom, she contended that this was the single charitable deed monster Tommy had ever performed, and quite likely, his last. "His last?" She ignored my confusion, adding that in hell his own nose would be busted with a crowbar and it would bleed profusely every month, and he wouldn't have brains enough to recollect the cause for such retribution.

"My god, Mother—stop this!"

"Stop what?" she yelled. "You're all alike. How's a kid become a prick? Beat it!"

"Mother, stop! I can't stand it!"

"*You* can't stand it!" Yes, at times, Mom was insane. (But who isn't if you scratch their surface a bit?)

Before I met Tommy, I was shy and backward in most social graces. Hangin' with him, though, imbued me with more courage and even a more appealing style. His example managed eventually to transfigure me, a pimply-faced wimp, into quite a charming, debonair lad. I say eventually—that is, by the time I reached my high school senior year. Yeah, proud he would have been of his handiwork. My class, by then, had twice elected me its president, and I had even cultivated a flowering love life. With whom? None other than that very same Sally Sue whom my buddy finger-fucked beneath my meditations on the combatants of the Peloponnesian War.

But maybe love and status wouldn't at all have impressed him; maybe he would have been impressed only with the brief but rabid period of licentious exploits that, during my freshman and sophomore years, I sped through like a March hare. Yet, he would have changed too, wouldn't he have? Maybe not. Mother (whose assessments of my girlfriends had become as caustic as had been those against Tommy) cautioned me that if I ever sucked Sally Sue's nipples (or "brown eyes" as Mom called them), I'd go as stone-blind as Tommy himself now was 'cause

Sal's jugs exuded the toxin of a woman debased. "Such women can kill you, darling." That was all there was to it. Kill me! Be warned, my darling! Apparently, I had outgrown Mom's influence somewhat, or managed to rebel against it, because "such women" had become the only sort to interest me—then and, for that matter, now.

All this, however, was later, after I lost him; and since this story is not about me, let me jump back to him.

Tommy rarely visited my house. Mom didn't forbid it; she merely preferred it that way, which was okay with me 'cause we lived on the wrong-way side of the tracks, and Tommy's family was way right. They even had a stable full of Arabian horses, and Tommy was teaching me to ride. Besides, his parents seemed never home, while my mother almost always was, at least during the daytime. She worked nights, waitressing at Longhorn's Bar and Grill, a rough, redneck joint that paid moderately well. It wasn't too unbearable, Mother maintained, if you could slap off a pinch and poke or you didn't *always* mind offering your own butt as the end of a joke. Tommy once revealed to me that "guys in town hung at that trashy two-bit tavern only 'cause your sexy mom shags tables there, kid." It delighted me, I confess, to hear him portray her as sexy, even though his large black eyes gleamed, and he wet his lips like a famished vampire when he did so.

"She's hot, you lucky putz!" He even inserted his thumb betwixt his index and middle fingers, sliding it back and forth, right up close to my face. With chagrin I turned beet red. "Yeah, she fires every rod in town. She's gorgeous, man," he pronounced. "But"—and I may have hated him for a brief moment when he added—"she's sure weird." Seeing my smile drop, he grinned, his glistening lips thinned, his eyes narrowed to a flickering dot, and he looked as evil as Bela's Dracula. Then he punched me sportively on the forearm, and I chose to conclude that he was merely joshing and forgave him instantly.

When Mother heard this, she prophesied that "a cunt would chew off his cherry pecker and spit him into the fires of hell." Her eyes focused on some middle distance as she spoke, and I smelled the bourbon on her breath. "No more hard-ons. Think about it, sweetie." Then she shouted, "Pricks! Don't fuck with us!" Us? Who? I flinched as though I'd been smacked. Did she intend for every prick in the world to heed that threat? I took it personally 'cause I was, after all, the only one of those in the room. I wanted to bawl.

My mother was beautiful. Who did she look like? I always believed Ann-Margret in *Viva Las Vegas* until Tommy modified my view. He and I were watching *Trapeze* at his place, when he burst out, "Your mom!" He pointed at Gina Lollabrigida! I scrutinized Gina—how glittering, how luscious—and yeah, she really did look like Mom. I was proud and tickled he saw Mother as so beautiful. But during one of the magnificent aerial scenes with Gina aloft, he shouted, "Fuck—look at that! No net, pussy swingin' free as a bird above yer fuckin' head. All the guys gawkin', prayin' she'll fall in their laps and straddle their bone! Christ a'mighty!" I was too tongue-tied to speak. Gina, my mom, straddling all those bones. How could I *not* picture it? I wanted to hide my face. And from the corner of my eye, I spied Tommy's own hard-on readying for the fall.

Later, Mother said, "He thinks I look like her, does he?"

"But you do, Mom."

"Hm. Well, I guess I've been hangin' and playin' without a net all my life."

"He meant it as a compliment, Mom."

"You'd have to break off his bone to get a real compliment. I don't need pricks praying I'll fall and land on 'em, sweetheart. I been nailed enough." With that she patted me gently between the legs. "You're all alike," she sighed and shook her head. (Yes, I came to appreciate belatedly, it is true how severely she felt impaled by men.)

On another occasion, Tommy disclosed that his father had once characterized my mother as having a bee in her honey box. The disquieting implications of that rattled me too much to question what exactly Mr. Henderson meant. (I must say, in those days, I seemed to never quite fully understand anything people said.) I now suspect that after my father—who never was her husband—abandoned Mom, she then ministered to her own embittered heart, which was, alas, imprisoned inside a voluptuous body, a body that persecuted men, whose desires, I'd bet, she refused to gratify. And although men buzzed 'round her beauty, and I believe her strangeness too, they must have resented her. They must have sensed she wished to send them all to hell.

"What is hell, Mom?" I once queried. (She frequently spoke of hell and the like, and yet, oddly, she had nothing to do with real religion. But hell certainly constituted for her something a bit more than the most awful abode conceivable elsewhere.) "It's a bone that can't shoot off, so it makes devils," she explained. I presume she meant unfulfilled desire creates the torments of the underworld—but not only the underworld. A drunken son of a bitch once beat her up and tried to rape her, but she cut his throat in the nick of time (with a penknife she just happened to have handy). Sliced him badly but not fatally. I can still see the bastard's blood staining her face and torn clothes, and gluing together strands of her tangled hair.

"Look at the mess he made of me," she wept. And gazing stupefied at her, so raw and mauled over, I wept too, holding her tightly, very tightly, 'cause I wanted my heart pressed as closely as possible to hers. She slumped to the floor, pulling me down, and we lay there wrapped in each other like a pile of wet rags.

Mother owned that she must, indeed, seem weird to men, "but only 'cause my bee declines to buzz 'round their flies." She giggled at her silly little pun. "Besides, that bee's a mad-as-hell hornet that'll sting any prick that pokes this box for honey. That bee protects me, sweetie-pie." *Please, Mother, don't tell me anymore of this,* I wanted to yell out but couldn't.

One night after Mother had gone to work, Tommy dropped over. We swiped a few Buds from the fridge, kicked those back real quick, and spent a couple hours foolin' 'round, gossiping, and swapping dirty jokes. We also "ear-fucked," as Tommy termed it, a dozen class cunts, meaning we phoned 'em, disguised our voices, and whispered our raunchiest obscenities. We called that "shootin' the receiver." We clocked each call to check our predictions of how long any particular "ear" took to "shut the fuck up." Great sport.

We played this game a lot, and occasionally, we got a big surprise— like that night when, for the first time, we rang Rita Yearling. Now, Rita was the president of the Teens for Christ Club, and she would—as she wrote in an essay she actually volunteered to read aloud in English class— rather expose her "vernal body" (she said *that*) to the searing sands of the Sahara than say "dammit." *Vernal body!* Well, yes . . . but totally oblivious, she failed to detect that in her reading she had blasphemed. I felt compassion for her, but along with the rest of the class I couldn't refrain from snickering.

Clearly, she hadn't an ounce of self-awareness (even less than I had). Exposed in the Sahara . . . *please!* She hadn't the least reserve about flashing (but unwittingly as 't'were) her chaste but no-less-carnal attributes, thereby agitating a guy's testosterone. (How often did I conjure spectacles of her nude body squirming on the scorching sand, imploring relief, whereupon I would—oh, never mind.)

Anyhow, after minimal soul searching, we phoned goody-good Rita. And what'd she do? She let us shoot off in her ear till we ran bone dry and were left with nothin' to do but simply hang up. Taken aback, we gaped dumbly at each other, like a couple of horny toads outfoxed.

Later that night, we of course found time for Tommy to copy my homework for social studies so he could hand in the assignment next morning. And as part of our well-rounded evening, we also watched

The Curse of the Mummy on the tube. (Notable, because the following day
in English class, this flick would figure into a discussion of Poe's "The Fall
of the House of Usher"—a tale of incestuous encryptment). Mr. Knoll,
or Know-It-All as we dubbed him, would observe, "You can never inter
evil—not entirely; it always comes unburied." "How's that, Teach?" "We
ourselves resurrect it." "But, Teach, why?" "Because, students, it's
inextricably confounded with our deepest cravings." "Huh?" "We'd rather
die than leave that stuff entombed." "We would?" "Yes, students. You
see, the undead embody the sorry state of our darkest cravings." *Embody?*
At that arid juncture, I'd be ogling Rita Wetear's high-thigh expo, and
sure enough, an evil configuration within my own dungarees would
revivify. My very own mummy. Out of the crypt into the light. A Poe
moment!

At one point in our evening, Tommy strutted out of the bathroom,
waving in the air, like a victory flag, a pair of Mom's skimpy black panties,
which she had washed that day and draped over the towel bar to dry. He
dangled the frilly trophy in front of his crotch, modeling it indecently.

"Hey, mind if I snatch these?"

"What!"

"Yeah, they're right next to the best thing, ain't they?"

"*What!*"

"Somethin' to flog the bishop."

"What bishop?" He tapped his penis. "She'd kill you, man!" He did
his fiendish Dracula grin and acknowledged that, yeah, she probably
would.

"But how would she know?" he asked.

"She'd know."

"Yeah—yeah, I guess she would." He let me grab the panties from his
hand, humorously conceding me the winner, the lucky stiff, to whom
tonight the prize belonged.

"Hey, look, tell 'er somethin'. Tell 'er I got a wild young colt, a real
bucker she can straddle bareback any ol' time she wants. Tell 'er, will
ya?"

"What! Do you wanna die?"

"That way? I might. Tell 'er."

"You're crazy!" I glowered at him.

"Yeah." He laughed, and I did too, finally.

(That night wasn't atypical—not for Tommy and me, maybe not for
most kids that age. But you know, the more you review your life, the
more you see how not uninsane you've been, and perhaps especially
during those hormone-driven years I'm now recalling. Anyhow . . .)

I narrated most of this to Mother. I shouldn't have. She was good 'n soused and it enraged her—truly enraged her. I was shocked; I had never seen her so furious. "He likes that fuckin' word *straddle*, doesn't he? Tell him to shove his colt up his shit-packed ass and yank the trigger," she shrieked. "See if it's a good *buck*." Tell him! Tell him? Never before had she directed me to tell him anything. (Conversing through me, they were!)

She went berserk, tearing at her hair, ranting and howling, as though completely demented, raking her hands savagely through the air as though she were clawing at him, or enacting both the role of the rapist and the raped. I stood with my mouth agape. I watched her jack up her skirt and yank down her panties. "Take the fucker these. Somethin' to shoot the bishop in." She flung them, and they struck my face. "Flog the motherfucker. Tell him they're bandages for his mangled manhood." *Mangled manhood!*

"Mother—my god! Please! Don't!"

"'My god'? What are you saying? If God doesn't jerk his nuts off, I will. *Do you understand me?* Tell your prick that! *Go on, goddamn it!* Get lost!"

"*What?*"

"I can't stand to see how you're growing up. Every prick in the world's the same." She exploded into a torrent of tears. I had never seen her weep so bitterly.

Do you understand me? Then? No, Mother, not then. I doubt I understood much of anything then. Why did I torment her this way? I knew something about him burned her up, something about Tommy and me—*and* her. Why did I keep bringing him to her, dousing gasoline on smoldering coals? Why did I continually subject myself to her frightening, insane cynicism, her hatred, her wounds, some of which I myself persistently inflicted? Such excruciating questions surfaced a decade later, after she had died of liver failure, when she wasn't near enough to distract me from unwelcome yet much-needed self-reflection.

But, "*Do you understand me?*" Yes, Mother, *some*, but only *now*, after it's too late. Forgive me. Christ, the more you reflect on your life, the more forgiveness you find you need. But again, I've digressed. This story's not mine; unless whatever we write's ours, whatever we read's ours. No matter.

There's a penultimate episode here—one before the last—that I hesitate to reveal because I'm still too embarrassed and afraid of what it might suggest. ("Tell me everything." She trained me well.)

The final day of the eighth grade, I came home and nearly collided with Mother as she bolted out the front door hurrying to work.

"Oh my! Aren't you home early, darling?" she asked, surprised. I was also surprised because she appeared so . . . I don't know, vibrant, even happy; very different from her usual angry or downcast self.

"Last day o' school. Out early."

"Marvelous!"

"*Marvelous?*" (A word she never used.) "Eh, yeah—well, it is. Ah—you look . . ."

"Yes?"

"Smashing."

"Really? Imagine that." She kissed me quickly on the cheek. "Warm up that spaghetti in the fridge. I chopped up some salad for you. And finish off the apple pie. See ya tomorrow. We'll go horseback riding or something."

"Horseback riding?"

"Whatever, dear. Celebrate."

"Celebrate? What?"

"The end, the beginning . . . whatever. It's summer. Love you. Be good. 'Bye." She dashed away. When she reached the car in the driveway, she turned, smiled, and winked at me. I had never seen her look so radiant. For a moment, I remained motionless. Was *that* my mother? She drove down the road, the gray Pinto shimmering in reflected sunlight. I was dazed, as though jolted by a heavenly vision.

Puzzled, I walked through the house to the kitchen, poured a large glass of cold lemonade, and leaned against the counter, thinking about . . . her radiance. I frowned and smiled alternately, wondering if I had ever understood anything about her. A creaking noise coming through the open back screen door startled me. I stepped out and was alarmed to find Tommy sitting in the old rocking chair, tilting sluggishly back and forth. He didn't look at me; actually, he seemed not to even observe my presence.

"Hey, man, what's up?"

"Nothing." Still, he refrained from looking at me.

"What are you doing here? Mom was home!"

"Yeah."

"*Yeah?* Did she know you were here?" He didn't answer. His head hung down; his complexion was ashen. He seemed subdued, despondent even, absorbed; totally unlike himself.

"What's wrong?"

"I gotta piss." He rose slowly and walked to the bathroom. A little stooped. And . . . was he limping? When he returned, without a word, he passed me, stepped from the porch, and headed off down the sidewalk. Hands pushed deep in his pockets, he leaned forward slightly, moving slowly, carefully, like an old man.

"A couple o' Eastwood flicks tonight, Dirty Harries. Wanna catch 'em?" I almost shouted because, although he wasn't that far away yet, I felt he really couldn't hear me. It was a little eerie.

"No, not tonight."

"What's wrong?"

"Jus' don't feel well, that's all."

"What's wrong?" He didn't respond. I watched him hobble down the street in broken motions, a stooped stick figure. A block away, he seemed to evaporate into the heat waves of the sidewalk as though incinerated by the bright June sunlight. I then went to take a pee myself, and I noticed on the white tile bathroom floor, near the toilet bowl, a fleck of blood. I stared at it. I thought it was Mother's. I spit on my fingers, whipped it up, and inspected the red stain on my fingertips.

I knew immediately, but too late, that I should not have touched that blood. For some crazy reason I perceived it as an indelible blemish that would discolor my very being. A cliché, I suppose. Blood on my hands. But still—how do you cleanse or cover such invisible sights if what they attest is true? All the perfumes of Arabia—Lady Macbeth in that Polanski flick, a few days ago—I didn't think I had comprehended a line of it . . .

I never related to Tommy any of Mother's expressed revulsion for him. I'm glad now I didn't. He surmised fairly accurately, I'm positive, her truculent denunciations of him. I'm glad I never told him because at the end of June that summer, he fell suddenly and acutely ill of testicular cancer and died quickly, even before the summer closed. I was deeply distressed over his condition during the couple of months he fought so desperately and agonizingly to live. During that time, my mother sought, consolingly, I really do believe, to persuade me that his horrible depredation was absolutely just, all ordained for the best by God who, as always, knew his business perfectly well. *And*—she just couldn't resist—it was all emerging as *she* had foretold.

(Why, oh why, had I related to her all those things about him? Why had I allowed the poisonous body of her hatred to embrace him? I posed these questions to myself a thousand times; the answers have all been disquieting. But there's no point in spelling them out. I'm not the focus here.)

Mother drove me daily to the hospital. Following a few visits, he scarcely even spoke. Often he slept or dozed half conscious under the effects of heavy sedation and pain medication. Occasionally, he was so delirious he even failed to recognize me. I would listen to him groaning and imagine that he already stood at the doorway to that inferno into which Mother had consigned him. It was dreadful. When he slept, I usually held his hand, and sometimes I could feel him holding mine—exerting a pressure deep from within his dreams or nightmares. The day before the end, he stunned me by whispering that he wanted to see my mother, a wish he had to repeat three times before I convinced myself I heard correctly. I rushed down to the car where she was waiting, reading a magazine, and I told her his request.

"No, that's not necessary, dear," she answered, without bothering to glance up from the magazine.

"Mother—*please!*"

"No. Are you ready to go?"

"Mother—*please. I beg you!*" Annoyed, she tossed the magazine in the backseat and sprang out of the car.

"I won't be long."

I waited nervously. The minutes crawled by. I don't know how long she had been gone—five minutes? half an hour?—before I bolted back into the hospital, taking the stairs, not the elevator. Why was I running this way, with such urgency? I think I was crazy. I intended to surprise them. But why? I had to find out what was happening.

When I reached his room, I paused outside the door, listening. For what? My heart pounded. Breathless, I forced myself to enter his room. Mother wasn't there. His eyes were closed, his mouth was slightly open, and his breathing rasping and labored. He was groaning and whimpering but appeared to be sleeping. Tears streaked the sides of his emaciated face. Through the sheets I could see the outline of his throbbing erection. I couldn't believe it. For a full minute I stared before averting my eyes. I had witnessed something forbidden. How could this be?

I ran from the room. Mother sat in the car, reading.

"Where you been?" she asked.

"Nowhere. Did you see him?"

"Yes, I did. He looks better."

What did you say, Mother? I think I've lost my hearing.

I gazed through the windshield at nothing I could see.

The next morning, I learned he had died. I cried harder than I ever had, harder than I would later at my mother's funeral (the only other loss that would matter). Even though I had been expecting him to die at any moment, his actual death sent me reeling. I became dizzy; I nearly fainted. It was beyond belief. I had known him not even a year. To think that I would never, *never* again see him, that he was gone forever, that he had now begun the eternity of his dreadful atonements, was all too terrible. My friend. My first friend. Gone forever. *Forever!*

What in the world *is* gone forever? Who made that up? My god! This gravest of all realities was too unreal for me to conceive. The undead— no wonder, even about the dead, we always imagine some kind of life. (Poe and Mr. Know-It-All were right.) I pictured Tommy now in his gruesome afterlife, suffering those cruel tortures prescribed—not by God, but by my mother—for all the sinful misdemeanors of his boyhood, for a boy growing into a prick. I visualized quenchless thirst; ceaseless, unendurable longing, the fulfillment of desire forever withheld; and castration. I saw his penis poised for Gina Lollabrigida's pussy to drop on it; saw his bishop beating beneath the sheet in a hospital bed, begging for a hand; saw Delilahs materializing out of the burning Sahara sands, saw them swarming 'round him, meretricious, pissed off, flaming pussies everywhere, a hair's breadth beyond his reach; saw acrobats flying above in a bloodred firmament, overplaying his head; saw brown eyes an inch beyond his parched lips; saw a mouth that looked like Mom's chewing off his cherry picker, making good the mangled manhood of a boy. I saw everything.

For a time I was delirious. I wanted to follow him into that perdition, wherever it was, and cut a deal with the devil in charge to pardon and release him. I didn't realize then that the only force that bound him in this state emanated from Mother's persuasion over my imagination.

Somewhere during that sorrowful day of his death, I reached beseechingly out for my mother. She wrapped her arms around me and pressed my head between her breasts, and I sobbed inside the warmth of that surrounding softness. Every man in town would have envied me my place of solace. I am ashamed to admit that amid my grief I thought of that, as though I were a victor. But I did think such thoughts—probably because I knew that right then, *there* in that very spot, Tommy himself would have died to be, instead of in that damnation where he now abided, inflamed by all those inaccessible women flaunting their bountiful bosoms and open vaginas—trying to torture him to death even more. Cunt that ain't free ain't worth havin', I wanted to remind him.

My mother rocked me back and forth, and I recalled him rocking on our porch, somehow damaged, absent already, crippling away, broken down, eventually evaporating into the thin air of memory. Had *he* rocked inside my mother's embraces? It seemed to amaze her that I was so stricken, so inconsolable. I wanted to bury myself in her. And she opened herself as wide as she possibly could to all my anguished outpouring. With her body enveloping me, through the sounds of my sobs, I heard her whisper, "At last," and I wondered whether he had ever heard her utter those words, with her moist lips stoking his ear.

Highway Zero

A cross untamed land they race, afraid with courage. Mail satchels saddled, from one relay outpost to another, from St. Joe to Sacramento, from country's heart to sea edge, they race amid stampeded buffalo and outraged Paiutes, tearing across the land. Hurrying letters and postcards, silent words horsebacked from far-off hand to hand, for eyes too far out of sight to see, to read. "Ma died today. Can't ya come home now?" "Frank James killin' with Quantrell. Whupped the blue-bellies at Wilson's Creek. The South's awinnin'." "Bad here. Sis sold her treasure for a buck. Can ya send a little somethin'? Love ya anyhow." "Where's Sacramento, Billie Ray? Ya lost me, love." Words galloped from here to there. Saddle sore, bone shaken, bedeviled with Cupid's cramp, arrows zinging past their ears, racing, zigzagging, then flat out. They speed, knowing where they're headed. Minus roads, but never that far off course. Always on Highway Zero, somewhere uncharted.

Richard Knott had been depressed lately, even confused. About what? Profession, marriage, age, money, friends—you name it. Tired, angry, fed up with everything, including himself, mostly himself. Here he was, nearly fifty-eight, a psychoanalyst, but unable to slay his own inner demons. What was going on? Midlife crisis? Call it that—a diagnosis as worthless as any other. Actually, wasn't he a bit beyond midlife? Shit! Anyhow, good to get away. Yes, and on his way to a class reunion, the fortieth. Looking forward to it. *The fortieth* . . . damn, had so many years passed? How many more remained?

He gazed out the window of the 747. Puffy white clouds bloomed like cotton balls beneath the plane, elegant, scarcely moving, going nowhere, content. What would it be like, he wondered, tumbling into one of these foamy cushions? So very inviting, so safe looking. Hard to believe you'd fall right through. But alighting on something real soft sounded awfully appealing. In a way, that's what this forty-year reunion promised—old friends, everything atingle with warm reminiscence and laughter, drinks, dancing with former sweethearts, maybe even tumbling

into bed with one . . . with Alicia Greene. (Ah yes, would she show up?)
A reunion. Yeah . . . soft, easy. Hmm . . . who *would* be there? It surprised
him that he hadn't considered that more. Who did he want to be there?
Did it even matter? After all, he hadn't bothered to attend the previous
three reunions, had he? But now he needed to connect with the past;
he felt ungrounded.

Yeah, ungrounded. His marriage teetered on the brink of dissolution.
His wife, Lilly, was sick to death of his moody self-absorption and disregard
of her. And he had indeed begun to view himself as unworthy; she'd
wasted her love on him because at love he was so inept.

"Go to St. Joe. Get yourself together. Find yourself," she said, as he
prepared to depart. "Bring me back what you find. It has to be better,
darling, than what we have here."

"Might not be."

"Gotta be. Do something adventurous. Fluff yourself up. Ride for
the Pony Express."

"Century and a half too late for that, Lil. Besides, I'm over eighteen."

"Okay. E-mail me then. 'Bye."

Across the aisle sat a woman with long heavy black hair, pale
complexion, full red lips, protruding cheek bones. Her breasts swelled
with her breathing, as though she were anxious or excited. Other than
that, she scarcely moved. She wore a bloodred dress. Richard couldn't
refrain from glancing at her; and although she seemed so inwardly
focused, a couple of times he thought she glanced at him, but he couldn't
be positive about that. She looked like an attractive witch. He wanted to
speak to her, but for some reason he could find nothing to say. That
somewhat surprised him because, generally, he easily made the
acquaintance of women. Not this time, however. Somehow she appeared
too forbidding. A bloodred dress. Jesus, in the summer heat. Well, you
can't win 'em all.

He pressed the button on the armrest, reclined the seat, closed his
eyes, and stared into the darkness. No, can't win 'em all. He was tired.
Hadn't been sleeping well. Insomnia—another problem. Yes, indeed,
nice to get away. Precisely what the doctor ordered, himself being the
doc. Physician, heal thyself. That had a lonely kind of echo to it. He was
a psychoanalyst. Right now, that too sounded lonely. All that dwelling in
the netherworld of heartache—dreams, madness . . . desires twisted by
guilt, anxiety, and shame into every imaginable demon. Takes a toll. You
don't battle monsters of the deep and exit unscathed. That was it: He
was a battle-weary warrior returning to the bosom of his homeland. Yes,
he *was* tired. Find a cave and crawl in . . . The plane hummed soothingly

through his body. Very relaxing. Perhaps all he required was this: just to stay nestled in this plane for days, not go anywhere. Imitate those clouds; yeah, either that or fall through one . . .

Who'd be there? In the dark enclosure of his eyelids, a woman encircled her luscious arms around his neck. All his troubles ebbed. Ah yes, here at the self-center of the world, Richard Knott now dreamed of himself snugly enfolded.

Around 9 AM the red-eye express landed in Kansas City. A quaint airport, uncrowded, manageable, in the heart of the country. He noticed the woman who had been seated across the aisle walking in front of him. That dangerous dress . . . God, what a gorgeous figure, long, mesmerizing legs. Did she right then glance over her shoulder at him? Hardly. "Excuse me, may I introduce myself. We were meant to meet. I'm—" Can't win 'em all. He swerved to avoid colliding with someone, turned back, and she had vanished.

From Avis he rented a car and headed north on I-29 for St. Joseph. No hassle. Easy as pie. It always astonished Richard how uncomplicated life could be once you escaped the insane congestion of the East Coast. He'd been born and raised in St. Joe, still . . . you forget how much simpler existence can be. You become so inured to the mangling your psyche suffers in an area like New York. Sure, it gives you everything, but everything is never what you need. Deals with the devil. But whoever learns that lesson?

Richard thought about this as he drove slowly, taking in all the lush green farmland. Oh, the glorious August morning sunlight! Cornfields, colorful meadows aflow with wildflowers, cows sauntering around lakes . . . bucolic, a tranquil place, Missouri. Oh yeah, tranquil—a place where Jesse James, Wild Bill Hickok, and Bonnie and Clyde had had a bang-up time. Still, calm enough now.

Unhurried he drove. Maybe he ought to just move back here. Yeah, ease out of his practice and move back. He'd dreamed a few nights ago that he was driving and his car began to wobble. He discovered one of his tires was flat. Well, of course that had abundant implications—none pleasing. But he now realized that it depicted something about retiring. Cute. And yes, he did feel his life wobbling. So, retire and return home. No, you can't go home again. Home? You can't get there from here. Sometimes you're too ruined to return to something really good that you once possessed, either because you simply outgrew it, or too young or too stupid, you failed to appreciate it. You're too ruined: Was that a correct way to put it? How could a psychoanalyst—a psychoanalyst, of all things!—return to St. Joe? In St. Joe, who ever heard of such an oddity? Well, nonetheless, here he was, in fact, on the road to St. Joe.

A party had been planned for eight o'clock Friday night. The reunion committee called it the Big Bang. Okay. Enticing. In his hotel, Richard eagerly showered and dressed, and then took out the directions that had been mailed to him. It was at Roger Maize's home in Glenn Creek. Richard didn't remember Roger. Frankly, he remembered very few of his classmates. Although Richard certainly knew his way around St. Joe—not a large town—he didn't recognize Maize's address, either. Well, there was no address, really—just a map sent by the committee as a guide.

The map was small, about three inches square. He studied it. It had been hand drawn and then photocopied. The lines were vague and the details rather scant. The more he examined the map, the less sense it made. Undoubtedly anyone living in St. Joe would know at a glance the location of Maize's home. Great . . . Richard had to smile—the ideal map for anyone who didn't need it! But yes, the lines and words were faded, even the north/south coordinates seemed imprecise. Points that Richard might have guessed lay south were marked as north. Was it possible that such a gross error had been overlooked?

Yeah, he couldn't even pinpoint where he was right now in relation to the map's geography. In a couple of spots, the drawing was slightly blurred, as though in the handling and packing, Richard himself might have smudged it. And there seemed to be some image bleeding through, an embedded figure . . . a face, maybe. Pretty weird. Was this a joke? The actual home site seemed located just off the very edge of the map. Presumably, this squiggly little arrow was meant to point to that; otherwise, it pointed to nothing. Hmm . . . what a useless document. Fairly humorous, though. Well, he'd show it to the desk clerk and get the directions straight.

Richard handed the clerk the map. "Have a look at this." After careful inspection, the clerk grimaced.

"What's this a map of?"

"Some part of St. Joe."

"Really? No—I don't think so. Well, maybe. Damn, I don't know. That arrow—Glenn Creek—could be pointin' at one of them new high-dollar sections south of town. Maybe it's just a house out in the middle of nowhere. Could be."

"It's not clear?"

"Not to me. Sorry. Wait a sec. What's that? See it? It's a face, ain't it? See? Grinnin'."

"Yeah, sure, kinda does look like a face."

"Funny, ain't it? Damn, and what's this say? It's a zero. What's that—Highway Zero? Damn! Never heard of it. Looks like Glenn Creek sets right off that highway."

"I didn't know there was anything in St. Joe that everybody didn't know about."

"Yeah, right. But that looks like the Faraon Street Overpass . . . sort of. And there's Pickett Road, I think. Yeah, I'd head south, see where that takes you. Sorry I ain't much help."

Richard smiled as he strolled toward his car. With these guidelines, he could wind up practically anywhere. How peculiar. He had flown halfway across the country to a town he thought he knew like the palm of his hand, and here he was—lost. He chuckled. All right, who really knows the palm of his own hand? Fine. Christ, St. Joe wasn't that big. What the hell, how lost could he get? Time to kill. He could afford to be aimless; in fact, he welcomed it. It felt kinda fun.

In the parking lot, entering his car, he believed he glimpsed the woman who had been seated across from him on the plane. She was in a car several yards away; she might have been looking at him, but he couldn't be certain because the late afternoon sunlight reflected on the window glass of the woman's car. He smiled and nodded at the glaring image and then drove off. What a remarkable coincidence.

He headed south on I-29 searching for Highway Zero.

Besides the class reunion, this vacation was to serve additional purposes. That morning he had visited his mother's grave. Sad, depressing—she had died so young, at fifty-five, of breast cancer. Twenty years ago. He had been very close to her. Oh, how she had doted over him, called him her savior. "He gives all the meaning to my life, to my marriage," she had often exclaimed.

Gazing with tear-filled eyes at the small, flat gravestone, the unsettling realization suddenly dawned that, as a son, he had been a failure. *A failure?* It sounded too harsh. He resisted this accusation, but a guilty little memory promptly rushed forth to bear witness against him. He hadn't even managed to be with her during her final hour. *Hadn't even?* "Better hurry out here," her doctor had advised. And didn't he intend to hurry? Yes, he did, right after he saw one more day of patients. Hadn't he booked a flight? Yes, yes . . . but too late!

Well, at the time, he had been—his defense persisted—in New Jersey and she was in Los Angeles at the City of Hope. How can you synchronize such matters? No, of course you can't. He had booked a flight. Yes, yes, but still, he had to admit, not being there to say goodbye did fit his profile, so to speak. Yes, because he was never entirely there for her . . . no, not for her, his own mother, and maybe not for anybody else, either (not for Lil).

"Just a little too selfish," his father had frequently observed, not cruelly, just as a matter of fact. "No, he's preoccupied," Mother would intercede. "He's trying to figure out the world 'sall. Quit putting him down."

Trying to figure out the world, he supposed that was true. (Surely one of the reasons he'd become a psychoanalyst, to peer into the underbelly of things.) Through so many childhood years, and probably far beyond, *she* had been the world to him, yes, and now she composed the very earth he walked upon. My god, how he missed her. He now recalled that at the gravesite he had placed his clinched fist upon his chest, as though his own heart had been excised. He had wanted to say he was sorry but no words came.

That visit had engendered some added pain. Near his mother's grave marker lay another, newly placed, one inscribed with his father's name and birthday, and with space allotted for the final entry. Richard was a junior, so the name chiseled in stone was also his own. For a second, this perplexed him because the grave next to his mother seemed to await him. Then the morose awareness of his father's not-too-distant death struck him. This conscientious preparation for burial sent a flush of nausea through his gut.

Later he had been with his aging father, who seemed afflicted throughout his body—arthritis, lupus, eyes that imperfectly aligned their separate visions, and a groin that itched during the night ("Only at night, son. Terrible . . ."). After breakfast together, Richard and Dad toured the town, reminiscing about different places. Dad showed him a grand casino recently built along the banks of the Missouri River. Even at ten in the morning, the parking lot held quite a few cars. Dad asked, "You wanta quick look-see, son? I've never even been in." Richard answered with a slight snicker, "No, that's okay." *That's okay?* What did that mean . . . and with that mildly demeaning tone?

Richard stared at the wide river, at the blinding sunlight glaring off its black slow-sliding skin. He assumed that painful memories from childhood had been evoked of what an inveterate poker player his father had once been. How horrible the tension resulting from the money he'd lost; how horrible the distress caused his dear mother. Years of tension, until—it seemed to happen in a day—his father abruptly stopped gambling. For the first time, Richard now wondered whether upon this had grown his conviction that any genuine change in people's lives was mostly inexplicable and ultimately miraculous.

They spent much of the day touring. They drove past a three-bedroom ranch house on Penn Street where the family had lived in the '50s.

"You used to mow lawns for a buck in this neighborhood," his father remarked. "You didn't like to work in those days."

"No, I didn't," Richard replied. "You remember what happened next door, Dad?"

"Next door? No. Something happen?"

"The Greenlease kidnapping. The boy, Bobby, they found him buried there in a lime pit. Back in '53, I think."

"Oh yeah. It was a big deal, but I sure forgot. What a thing to remember."

"Yeah, well, I'd asked to mow that lawn too. Bonnie Brown Heady's house. Kinda glad they said no. Couldn't sleep for a month after they discovered the poor kid's body . . . eroded."

"You always were real jittery about going to sleep nights. Had to sleep with a flashlight," his father observed, smiling. "Your mom said, 'Let him keep the light. He wants to see in the dark. He's afraid of getting lost.'"

"She said that? I still don't sleep well."

"Yeah, well, nothing changes much till you're old enough to die, I guess."

They drove out to Lake Contrary. Richard recalled the lazy summer days there fishing for catfish with his father. Contrary . . . what a name. Currents that contradicted, a disposition or will that opposed your own, like those times the lake refused to hand over a single catfish.

"This used to be such a splendid place, marvelous amusement park and all. Just the lake's left," Richard commented. "Dances, big-name bands."

"Yeah, well, everything goes to hell. Town's just a hole in the wall now."

Richard remembered witnessing in the park, at the age of maybe eight or nine, a tightrope walker perform. His father knew this strong, skillful man, and while his father was talking with him after his performance, the man leaned over and squeezed Richard's biceps. The man scowled and shook his head with disappointed concern. "You gotta do something about this, son. Push-ups." And that was what Richard did—push-ups, chin-ups. He exercised obsessively, ordered a Charles Atlas manual. He became fit, even a good football player in high school. His father had encouraged this body building—his father, who once seemed the strongest man in the world . . . and now . . . old, ill, and cynical, with two eyes that regarded the world differently. (Those eyes, how uncanny. Damn, if they didn't reaffirm a childhood conviction that Dad always saw more than he, Richard Junior, ever could.)

In the middle of downtown, they passed the black statue of the Pony Express rider—frozen in a posture of breakneck speed. "Now there's a guy headin' nowhere in a hurry," his father said.

They drove past St. Patrick's . . . Oh, the hours spent on his knees at Sunday Mass (up to the age of ten) begging forgiveness for jerking off, window peeking, allowing his mind to fill with filthy fantasies, and other childhood perversions. Begging, fervent as a medieval penitent. Maybe that was the door where he should knock. "Father Fagan. Hi. It's me. Lapsed but back . . . Incidentally, where's Highway Zero?" "Well, outside Holy Mother Church, it's every road you're on, my son." Ah yes—next stop.

"You said you wanted to visit Jesse James's house. Why?"

"Don't really know."

"Wanta see the bullet hole where Bob Ford nailed him?"

"The bullet hole, yeah, sure . . . the whole house. Jesse is part of St. Joe's history—what makes this place the place I grew up in."

"You think Jesse's place affected you, son? We got the Pony Express barns here too, remember. What about them? They count for anything? They're just down the street from Jess."

"Sure, those barns count. It's what made me, Dad. Background."

Richard cruised south on I-29 searching for . . . well, what? Did he know exactly? Highway Zero. Yes, of course. It felt comical, tracking down a road called Zero. Comical, yes, but something was troubling him. What? Oh, maybe nothing, really. No, something . . .

He continued to muse over the day he had spent, letting his attention drift about from one thing to another, looking for a clue to his unease.

Jesse James, one of those outlaw golden boys, assassinated . . . that bullet hole in the wall . . . famous spot. For over a century, folks had trekked here to gawk at that dot. Why, for christ's sake? Why had he himself gone? It's what made me, Dad. Background. Looking with eyes misaligned, his father said, "I see two holes. Was he shot twice?" Something eventful had played out in Jess's shack. Right there. Well, strictly speaking, not right *there*, since Jesse's abode had literally been relocated a couple of times. Presumably, they'd trouble settling on a permanent site for that little hole in the wall. Could neither trash it nor decide where to conserve it. Like some of Richard's patients who refused to chuck anything because they just might need it ten years from now.

Throw Jesse's death hole out—never! Richard smiled, thinking how we worship these shrines of infamy where some evil erupted, doubtless some evil buried within ourselves. Standing at such locations, we secretly enact the roles even as we insist, *"This isn't me!"* Recalling the scene of assassination did induce some unease, but he didn't know why. (This isn't me.) Funny, all the years lived in St. Joe and he'd never before visited the James house. Why today? He didn't know that either.

Highway Zero, no trace of it. As dusk slowly descended, Richard began to doubt that it existed. He didn't care to be scouring around for this obscure place after dark. He had been driving for quite awhile; he must have been twenty miles south of town now. Christ, keep going like this and he'd pretty soon be back at the KC airport. A quote from somewhere popped into his mind: In our beginning is our end. Who said that? Jesse James? Lilly? Maybe.

No, nothing here was adding up. Would they really throw this reunion bash so far outside city limits? Probably not. Something about this was a bit off. He decided to pull into a Texaco truck stop and seek better directions. If they didn't know the roads around here, no one would.

He parked and approached a trucker slumping against his rig waiting for its tanks to fill.

"Hi. Where's Highway Zero?"

The trucker grinned. "Highway Zero? You serious? Someplace down in hell would be my guess." He laughed. "Sorry, beats me." Richard also laughed. Maybe someplace down in hell. Well, he hadn't considered that, and it didn't sound all that crazy, either.

He entered the truck stop, a small general store with a few customers milling about. The heavyset woman at the register greeted him with a jovial nod. Her name tag read "Ruby." "What can I do ya for, hon?"

"Ruby, I'm lost."

"Who ya huntin', hon? Gimme a name."

"A name? Okay. Roger Maize."

"Don't live round here. Who told ya he did?"

"High school reunion party at his place tonight."

"Well, I don't know 'im, and round here, ain't nobody I don't know."

"I got a map."

"Let's have a gander." She examined the map, turned it about as though it were a puzzle, then puckered her lips, kissed the air, and shook her head. She passed it to a man leaning on the counter. Perplexed, he shook his head, too.

"Ain't got much to do with St. Joe. Roger Maize? Let me check the phonebook anyways." She checked. "Ain't listed. Sure yer in the right town?"

"I got a phone number. Would you mind calling?"

"Sure. Don't mind." She dialed and handed the receiver toward Richard.

"No, when they answer, ask where the hell their place is. It won't mean anything to me."

"Got an answering machine."

"Say, Richard Knott's looking for you. He's lost. Call back quick as you can." She repeated the message over the phone, gave her number, and hung up.

"Look, all I can tell ya is try that side road over there for a few miles. Yeah, that one, back toward St. Joe. Won't find much. But ya gotta be too far out, don't you think? Ain't no parties round here. I'd know. If there ain't nothin' down that a way, head back. Check if Roger Maize has rung ya."

So he took the road Ruby recommended. It was gravel, and in the rearview mirror Richard could watch the billowing gray dust clouds he produced. "What a mess I'm making," he muttered. He drove for several minutes. No cars appeared, but half a mile ahead he spotted a tractor moseying along. By the time he approached to pass, the tractor's dust had thickened into such an opaque fog, Richard was, for a moment, driving blind. In fact, for a scary second, he steered off the road's shoulder. He slowed, craned his neck, and glowered at the man on the tractor, an old man who seemed not to notice Richard at all.

Richard's temper quickly cooled as he realized that this old man was now, quite literally, eating *his* dust. He felt an urge to stop and apologize ("Sorry, Dad!") and then ask where the hell Highway Zero was. If anyone would know, wouldn't this old geezer? But no—all the dust would drench him as well, ruin his clothes, probably turn him pale as a ghost. He imagined striding into the reunion looking like a dead man. "Sorry, folks, huntin' for the place killed me." Pretty humorous sight. So, no, keep driving. Sorry, Dad.

Richard now recollected an exchange that had occurred earlier in the day. His father introduced him to a man who had recently moved into the neighborhood.

"Ned, here's my son, Dick. In from New York. He's a psychoanalyst. Hell, we all need one. Son, meet Ned Thomson. Both of us old enough to complain about everything. And do."

"Same name as Dad's? Okay. Ya look alike too. A psychoanalyst, ya say? What exactly is that?" Ned asked. "I mean, what exactly do you do, Dick—work with crazies, right?" How often had Richard been waylaid by this conversation?

"Work with unhappy people, Ned, people who suffer emotionally, you know . . . people depressed or anxious, frequently for reasons they don't understand."

"They don't know why they're hurtin'?"

"Generally, no, not sufficiently. And it's the part they don't know that causes the most trouble."

"Well, I sure know what causes my troubles."

"Well, that's good, Ned. That can sure help folks deal with life."

"I don't know, Doc, if it really helps me all that much . . . the knowin'. Maybe. So what do you do with these hurtin' folks?"

"Talk to them."

"Talk to 'em? That's all?"

"Yes, that's all."

"What about?"

"Oh, everything. Thoughts, dreams, feelings, relationships. Everything."

"And that does the trick, gets 'em well?"

"Yeah, sometimes. Not always, Ned, but usually, yes, it helps."

"How much does this cost? Can I ask ya that?"

"Hundred and fifty bucks a session."

"A session?"

"Forty-five minutes."

"Jesus! Talk ain't cheap. And how many sessions does this talking take? Can I ask ya?"

"It varies. Maybe a thousand."

"*A thousand?* Who in hell's got that kinda bread, Dick? Damn! And you say *usually* it helps. Aren't any of you guys in St. Joe, are there?"

"One. Right here talking with you, Ned."

"Sure hope yer pa's footin' the bill here."

Yes, a conversation not uncommon. Just well-meaning folks trying to grasp, in a minute or two, what the hell psychoanalysis was all about. Surprisingly, however, this little dialogue today disconcerted Richard. He felt like an alien in his own hometown; people didn't know what he was. How could they welcome a son they no longer recognized? "I'm a witch doctor, Ned." That, they might have accepted.

Richard continued another five miles or so, found nothing but shadowy pasture land sprinkled with houses where no one appeared to live. Of course this was unlikely, but none had lights on, although it was now dark enough. If he detected one exhibiting some sign of life, he thought he might knock on the door and ask directions. They'd be real glad to help if they could; everyone was friendly in St. Joe. But he saw no lights.

How long do you just keep driving? *Enough!* he concluded, and in a driveway that seemed to lead nowhere, he U-turned and headed back.

Now with night having fallen, the journey felt lonelier, more isolated. He watched for the farmer. Richard wanted to stop, chat, have a beer with him, something to interrupt the isolation, someone to be in touch with. But evidently old Dad had reached his destination.

Back at the Texaco station, Ruby tilted her head, recognized him, and smiled sympathetically.

"Ain't no luck, hon?"

"Saw lots of Missouri. They call?"

"Nope. Disappointed, ain't ya, hon?" she said, her tone as compassionate as a mother's.

"Well, where to from here?"

She shrugged. "Find yerself a gal somewheres."

Find a gal. Not a bad idea. Sure would help rescue the evening. What about that woman on the plane, in the hotel parking lot? They seemed fated to meet, didn't they? He had thought of her throughout the day. Very attractive. A trifle unnerving though. All that blood red . . . Shit, everything about this day was a trifle unnerving. Fishing in Lake Contrary all day, all night, catching nothing. Oh well. Why not call it quits, return to his hotel, and read a book? He had bought one at the Newark airport, *Primal Scenes: Stories of Radical Witness*, by some guy he'd never heard of. But the title intrigued him. Yeah, kick back a beer or two and just read, maybe e-mail Lilly and narrate the day's nonadventure. "Dear Lil, Spent the day among the dead and dying." She'd respond, "Sounds like you're right at home, my St. Joe boy." "Nothing but driving in circles, Lil." She'd respond, "Guess that's one way to circumvent the heart. You've been lost a lot lately, Dicky."

Yeah, call it quits.

On the return trip, however, he decided to give it one last try. After all, it *was* still early. So he pulled into another truck stop (in Missouri these places abounded). Again he displayed his bizarre map. Again, it baffled the woman at the checkout. "Highway *Zero*? Damn, ya got me, sweetie." In an effort to assist, she even phoned her grandfather, who, she maintained, "Knows every blessed thing about St. Joe. Here when Robidoux laid out the streets." But the man as old as the town claimed, "Ain't no such a place, never were, ain't gonna be." Utterly perplexed, Richard threw up his hands.

"I know where Highway Zero is." *What?* Richard whirled. A young man, maybe nineteen or twenty, had spoken. Richard could smell that he'd been drinking. "Yeah, head on north toward St. Joe, mister. Couple miles. Take your . . . ah, second right, yeah, then your first left. Keep goin' a ways, till you come to a crossroad. Go . . . ah . . . right again . . .

for . . . I don't know. Don't worry. You'll hit a dead end. That's Highway Zero. Not much of a highway, but that's it."

Richard chortled appreciatively, feeling elated. "Son, look, for twenty bucks will you guide me out there? I'll follow you. How 'bout it?"

"Sorry, mister, can't. You can't get lost."

"No, trust me, friend, I can."

"Sorry, really . . . wish I could. Where ya want Zero to take you?"

"Place called Glenn Creek."

"Hmm, don't know it. Well, Zero goes right and it goes left. Good luck."

The directions seemed reasonably exact. But could he trust a half-drunk kid? Well, he wasn't trusting him with his life. With no other leads and still some time to kill, why not?

Turning to leave, it stunned him to see the mysterious woman he had been encountering here and there. She was dressed in white (a witch disguised now as a virgin). Although she gazed directly at him, her large deep-set eyes seemed lasered upon things deep within herself.

"Hello," he said impulsively. She frowned and didn't reply. "I sat across from you on the flight into Kansas City. And I saw you at the Drury Inn. I'm there too."

"Oh yes?" It did seem to be a question. He now immediately understood why he hadn't spoken to her before. She wasn't what he'd call receptive. Nonetheless, here she stood, right in front of him. Why not go for it?

"Perhaps we could have a drink later."

"Perhaps we could have a drink?" Was that another question? Unsure how to respond, he hesitated. She smiled faintly, but whether at *him*, he couldn't tell. In any case, she simply walked away. He watched. When she reached the door, she turned and smiled again, but not expressly at him. Disconcerting . . . but by god, when he returned to the hotel he would get her name somehow, yes, and . . .

A hundred and ninety relay stations, lots burned down by Indians furious with these incursions into their land. Carry the mail. Time of the essence. Fast, fast as you can go, Dick. Pony Express mount . . . jump over the horse's rump. Go baby! Go! Eighty riders. Long, long lonely days. Lasts a year and a half—April 1860-October '61. Not long. Delivery. Lightweight saddles, mochila mail pouches. St. Joe . . . the origin, the heart . . . Go forth, mail seeds. Knowing where they're going, unless too overcast they lose the North Star. Then—Return to Sender. How did they handle that—returns? No return. Words that could not come home again.

So he resumed a northward course, back toward St. Joe. Back and
forth, running down his reunion. Take your second right, the kid said.
So he turned off I-29. Except for the moonlight, it was dark now. He
glanced at the dashboard clock—9:10. No doubt the party was in full
swing. Who was there? Alicia? Get yerself a gal. Now, *there* was one to
get, get again . . . first long-term sweetheart, first all-the-way sex, hot as
living hell, but, man, it *was* love, *it* was love. (Wasn't it? Hard to say, because
in the sex-crazed days of teenhood, he construed a sunrise as an erection.
And Dad in his eighties with an itchy groin; hell, did it ever stop?) Yeah,
would Alicia be there?

Kind of forsaken out here. Only a few other cars, all speeding the
opposite direction, no one, apparently, traveling his way. With amusement
and a hint of anxiety, he thought, "Who wants to go nowhere? Sounds
like a place in hell to me."

The road kept twisting, not rushing to arrive anyplace. Soon no other
cars at all appeared; it was as though he had crossed into a zone of
desolation. He found himself becoming fatigued, fed up with *this*. This
what? He wasn't sure what this was: Being so ridiculously lost, searching
for something that became evermore elusive, searching for nothing? An
odyssey in a teacup. Wasn't this trip for R and R, for fun? The day had
actually been unpleasant. But really—how could it have been otherwise?

A visit to his mother's grave, and finding next to her a marker bearing
the name of Richard Knott, then reminiscing with his ailing father over,
well, fairly gloomy topics; a mysterious woman who, because of their
continual encounters, seemed to imply some importance (a knockout
red herring, if ever one existed). And everything else . . . No, the day
had to be a downer.

What had he expected? Fine—now add this evening . . . add this
perfectly hopeless, exhausting search; a search, by god, still going on!
Snaking his way along this interminable road, it occurred to him that he
had virtually forgotten the purpose of this journey—a party, a reunion,
wasn't it? Yes, well, somewhere along the way that destination appeared
to have yielded to another that had insinuated itself.

According to Richard's sense of the young man's directions, Highway
Zero now had to be close. And why was that? Could he trust his sense of
anything today? Hadn't he, honestly, made a turn or two that represented
guesses rather than accurate recollection of the directions he'd received?
Still, he had to be close. Or he didn't have to be.

But yes! There, right up ahead, he discerned a fork in the road.
That had to be it. And yes, it was. For the road veering to the right, his
headlights lit the sign *Hwy Zero*. My god! His mouth dropped open; he

stared, disbelieving, as one would at a great revelation, or a great mystery solved or a pot of gold or (parked at this v-section, from nowhere the whimsical notion struck him) the vagina of a woman. *The vagina of a woman . . .* Oh boy, is there a man who isn't an adolescent all his life? Abruptly, he broke into laughter. Sure, why not?—the womb of the world. Where else could Dick have been going?

He felt mildly exhilarated. Dear god, here it was. Highway Zero. Strangely, though, he suddenly felt that he was about to cry. In fact, he did. Tears rolled down his cheeks. He didn't move. His reaction bewildered him but he let it flow over him. He was tired, and—damn!— maybe at this stage, a touch demented. It had been a screwy day. He shut his eyes and beheld his mother smiling at him; he seemed to be a little boy. He wanted to say something to her. "Mother, I'm sorry. I don't know how to love. Forgive me."

Time passed. He became aware of that. How much? Enough to cause him to wonder whether he'd fallen asleep. Christ, had the whole day been a dream? He didn't quite comprehend his condition. His condition? How odd, he thought. Did he have *a condition?*

Another question now voiced itself: Where to from here? Something eerie about that too. He had been so busy hunting for this cursed highway, so concentrated on that task, he had evidently ignored the fact that the enigmatic map, with that weird facelike image bleeding through, had made no sense to anyone. He was dumbfounded. Doubtless some kind of magical thinking had persuaded him that once he arrived at this juncture he could figure out the next step.

Well, there it was—Highway Zero. Now what? The kid was wrong. Highway Zero didn't go to the right and to the left; no, it went straight ahead. Maybe the kid had never been here; maybe Richard was the only person who had ever been here. What a spooky suspicion that was. But straight ahead it went, and that's the direction Richard now chose. Why not? He'd come this far for something, surely. For a moment, he envisioned himself as someone acting out a posthypnotic suggestion. *"When you wake, you will not consciously recall any of this."* Okay. Where, then, he wondered now with anxious curiosity, was he supposed to go? Was *his condition* one of passive compliance? The idea at least lent some intention to his wanderings; something at least was guiding him, guiding the blind. Who had once told him, "We are all God's posthypnotic suggestion"?

Outta St. Joe. Words go. First yer ferried cross the Mo River. Horse and rider. That always ain't a picnic. Had a buddy drown. Couldn't swim a lick. Then lickety-split, beatin' leather 'til yer butt and balls crack. One relay post to the next. Two-minute changes. Git! Expectin' nothin' good, hopin' hard you git spared the worst. Bears, mountain lions, rattlesnakes, redskins yelpin' after yer skelp, shit weather, madness. Everything out to kill ya. Treat yer horse like the Mother of God. Long land. Long delay. Don't hold yer breath, honey, but the mail's acomin'. Keep in touch. Words embody dead bodies deciphered into life. Ain't history a bitch, Dick? Haunts yer fuckin' ass, don't it? Gits ya lost, don't it? Keep in touch.

Richard observed barriers stacked at the edge of the road. Obviously they had served to designate some construction work. But the road now lay wide open. He proceeded slowly with high beams on, trying to see as much as possible. He was, after all, searching for something. A class reunion, wasn't that it? All this still contained some point, didn't it? Turning his head to the right and to the left, leaning forward, straining his eyes to make out various shadows, he certainly resembled a man searching. But other than moon-tinted trees looming darkly everywhere, he saw nothing special. Zero. Hard to imagine any class reunion out here. Christ, had he ever experienced anything quite as meaningless? Paradoxically, he supposed that that in itself held some redemptive worth. He had spent his life deciphering meaning, interpreting every blessed thing his patients said, thought, dreamed. Why, yes, look at it that way: redemptive, a holiday from meaning!

He was getting rather sleepy. Maybe he ought to pull over and take a nap. He was confused. Hadn't he already taken a nap? Hmm . . . maybe. In any case, he wanted to continue a little farther, just in case. Just in case of what? In case the big reunion bash suddenly eventuated. Bingo! Yeah, suddenly just clogged the whole damn road, the whole infernal Zero. Old friends swarming everywhere. Dancing madly about. Naked. Drunk with joy. Indecent, maniacal . . . drunk. A carnival. Shouting, *Hellooo, Dick! Welcome home, honey.* Yeah, forget the R and R. Fluff yourself up. Ya need a jump-start, love. A big bang.

He had driven perhaps five miles when he detected something ahead in the road. He slowed to a stop. What? There were half a dozen bales of hay blocking the road. A damn good thing too because—he couldn't believe it!—the highway simply ended. He got out of the car, and for a minute, stood staring in astonishment. His heart was racing. Without knowing why, he was afraid. He walked over to the bales of hay as though approaching something sleeping that might prove deadly if wakened. He scrutinized the hay. Was someone playing a trick on him, and these ordinary bales of hay really weren't what they so obviously were? How in the world . . . He reflected a moment, then inferred that those barriers he'd noticed at the beginning of the road were meant to prevent traffic from coming through. Yes, and they had either been inadvertently removed or some pranksters had shoved them aside. Whatever.

He looked up at the sky. Millions of stars and a bright full moon. He walked back to the car, switched off the headlights, returned to the bales of hay, and sat down on one. The heavy heat of the August night oozed around him. He could smell the sweetness of the hay. He gazed out into the moon-silvered, empty night. No, not empty, umbrageous; trees hovered darkly around him, motionless, except for the faint rustle of leaves. Unreal. Rather ghostly. Didn't some people espouse that trees embodied the dead? His mother, Jesse James, Bobby Greenlease . . . maybe lots of embodiments out there.

With his slightly skewed eyes, how many of these dead souls would his father see? Was a tree awaiting his father and one patiently awaiting him, Richard Junior, as well? Which tree was Junior's? What difference did it make? All these incarnations resembled each other.

But Richard did feel that he was *among* these shadowy forms. Yes, somehow among them. Gathered in. A strange reunion, indeed. Trees . . . the dead . . . still life. Nothing going anywhere. Stillness. Jesus, this dreadful day and too many nights of poor sleep, he suspected, had made him half psychotic.

This was where he was. Strangely, he found this unremarkable observation curious. Yes, this was where he was. Everything in his life, he expected, had delivered him to this place, sitting on a bale of hay, staring down a dirt path sketched out for a road that hadn't been finished. There was no heavy construction equipment, no backhoes, bulldozers, front-loaders, not even a pick or shovel. Abandoned. What was this place? (Outside Holy Mother Church, every road's Highway Zero, my son.) Maybe a project they had no intention of completing. Maybe they didn't know where they were going either. No wonder no one knew this highway. It didn't quite exist.

Again, he began to sob. My god, what was wrong with him? What was he crying about so much? Oh hell, wasn't everything in the world worth crying about, if you paid it two seconds of serious attention? The whole day flowed over him, everything about it so fucking sad. He looked up at the enormous sky. And here he sat, under the Milky Way, a mere speck. A mere nothing. He wept. Had he ever felt so forlorn? Yet amid his tears a weird kind of joy circulated inside him, a nostalgic comfort, an elusive apprehension—a crazy mix of emotions not fully explainable. He thought, "This is the end of the line, where God wishes for me to die." How much the idea of death had always terrified him. And yet right now, right here at the end of Highway Zero, it appeared not so terribly alarming.

What a day it had been, though. The more time that passed, the more oppressive and dreadful it had come to feel. And that mysterious woman he kept discovering . . . those large, black eyes so inwardly engrossed. Cold, but how exceptionally beautiful in an otherworldly way. Blood red, and white. Undoubtedly he'd made a fool of himself trying to chat her up; or her response had made a fool of him. Probably didn't like men hitting on her. Hands off the grass, please. Got a zero there!

To get into her—but no, the closest he'd come to anyplace like that today was the Y-joint of Highway Zero. Pathetic. He could cry or laugh; oddly, they seemed to express the same thing: self-pity. Anyway, those brief engagements with her had lit the only sparks of excitement in a day otherwise overcast with—with what?—death shadows. There had certainly been no reunion, unless it was with some aspect of death.

Highway Zero! What a joke. Hadn't someone today even pointed out that possibility? It's a joke, brother. Richard pictured the quirky little map. That blurry face . . . it was a face, wasn't it? Yes, now in memory it appeared much more clearly so, and a mocking face at that. In his mind he stared at the map. Actually, it didn't say "Zero," it said Highway O. But the road sign read Zero. Oh fuck, did it matter? He sat pondering this question. Did it matter? Hmm . . . well, he supposed, in a way, it did. Zero, O, oh—

He was startled. His heart jumped. A nauseous thrill swirled through his stomach. He glimpsed something beneath one of the trees that had just stirred. It glistened; two glittering eyes. It rose up. In the moonlight he could see it distinctly now. A large black and tan dog, about thirty feet away. My god, how long had it been there? It stood still, leaning forward, growling. Richard froze. They stared at each other. Did someone once warn him never to stare back into the eyes of a strange dog who was staring at you? Crouching, the dog inched forward, baring gleaming teeth. Its head was lowered, ears slightly down, its tail perfectly still. Hackles erect as a porcupine's. Snarling. A fiend from hell with attack on its mind. God means for me to die here. Richard had no idea of what to do, or of the safest thing to do. Don't run. No, definitely don't run. Trembling, he extended his right hand. The dog paused, cocked its ears, closed its mouth, and tilted its head. It held that pose. This Richard interpreted as a good sign, more benign—had to be. Talk to him . . .

"Hey there. Hi. What are *you* doin' out here, big fella?" The dog wagged its tail a couple of times and then remained motionless. Quizzical. Evidently a little ambivalent. It was a German shepherd, and Richard surmised, a rather young one. These beautiful, powerful animals had always scared the bejesus out of him. This dog could kill him in one minute. "Come on over here. Let's talk. Yeah, whadaya say?"

The dog began to wag its tail again and then to haltingly advance. "Oh well, okay. Sure, come on over here. Be friends." With greater resolve, the dog stepped forward, gave a little whine, and licked the palm of Richard's outstretched hand. "Well, now, aren't you the friendly one?" Richard relaxed and smiled, patting the dog's head. The dog pressed against the side of Richard's leg. Lord in heaven, he'd escaped the jaws of death. He leaned over the dog, petting him enthusiastically. He felt glad, awfully glad, that this dog was here. "Aw, baby, how'd you get out here? Damn, how'd you find this place?"

The dog rubbed his head more firmly against Richard's knee. Richard slid down off the hay and sat bravely on the ground. The dog licked his face. The wet, rough tongue felt wonderful. Christ—death kissing him! Yes, a wonderful, warm wetness. "What's your name?" Richard waited as though expecting a reply. The dog wore no collar. "No name? Okay . . . oh, how 'bout 'Zero'? Okay with you?" The dog was whimpering, obviously very happy. "Pretty lonely, were ya? Sure, you were; so was I."

After a while, the dog sat down close and placed his large head in Richard's lap, his big eyes shining warmly up with what had to be happiness. Richard scooted down further and propped the back of his head against the hay bale, and Zero snuggled against him. How absolutely peaceful. How very peaceful. Richard gazed up at the huge sky, the brilliant moon, the myriad stars. Everything up there so stationary. Going nowhere. Nowhere to be gone to.

How amazing that the day had converged upon this strange rendezvous. Preternatural it was, yes. The dog now had his damp nose touching Richard's ear. Richard listened to the soft breathing and felt the delicate touch of warm air. The interminable sky. God's imagination. "Zero, I'm taking you home with me. Somehow I'm going to. Don't say no." ("Lil, meet Zero. Zero, Lil. I found him. He found me.") Richard's entire body tingled as the warm, damp breath lightly stroked his ear. He fancied that something profound was being whispered to him but that he was just too unprepared, maybe too undeserving to hear, to understand. He felt incapable of measuring up to the gift that he'd been given here. Listen. Listen. Life seeping into him. A day full of death fading . . . reembodied.

Richard smiled up at the vast, hypnotic canopy of sky, at the inert constellations—the Big Dipper, the Little Dipper, mighty Hercules, unlaboring, now at rest, locked in space. He placed his arm over Zero and hugged him tenderly. Over there shone the North Star. With a roaming eye and a dash of imagination, Richard selected a dozen stars and sketched out a Pony Express rider. Not too hard to do . . . projecting our mythology into the heavens. And yeah, Dad, he's headin' nowhere fast. Richard was very tired. A long day. Still as stone, he gazed. How breathtaking the sky—lifeless, though. Most of the universe . . . lifeless. But not this speck he was, this speck Zero was.

Some say the dead inhabit the body of animals. Apparently the dead can inhabit anything. Did such a spirit dwell within Zero? The perfect rhythm of Zero's breathing indicated that he was sleeping. Sleeping! What had Richard done to deserve such unqualified trust? Reached out his hand, yes, to something that he had feared. Not for a moment, however, did he believe that what he feared had disappeared. No, he had merely chanced upon a different way of accommodating it. No, the dead were everywhere; he was among them. Still, still, he lay in a state of awe. There was something very—well, he didn't know exactly— inexplicable, something almost holy occurring here, something certainly unfamiliar, nameless, but yes, holy.

Zero, Zero. How in God's name had Richard arrived here—at the end? Not quite the reunion he had anticipated. When you wake you will recall none of this. You will not. All those stars, the moon, all those silent trees hovering around him. Gathered around him. Perfectly still. Going nowhere. Which one awaited him, his host? Not so terrible. He felt found, grounded. Filled by the breath of this majestic creature, he felt as close as he had ever been to anything in his life. Something immense, yet light as a feather, had landed on him. Blessed, he fell asleep . . .

. . . and beheld millions of stars interlaced by millions of crisscrossing lines, causeways to everything that ever existed. He recognized at once the map of universe. It was too intricate, of course, to read. Ancient pathways of navigation. (Ain't history a bitch, Dick. Ain't it all made up, honey?) He did, however, decipher, woven into the firmament's fantastic tracery a gigantic grinning face. Richard smiled back, uncertain whether this was merely a joke. Although grossly distorted, it did look a little like himself or his father, or . . . well, everyone whom he'd ever known, or . . . well, no one who had ever existed.

He wanted to wake Zero and show him this ridiculous face. But he couldn't do that because he was, he vaguely knew, asleep himself. My, God, look at that—all those stars. What a concatenation! And where were Zero and he in all this immensity? Since he had nothing better to do, his vision began to travel from star point to star point, looking for Highway Zero, because if he found that, he'd find himself and Zero because that was where they were. But in this tangled and bewildering scheme, where was that? Ah . . . he finally saw. Here—in this gathering of all.

As Marilyn Lay Dying

August 4, 1962, around the world the headline read: MARILYN MONROE IS DEAD.

August 3, sometime between 8 and 10 PM, she was exhausted, but as usual, unable to sleep . . . not really sleep. The drugs hadn't helped yet, not totally helped. They had induced a kind of half coma wherein sleep and waking interwove indistinguishably. Drained, she felt sucked by a famished vampire. Indeed, of all the vampires who bled her, this wake-sleep malady had proved the most tenacious and debilitating.

She had named this particular vampire Bela. Early in her career, at a cocktail party, Bela Lugosi, with thick Hungarian accent, had asked, the second they met, "May I sink my fangs into your sweet neck, my pet?" Embarrassed and taken aback, she paused; then giggling, coquettishly responded, "For immortality . . . anything." He, devoid of any glint of humor, simply glared at her with mesmerizing eyes. And right now—tonight, in sleep or not-sleep—she was again recalling how much his expression had astonished her. He *was* Dracula, had become *that* which he had once only pretended to be.

For the first time she feared that everyone in Hollywood was demented. Here reality was so obviously invented; every bit of it invented! Dracula had not only presented this incredible idea to her but had revealed the horror embedded in it. Years later, when she recounted tormenting bouts of disorienting insomnia to her psychoanalyst (Ralph Greenson), she would sometimes say, "Bela slept with me again last night, Romey." (*Romey*, because Ralph's real name was *Romeo!*) She would tell Romey tomorrow that Bela had been at her again. Oh, she was so tired. How far away was tomorrow?

Startled, she felt her body being moved. My god, was someone else in the room? She wanted to scream, but couldn't; her voice was missing. She wanted to fling her fists out, strike her tormentors (real or fantasized, present or not), but couldn't; she was paralyzed. What were they doing? Or . . . what had they done? She didn't know whether something was in fact happening to her or whether she was remembering what had already happened, or whether she was altogether imagining things. Sometimes she certainly overimagined things. However, she *did* feel something penetrating her, didn't she, something . . . behind? What? Bela?

Once granted permission (and hadn't she granted them all permission?), vampires could ever after freely enter any door of yours they wished. And tonight, Marilyn Monroe suspected that Bela had chosen her anus, as he commonly did. She gasped and held her breath. No, he wasn't hurting her, not presently. She hoped his visitation wouldn't become insufferable. Typically it did. But she'd manage somehow, she reassured herself. If nothing else, she was a survivor. Yes, and maybe nothing *was* happening beyond her own imaginings. Yes, only that. "So, think peaceful thoughts." Was that Romey advising her? He was always in her ear. Peaceful thoughts . . .

Her mind drifted fitfully back and forth across wavering borderlines hunting for peaceful thoughts (a futile search, she knew, with Bela menacing her). She stared into the dark and that curious performance appeared—singing "Happy Birthday" to the president of the United States. When was that? Weeks ago—in May, yes, though it was vivid enough to have been yesterday; or fantastic enough to never have occurred. Perhaps the pinnacle of her life, the more she dwelled on it, the stranger it grew. In these insomnious realms, it frequently reappeared, somehow always troubling her. Bela, of course, invariably cast matters in a troubling light. But to her, that event had always seemed so surreal; and evoking it with Bela around led her to wonder whether she might be dreaming, dreaming again what had only been a dream to begin with. In a moment, the scene flickered and faded.

August: How uncomfortably sultry it was and yet a streak of cold sped along her spine. Oh dear—sometimes everything about her life resembled a dream. When she related that to Romey, she believed that he thought she was crazy. And how often she feared that she was as insane as her mother. "Oh, Mother," she sighed, picturing the old woman crouching in some bleak snake pit of the sanitarium where she was confined, weaving realities too intimate for anyone to comprehend. "Oh, Mother," she whispered (or didn't whisper, but only imagined), "you're probably not as drugged as your daughter now is, and with all your fantasia, you're probably not as fabricating as she, either." (*Fantasia* . . . where had she found that word? In Rilke, perchance, in his *Elegies*? Who could say? Bela cast her mind into such disarray. As from a scrap heap, dumping whatever he uncovered upon her attention, keeping her as deranged as possible. The very worst kind of lover. Not unlike so many she had known.)

Deranged. Oh, poor Mother. With chilling recollection, she saw herself—or saw Marilyn Monroe the movie star—locked against her will in a padded cell at Paine Whitney. An asylum. *There*—dear god! Marilyn Monroe in a padded cell, stripped naked, pleading, with all the terror of someone certifiably insane, to be released. Her New York analyst, Marianne Kris, had her incarcerated in that horrid dungeon and then had abandoned her. "Nightmares—the most exquisite enactments of our most private horrors. Yes?" Marianne had once elucidated. "Desire turned monstrous. Yes?" And Marianne who, like Romey, seemingly knew everything possible to know about Marilyn Monroe, had delivered her into the most exquisite nightmare she had ever suffered. Her most despairing thought now reemerged: *You'll always be an orphan, Norma Jeane.*

Ooh . . . something *was* pricking her rectum . . . a fingernail? Something, or nothing. But wasn't she alone? "Don't you even know whether you're alone, honey?" a voice that sounded like Marilyn Monroe's asked with annoyance, and yet the question seemed not to come from her. No—Bela was imitating her again. (Vampires could do exact impersonations.) But evidently, she had lost the source of the echoes she now detected. What was real? Ever present, that nagging doubt. Was everything about her made up? Oh, if she could only sleep, really sleep! But right now maybe she was asleep, dreaming she couldn't sleep, dreaming of herself singing to Jack; that surely was a dream. But was this as well? "All a dream I can't let myself wake from," she murmured. "Oh, dear Lord, am I all a dream, then? Desire turned monstrous?" She felt so disturbed. "Dear God, let me sleep. Please let me sleep," she mumbled over and over. "I'll do anything." If Death came to enfold her now, she wouldn't protest. She longed for some powerful being to carry her off, a power that wouldn't fuck with her mind. Come on—stab your fangs into my veins, Bela.

What's that? She was again startled, again bewildered by something underneath her, crowding its way in. But didn't she have some inkling of that already? She tensed the muscles of her vagina and anus. And then a prickly warmth tickled her, and she relaxed her resistance. Nothing to fear. Besides, maybe it all had already happened. Besides, Romey watched over her, didn't he? Hadn't he accompanied her nearly the entire day, listening to her endless woes, stroking her, injecting her, popping pills into her like candy? Oh, she'd spent such a glorious morning, yes, until . . . until Romey arrived to exorcize her demons.

By four o'clock, she was so out of it she couldn't tell up from down. Thank god Peter Lawford had phoned in time, just a while ago. Yes, she was pretty sure he had. At least she said goodbye to him. She was groggy, confused . . . " Say goodbye to the president, and say goodbye to yourself, because you're a nice guy . . . I'll see, I'll see." And these were her last words. *Last words? The late Marilyn Monroe? Say goodbye?* She mulled all this over. What was this kind of talk about? Her thoughts roamed in search of an answer. Where was Romey now? Always behind her, never far. "Romey, what am I talking about?" I'll see, I'll see. See what? Open wide. Say goodbye.

Her cheekbones and mouth tingled. Briefly, she believed somebody—not her Bela, please!—was tenderly kissing her lips. But no, there was no one. The night got hotter. Sweltering. Oh dear, a body could incinerate in this furnace. In her nakedness, she turned back and forth across the moist bed, seeking some enfolding space—other than the arms of her vampire—to crawl into, to escape her aloneness by disappearing into something. A womb would be fine. Or maybe she didn't turn; maybe she only imagined movement; maybe she was already stung into utter immobility. Maybe someone else was shifting her body about. She couldn't discern what befell her because her vampire tormented her relentlessly, poisoning her awareness with malevolent uncertainties. Alone she lay with him, and with whoever now lurked around her exposed body; her ass, valuable as the Hope diamond, up for grabs.

And only a few hours ago—no, back in May—a garden of millions had beheld her, called her a goddess. Who were they talking about? She heard someone introducing the late Marilyn Monroe. Who were they talking about? That wasn't even her name, was it? "Mother, do you know who I am?" That question sounded absurd. She regularly spoke to her mother during these sleep ordeals. "You're Norma Jeane, aren't you, sweetheart?" "Not really." "Yes, really." "No more, Mother." A pregnant silence intervened, as though from within the twisted bowels of her mother's madness a reply was brewing. "Not Norma Jeane? Then I'm not your mama, am I? Go away, my child." She turned on to her side, and the mattress moaned sympathetically. If her own mother refused to recognize her . . . her father? She had no father whom she knew of. She was nobody's daughter.

I am not what I am. Who said that? She'd memorized so many lines, which were hers? How much had she copied?

"Who made Marilyn Monroe, folks? All of us. She's a figment of America's imagination." Some newspaper reporter had written that. Often she mused upon what it meant. Was she just a bit of everybody's fancy? Oh, she wanted to sleep, to be relinquished at least from her own mind. She was barely thirty-six. How much more of her remained?

No more. Marilyn Monroe is over with. She saw a reflection of herself in a mirror speaking. It scared her sometimes—like right now—to realize how much she deferred to mirrors, because she rarely recognized the image. Had Jean Harlow, her girlhood idol, faced her there, she could not have been more perplexed. But this mirrored glamour *now* was Marilyn Monroe. Sometimes she did indeed squint and tilt her platinum head and find Harlow peering back at her from the mirror. And she would ponder what Jean Harlow saw in *her*. Jean . . . Norma Jeane.

Now she closed her eyes—had they been open all this time? I'll see, I'll see—and again remembered that gala birthday. During the morning she had thoroughly rehearsed the song, and although nervous as a kitten, by show time she was ready to go. But she was late, as usual. Awkward . . . funny, in a pathetic way. Everyone had to improvise frantically. Moderator Peter Lawford, though disconcerted, extemporized with forgiving humor. As her dear friend, he was accustomed to her disregard of punctuality. What was her problem! Friends teased that she'd be tardy for her own funeral. Well, yes, perhaps for *that*, but for the president's birthday? What was it she wanted to keep everyone waiting *for*?

"Mr. President, the late Marilyn Monroe," Peter ad-libbed to introduce her. She saw herself step to the stage, gleaming. She viewed herself as would one of the thousands seated in Madison Square Garden. But who was that someone whose eyes she now borrowed to assess herself? She watched herself (a version of herself) advance toward the microphone, with fast tippy-toe steps because her dress was so tight. Thunderous applause. The lights blinded her from seeing anybody amid the mass of people gazing at her (and of course, the hordes of others viewing her on TV were hidden too). She shaded her eyes with her hand for a second and immediately spotted the birthday king, there in his garden looking up at her, with a smile as big and winsome as only a JFK smile could be. Here in her bed, she groaned. How many had already known he'd fucked her? Yes, only a few weeks earlier. In fact, from that carnal fling had sprung the bright idea of her singing to him that night, "pouring on the sex," he said, with the mischievous grin of an adolescent.

Wearily, she turned over, feeling heavy (overweight again!) and as though she were sinking a little deeper into the mattress, into quicksand. She gasped, momentarily as panicked as someone being buried alive. No! No!—if sleep meant falling into a bottomless hole . . . Romey had told her she feared death. Why am I trying to kill myself, then? No, you only wish to kill the inner demon who tortures you, and then, once free, to live on as a new being. Suicide's a birthday. And if the demon's too entwined with all the rest of me . . . then it's out, brief candle.

Her mind continued to rove. Was she truly the world's most beautiful woman? Mirror, mirror on the wall, who's the fairest of them all? She couldn't recall the answer, or even who had posed that arrogant question. And what if she were (not always, but most of the time)? Right now, it hardly mattered, did it? Could she barter any of that priceless beauty for one night's rest? *Would she* if she could?

She saw herself approaching the podium and removing her ermine jacket, displaying herself in a sequined gown so skintight she seemed to present a glimmering nude body. "You were dazzling!" afterward the mirrors would attest. *"Stunning! Stunning!"* Who said "All that sex in my face, honey bun. I can scarcely breathe"? You overdo yourself, doll. Romey, do I?

Down, down I come, like glist'ring Phaethon.

A horn honked (or it didn't). Her eyes snapped open and stared into the empty room. *Was* the room empty? Was it ever? It was scary—very scary, because she couldn't trust her awareness to tell her the truth even about that. Who's there? No one said anything or anything she heard. With apprehension, her heart pounded; her eyes, either open or closed, scanned a vacant blackness. I'll see, I'll see. Who's there? No . . . nothing, no one, only you.

Whoever . . . they had passed by. Marilyn Monroe lying naked, Nembutal paralyzing her, the door ajar, and they passed by. She dreaded being invisible; it recalled her childhood when adults seemed so unseeing of her hungers. Well, with a miraculous makeover, everything about her now glowed nakedly evident and compelling. True, she'd put out plenty, but hadn't everybody finally given her everything she said she wanted? Shouldn't she be sleeping blissfully now?

A hundred photographs of her flashed before her, a hundred exposures. *Look at me!* Yes, we can't help but look at you. We love to look at you! *Now what?* What astounding resources you had! My god, *you created Marilyn Monroe,* the most coveted woman on the face of the earth. American-made too, perfected and spit shined! *Awesome!* "Awesome's right. But, Marilyn, aren't you—be honest—configured to gratify only the wishes of pricks?" *Configured* . . . some brash young woman had thus once rudely confronted her in an interview. "Designed for pricks," another bitch—who? Joan Crawford?—once had trashed her. Another: "Dick's dream." "It's these harpies who bedevil your sleep, my love," Arthur Miller had observed. Yes, they do, and so do you.

She stared at her photographs. How could so many mistakes turn out so beautifully? Nothing added up. A beastly joke she had played on herself. She wept. Or had she already wept? About what? How could anyone have so spectacularly mispresented her own longings? Marilyn Monroe portrays your longings beautifully—just not *all* of them, not the ones that want to kill her. Who said that? Everyone has a say in her. Twisted in her confusion, she conjured more pictures of herself and stared at them, as mystified as a child would be if granted, magically, a chance to preview the beguiling sight of what she will one day become.

According to the wishes of pricks . . . displayed herself as a gleaming body. Oh, she knew the intoxicating effect she had on others, men, of course, most obviously. But women too—they emulated her, or struggled mightily not to. Yet, who the *person* was who was affecting everyone, she couldn't figure out. You lost yourself amid the trappings. She was as much a spectator of her masquerade as anyone, as much amazed as anyone by the spectacle, by the worldwide commotion she provoked.

How maddening! How could anyone sleep amid such upheaval? Intrigued, Norma Jeane looked on from afar at this bizarre double, as she would at a mirror in a fun house; and Marilyn looked back with equal fascination, neither fathoming the other. The deadly absorption of each by the other had grown ever more excruciating. "I worry one will eventually suicide to annihilate the other." Marilyn couldn't articulate this—Romey did. It was by now a plot fully formed, one she played out obscurely, with enough stealth to fool one or the other.

Her skin felt clothed with the damp August heat, naked though she was. She longed to take something else off. She wondered if she had remembered to remove her makeup. Who was she without it? Everything's appearance—*that* she had learned long, long ago. "Everything's surface with you, darling." Who said that, some husband? Jealous Joe perhaps? Or no one yet? The mirror? Drop the mask. What's left, then? Another mask. A bit of make-believe to fasten you together, something at least to face, to present, real or not. It assembles you, makes you something . . . a baseball hero, Joe DiMaggio, for instance. Real's a mask too. "You're a fuckin' myth." I know. Absolutely everything made of nothing.

All this darkness encircling her . . . she couldn't see anything. She liked the bedroom completely dark. A mere sliver of light could disturb her. She longed to merge with the dark . . . *What's that?* Something slithering up her rectum? The vampire's coffin house. They say the undead slumber in their native soil, bowels of the earth. Oh, her illustrious body . . . even Beauty has an asshole. Nothing we worship has an asshole!

Well, Bela found it. Too many cracks to slip into, she couldn't slip out of. Cracks everywhere. Crazy thoughts. Pieces. Was she disintegrating? Romey, hold me together. Get me out of here. Use the exit, my dear.

Something white was rustling across her face. A wedding veil? No. Was that her own dress billowing up above her head? Oh, jealous Joe, over there scowling. Her father/protector. Another one. That sex stuff's gross! Disgusting! Cut it out! *You're my wife!* Oh, my Joesey, I'm Marilyn Monroe. You want me in your pocket . . . you ballplayer. It's only a subway breeze, sweetie, sweeping up my skirt. "With cameras rolling. Goddamn it! Men gawking. *You're my wife!*" These things happen, love. Only to Marilyn Monroe. Who? She's just a part I play. Stop trying to kill the Lorelei you married, slugger. If I'm not what I seem, I'm not what you want—not enough of what you think you want. Joltin' Joe . . . ooh, stop killing me!

He slapped her hard across the face, again. Her cheek flamed. Couldn't hit a homer any other way. "Is he too dumb for you?" Romey, her father/protector, had suggested. Aw, Joesey means well. "Sure, dummies always do." How unkind . . .

Someone's gentle breath then spread over her body, to cool or warm her she couldn't tell. Words tapped softly against her. "We want to display it,/"—Rilke, is that you?—"to make it visible, though even the most visible happiness/"—Rilke?—

> can't reveal itself to us until we transform it, within.
> Nowhere, Beloved, will world be but within us. Our life
> passes in transformation. And the external
> shrinks into less and less.

Rilke, is that your touch laid on my flesh, weightless as a tongue of fire? Oh, make me a poem, a poem of me.

"Everything about you's so suspiciously manifest. Are you for real?" *Suspiciously manifest?* Who used language like *that*—Romey? He too had such a way of scolding her. But Romey also wanted her; she knew that. So out to make her, make her better, make her over—make her. Everyone wanted to make her; fucking was the least of it. Pygmalions all of them. She their Galatea. Am I a statue then? Oh, how she had prayed for everyone to desire her. Romeo, Romeo, am I your Juliet? The gods heard, nodded, and decreed that it should be so. And now she felt devoured. She wanted to cry. Maybe she was crying. Dear Arthur Miller, her father/protector, a mere three days after their wedding, had warned her that she had misconceived her own hungers. *Misconceived?* Yes, misconceived. Oh, make me a whole then, will you? Write me over, she had begged him. And he sure tried. Wrong script. Again, again, again . . . misfits . . . after the fall.

What a metamorphosis she'd undergone. She couldn't get over it. Gentlemen prefer blondes . . . or kittens, really; they want sex kittens. A woman who's a girl. What? What did they want? At first, she couldn't believe it was really that. *Her!* Through a glass darkly, perhaps, all seed, as yet unformed—but *her!*

"My name's Lolita"—she remembered lyrics she'd once sung. "I'm not supposed to play with boys. My heart belongs to Daddy . . . You know, *propriétaire.*" She strained to sing the words now, but she was voiceless. "Innocence and sex amalgamated." Someone had once tried to explain the phenomenon of Marilyn Monroe to her. "Incest thinly concealed. America loves its pussy to death." Incest with a missing daddy. Romey . . . that's my unique achievement? More crazy thoughts. She felt her understanding tipping over now into insanity. Or had it already done that years ago?

She rolled over onto her back and spread her golden legs apart. Or did she roll on to her stomach and open the crack of her ass to Bela, or whomever? It didn't matter, up was down; down, up. However she revolved, everyone wanted to rescue her—men, naturally, but also women. Marianne Kris imprisoned her in a madhouse. Come then. Anyone could have her now—cheap as dirt, for one full night's sleep. No takers. No one could put Humpty Dumpty together again. Not now. "Aah, Marilyn, you made yourself too much for us to handle," someone coldly remarked. "But handle me you have," she replied.

Suddenly, she remembered she was late for . . . for what? She couldn't recall where she had to go, so she let herself delay. Besides, being late was an inevitable part of whatever she did. Naturally, it enraged everyone. I'm sorry. Pretty bad thing to do. I'm sorry. How often had she waited, to the point of insanity, for Morpheus to descend? Waited for love? Some kind of special love nobody ever showed up with. Ooh, waiting was awful, but she just couldn't get anywhere on time. Romey, with exasperation, flung interpretations like darts. "Withholding from others as you were withheld from as a child. Do unto others as you were done unto. Where's Mommy? Gone mad. Where's Daddy? Gone before day one."

Guess it's an old story. What were those sad lines? "Give me to drink mandragora/ That I might sleep out this great gap of time/ My Antony is away." Poor Cleopatra . . . her Antony, only him, only one. But I've lost them all. "They're all as starved as you once were, as you still are," Romey elaborated. "Out to suck you dry. Yeah, put that bloodletting off as long

as you can. Postpone your consumption." My consumption? I need their
hungers; let them eat me. I want a baby. Like Cleopatra's dying words,
with venomous asp at her breast, "Dost thou not see my baby at my breast,/
That sucks the nurse asleep?" "Oh please! What would MARILYN
MONROE—nipples aleaking with barbiturates and amphetamines—do
with a kid?" Change. "Let's get real for a change, shall we?" Okay, I'll
wait. I'm late. "They're waiting for Marilyn Monroe, and you never have
time enough to prepare for that part." That's right. "Cocks are good
only as long as they're waiting." Yes, yes, yes. With her sphincter as tight
as a crab's, she pitted her will against his. Make me! And he waited in
vain, his ego smoldering, for her to change.

Again, with exertion, she rotated to her side and extended her hand
to search around the bedside table for the bottle of sleeping pills. (Or
maybe she didn't do that. It didn't matter; she had done it so many times
before.) Finding it, she fumbled to unscrew the lid. (Or maybe she only
imagined she unscrewed the lid.) Would one be enough? It hadn't been
so far. All day, she'd been eating these things—uppers, downers. Would
one be enough, or two or three? Enough for what? Maybe it was time to
liquidate that demon, get some sleep, get real for a change, recast herself.
Not a new idea. But these birthdays had never succeeded.

And Romey would be furious, have her stomach pumped, have her
"irrigated" (he called it), as he had before. "I'm dying. I've been dead
since childhood," she mumbled to some anonymous presence. Tossed
in turmoil through these hours of sleep/not-sleep, she always lost track
of who was speaking. Everyone played so many interchangeable parts.
Bela, I'm like you—undead. You must have been my lover when I was
five. She overheard voices practically everywhere, some of which she was
certain had never spoken to her before.

Mr. President, the late Marilyn Monroe. Oh, Peter! No wonder you
phoned tonight—so worried, were you? No wonder. You disclosed my
death, darling. *Me*—undead. My god, was everything anyone said about
her somehow true? She took one pill in with her tongue (or maybe she
didn't, or didn't take just one), washed as much saliva around it as she
could, and managed to swallow it. She saw her analyst sticking candy in
her mouth, lifesavers, commanding her to do as ordered. Sometimes he
smacked her. Devoted, he'd do whatever was medically necessary to get
her well.

Everyone had a better idea of who she should be. They all seemed to
believe that the only way to treat Marilyn Monroe, to save her from herself,
was to eliminate Marilyn Monroe. Their desires grabbed her, the epitome
of all they had yearned for, but then they sought to remold her out of

existence. They wanted more, *more* out of her. Dear jesus! She groaned like a prisoner, her buttocks now and again being probed. Alchemists, they labored to convert her shit into gold. No place remained to hoard even a small portion of herself. She couldn't surrender enough. Take me; take what's left of me. The perfect dream goddess—sexual clay, anything you want . . . till you wake. Then let me sleep. *Please!* I'm empty, purified, nothing, not myself, saved. Dear Lord, send a redeemer to save me from my saviors. Let me sleep. Down, down I come.

"You're just a cunt all decked out." Who had said that? Anybody could have. Well, at least she was something to someone. To everyone? Oh please, no. "What about these nude shots, baby? This nude calendar?" What about them? "Are they you?" They look like me all dressed up. *Burn the witch! Purify, purify! We're Americans!* Oh, she'd been shot so many, many times. Most of her lay captured in pictures. She *was* her photographs. She wondered, how many million shots of her existed in the world? All those copies . . . She contemplated this, as she had during other sleepless nights. Yes, and here she was, lying here in pieces, the real thing, whatever in god's name that was—sleep starved, alone, afraid of the dark, scattered everywhere, a wanton flirting with Death, her only lover. Down, down I come glistering.

Flirting with Death? The thought seemed to jump from nowhere— it always did—and yet, it was unmistakably her own. All the times before, it seemed to jump from nowhere, too. (Hadn't she thought of Death like this only recently?) And now, as on those previous occasions, she stretched and spread wide her famous legs, as though to accommodate this most imposing of all paramours. Placing her hand between her thighs, she moved her fingers about, combing through her golden fleece for something—a wound, perhaps . . . something painful enough to prevent the sleep she craved. *Something* . . . but there was nothing—no, only the hole every man sought as the passage into her, the spot to nail her down. The only goddess Americans have ever had, now nailed down like Christ on a cross.

Was she sleeping yet? Sometimes she couldn't determine that unless she happened to recall having dreamed. Yes, only if things slid far enough into the starkly bizarre could she be confident of having slept, although sometimes she couldn't tell even then, not with Bela hovering near. After all, dreams could resemble movies . . . dreams and everything else as well. Life for her was not even from real to reel, but from reel to reel, unable to extricate herself from a silver screen. Was she dreaming herself? Even in her dreams she was a movie star and had been since the age of five.

Now she viewed herself etherized upon a gurney, sheathed in a pale gray gown, as diaphanous as the air. She felt so composed. Dr. Frankenstein was transforming her into a bride for his lonely, love-starved monster. He had stitched together body parts stolen from everywhere. With the surgery finished, he ogled her. She was flawless—his masterpiece. And now, applying the final touch, he reached beneath her gown and inserted the precious suppository.

Immediately something squiggled hotly through her colon, secreting its life-giving balm. So, *this* was what had been going on tonight—an operation. Of course this scene could be a movie. Was Boris Karloff skulking round the lab? Yes, she assumed he was. She now overheard the infamous scientist conferring with himself. "Perfect! To appease the monster in us, something monstrously beautiful."

"So this is what I'm for," she noted to her unconscious self. The doctor's words had illuminated a mystery. Enlightened, she couldn't wait to wake and set to work appeasing the monster in us all. But strangely, the elixir was not arousing her as expected. Definitely, however, this was a dream; she must be sleeping. Oh, how wonderful! She was quickly reminded of her fatigue. How could she have forgotten? No . . . She now hoped the resurrection wouldn't occur for a long, long while. No. Stiff as a board, Boris would just have to cool his heels.

Like Dr. Frankenstein, you're tormented by your creation . . . Romey?

Oh, one weird association pursued another—

"You're too fantastic, darling." Not without heroic effort, darling. Every day a makeup artist made her up, sometimes several times a day. Everything's fantastic. That's given. We are fantastic—a curse, as indelible as original sin. (Did Gable's friend Bill Faulkner say that? Hmm . . . she felt she was playing the corpse in *As I Lay Dying*, confined, full of confused awareness. Oh, she'd read that creepy novel . . . part of it . . . enough.) What's not a cover-up? "Did Freud say that, Romey?" "I did." Well then, was this a movie she was starring in, *The Sleepless Maiden?* Take one, take two, hadn't she played this excruciating scene myriad nights before? Sleeping Beauty, right before that benumbing spell knocks her cold. Oh, to sleep a hundred years. Please, God, punish me that way. The meds are making you nuts, baby. Whoever said that, did they mean the uppers and downers or her doctors? Both—they're one. "Mother, is madness a relief?" "You should know, Norma."

As she so often did, she stuck her thumb in her mouth and sucked it like a nipple or a penis, or like a penis that was a nipple. How long did she do that—a minute or two . . . or for the rest of her life?

Right up her rear end something had gone and was nettling her unpleasantly. Maybe she would expel it. One moment her rectum felt as though a hot poker had been rammed up it, the next as though it were a cavern of ice. Now, however, only a soothing warmth oozed through her bottom. Romey . . . was he tranquilizing her again? All his magic potions: pills, injections, suppositories (was it chloral hydrate up her ass tonight?), trying to rein her demons, trying to rein her. I trust you, Romey; I trust you. *Trust him!* Give us a break! She heard the anti-Romey chorus railing. What's this rat doing burrowing up your butt, we'd like to know? Doctoring you, Greenson lost his marbles. Pathetic fucker. Not hard to see how he did. Anyone that wrapped up in you is doomed. Possessing you's not easy to do, not for anyone, not for you. But doc's dosing your sweet ass real good now! Shit, you should've listened to us, love. Your suicide was the consent you give to all these crazed assassins to slay this or that in you. *Was?* Am I dead, then? The late? Say goodbye to yourself.

She was drifting off. Maybe . . . searching . . . She looked around, and again beheld herself, or that rendition of herself, up there on the stage, exhibiting herself before Jack and company, glistering, singing that stupid, stupid nursery tune. We do a double take. How are we supposed to take you, lovely? The world's most gorgeous woman singing the silliest song in the world. The queen of hard-ons, acting naked, reciting childish nonsense, pretending not to be what she so clearly is, so clearly is at least to everyone other than herself. On the surface, on the surface, yes . . . it's the undercurrent that keeps us up nights. Had a reporter published that in *The Times* the day after? She couldn't retain everything everybody found in her.

Hmm . . . she thought of a story she had once read about herself in some tabloid, or read in the troubled eyes of some unknown man or woman at whom she fleetingly glanced. She read: "The only goddess Americans have ever had. A blue angel, a nameless evil, Americans know that, but until they have a more revealing name for Marilyn Monroe, they can go on worshiping her." Yes, someone had written that. More revealing of what?

And: "She's such a little girl; we can't burn anything that underage. She's not dangerous. The hard-ons she makes out of us are toys, playthings." It read: "Would the witches of Salem recognize their triumphant sister? No, not dressed to look undressed. The Empress's New Clothes." Oh, that revealing. I see. Where had she read that?

Her thinking was dreadfully muddled. In such tatters, how could she sleep? A crazy quilt. "She really is a witch, of course, driving men to distraction, beating the pricks at their own game." Where had she read that? Her mind was awash with this odd debris. Is this what's beneath? A riverbed clogged with detritus? A bed of shit? Oh dear. Yet look at her up there on that stage before the whole world, shining. From reel to reel. She wished she knew this celebrity she had invented, the one myriads had invented. She couldn't even recognize who was reaming her out (if anyone was), pounding a stake up her ass to impale the witch or break Bela's diabolic heart. The river of no return . . . Was that a song she couldn't recall?

Happy birthday to you, happy birthday to you, happy birthday, Mr. President, happy birthday to you. Slow . . . slow, breathy . . . sultry. Open, oozing sex. It was all another comedy, a spoof. Wasn't it? She wanted so much to play more serious roles. But until then, play Marilyn Monroe; that'll keep you busy, hon. Loud applause. *She*, someone whom she barely knew, had brought down the Big Apple, set the palace garden ablaze. Unbelievable . . .

She felt the weight of a world of lovers pressing down on her. Her fame, the phenomenon of her simply crushed her. How could sleep contend with the incredible presence of Marilyn Monroe? A sex goddess. The sexuality she embodied burst from her skin. How could the roots of her existence sustain all of this, withstand all this? How could she sleep a single night without drugs—more and more drugs? "Desire's possessed you, honey bun, in ways too overwhelming to comprehend." Who's talking? If only her mother weren't so crazy, maybe she could curl up in her lap, be born again. She was ready, balled into a fetal position right now, wasn't she? Oh, if something could just wipe her out. Maybe Death *was* the only master strong enough to cope with the gargantuan shape of her desire. For all she had to eliminate, perhaps her anus was the perfect site to focus on. But that happened to be the only hideout left to conceal whatever remained of something precious she had lost or displaced.

"You're too frail for your fame, hon. You can't maintain everything you've become. The picture exceeds the frame." Yeah. She'd framed herself.

Dear god, had everything in the country converged on her—art and politics? (With fleeting urgency, Khrushchev had shaken hands with her as if she were the doorknob to a life more transcendent.) And crime? There was Sammy Giancana—"death without a drop of poetry, not worth pissing on, sweetie," someone had told her. And religion got its savage licks in, trying to scourge the whore to death. That hurt. On the radio she'd once listened to a Baptist preacher railing against her as the harlot of illusion, "addlin' our brains and causin' us to misperceive hellish lust as heav-en-ly. Vanity, vanity."

She suspected that many of these red-hot crusaders struggled bodily with her in their beds. She was heartily sorry they agonized about her so. If she could cool their burning souls, she would. Now and then she wondered—and maybe she did again tonight, right now—whether the pope ever dreamed of her (he *was* a man, wasn't he?), whether with infinite kindness he ever dreamed of persuading St. Peter to introduce her to her true father, her true maker. *Here*—the late Marilyn Monroe! No, probably not.

Ooh, and all the daughters of music are brought low.

She sucked her thumb furiously, or she thought she did, because she tasted, or thought she tasted, what seemed to be blood. Sucking her own blood. Bela, suck the poison out of me. Blood, blood . . . who pricked me? "Now, what do you associate to that?" she heard Romey say. "Sleeping Beauty pricked her finger on a spindle and slept a hundred years." "Yes, and what else?" "Punishment for playing with yourself." "That's right." But Beauty slept.

From reel to reel.

In her anus, the movement of something—imagined or not—continued, a bit more vigorously now. She hoped she wouldn't soil herself. No control left, flushed out. Finally, only shit. The soil of beauty.

Another shrink, one Dr. Geha, had once called her *an inkblot* . . . the sum of a million projections. Not the most astute of her commentators, but for just a second an inkblot now appeared before her. "What do you see, Miss Monroe?" An inkblot that's very despondent 'cause everybody sees it as something else. "Like what?" A star. "A star?" Falling. Coming like glist'ring Phaethon.

Romey, I think I'll remarry Joe. Huh? Put a gun in your mouth and pull the trigger. That'll get you where you wanta go quicker.

She sensed a disaster at hand . . . or a disaster that had already befallen her, of which she was now only the aftershock. "Ah, you're too young, my dear, and too—well—unwise, to deal with such sudden and cataclysmic transformation." Which shrink had told her that? No matter, she had always sensed that it was true. Too young, too unwise, yes, but who could step through the looking glass into such fabulous alterations and confront such enormous attention from others without fatal results? Oh, as a child, how much she'd loved Alice's wonderland. But her own rabbit hole . . . once in, the path back disappeared.

Some dreams you can't escape, she thought in a dreamy kind of way. She recalled a lecture that she and Arthur had attended in Manhattan:

"Some dreams are so aesthetically rendered," the speaker maintained, "so dramatizing of all the contradictions that make us up, that we become captivated irredeemably in their configurations of us. Such dreams are the ultimate works of art. Perhaps enactments of sheer madness." Oh my . . . was her life such a dream? Was this night such a dream? From reel to reel. Down the rabbit hole. No return. No return.

What was that ringing—a phone, the alarm clock, a fire alarm, just a ring in her inner ear? My god, was it time to get up already? Lawford calling, Romeo, the president, Dracula, Peter Rabbit, everyone who loved her, all calling her to come back. She shut most of the noise out of her mind. They'd have to wait. She had to suck her thumb right now and get some sleep. Say goodbye to yourself. You were a nice guy.

Then she realized, at first dimly bemused, that something as hard as a bone had, indeed, been insinuating its way into her. (Bemused, because at first it felt like "a dog burying a bone in the dirt," as she always referred to her "backdoor lovers." Nasty, nasty, but, oh, let 'em do what they want. Good for constipation.) Or it was hard as a bone *by now*, or it had been hard and up inside her for years, throbbing, a time bomb ticking.

Hard on her. Her body had been so numb; evidently she had failed to notice how very serious this situation really was. Was it sleep, belated sleep, coming round at last? Petrifying her through and through. Always late. Had Bela finished driving her nuts and returned to his coffin, constipating her again? No, she was coming out of her own ass—giving birth to herself, again. Her relinquishment was now apparent. She shoved that awful realization to the background and went on sucking her thumb (or went on with a dream of sucking). She felt half dead. She often did. It was difficult to tell what was new here, to distinguish what was happening now from what had already happened, or from what was happening again and again. Her body, the only thing worth clinging to, she was now losing touch with. But something—not a penis, oh no, not this time—had definitely been worked up into her . . . something, warm, melting into her, through her vagina or her anus, down there, a long ways away. She realized that this was hurting her. Ah, where you been, baby. It's been hurting for years!

She sucked and tasted what seemed her own blood. (Or was it the blood of others she had sucked? At this stage, she guessed the river of blood was comprised of everyone.) Oh, but this wasn't funny anymore; no, not at all. I see. She had to hurry now; she was running late. Had she given away too many pieces? Allowed her soul to be snatched from her? Now you ask! Had she so terribly misconceived what had been made of her? Miscalculated how much she could lose and still hang on?

Sometimes you don't realize how close you are to the edge, hon. Maybe someone once said that. But yes, oh, she'd had such a glorious morning—LA sunshine, vibrant flowers bursting with color . . . vibrant hope! Oh, I'll see, I'll see. "A lightning before death," the real Romeo would have called it. She felt that a match had been struck inside her anus, setting her ass aflame. Your ass has always been aflame. Oh please, don't be mean to me now. Liquid fire spread up inside her and ran down her legs. Down, down, I come. Wasted. Reel to reel.

The price was high, love. Too high? To have been Marilyn Monroe? What do you think? With whom had she had that little chat—Gable, Brando, Jane Russell, even Faulkner, maybe? So many had a say in her. *To have been Marilyn Monroe?* The late. She knew—this was it. Say goodbye to yourself. It terrified her. But you said you wanted peace and quiet. Yes, but how often had she been undone by prayers answered? Hurry up! You're late. Aw, jesus, this was it!

Those whom the gods love die young. Small consolation there. She sucked her thumb dry. Rilke . . . Rainer Maria, love, make me a poem . . . alight with angels of dread and happiness descending . . . indescribably beautiful (ineffable, you'd say), but not—please, no—not totally unrecognizable. Not again! "Don't think that fate is more than the density of childhood." No, no, I wouldn't. Have I?

Ooh . . . Some kind of alarm was still ringing, but she had no clue how to respond, or whether it even had anything to do with her. Marilyn, it's your birthday. Blow out the candles. She would, but she couldn't budge an inch, couldn't even take a deep breath. She, who had fired the sexual passions of the world, lay stung into paralysis, aflame with waste. They must be administering an enema (or they already had)—yes, doing everything they could to induce sleep.

Enemas had worked before. (With Frankenstein, just a dream or two ago, they hadn't.) Work for what? Dieting, constipation, purgation. Lose the weight she had been lugging all these years as the world's most ravishing woman. Meds had frequently gone up her ass—a shortcut. To the heart of it. Not to worry. A fire had been kindled all right. *Hurry! Hurry!* Romey was on the scene, shielding her. I trust you, Romey. Fear nothing. He had watched over her all day. "I've a dream for you to analyze, Romeo." Oh yes, remember—tell him this one. "No, I didn't see you there, but it was you."

His caring finger screwed with insistence up her butt. His finger or some other. But it was you, Romey. I know your touch. At that point directing everything. We tell you he's lost his marbles. *Hurry! Hurry!* But you can't *be* late for this. This is how it had to end—with guardian angels presiding over her. Caretakers. Our only goddess. We worship you. I see, you do. My ass. We'll screen you. Don't worry. So long as evil has no name we know.

"Mother, it's me—Norma Jeane." *Who?* A fire had snaked its course up and around the lining of her guts. It had taken thirty-six years. Not long. Gradually it became unbearable. No, unbearable since I was a little girl. Not this unbearable. I see. The absolute sleep that she'd die for had at last arrived. She began to sob, hoping enough tears would put out enough fire so she'd not be reduced completely to ashes. Bela, anything for immortality—remember? Josey? Remember your promise—send me flowers forever after I'm gone. We'll remember. You'll never die. Who am I? I'll see, I'll see. The fire was pretty much all she was now. *Mother, it's me!* Oh, sweet jesus, were they burning her alive—purifying her? She hoped she wouldn't soil herself like a baby.

MARILYN MONROE IS DEAD.